Also by Cindy Gerard

Feel the Heat

Whisper No Lies

Take No Prisoners

Show No Mercy

CINDY GERARD

RISK NO SECRETS

Pocket Books

New York London Toronto Sydney

Pocket Books
A Division of Simon & Schuster, Inc.
1230 Avenue of the Americas
New York, NY 10020

This book is a work of fiction. Names, characters, places, and incidents either are products of the author's imagination or are used fictitiously. Any resemblance to actual events or locales or persons, living or dead, is entirely coincidental.

First Pocket Books paperback edition June 2010

POCKET and colophon are registered trademarks of Simon & Schuster, Inc.

For information about special discounts for bulk purchases, please contact Simon & Schuster Special Sales at 1-866-506-1949 or business@simonandschuster.com.

The Simon & Schuster Speakers Bureau can bring authors to your live event. For more information or to book an event contact the Simon & Schuster Speakers Bureau at 1-866-248-3049 or visit our website at www.simonspeakers.com.

Cover design by Lisa Litwack

Manufactured in the United States of America

10 9 8 7 6 5 4 3 2 1

ISBN 978-1-4391-5361-1
ISBN 978-1-4391-7704-4 (ebook)

As always, this book is dedicated
to the men and women of the United States military
for their unfailing dedication to duty, to country,
and to defending the American way.
I am forever grateful.

And to Joe Collins—my friend
and my go-to guy for all things that go boom!

Acknowledgments

No book ever hits the shelves without a collaborative effort between the writer and the editor. I have been particularly blessed to have partnered with Maggie Crawford, editor extraordinaire, with not only this book but the first four books in the Black Ops, Inc. series. Thank you, Maggie, for not only making these books better but for making me a better writer.

The truth of the matter is that you always know the right thing to do. The hard part is doing it.

—Norman Schwarzkopf

1

The old cargo van caught Sophie's attention the moment she stepped outside the Baylor Middle School's double front doors. Instantly wary, she stopped on the top step and squinted into the blinding El Salvador sun. The vehicle was black and beat-up, the windows tinted dark. It was also as out of place as a tank on this street lined with school buses and high-dollar limos parked right alongside used compact cars driven by parents or nannies or maids waiting to pick up their kids on the last day before the school's summer break.

The van crawled like a heavy-bellied lizard stalking prey through street traffic that was thick and harried, stop-and-go. Students laughing and happily leaving the campus jammed the cracked sidewalks, the dirt-packed schoolyard, and the littered curb. All of the kids were anxious for summer to start. All of them were looking for their rides. All of them knew to beware of strange vehicles. Yet in their excitement to start their break, they all seemed oblivious to the possibility of a predator among them.

Sophie had made the difficult decision to dismiss classes three days earlier than planned. It was a precautionary measure after a rash of kidnappings for ransom had paralyzed the community. Her heart ached for the two children who had not yet been returned. Her anger boiled at the thought of the ruthless monsters who preyed on a parent's terror and for the corruption and ineptitude of the San Salvador *policía* who had been criminally incompetent in their efforts at recovery.

Not again, Sophie thought, never taking her eyes off the van as she dug into her pocket for her whistle. Another child was not going to be abducted. Not from *her* school and not on *her* watch. Her students were well versed in what to do if she or any of her teachers sounded three sharp, shrill blasts. She was just about to sound the alarm when the van moved on down the street and disappeared.

She drew a deep breath, let it out with a mixture of relief and embarrassment. Vigilance was one thing. Panic and paranoia, however, did not look good on a school administrator. It wasn't very reassuring to the children, either.

"Whoa." Sophie laughed and caught her balance when little Juan Gomez ran up to her and wrapped his arms around her hips.

"Le echaré de menos, Señora Weber."

Sophie bent down to return Juan's hug. He smelled like youth and summer. The ten-year-old was a darling little boy. He'd come a long way from the shy, illiterate waif who'd arrived two years ago, wide-eyed and frightened and on a track to follow his older brother's footsteps straight into the violent Mara Salvatrucha gang.

"I'll miss you, too, sweetie, but I'll see you in the fall, okay? In the meantime, don't forget your summer reading."

"I won't."

No, he wouldn't, Sophie thought as the child waved good-bye and skipped down the steps. The Baylor School had opened up a new world to Juan. A future that promised something more than poverty and despair. She grinned as he disappeared into the milling crowd of students, some of whom were privileged and some of whom were poor. To ensure minimal class distinction, they all wore the standard school uniform of white short-sleeve shirts and khaki shorts or skirts. To ensure equality, many of them had been awarded scholarships that came with the promise of a future they would never have had without her school. Juan was one of those children.

She breathed deeply of the fragrant blossoms of a row of mature white coffee-bean trees lining the schoolyard. She would miss that scent and her kids during summer break. She worried about them, encouraged them, stood up for them. Granted, only one of the two hundred and fifteen middle-school students was actually her child, but she considered all of them her kids. Because this was her school. The school she'd made happen five years ago in a part of the city where those most in need usually did without.

Her sense of satisfaction was tempered with the wish that she could do even more. With Diego Montoya's help, perhaps she could.

She thought about the handsome coffee baron, knew he was still waiting for a response regarding his invitation to take her and Hope to Honolulu, where he wanted to show them Punahou School, a progressive college-prep school that could serve as a model for further development of Baylor or one of the schools she hoped to open in the future.

She sighed deeply and wondered what she should do about Diego. He was persistent, she'd give him that. Had been ever since her divorce. Since he was also a major benefactor not only to Baylor's scholarship fund but also to the general operation budget, she couldn't afford simply to brush him off. Frankly, she wasn't sure if she wanted to. Diego was . . . well, he was a very attractive man. A very powerful man. At times, he could also be an intimidating man, and he'd made it very clear that his interest in her went beyond professional. She supposed she should feel flattered, but in actuality, she wasn't sure what she felt.

It wasn't that she didn't trust him. He'd never given her reason not to. But something—she didn't know what. Couldn't pinpoint it, but for all of his polished manners, good looks, and generosity, he made her a little bit uncomfortable. Maybe it was simply all that overstated Latin charm. She wasn't accustomed to such blatant and unabashed attention.

Tomorrow, she thought, would be soon enough to tackle that problem. Today, she still had paperwork to finish up before she could call it a day.

"You can smell the freedom in the air, can't you?"

Sophie grinned at Maris Hoffman when her vice principal joined her on the front steps, her pretty brown eyes sparkling, her native German tongue barely discernible anymore when she spoke English.

"Do you remember that feeling?" Sophie asked her, congratulating herself again for having had the foresight and good fortune to hire Maris two years ago. Maris had proven to be an exemplary educator and administrator and also a trusted and cherished friend. "Being young and free with nothing ahead of you to worry about but summer sun and fun?"

"Oh. You thought I meant the kids?" Maris laughed and brushed a straight fall of auburn hair out of her eyes. "I was talking about *me*. Two months without calls from parents, schoolboard meetings, and doling out detention. Ah, yes, the sweet scent of freedom."

"If I didn't already know that the next couple of months, you'll be pouring your heart and soul into curriculum content and ways to increase the quota on scholarship students, I'd buy that line."

Maris lifted a shoulder. "Oh, well. A girl can dream. So what's on your agenda for the summer?"

"Haven't thought that far ahead." Well, if she didn't count Diego's tantalizing yet somehow manipulative offer of that trip to Hawaii.

Maris pushed out a huff. "And you accuse me of being dedicated."

Yes, Sophie thought again, all the stars had aligned when Maris interviewed two years ago. "Lunch next week?" she suggested as Maris turned to go back inside.

"Sure. Give me a call in a couple of days. I've been dying to try that new place that was written up in the paper last week."

Sophie turned to follow Maris back inside and hit that paperwork but paused and smiled when she spotted Hope. Her lovely yet currently gangly daughter stood by the curb, chatting with her "BFF" Lola Ramirez, while waiting for Lola's mother to pick them both up. Peas in a pod, those two. Both wore their dark hair straight to the middle of their backs, with thick bangs falling over their foreheads. And both so wanted to be older than twelve.

Too soon, she thought, watching them. Too soon, Hope would get her wish. Her daughter was growing up, a truth that both saddened and thrilled her.

Hope caught her eye just then and waved. When Lola also spotted her, she waved to Sophie, too. Smiling widely, Sophie lifted her hand to return their greeting— then froze on a sudden clutch of alarm when the black van reappeared out of nowhere, careening down the street, motor racing.

The van wove recklessly among the waiting cars, then screeched to a stop by the curb where her daughter stood.

Sophie's heart slammed into her ribs like a fist. She grabbed her whistle, gave it three short, sharp blasts, and sprinted down the steps, her heart racing as fear shot adrenaline through her blood like jet fuel.

"Run! Hope, run!" she cried as the side door of the van flew open.

A man jumped out; he headed straight for Hope.

"No!" Sophie yelled, her breath catching as knots of frightened children cried and screamed and ran for safety.

She raced toward her daughter, but by the time she reached the street, it was too late. The driver gunned the motor, took the corner on two wheels, and sped off—stealing a piece of Sophie's heart as the van disappeared.

2

Wyatt Savage was a true child of the South. Besides growing up hunting and fishing and playing war with his buddies in the woods behind his daddy's south forty acres, he'd been raised on fried chicken, peach pie, and meddling for as long as he had memories. He was up for everything but the meddling—no matter how well intended. That was one of the reasons he hadn't been home for a while.

"Two years is not a *while*," his momma pointed out.

Wyatt sat beside her on the wide swing on the front porch of the only true home he'd ever known, sipping sweet tea before supper. The mouthwatering aroma of frying chicken drifted out of the house through the screen door.

Beside them, his daddy sat in the green metal spring chair that had been a staple on the porch for as long as the swing; the look on his face said that Momma was right. It had been too long since Wyatt had been back to Adel, Georgia. The new lines on Margaret Savage's face told him how long. The stiffness in Ben Savage's arthritic fingers and the hitch in his shuffling gait were yet more proof of the march of time. And the loss of Wyatt's railroad-engineer grandfather last year emphasized the inevitability of death. Wyatt had been deep undercover in Guatemala at the time. Hadn't known about his passing until six months after they'd buried him. A fact he would always regret.

"No, ma'am," Wyatt admitted with no small measure of guilt, as a slow-moving ceiling fan and a muggy summer breeze labored to cut the steam out of the July heat. "Two years is a lot more than a while. I'm sorry for that."

"Well, you're here now." His momma's face looked younger when she smiled, the gray hair at her temples not as pronounced. Her Southern drawl grew thicker. "That's what's important."

Yeah. It was important. He'd sat up straight in his rack one morning a week ago and thought, *I need to see them.* They'd both retired within the last three years— his Mom from teaching at the elementary school and his dad from farming. And while he called regularly, it wasn't the same as seeing them face-to-face.

So he'd flown into Atlanta from Buenos Aires and surprised them yesterday afternoon. Just shown up. He wasn't sure why. Guilt? Fatigue? The need to refuel on something as constant, simple, and pure as home?

Whatever the reason, his momma was dead right. Two years was an eternity—at least, it was in his world, where a single night could last forever, because his world was too often about death and destruction. Anyway, it was if he did his job right.

His Black Ops, Inc. team members were back in Buenos Aires. He couldn't help but wonder how deeply they were entrenched in scuttling an arms shipment en route to Mexico via Argentina that had originated in Tehran. Never a lack of bad asses to burn, particularly bad asses with a vendetta against Uncle Sam or democracy in general or some private citizen who might be the current target of their wrath. Yeah, his world was full of scum who profited from human trafficking or the illegal drug trade or who sold out their country and preyed on the weak in the name of jihad.

A part of him wanted to be back there, fighting in the trenches with the BOIs. Another part was damn glad he wasn't.

That was the part that was weary. Battle-weary. Bone-weary. Soul-weary.

"There they are!" The old porch boards creaked under his momma's slight weight when she rose from the swing. Smiling with excitement, she walked to the railing and focused on the road that led to the old white farmhouse.

Shielding his eyes against the glare of a low-hanging sun, Wyatt followed her gaze to see a snazzy late-model tan Ford pickup speed toward the house, a billowing trail of sand-colored gravel dust riding in its wake.

"I see she still drives like a bat outta hell." He couldn't stop a grin as the pickup flew into the driveway and skidded to a stop. His kid sister, Annie, shouldered open the driver's-side door, slammed it shut behind her, and sprinted to the house.

She loped up the porch steps, her smile wide and white. "I'll be damned. He *does* know the way home."

God, he'd missed that grin. "Hey, Spanky."

Wyatt rose and braced himself as she launched herself at him. He caught her in his arms with a laugh. She still smelled like the perfume she used to splash all over herself when she was a teenager. The scent was as sweet as it was innocent, and it brought back a ton of memories of the vital and vibrant girl who was now an amazing and beautiful woman.

"Whoa, there. You're breakin' my back," he teased. "You put on a pound or two, by the feel of it."

"Yeah, well, it doesn't feel like you've missed any meals, either," she shot back, laughing as he set her on her feet. She stood back so she could really look at him. "Damn. Look at you!"

Wyatt knew what she saw. He was rock-hard, his skin leather-tan, his brown hair buzzed short, his jeans stiff and new—his concession to conformity—and not nearly as comfortable as the cargo pants he was used to wearing. Because she was looking too close, searching for something to be concerned about, she also saw only what he wanted her to see.

I'm fine, his smile said. Because she wanted to believe it, she let it be.

"Motherhood agrees with you, Spanky. Where *is* the little tricycle motor, anyway?"

Another truck door slammed just then, and his brother-in-law, Jed Cooper, walked toward the gathering on the porch, a tow-headed toddler in his arms. "Did I hear someone ask for trouble?"

Wyatt exchanged a quick hello and a smile with Jed, noticed that the former high school all-conference quarterback still kept himself in good shape, then focused all of his attention on the boy.

"Holy God." He glanced at Annie. "He could be your clone."

The little guy was close to two—Wyatt knew that because his mother had told him about Will Cooper. Will had Annie's silky blond hair, sky-blue eyes, and devil grin and his daddy's athletic frame.

"Down," Will demanded of his father, who set him on the grass beside a brick walking path that led to the house.

"Not so fast, little man. Someone wants to meet you." Annie ran after her son, who had made a beeline for the tire swing Grampa Savage had hung from a bough of the ancient live oak that shaded the west side of the house.

Annie scooped him up, nuzzled his neck until they were both giggling, then carried him back to the porch. "Meet Kid Chaos." She delivered approximately thirty pounds of wriggling boy into Wyatt's arms.

"Hey, big guy." Wyatt smiled into Will's bright blue eyes and, out of nowhere, felt a tug of longing so deep and so unexpected and so painfully out of reach that it stole his breath. This child was vital and beautiful and a living extension of his sister, and damn, it hit him that maybe the absence of this kind of innocence, this kind of hope and promise of tomorrow in his life, might have been what had brought him home.

He looked into those trusting blue eyes and thought of Sam and Abbie's little guy, Bryan, and finally understood why Sam had left BOI and come alive as Wyatt had never seen Sam before.

Talk about awakenings. And talk about pain, when the little guy's grin changed to pure ornery, and he hauled back and smacked Wyatt in the nose with a tiny fist.

Both Annie and Margaret gasped in horror.

Despite the pain, Wyatt let go with a whoop of laughter. "Yep. Just like your momma."

"Sorry. Shoulda warned ya," Jed said with a smile that held as much amusement as apology.

"He's probably just hungry." Wyatt reluctantly handed off the toddler to his sister. "Speaking of which, since everyone's here, maybe we'd better eat that supper you fixed, Momma." He gingerly touched his fingers to his nose. "Feed the boy before he draws blood."

Wyatt caught the look his momma and Annie exchanged and felt his gut clench. He knew that look. "What? What did you do?"

Annie hitched Will higher on her hip and stared at their mother with narrowed eyes. "You didn't tell him?"

"What's to tell?" Margaret said with a dismissive shrug. "It's not like Carrie's company or anything."

Carrie? "Carrie Granger?" Wyatt glared from his mother to his sister, already knowing what came next.

"Momma invited her to supper."

Margaret blinked rapidly and hurried for the door. "I'd better check on the chicken."

Wyatt turned to his daddy.

"Don't be lookin' at me, son." Ben Savage rose slowly from the chair. "I learned to stay out of that woman's path a whole lotta years ago."

"Welcome home," Jed said with a man-to-man and very sympathetic grin as he walked past Wyatt into the house.

Fried chicken. Peach pie. Meddling.

Yep, Wyatt thought, as he spotted the dust trail of another vehicle bearing down on the Savage place. He'd hit the Margaret Savage trifecta.

Night had fallen by the time supper was over. Outside on the porch, a miller fluttered against the window screen; crickets chirped in the dew-damp grass. Summer smells filled the night air, but the scent Wyatt remembered best was the subtle fragrance of the white Cherokee roses his momma had planted all around the porch years ago. He breathed deep as he lifted a hand, indicating that Carrie should sit down on the swing, and worked on forgiving his mother for putting them both in this position.

"So," Carrie said, breaking an uncomfortable silence as she took a seat, "should we just talk about the pink elephant and get it out in the open?"

It was hard to believe that Wyatt had forgotten how pretty Carrie Granger was. And how smart. "Sorry about—" He lifted a hand, debated what to call it, and finally settled on "the blindside. I shoulda seen it comin'."

"For what it's worth, I missed it, too. Your momma told me this was a welcome-home party."

The chains holding the swing from the ceiling of the porch creaked when he eased down beside her. Inside the house, his momma and Annie washed the supper dishes, while his dad and Jed, with little Will asleep in Jed's arms, caught a baseball game on ESPN, conveniently leaving Wyatt and Carrie alone.

Margaret had insisted. "Go on outside now, you two. Enjoy the lovely evenin'. Can't imagine how much catchin' up y'all have to do. We can handle these dishes."

"It sounded like there was going to be a lot of people here. Not just family. And me," Carrie added, sounding a little embarrassed and looking mighty fine.

"Momma has a way of understating what should be obvious." He felt relieved when she smiled.

He also remembered why he'd always liked her. And why he'd been so hot for her in his randy youth. The soft rays of the porch light cast flattering shadows on her face, accentuating her model cheekbones and perfectly arched brows and a cupid's-bow upper lip he used to just love to nibble on. Man, he'd had a big bad thing for this blue-eyed blonde. She'd been pretty back then. She was gorgeous now. Sophisticated. Poised and all woman.

"So tell me something, *Miss* Granger." He smiled

when she tucked a shiny fall of long blond hair behind her ear. "Is there not one man in the county smart enough to realize that women like you are as rare as a cool breeze in August?"

She smiled at the hands she'd clasped in her lap, then turned amused eyes on him. "You mean other than Jim Bob, Ray Bob, Joe Bob, and Bob Bob?"

Wyatt chuckled. "Yeah. Other than them."

"Well, then, no. Apparently, you were the only smart one, and you left," she said, tongue in cheek.

Yeah, he had left. A long time ago. Just like it really had been a long time ago when they'd been an item. He appreciated that she hadn't made it sound bittersweet. Just sweet. They'd been kids, and they'd both moved on—at least, he had. Something in her eyes, though, something soft and vulnerable and interested, made him realize that maybe she hadn't moved quite as far as he had.

"I really am sorry Momma put you in this position."

"Hey." She lifted a hand. "I scored Margaret Savage's famous fried chicken and peach pie out of the deal. And I got a chance to catch up with an old friend. What's to be sorry about?"

"You always were a generous woman, Carrie Ann," he said, looking past the porch rail toward the yard, where lightning bugs glided in the warm summer night.

"So how are you, Wyatt? Other than single and in dire need of a wife?"

He grinned again. "Other than that, I'm doin' fine, sugar."

"It's the little guy, you know," she said. "Margaret's got a taste of grandbabies. It's in her blood now. Like a fever. She wants more. Annie can't do all the heavy lifting."

"He's quite the boy," Wyatt admitted, and felt that tug of longing again. "I'm glad I got a chance to meet him."

"How long are you home?"

He looked at her sideways, intrigued and a little uneasy about an almost undetectable edge of hope riding lightly on her question.

"Just for the week. I felt the need to check up on them. Touch base, ya know?"

When her bright expression wavered ever so subtly, he felt a little pang of guilt. She'd been hoping for a different answer. Maybe something that hinted at long-term.

"So . . . you're checking on the folks . . . and maybe reconnecting with home?" she suggested after a short silence. "Getting a good dose to carry you through whatever lies ahead?"

Whatever lies ahead. He wondered what she knew — or what she thought she knew about what he did.

"There's talk," she said, when he said nothing. "Ever since you blew out of here all those years ago, people have been telling stories about you. Speculating."

"Now, that's a sad and sorry commentary on Adel if I'm the most excitin' thing they've got to talk about."

"You know how it is. Local hero and all."

He grunted. "I'm no hero."

She looked at him askance, and there it was again.

That faint but unmistakable look in her eyes that said she still thought he was someone special. "Anyone who leaves here is a hero."

Yeah, in some people's playbooks, he supposed that was true. Not much happened in Adel, Georgia. That's why he'd left, after all. Traded the slow pace and the easy grace of the South for the "thrills and chills" of the spook world. And when he'd parted ways with the CIA, Nate Black and his team at Black Ops, Inc. had been waiting. *Out of the frying pan, into the fire.*

"Word is you're one of those shadow-warrior types who disappears into jungles full of bad guys with nothing but a knife and a length of piano wire."

Oh, yeah. She saw him as a hero, all right. He grunted again, then put things in perspective. "Right. Well, except that I always take my manservant along to press my fatigues and buff my nails."

She smiled. "It's okay, Wyatt. You don't have to talk about it. Probably couldn't even if you wanted to. Just know there are people thinking about you. Thanking you. Praying for you."

Jesus. What did he say to that?

As it turned out, he didn't have to say anything, because Carrie shifted on the swing so she was facing him. Her blue eyes sparkled with that old familiar mischief that had drawn him like a bear to a honey pot, and he knew even before she leaned toward him that she was going to kiss him.

Just as he knew he was going to let her. For old times' sake. For her sake. Maybe even for his sake.

Nice. Very, very nice, he thought, as she slowly pulled away from a kiss as sweet as a long-ago memory of the two of them making out on a blanket under the stars in Old Man Larson's pasture.

"That's so you know I never forgot about you, Wyatt Savage."

He touched a hand to her cheek, brushed his thumb along her hairline. "You always did know how to knock the pins out from under me, sugar."

Back in high school, she'd knotted him up ten ways from Sunday with a certain look, a flirty smile, a spontaneous kiss like the one she'd just surprised him with, and taken him back to a time of such simple innocence that for an instant there, it made him want it all back.

Clocks didn't march backward, though, and neither could he.

"Carrie," he said, as her eyes searched his, then transitioned from expectant hope to understanding regret.

"No. It's okay. And it was worth a shot." She forced a smile and attempted to make light of her action. "It's those damn baby blues. Guess I'm still susceptible."

Aw, damn. He'd hurt her. "Sugar—"

She shook her head, cutting him off, then leaned in and kissed him once more, this time a quick, soft peck of friendship to undo the expectation of the other kiss.

Just that fast, she shifted back into safe mode and, smart woman that she was, pretended the kiss had never happened as she started talking about mutual friends, filling him in on who was married, who was divorced, who had children, who had surprised her.

A good woman, Wyatt thought as he used his foot to rock the swing and listened to the soft Southern cadence of her voice. A real good woman. If he had a lick of sense, he'd do exactly what his momma wanted him to do. Settle down. Get married. Raise those babies he hadn't even realized he wanted with a woman like Carrie Granger, who was clearly open to all kinds of possibilities involving him and her and a future.

"Now might be the time," he heard her say, and wondered if he'd spoken his thoughts out loud.

"For me to make my getaway," she clarified when he jerked his head her way. "While everyone's busy inside."

"You don't have to go," he said, suddenly realizing he wanted to see more of her but knowing it would be unfair to ask that of her when he couldn't offer what she wanted. "Although I wouldn't blame you. I haven't exactly been stellar company. Someone's bound to break out a deck of cards soon. If I recall, you play a mean game of Spades."

"This is true," she agreed with a smile, "but I'd hate to have to beat you in front of your family—being they think you walk on water and make it rain and all."

Yeah. She was pretty, smart, and funny.

"And I very much enjoyed your company, Wyatt. It's just that I've got an early morning. I'm approaching the hospital board first thing about funding for a dialysis center, so I need my game face on."

Sometime during supper, his momma had pointed

out that Carrie was the hospital administrator at Adel Memorial. *What a catch*, her smile had said. His momma was right about that.

"It's really been great seeing you, Wyatt."

He stood when she did, then walked her down the porch steps and down the brick path to her car. "You're an amazing, beautiful woman," he said, because it was important for her to understand that he knew. "Too good for the likes of me. I did you a favor when I left town."

And he'd be doing her a favor when he left again.

He opened her car door for her, and she turned and looked up at him with more than a hint of regret shining in her eyes. "Guess we'll never know. Stay safe, now, Wyatt." She hugged him then. He hugged her back, both of them clinging for a moment, remembering what it had been like to be young and in love, with their entire future still ahead of them. "Thank your momma for me, okay?"

"Will do. Take care, now, darlin'." He let her go, then worked at convincing himself that what he saw in her eyes in that brief moment was simply the same kind of wistfulness he was feeling. They were both missing their lost youth.

"You, too." She flashed a quick smile and was on her way.

Fingers tucked in the hip pockets of his jeans, Wyatt watched her drive down the washboard road, thinking that he probably *was* a fool for letting her go. Thinking that there was a scent of rain in the air. Thinking that he really had missed this place called home.

He turned and strolled slowly back toward the house

while a whole bunch of unexpected feelings closed in. Melancholy for one. Maybe even a little regret.

"Wyatt?"

Annie hurried down the porch steps, carrying the portable phone. "You've got a phone call. She says it's urgent."

He stepped up his pace. "*She?*"

"Said her name was Sophie. That you'd know who she was."

He damn near dropped the phone when she handed it to him. He knew only one Sophie, and he'd been working on erasing her memory for the better part of twelve years.

Stupid, yeah, but even after all this time, Sophie remained the main reason he hadn't encouraged Carrie just now. No woman deserved to play second chair to the one woman Wyatt would always put first.

He pressed the receiver against his chest to muffle the sound. "You sure she said Sophie?"

Annie nodded, her brows knitted in concern.

God.

Heart slamming, he turned his back to his sister and lifted the phone to his ear. "Sophie?"

"Wyatt. Oh, Wyatt, thank God I found you."

She sounded breathless and hoarse, but he recognized her voice. Would recognize it anywhere. The sound knocked the breath out of him. "Sophie—"

"I need your help," she cut in, her desperation sharp and thick. "I need—" That was all she got out before a heart-wrenching sob stopped her.

He clutched the phone tighter. "Sophie, where are you? Are you hurt? Are you in danger? Talk to me."

"No. No, I'm fine. God, I'm fine, but—"

"Hugh?" he interrupted, concern for her shifting to concern for her husband and his old friend. "Jesus. Did something happen to Hugh?"

"No . . . it's not Hugh. But I can't reach him. He's out of touch, some op in God knows where. Oh, God, Wyatt!"

"Slow down, Sophie. Deep breath. Tell me what's going on."

"It's our daughter." She fell apart again then.

For about a nanosecond, so did he, as he processed the fact that Sophie and Hugh had a child. They were married, for God's sake, for damn near twelve years now. But a child? He hadn't ever let himself think about that. About a child with Sophie's eyes and Hugh's lanky good looks. He'd never wanted to go there. Wished he didn't have to now.

"Sophie." He hardened his voice. "Pull yourself together. I can't help you if you don't tell me what's happened."

He sat down on the bottom porch step and listened, his palm sweating on the receiver.

"Jesus," he muttered, when she'd finally gotten it all out. "I'll be there. Just hold on, okay? I'll get there as soon as I can."

He gave her his cell number, got hers, and told her he'd be in touch. Then he pressed the disconnect button. For a moment, he just sat there, stared at the phone, then stared into the dark.

"Wyatt?" Annie sat down beside him. She laid a hand on his arm. "What is it?"

He'd forgotten she was even there. "I have to go."

"Yeah, I got that. Who is Sophie?"

He turned his head, looked at his sister, but didn't really see her as the porch light spilled into the dark. Instead, he saw the image of the only woman he'd ever loved. Rich coffee-brown eyes, sable-brown hair, a smile that had glowed with happiness the day she married his best friend.

She hadn't needed him then. Hadn't needed him since.

Yet she needed him now.

"Wyatt?"

He snapped out of his momentary trip down Bad Memory Lane. "A friend. From a long time ago," he said, rising. "Look, I need to check on flights out of Hartsfield. Then I could use a ride to Atlanta."

"Sure." She stood up with him, understanding the urgency. "Jed will drive you."

"Look, Annie—"

She stopped him with a shake of her head. "Don't worry. I'll handle Momma. Just go do what you have to do." She hugged him hard. "Then you get your sorry self back here, ya hear? You still owe us five days of the week you said you'd stay."

He hugged her back, sorry to be the cause of the worry in her voice. "Count on it."

3

At nine the next morning, ten hours after he and Jed had left the farm and the concerned look on his momma's face, Wyatt stepped off a direct flight from Atlanta Hartsfield to Comalapa International Airport south of San Salvador, El Salvador. It probably should have been, but it turned out that ten hours wasn't nearly enough time to prepare himself to face a past he'd been trying to outrun for twelve years.

One phone call had managed to reach out, grab him by the throat, and knock him on his ass.

He hadn't seen either Sophie or Hugh in all that time, and one look at Sophie—who was waiting at the arrival gate fifteen yards away—damn near sent him to his knees. Sophie Baylor Weber was the reason he'd let more than one good woman like Carrie Granger walk away.

Jesus. He was thirty-seven fucking years old, and his heart was slamming so hard it felt like a bass drum pounding against his ribs.

Kaboom. Kaboom. Kaboom.

He'd experienced this gut-knotting, heart-clenching, visceral reaction the first time he met her. What he felt when he saw her now was just as pure, just as primal, and just as it had been then, one-hundred-percent involuntary. If it was only about desire, he could handle it. But it was more. It was hunger. It was craving. It was an overwhelming need to protect and possess her. To be possessed by her.

And damn it, it was still love.

He was so fucked.

She hadn't spotted him yet, and as he advanced by inches in the slow-moving line of disembarking passengers, he took advantage and looked his fill. The fact was, struck by the notion that this sudden, close proximity had reduced twelve years to a heartbeat, he couldn't look away.

She still had that same endearing little head tilt, the same pinch between her arched brows when she concentrated, the same gentle curve of her slender neck that had always made him long to press his lips there, right there, where he knew a tiny strawberry birthmark stained her nape just below her hairline.

Yeah. Okay. He needed to rein himself in, because, damn, he was way out of line. But she looked so amazing. Like she always had. Hell, she could wear a sweatsuit and look sexy. In the plain cream-colored tank top, slim brown Capri pants, and leather sandals she wore today, she managed to look like she'd just stepped out of a fashion magazine. Style. Sophie had always had it in spades. Nothing had changed on that front over the years.

Years that had matured her, yes, but not aged her. Years that had been damn kind. Benevolent, even. She was stunning.

She still wore her dark brown hair long and straight and chic. Even though her expressive brown eyes were wide with worry and her slim, curvy body stood tall and rigid with tension, her bearing told him what he needed to know about her state of mind. Her fear had cracked but not broken her spirit. She looked a little lost yet brave and strong and even more beautiful than Wyatt remembered.

Desire hit him like a comet. Hot and fast. God, he still wanted her.

But if desire was the comet, guilt was its tail. He had to pull it together. She was married. Not just married but married to a man who had once been his partner and his best friend. If that wasn't enough to feel guilty about, the gravity of her problem was. He'd come to her because she had trouble, big trouble, and that had to be his priority.

A commotion to his right drew his attention away from her. Half a dozen uniformed guards carrying AK-47s—not your garden-variety airport security rent-a-cops—marched toward their line and formed a make-shift barrier to hold them all in place.

What the hell?

He glanced around and saw the reason for the security detail. A private jet with the seal of the United Kingdom on the fuselage had landed just behind his commercial jet. A UK embassy bigwig, most likely.

When he saw a very aristocratic-looking gentleman flanked by four watchful men disembark and walk across the tarmac toward the terminal, that pretty much soaked it. The men were clearly personal security. They all had the look of Secret Intelligence Service. The SIS was the British equivalent of U.S. Secret Service, which meant that nothing and no one was leaving this section of the terminal until their guy was clear of any possible threat and tucked safely inside an armored car.

Must have been a snafu, he decided, or there would have been a car waiting on the tarmac. That kind of screw-up made him uneasy; it reeked of either incompetence or a setup. Since SIS didn't screw up, that left door number two. And that could mean problems.

His gaze swept the terminal, looking for signs of trouble. He saw nothing—which he knew from experience meant exactly jack shit. He glanced past the guards to Sophie and felt another jolt of awareness slam inside his chest when he realized she was staring at him. The look in her eyes told him that she'd been watching him for several moments. The catch in his breath told him he had to get his act together.

She raised a hand, offered a tentative smile. He forced a return smile, then, reading the frustration and desperation on her face at the delay, mouthed, "Hold on."

She nodded, understanding that he was stuck for a little while longer.

Finally, the exterior door to the tarmac opened. The Brit, smelling of expensive cologne, and his SIS guards, smelling of gun oil and the sharp edge of vigilance, filed into the terminal and walked swiftly past them. The guards with the AKs relaxed the perimeter. Not the SIS. They stuck to the diplomat like armor on a tank—as they damn well should until they could get him safely out of the terminal and into an armored transport of some type.

Wyatt didn't like this. Couldn't wait to get the hell out of there. El Salvador was like the wild west on steroids, with no Marshall Dillon in sight. Violence, drugs, and abductions were standard fare, which, sadly, was why Wyatt was there. Didn't matter that he was weary of the violence and pushing his capacity to bear witness to yet one more horrific instance of man's inhumanity to man. It was what he did. He fought the bad guys. And because it was what he did, his sixth sense told him he needed to get Sophie out of there ASAP.

Finally, the line started moving. On a deep breath, he broke out of the pack and headed for her. She reached out a hand as he approached and folded her arms around his neck. Digging deep for restraint, he wrapped a single arm around her, determined to maintain a professional distance. But when she turned her face into his throat and whispered, "Thank you," he thought, *Fuck it*.

He dropped his go bag on the floor and embraced her. She needed a shoulder; hell, he'd been one for her before.

Old habits. Old feelings. Old needs. Seemed every damn one of them was stronger than his resolve.

"I wasn't sure you'd come."

He breathed deep of the fragrance of her hair—fresh, female, and, after all these years, still familiar.

Not come? She'd had little reason to worry. Sure, he'd considered saying no. For about five seconds, sanity had ruled and he'd told himself to stay the hell put. It was kind of like hoping for a bomb not to go *boom*.

He reluctantly released her. They had to make tracks. Too much time had passed already. The first forty-eight hours in an abduction situation were the most critical; they'd already burned eighteen hours since the child was abducted yesterday afternoon.

"Let's get out of here."

"This way." She took his hand, following the British entourage as they headed for the main exit.

The terminal was small, fewer than twenty gates total, which meant they should be outside and heading for short-term parking in no time. And they would have been if a barrage of AK-47 fire hadn't cracked through the terminal and sent him diving for the floor, jerking Sophie down with him.

"Head down!" Wyatt shoved Sophie beneath him as deafening return fire answered the initial rifle salvo a split second later.

Panicked screams erupted all around them, as passengers as well as airport employees and shop vendors ducked for cover.

Shielding Sophie's body with his, Wyatt took a chance and lifted his head high enough to get a read on the location of the shooters and ID their target.

The main terminal was fairly small, a long, wide corridor with no more than sixteen gates flanking the north and gift shops, a food court, and several small kiosks lining the south perimeter. The exterior walls were glass, the interior a mix of concrete, steel, and more glass. Everywhere Wyatt looked, terrified travelers had ducked behind any protection they could find—arrival and departure desks, newsstands, trash cans, anything that would act as a barrier between them and flying bullets.

There was good news: Sophie didn't appear to be the target. As he'd suspected, the British diplomat was. The SIS, shielding their man and apparently seeing no chance of extracting him from the kill zone, had hunkered down behind the marginal protection of a newsstand.

Then there was the inevitable bad news: He and Sophie were stuck between the attackers and the Brits, smack in the middle of what was rapidly escalating into a full-out firefight.

"What's happening?" Sophie flinched as another deadly volley flew over their heads.

Wyatt pushed her cheek back to the hard concrete floor and braced against a spray of splintered ceramic tile as an answering round of rifle fire hammered the walls.

"Apparently, someone's got a big bone to pick with the Brits, and we're caught in the crossfire. We're like sitting ducks out here." He reconned the area and made a decision to head for the counter of a fast-food eatery near an exterior wall. "On my go, stay low and make

like a leopard. Crawl left, and keep crawling until you
can't go any farther. Got it?"

"Got it." She sounded breathless and scared but together as the battle heated up to a war.

The automatic-rifle fire rattled in constant, frenetic
bursts. Wild rounds broke glass and sheared through
walls and ricocheted wildly off metal handrails and I-
beams. Wyatt counted ten, maybe fifteen, individual
rifles interspersed with a couple of pistols, a mini Uzi,
and an H&K. None of them was sparing the ammo.

"Go!" he yelled above the shouts and screams and
the deafening explosions of rifle fire. Not two feet from
them, a wall of plate-glass windows shattered and fell in
a shower, splintering into thousands of shards of poten-
tially lethal flying projectiles.

He scuttled left, keeping Sophie in his sights as she
kept pace with him. Finally, he reached the counter.
He reached for her, dragging her the final yard, then
pushed her between him and the base of the counter.

They were still on the periphery of the battle, but at
least they were no longer out in the open. Breathing hard,
he wiped a trickle of blood from above his eye—glass cut.

Another spray of gunfire whizzed overhead, and a
ketchup bottle on the edge of the counter exploded,
splattering ketchup on the floor in front of them.

"Crawl around to the back side of the counter," he
ordered. "Watch out for the glass. Go."

Right on her ass, he scrambled on all fours to the
edge of the counter and ducked around behind it. Wyatt
half lay, half leaned against the interior side of the wall

and tucked Sophie snugly against him. They were out of sight of the gunmen but not out of danger, with only a partition of wallboard and stainless steel standing between them and any stray bullets.

If this had been his fight, he'd be figuring out a way to arm himself. But it wasn't his fight. Not today. Today, his main priority was getting Sophie out of there in one piece.

"There's gotta be a back way out." He rose to a crouch and, grabbing her hand, headed for what he hoped was the kitchen and a delivery entrance.

"Wyatt—" Sophie pulled against his hand. He glanced back at her, saw the look on her face, and followed her gaze to the far side of the room.

Five long, smack-in-the-line-of-fire yards away, a young woman huddled in a ball on the floor, hiding behind an overturned table. In her arms was an infant. The baby couldn't have been more than a couple of months old and was wailing at the top of its baby lungs. The mother was paralyzed with terror. The thousand-mile look in her eyes said, *I've gone away and you can't make me come back.*

And bearing down hard, using the cover of an angled exterior wall to conceal his approach, a masked gunman crept slowly toward them. The shooter wasn't aware of the woman and child yet—they were out of his line of sight behind the table—but that was all gonna change when he worked up the nerve to poke his head out from behind the protective wall.

Wyatt would stake his life savings that the gunman

didn't give two figs about collateral damage. High on adrenaline and fear, he'd point and shoot at anything that startled or scared him—then the baby wouldn't be crying anymore.

"Shit." All he wanted to do was leave the Brit's protection to the SIS and the local security detail, avoid getting caught in the middle of an international incident, and get Sophie gone.

Right. Since when had he ever gotten what he wanted?

"We don't have time for this." Wyatt huddled over Sophie as she knelt on all fours, attempting to talk the terrified young mother into crawling the five yards toward them and relative safety before the gunman or a stray bullet found her there.

"Give me another few seconds. I think I can reach her."

Shrapnel from glass and tile and concrete flew over their heads like missiles; the relentless hammering of the AKs battered their eardrums.

Screw this. "We've already pushed our luck as far as it's gonna go. I'm going after them. Hold your position here, then be ready to hustle them toward the back door when I grab them, okay?"

She nodded, even though she had to be well aware that she could still get caught in the rifle fire. Damn if he didn't think she was about the bravest woman he'd ever known. Considering he knew some damn brave women—among them Crystal Reed, Abbie Lang,

Jenna Jones and B. J. Mendoza—that was saying a lot about Sophie.

Gauging the distance between the counter and the wailing child and mother, who now appeared to be catatonic, he inhaled deeply, let his breath out on a rush, and dove for the terrified pair. He was airborne for most of the first three yards, a big damn bull's eye of a target, skimming horizontally a foot above the floor. He hit the cement floor on his belly and skidded the final two yards until he reached them. There was no time for small talk or reassurances. He got his feet under him and, keeping his profile low, scooped both of them up just as a spray of bullets riddled the wall above their heads. Then he ran like hell for the back of the restaurant, the baby screaming, the mother still too terrified to react.

And the damn bullets just kept cracking.

Sonofabitch.

He handed the pair off to Sophie. "Find that back door! Go!" Then he turned back to deal with the shooter.

He'd tried, damn it. He'd really *tried* to stay out of this. But it was personal now, because that last round of fire had been aimed at him. Worse, it had been aimed at Sophie and that mother and her baby. The gunman didn't know it yet, but he'd be wearing a toe tag before this day was over.

Wyatt ducked back behind the counter, scuttled over to the deep-fat fryers, and lifted a mesh basket full of burned French fries out of the boiling grease. Holding the basket away from his body, he scrambled back over to the counter. He reached the far end just as a pair of boots hit the floor in front of him.

He shot up with a roar, slammed the basket over the shooter's head like a net, and jerked him off his feet. The guy screamed in pain, dropped the AK, and grabbed frantically at the basket, as hot fries and grease burned his face and neck.

Wyatt dove for the rifle as it skidded across the cement floor toward the center of the terminal. When he finally reached it, he scooped it up and rolled onto his back. The gunman was back on his feet, howling in pain, a knife in his hand, and bearing down like a wild man.

Wyatt didn't bother to shoulder the gun. Shooting from the hip, he aimed and leaned on the trigger, firing off three quick bursts as the guy advanced. A jagged row of crimson stains gushed from his chest. He stopped dead in his tracks—literally—then crumpled to the floor.

It would have been a perfect time for a ringing silence, Wyatt thought, as the acrid scent of gunpowder and blood filled the air, but he knew that wasn't in the cards. The gunfire continued around him as he lay on his back, fully exposed, dead center in the middle of the melee again.

He glanced to his left and saw another masked gunman rush the SIS's makeshift stronghold. Wyatt's reaction was instinctive and automatic. He rolled to his knees, shouldered the AK, and emptied the magazine. The shooter dropped like a stone.

A head popped up, and an SIS agent looked from the dead guy to Wyatt. Surprise registered first when he saw he had an unexpected ally, then he gave Wyatt a clipped nod of thanks. Before Wyatt could return the gesture, the SIS agent shouldered his own weapon and fired several rounds above Wyatt's head.

"Jesus," Wyatt swore, jerking his head in the direction the SIS agent had fired. Not six yards away, another masked gunman dropped to his knees. Blood oozed out between the fingers he clutched to his chest before he toppled, face-first, onto the cement floor.

Wyatt looked back at the SIS agent. *Tit for tat*, he acknowledged with a nod, and scrambled like hell to get back to Sophie while the battle raged on all around him.

"It's locked." Sophie looked up from the back door of the restaurant, where she crouched with arms around the mother and child beside her.

"Of course it is," Wyatt grumbled under his breath, because, hell, he needed something else to fuck up what was already a fucking fucked-up mess.

4

The back door of the restaurant was metal, window-less, and yeah, Sophie was right, it was locked. Wyatt stood back and kicked it dead center, near the handle. It didn't budge. Didn't budge the second time he laid into it, either.

"It sounds like they're moving this way!" Sophie huddled over the trembling pair.

The gunfire *was* getting closer. Wyatt just hoped to hell the good guys were winning. Sweating from exertion and heat from the close quarters and the bubbling deep-fat fryers, Wyatt inched around the corner and spotted what he hoped was a closet. A broom, a mop, and a stack of red work aprons was all he found inside.

With the AKs still cooking off like fireworks in the background, he scuttled back to the exit door, swearing when something sharp pierced the back of his upper arm. Ignoring the pain, he grabbed the empty AK. The wooden stock had a metal butt plate; he used it to lay into the door. On the fifth smash of the stock, the latch finally popped.

"Thank God." Sophie shepherded the mother, who had come back to herself enough to have a death grip on her baby, out the door, with Wyatt hot on their heels.

A hail of gunfire strafed the metal door as he slammed it shut behind them. They were in a long, windowless hallway lit by dim bare bulbs hanging high overhead. The baby's wails echoed through the cement and metal walls as Wyatt scooped the mother up into his arms and shot off at a sprint in the opposite direction of the gunshots. "Stay with me!" he shouted over his shoulder.

"Just try to lose me," Sophie said, two steps behind him.

Not more than fifty yards later, they encountered a pair of double bay doors. Receiving, Wyatt thought. This was where the trucks pulled up to deliver supplies. There wasn't a soul to be found.

"Where is everyone?" Sophie asked as they hurried down several steps to a regular-size door, where a red *Salida*—"Exit"—sign glowed above it.

"Where would *you* be if you heard a war break out?" he yelled over the baby's screams.

"Right. Gone."

"Which is what we're going to be just as soon as I can make it happen," he assured her.

"Please don't let this door be locked, too," Sophie whispered when she reached for the handle.

Finally, a break. The door swung open to a burst of blinding sunlight, unimaginable heat, and suffocating jet-fuel fumes. Wyatt herded them all outside, set the woman on her feet, steadied her, and got a bead on their location.

They were at the far south end of the terminal. It wasn't yet ten a.m., and the heat and humidity covered them like a heavy blanket that had been soaked in boiling water. The muffled sound of continued gunfire punctuated the fact that while they were out of the direct line of fire, he still needed to get them away from the airport.

"Where's your car?"

Sophie had thrown a comforting arm over the mother's shoulders and was talking softly to her in Spanish. The baby had finally cried itself out and was sleeping in its mother's arms.

Sophie looked up and around to get a bead on their location, then notched her chin toward the west. "Over there—about four, maybe four and a half blocks away."

She started talking to the woman again in that soft, soothing voice of hers. Wyatt was far too aware of the need to get the hell gone from the airport, yet the sound of her voice took him back in time. He'd heard that voice in his dreams for years. Her soft, steady cadence, a little husky, sexy as hell, confident, and undeniably female.

"Oh, my God, Wyatt, you're bleeding."

Her eyes welled up with concern as he felt a fresh trail of blood trickle down his forehead. He wiped it away with his sleeve. "Just a glass cut. I'm fine. How about her? She with the program yet?" he asked as he located a piece of glass biting into the back of his arm and jerked it out.

"Getting there."

"Then let's move."

"Wait." Sophie gently pried the baby from the woman's arms. The mother gradually relinquished her hold as Sophie continued talking to her, offering reassurances, promising they'd get her to safety. "Okay," she said. "Let's go now."

He supported the mother with a hand on her upper arm, and the four of them headed for the open parking lot at a jog trot. The baby slept on as the distant screech of sirens grew louder.

"The local *policía*," Sophie said keeping pace beside him.

About damn time, he thought as the first brace of police cars roared past them, lights flashing and sirens blaring. A pair of ambulances flew by on their heels.

Wyatt stepped out into the street and flagged one down. Thirty seconds later, satisfied that the mother was being treated for shock and the infant was physically okay, Wyatt gave Sophie a discreet nod. They quietly slipped away and ran to the parking lot. The last thing either of them needed was to get embroiled deeper in a situation that was becoming more explosive by the minute.

They were both breathless and dripping with perspiration by the time they reached her vehicle. It was a late-model SUV. Black, with dark-tinted windows, four-wheel drive. Wyatt had no doubt that Hugh had

selected it for its ruggedness, versatility, and off-road ca-
pability. He'd yet to meet an operator who would drive
a car over an SUV.

Sophie hit the keyless remote and climbed behind
the wheel. "For God's sake, get in," she said when he
dug in his pocket for a handkerchief and tied it around
the puncture wound in his arm so he wouldn't bleed all
over her seats.

She was already cranking the key; hot, stale air blew
out of the air-conditioning vents when he ducked into
the passenger seat. Another pack of police cars sped by.
Three military choppers zoomed in low, their main ro-
tors kicking up dust and debris, the *thwump, thwump,
thwump* of their engines deafening.

"I'll say this much." Wyatt had to yell to be heard
above the noise. "El Salvador welcome parties are a little
livelier than the ones they throw back home in Georgia."

Sophie pushed her hair out of her eyes and smiled.
"I'm so glad that some things never change."

He shot her a puzzled look.

"Once a hero . . ." she said, a world of appreciation
filling her eyes.

He reluctantly smiled back. "Yeah, well. I'm still
workin' on that little character flaw, sugar. My momma
tells me I'll live longer if I quit stickin' my neck out."

"She's right," Sophie agreed, a bit sadly, and shifted
into gear, "but, damn, I'm glad you didn't listen to her."

Take charge. Take care. Take control. Same Wyatt.
Same solid, stand-up warrior, Sophie thought as she

waited impatiently at a light, then punched the gas when it finally turned green. He and Hugh were alike in that way—yet in so many ways, they were different.

An electric aura seemed always to surround Hugh, setting everything and everyone around him on a razor-sharp edge of excitement that could be as exhausting as it was exhilarating. Wyatt, on the other hand, had always been so easy to be around. He was a warrior, there was never any doubt about that, but he never wore it the way Hugh did. Hugh was all about flash and swagger, while Wyatt was about understatement.

Heads turned when Hugh walked into a room; she'd even heard women gasp when they first saw him, he was that stunning, commanded that much attention, with his dark hair and eyes, Hollywood action-hero looks, and tall, rangy frame. Wyatt's bearing and quiet good looks would never draw a gasp. He was a good four inches shorter than Hugh's six-foot-two, carried his weight more like a football player than the runner Hugh always made her think of. Now, as the first time she'd seen him, Wyatt wore his sandy brown hair in a buzz cut, military short, a crisp, stark contrast to Hugh's, which always looked as if he'd just stepped out of a photo shoot. And while Hugh's dark eyes could pierce like lasers, the gorgeous light blue of Wyatt's eyes made her think of a low-burning flame. Steady, warm, embracing, yet barely masking a simmering sexual heat.

No doubt about it, Wyatt was handsome in his own understated way, but it took a closer look to see just how much of a man he was.

If she'd been older, wiser, less blinded by Hugh's brilliant light, she might have appreciated that more when she'd known him back then. Might have looked past her impressions of Wyatt Savage as a man who, while funny and smart, lacked the excitement that drew her to the lightning bolt that was Hugh. Wyatt had been comfortable. Papa Bear, Hugh had always called him. Wyatt had been a protector. A mediator. A level head.

In retrospect, she realized that she'd been wrong the many times she'd tried to delegate a "safe" spot for Wyatt in her mind. Safe, like a favorite old shirt, all snuggly and warm and stable. Safe, because Hugh had always made her feel as if she was straddling a razor-thin edge of danger, and she'd needed Wyatt's stability to counterbalance Hugh's volatility.

She needed stability now. God, she was relieved that he was here. She'd been nervous about seeing him again, and not just because of her concern over Hope and Lola. Twelve years was a long time to miss someone. Twelve years was a lot of time for a person to change.

Like Hugh had changed.

Wyatt hadn't. Thank God. She'd known the moment she laid eyes on him in the terminal that he was the same Wyatt, and she'd been thanking God ever since and indulging in the solid, steady strength of him.

"You look good, Wyatt. Well, if you don't count the blood," she added with wry concern. "I am *so* sorry. Are you sure you're okay?"

"Quit worryin' 'bout me. I was a pint over my limit anyway."

She glanced at him then. Even in the worst circumstances, Wyatt had always been able to make her smile with his down-home Southern drawl and quirky sense of humor. Circumstances didn't get much worse than this.

"Any idea who might have been on that welcome committee?"

She turned back to the highway, her hands gripping the wheel tightly as the air conditioner finally started blowing cool air. "Best guess would be the Guerrilleros Nacionales."

"The Guerrilleros Nacionales?"

"The GN is an ultra-nationalist group committed to the purity of El Salvador."

"I know who they are, sugar, but what's their beef with the Brits?"

"What *isn't* their beef—with *any*one—Brits, Americans, Germans. Pick a culture. They're violently against any intervention from or even fraternization with outside governments, and they don't care who gets hurt if it furthers their agenda. Kidnapping for ransom, by the way, is also one of their favorite tactics," she said bitterly, and changed lanes.

"You figure they're in the thick of your situation?"

"It fits," she said, nodding. "They're nothing but terrorists. Usually, they aren't bold enough to stage a daylight and very public attack, though. The airport, for God's sake. I can't believe what just happened." She shook her head. "God, I hope no one got hurt back there."

"News at ten," he said.

Yeah. The attack at the airport would make the news, all right. Just as the abduction had made the news.

She looked sideways at him again, at his clean, crisp profile and the hard, world-weary look that men like him always wore, and felt a heavy sadness flood her heart. She'd often wondered what Hugh had done and seen in his lifetime. More often, she'd been content not knowing. Seeing Wyatt wearing that same look was somehow more disturbing than seeing it on Hugh. Wyatt had always been so . . . well, *sweet* was the word that came to mind, although she knew he'd roll his eyes at the notion.

But he *had* been sweet, she thought as the traffic slowed, stopped, and started moving again. She couldn't imagine Wyatt enjoying what he did the way Hugh did. The way Hugh always had. But she could see Wyatt doing his job. Like he'd done it today. Competently, professionally, but with resignation, not relish. Hugh thrived on adrenaline. He always savored an operation.

She flexed her fingers on the steering wheel, thinking about the differences between the two men that she hadn't seen or understood back when they'd all been young and idealistic and green . . .

Langley Air Force Base, Hampton, Virginia
Twelve years ago

Sophie glanced up from her desk as her last two new students sauntered into her adult-education Spanish class.

She did a double take, then shook her head as the two men sized up the room.

"God," she murmured to her TA, Dana Long. "Does the CIA really think they're fooling anyone when they send me their 'spooky boys' under the pretense that they're"— she stopped, checked the class list, and laughed—"U.S. embassy clerks?"

"Must have missed the Subterfuge 101 class," Dana said, following Sophie's gaze. "At least they could try not to be so obvious."

Right. If these guys were clerks, Sophie was a tank commander. Just as it was hard to mistake the lingering scent of the disinfectant the janitorial service used to clean her class room as anything but industrial-strength, it was hard not to recognize CIA operatives as anything but spies. More than anything, their eyes gave them away. Watchful. Vigilant.

She'd taught this adult Spanish class in the same classroom, with its gray walls, acoustical-tile ceiling, and metal desks, for two years now. She'd gotten good at recognizing students who weren't what they presented themselves to be.

"They're pretty cute," Dana said behind her hand as the two men found seats in the back of the small room. "Especially the tall one. What a stunner. What do you think? He remind you of anyone? Wait. I've got it. George Clooney—only with sharper, sexier edges. Man, I'd like to see him naked."

Sophie couldn't stop a quick bubble of laughter and intentionally misunderstood. "Clooney?"

"Well, yeah, him, too." Dana grinned. "The way this guy's looking at you, I'd say there's a good chance you might actually get to see a grand unveiling."

Sophie glanced toward the back of the room, and sure enough, Mr. Tall, Dark, and Handsome had rocked back on two chair legs, tilted his head and was sizing her up with an openly appreciative grin.

"Now, the other guy," Dana continued, "he's not exactly TD&H but he's hot in his own way, you know. He's got that crisp, clean-cut, all-American man-boy look going on."

Another astute analogy, Sophie thought, with a glance at TD&H's buddy. He was a few inches shorter than his partner in crime, a little heavier-built. Not that he was overweight. No, he was rock-solid, all muscle, and while he wasn't fair-skinned, his buzz-cut light brown hair bounced him out of the dark part of the equation. He wasn't what she'd call strikingly handsome. Dana was right. All-American suited him better. And that slow, conspiratorial smile he slid her way, well, what could she do but smile back when those dazzling and intelligent blue eyes caught her checking him out?

Trouble. Both of them, she realized, and decided it was time to earn her pay.

Sometimes she felt so fortunate to be doing what she did that she'd almost be willing to teach the class for free. And while she'd never get rich on her teacher's salary, it was nice to know that as long as what she did made her happy, she'd never feel pressure from her family to "raise the bar" in the aspiration department.

Not that she didn't have goals. Lofty goals. Goals that included her own school someday, where she would teach children instead of adults. She had her parents to thank for that dream, too.

Her father was a high-ranking U.S. embassy official, and her mother was a "proud and practicing" socialite who had been dedicated to various charitable causes her entire life. Because of her father's embassy assignments all over the world, Sophie had acquired a taste for exotic places during her globe-trotting childhood. She'd also developed a strong sense of service from her mother, who Sophie knew would continue her philanthropic work even after her father retired.

Many of the impressions Sophie had taken with her from her childhood as they had settled and resettled around the world had been of the poverty and deplorable illiteracy rates, particularly in the many Central American countries where her father had been stationed. That's why, at an early age, she decided to make teaching her life's work. Because she herself had received an excellent education in schools attended primarily by children of U.S. military and embassy employees, her personal goal was someday to found a school somewhere in Central America that would offer scholarships to local children so they could have the same educational advantages as American children like her who were essentially visitors in their land.

All dreams started with small steps, however, and Sophie understood that she had to establish herself and her credibility as an educator in the right circles before she could see that dream to fruition. That's why, after graduating with degrees in both education and administration with a minor in Spanish, she'd taken a position with the State Department as a Spanish instructor for embassy employees.

Employees like the cute "spooky boys," who were sure to give her trouble before the three-month class was over.

"All right, class," she said, addressing the room of fifteen students. "Glad you could all make it. I'm Sophie Baylor. This is my teaching assistant, Dana Long. My credentials are posted on the school's Web site, but I figure you already know what you need to know about me, or you wouldn't be here, right?"

She smiled to the room at large. "So, how about you tell me a little bit about yourselves and why you're taking the class? Anyone want to start?"

Two hands shot up at the back of the room. Of course, it was TD&H and his sidekick; both men were grinning from ear to ear. Brother. She was used to the occasional flirt, but these guys took it over the top.

She pointedly passed them by and smiled at a pleasant-looking middle-aged woman in the front row. "Let's start with you, okay? Then we'll work our way to the back of the class."

It wasn't the first message Hugh Weber and Wyatt Savage hadn't gotten during the three-month crash course in Spanish. But those sexy grins were the first of many unmistakable messages they both sent her way . . .

5

"Sophie?"

Sophie jerked her gaze away from the road and her memories to see Wyatt watching her with concern.

"I'm sorry. Shell-shock moment. Guess I'm having a bit of a delayed reaction. It's not every day that I get to dodge bullets," she added, attempting to make light of her lapse in concentration.

There was more than a grain of truth in what she'd said. The incident at the airport had rattled her. Seeing Wyatt's blood had rattled her.

The abduction was making her crazy.

"You want me to drive, sugar?"

"No. No, I'm fine." *Damn.* Tears filled her eyes. She fought them back. "Okay, I'm not fine. But I need to be." Because she needed to keep it together.

"Maybe we should wait until we get wherever we're going before you fill me in."

Again, typical Wyatt, trying to take care of her. The first time she and Hugh had had a fight, she'd run to Wyatt.

"That's what these shoulders are for," he'd said, and had let her snivel all over him before he'd sent her back to Hugh.

She was determined not to cry now.

"So, how's your daughter doing?" he asked.

"Hope is traumatized. Terrorized. Riddled with guilt. Lola is her best friend. Hope knows that she was the target and that the kidnappers took Lola by mistake. Her heart is broken. Ramona, Lola's mother—God, she's devastated."

And so was Sophie.

"Why are you so sure Hope was the target?"

"Hope heard the man behind the wheel instruct the bastard who grabbed Lola to 'Get the Weber girl.' With Lola and Hope both wearing the school uniform, he took the wrong girl.

"Besides," she added, "why would they take Lola? She's one of my scholarship students. There's no money, no reason to take her. Ramona was unemployed a year ago. She and Lola were staying with Ramona's brother until I hired her. Now she and Lola live in my little *casita* behind the house."

The little guest cottage had been a perfect fit for the two of them, and Ramona had proven invaluable to Sophie.

"I don't know what I'd do without Ramona. She manages the house, watches both girls." She stopped, her breath thick in her chest. "How can I feel so thankful and relieved that Hope is safe when poor little Lola is going through a nightmare?"

"Hope is your child," he said. "How can you *not* feel relief?"

Intellectually, she knew he was right, but it didn't stop the guilt.

"Why abduct your daughter?" Wyatt pressed because he was a smart man. He knew she needed to keep focused, or she'd flounder in guilt and fear for Lola.

"This is El Salvador," she stated, not even trying to hide her bitterness. "Kidnapping for ransom is a national pastime."

He nodded with the certainty of a man who had had too much experience with bad, bad men. "What do the police say?"

"They're useless. Of course, they point fingers at the usual suspects. MS-13 is at the top of their list."

"MS-13 is always at the top of everyone's list," he muttered.

She couldn't argue with that. The violent street gang, also known as Mara Salvatrucha, had started in El Salvador and spread not only to most of Central America but also to California and several other areas in the States. Its members were violent and vicious and totally void of conscience or remorse. Drugs, tattoos, and kidnapping were their MO.

"They also suspect the GN," she added, frowning when she thought about the group that was most likely behind the attack at the airport. "They've been opposed to my school since I opened it five years ago."

That drew his interest. "Because?"

"Because they see the school as interfering with their

'purist' doctrine. We integrate international as well as national customs into our curriculum. Instead of seeing it as good exposure, they see it as diluting the traditional El Salvadoran culture."

"So it's not a stretch to point a finger their way."

"I just don't know, Wyatt. It's true that the GN has never been happy with our cultural interaction. I suppose they could be trying to scare me into shutting down. Or possibly to bring negative attention to the school. Too many incidents like this could make a case for my school not being a safe environment. My grants could be pulled. That would be the end of it."

"I still hear a 'but' in there," he said.

"But I just don't think that they'd put this much energy into shutting me down. They've got bigger fish to fry."

"Like the British diplomat," he concluded.

"Right. I'm actually more inclined to think it's MS-13. But then the FMLN could be behind the kidnapping, too."

"Farabundo Martí National Liberation Front?"

She nodded. "They've also been behind a number of kidnappings for ransom over the years. It's their power play of choice."

"If I remember right, the FMLN was granted legal political-party status more than a decade ago."

"A thug by any other name is still a thug. And at their grass roots, they're still a terrorist organization. But the fact is that since they've been legitimized, no one has had the guts to stand up to their terrorist tactics, especially not the police force."

"I take it you suggested the FMLN to the police as a possibility?"

She snorted. "Oh, they concede that it's possible the kidnappers could be fringe members of the FMLN—many Mara Salvatrucha gang members can even be traced back to the FMLN—but since the *policía* are scared to death of MS-13, it's highly unlikely that they'll do anything at all."

She braked for another light and finger combed the hair back from her face while Wyatt digested and processed information.

"Talk to me about other possibilities," he finally said.

The light turned, and she hit the gas. "I've racked my brain trying to come up with an answer. It could be anyone. The police force's antikidnapping task force is a joke. I wouldn't even be surprised if they were involved. The entire force is noted for its corruption—right up to the higher-ranking police officials—and the task force has never been effective in finding abduction victims. They're in bed with the local drug cartel, which is rampant in certain sections of the city. Hugh's been more effective lately at recovering kidnapping victims than anything the *policía* have done."

But Hugh wasn't here.

"We can't discount the possibility that the abduction was intended to hurt Hugh. He has to have made a lot of enemies over the years," Wyatt said quietly.

"I know. I've thought of that."

"Have you heard anything from him?"

She shook her head, biting back her frustration. "Not yet."

She felt sick to her stomach thinking about Lola in the hands of ruthless, heartless men. God, the things they could do to her.

"Okay, who else could be responsible?" Wyatt's voice snapped her away from her grisly thoughts. "What about competition? Would another school have a reason to cause trouble?"

"No," she said, and forced herself to focus on something useful. "I can't see that. Schools are overcrowded. Baylor is actually taking some of the heat off the public education system."

"Has there been a ransom demand yet?"

She'd been waiting for this question. Dreading it. "No." She felt tears well up again. "And bottom line, I don't have the money to pay one."

Wyatt was silent for a moment. This didn't compute. He'd made a conscious decision to keep his distance from Sophie and Hugh after they'd gotten married. Yeah, it had been the coward's way out, but it was what he'd needed to get over losing her. Still, he'd heard things over the years. CIA and post military circles were tight. He'd known Hugh had started his own private contracting business several years ago after he'd parted ways with Uncle. If Hugh had experienced half the success that Nate had with Black Ops, Inc., then raising ransom money shouldn't be an issue.

He wanted to ask Sophie about that but decided to respect her silence—for now—and hope she would eventually bring up the subject.

"What about your parents?" he asked instead. "Could they help?"

A strange look came over her face before she said quietly, "I . . . I can't ask them. I can't involve them in this."

Again, her response prompted questions he might have to explore later. The lady had some secrets she didn't want to risk sharing with him, secrets that he hoped had no relevance to Lola's abduction. Okay, fine. For now, he'd take his cues from her.

"But someone might assume you would ask them for help," Wyatt said, instead of asking why she was being so evasive. "Someone could find out enough about you to be aware of your family's finances, figure you would tap them for the cash. Not that it narrows the pool of suspects. Anyone with access to the Web could find out damn near anything about anybody. Case in point, you found me."

"I got lucky," she admitted, using his example to veer away from the subject of her parents as she turned off the main thoroughfare onto a quiet side street. "I remembered that your parents lived in Georgia, remembered their names, and yes, I did a Google search of the Georgia white pages. Found them on the first try. I was stunned when you were actually there."

She was stunned? He wasn't a fatalist. Wasn't much on "signs." But what were the odds of him being at his parents' at the exact time she had needed him? Slim and slimmer. He decided not to question it. Besides, his dad always knew how to reach him in an emergency. If Wyatt hadn't been home in Georgia, Sophie would have persuaded Ben to contact him. Still, the timing, with Hugh out of touch, made a man wonder about kismet and karma and forces of nature. And cruel twists of fate, because, damn, with Hugh temporarily out of the picture, it was too frickin' easy to imagine painting himself in.

"I'll figure something out on the ransom."

The tension in her voice cut into his thoughts and slammed him back to the immediacy of the moment. "Let's hope it won't come to that."

"It always comes to that," she said with a fatalism that broke his heart.

"How about beefs with your neighbors?" he continued, getting back on track. "Other parents? Maybe parents of kids who wanted into your school but didn't make the cut?"

"No. Nothing like that. At least, not that I know of." She slowed down, then turned onto a cul-de-sac in a quiet, affluent-looking neighborhood and pulled into the first driveway. Red and pink hibiscus, squat pineapple palms, and low-growing waxy green ground cover were all neatly manicured in beds surrounding a white single-story house topped with a terra-cotta tiled roof.

"As for the school," she continued after shutting off

the motor, "except for the students on financial scholarship, most of the kids attending Baylor are locals and a mix of children of U.S. embassy and military personnel, so I think you're heading down a dead end there."

She sounded weary and frustrated. And very much alone. Wyatt felt a surge of anger toward his old friend. *Hugh should be here, damn it.* Hugh, not he, should be here, getting a handle on the situation and taking care of his wife and family.

"Come on, let's get inside," she said, looking across the seat at him. "Hope's next door with Carmen, my neighbor and one of the school security guards I hired to watch over them until I got back. Thank God for Carmen," she added with feeling. "She's always been like a surrogate grandma to both Hope and Lola. And as upset as she's been over Lola's abduction, she's held it together for Hope's sake."

She stopped abruptly. "God, I'm rambling. Sorry."

"Deep breath, Sophe," he said, sympathizing.

She smiled. "Come on, let's get you cleaned up before you meet them. I don't want Hope and Carmen to see the blood."

She glanced at his forehead. "And please, don't mention the attack at the airport. Hope is frightened enough. I don't want her worrying that something could have happened to me, too. If either of them hears about the incident on the news, I'll just say we were already gone when it happened, okay?"

Mother Bear, Wyatt thought. Protecting her cub and those who were important to her. "You got it." He opened his door and stepped out of the air-conditioned car and into the wet El Salvadoran heat.

He'd been in the country for roughly two hours. So far, he'd gotten caught in the middle of a terrorist attack, killed two men, saved a mother and a child, and bled all over one of his favorite shirts. And it was still more than an hour until noon.

A typical day in the life of Wyatt Savage. *Jesus.* Not for the first time, it occurred to him that he really needed a new line of work.

"You can leave your bag in there," Sophie said after she'd led Wyatt quickly through a large living room that opened to an airy kitchen.

He'd caught brief flashes of vibrant colors, large arched windows, and soft, stylish furnishings before she'd hooked a left down a wide hallway with a floor covered in travertine tile the color of eggshells and walls painted a rich terra-cotta. High ceilings and the slow rotation of ceiling fans stirred the air and helped what he figured was a central air-conditioning unit cut both the heat and the humidity.

As instructed, he tossed his go bag onto the floor of what he assumed was a guest bedroom, then joined her across the hall in a tiled bathroom. She was busy setting first-aid supplies on the vanity.

"Sit," she ordered, pointing absently to the closed lid on the toilet.

"Yes, ma'am," he said smartly.

That brought her head up. Red flamed in her cheeks.

"Oh, God, I'm ordering you around like you're one of my students. I'm sorry," she added as he sat. "I'm just . . ."

"Upset?" he suggested to put her at ease. "A little shocky from the fiasco at the airport? Exhausted, maybe? Have you even slept since the girl was taken, sugar?"

Her shoulders sagged, and for the first time, Wyatt could see just how big a toll the abduction had taken on her.

"I grant you absolution," he said with a soft smile. "So, order away, Teacher Lady, if it makes you feel better. And I promise to be a good Southern boy and grin and bear it."

Her deep breath and the slow smile that followed told him he'd managed to ease some of her tension. "Like you were a good boy in my Spanish class?"

"I was a *very* good boy. I never missed a class."

She snorted and ripped open a package of antiseptic cleansing wipes. "You never missed an opportunity to give me grief, either."

"Darlin'," he said as she started dabbing at the blood on his forehead, "I missed a lot of opportunities with you."

One in particular, he thought with regret.

When her hand momentarily stilled, he wondered if she was thinking about that day, too. That sweet, sunny Sunday when things had gotten out of hand between them.

The bathroom became very quiet. And very small. He'd been trying hard not to think about where she was standing—which was directly in front of him, her breasts at eye level, her scent surrounding him. The hand she'd used to hold his head still so she could clean him up was an intimate and tactile reminder of everything female about her.

Her right leg was wedged between his thighs, where his hands, clenched into tight fists, rested. A fractional shift forward, and his hands could be encircling her waist, his breath could be warming her nipples.

He closed his eyes, willed himself to get it the hell together. Not happening. He was angry. Angry that he was here. Angry that the one thing he'd wanted for most of his adult life was within his grasp, and he still had no right to take it. Couldn't take it.

Neither could he stop himself from asking the question that had been burning in his gut since she'd called him. "Sophie, why can't you reach Hugh?" A husband left his wife a contingency plan for emergencies. "Where the hell is he?"

She expelled a fractured breath, as if she, too, had to struggle to come back to a reality that existed far outside the confines of this moment. With renewed vigor, she went back to work cleaning the blood off his face.

"Hugh is where he always is," she said, her tone thick with resentment. "Off in some Third World corner of the globe, protecting some high-ranking official from a coup or training someone how to do it or something equally dangerous."

Her face grim, she continued working on his head. "Why do head wounds have to bleed so much?" she muttered rhetorically. "It's just a little cut."

"I told you, sugar, I'm fine," he reminded her, then winced when she took out some of her frustration at Hugh by scrubbing a little harder.

"Take off your shirt," she ordered, apparently satisfied that she'd done what she could on the head wound. "I want to look at your arm."

He slowly undid the buttons, then shrugged out of his shirt, wondering at the wisdom of getting half naked in front of her.

What? You think she'll attack you?

The troubled look on her face dashed those hopes and, thank God, the distinct possibility of a major hardon. She glanced at him, then quickly looked away.

"What?" he asked, sensing that she had something on her mind that had nothing to do with close quarters and his stupid fantasies.

"Hugh's changed, Wyatt," she said, sounding sad and resigned. "I'm not sure you'd know him anymore, much less like him."

He was still processing the acrimony in her words when she dropped her next bomb.

"We've been divorced for almost two years now."

6

It took several heartbeats for Wyatt to process what she'd said. Several heartbeats where he couldn't move. Couldn't speak. Could barely breathe.

Divorced. Sophie and Hugh were divorced.

He didn't know what to say. Wasn't sure he knew what to feel. Shock. Disbelief. Sorrow.

Elation.

He hoped to hell she couldn't see his heart jumping in his chest as he sat there. The sharp sting of alcohol leaching into the open wound in the back of his arm was the only proof that he wasn't experiencing some kind of out-of-body experience.

Hugh's changed . . . I'm not sure you'd know him anymore, much less like him . . . divorced . . . almost two years.

Yeah, the kind of work they did could change a man, could take over his soul if he wasn't careful. But for Hugh to let himself lose a woman like Sophie? *Jesus.* What the hell had happened?

Still reeling, Wyatt let himself glance up at her.

All he saw on her face was concentration as she worked on his arm. At least, that's all she let him see.

"This could probably use a stitch or two," she said, frowning, "but I think we can make do with a butterfly."

He couldn't take his eyes off her face. He didn't know what he was searching for. A broken heart? Regret? Relief? Joy? Anything to give him a clue about how she felt.

He got nothing. She gave absolutely nothing away. *Divorced.*

"All set." She backed away from him. "And none too soon. I just heard the back door. That means Hope is here, probably Carmen, too. Maybe you could, um, put a fresh shirt on before they see you?" she suggested, gathering up his bloody shirt.

"Yeah. Sure," he mumbled absently. Like an automaton, he stood and squeezed past her and out of the small bathroom. He walked across the hall to the bedroom where he'd stashed his go bag, closed the door behind him, and leaned heavily against it.

"Jesus." He scrubbed the heel of his hand over his bare chest.

Sophie was single.

Which meant . . . hell, he didn't know what it meant. For the time being, he didn't need to know, he reminded himself, pushing away from the door in self-disgust. He didn't need to think about it. Couldn't think straight about it if he tried.

The clock was ticking. A child's life was at stake, and

for the moment, the best hope that child had of coming home alive was him.

He unzipped his bag and rummaged around inside. He finally came up with a clean white T-shirt and dragged it over his head. Then he drew a bracing breath, swung open the bedroom door . . . and found himself staring down into the upturned face of a wide-eyed El Salvadoran girl.

"*Buenas tardes, señorita*," he said when it was clear that he'd scared her half to death.

She was a beautiful girl. Huge black eyes, long dark brown hair, lithe and slim, with toasted-caramel skin. He wasn't good at ages, but if he had to guess, he'd put her somewhere between ten and twelve. Sophie hadn't mentioned that Lola had a sister, but he couldn't help but wonder if this, too, was Ramona's child. Or possibly her neighbor Carmen's granddaughter.

He extended his hand. "*Me llama Wyatt.*"

"*Sí.*" She hesitated, but when he smiled at her, she laid her hand in his. "*Sé quien es.*"

So she knew who he was. And she was still a little afraid. He didn't blame her. His big mitt looked like a bear paw next to her delicate little hand.

"That's a very pretty necklace," he said, commenting on the heart-shaped disc that dangled from a delicate chain. There was something engraved on the silver, but the letters were so small he couldn't make them out.

When he didn't get any response from her, he tried again, in Spanish this time.

"Cómo te llama?" he asked hoping she'd feel comfortable enough to tell him her name.

Footsteps on the tile brought his head up to see Sophie walking toward them.

"Hope," Sophie said, her gaze riveted on the girl, her expression full of warmth and what could only be love as she looked from the child to him. "Her name is Hope. She's my daughter."

He cut his gaze from Sophie to the lovely Latino girl, unable to hide his surprise. It had never occurred to him that Sophie and Hugh would have adopted a child, yet it so fit what he knew of Sophie. Her heart had always been kind and generous and open, and the proof that she hadn't changed was right here in front of him. He slowly absorbed the shock waves of yet one more bombshell.

Before he'd fully digested this latest bit of information, she hit him with one more explosive blast.

"Wyatt," she said so quietly that he understood something had happened.

He met her worried eyes.

"We just got a ransom demand."

A few minutes later, Sophie joined Wyatt at the island separating the kitchen from the living area, where he was studying the ransom note and working on a mug of coffee. She glanced into the living room. Hope sat cross-legged on the floor in front of the TV, watching a *Hannah Montana* episode dubbed in Spanish. Only Hope wasn't really watching it. Her daughter had withdrawn into herself. Even though Sophie understood that it was Hope's subconscious attempt to escape the horrible reality of Lola's abduction, it was still difficult to watch.

Just as the ransom note had been difficult to read. It had been mixed in with the bills, unsolicited advertisements, and Sophie's morning paper. The plain white envelope appeared as innocuous as a greeting card. There was nothing innocent, however, about the contents. Handwritten in Spanish, it advised Sophie that if she wanted to see her daughter alive again, she was to pay $500,000 in unmarked American bills by noon on Thursday. At that time, she would receive a call with instructions on where and exactly when the exchange would be made.

She felt sick. She didn't have half a million dollars.

"It's significant that they're giving you three days to get the money."

Her head snapped at the sound of Wyatt's voice. "I'm sorry." She turned to him, knew he'd said something important. Knew that she wasn't tracking on all fronts. "What did you say?"

He studied her with concern. "Maybe you should get some rest, sugar."

"No. No, I'm fine. It's . . . it's just a little difficult to concentrate."

His frown deepened, but he didn't press her. "I said it's significant that they're giving you three days to get the money. And it's going to help that our window of time just expanded by"—he checked his watch, did a mental calculation—"seventy-six hours," he said. "Good news for us."

Good news for them but bad news for a terrified child who wanted to come home.

She couldn't stop thinking about Lola and her mother, Ramona. Overcome with grief and worry, Ramona had allowed her brother to take her home with him to her parents yesterday. Sophie couldn't get Ramona's face out of her mind. The young woman had aged years in a matter of hours.

"Why is it significant that they're giving me three days?" she asked, her soft tone matching Wyatt's so Hope couldn't hear them.

"It means they know you'll have to go to an outside source for the money, which means that whoever is behind this knows enough about you to realize you won't have the cash."

"Yet they don't know enough to take the right child." She stopped when she realized what she'd said. "Oh, God. *Right child*? There is no *right* child. There is no—"

"Sophie." Wyatt covered her shaking hand with his. "We deal with what is, sugar, not what should or shouldn't be. Keep it together, okay? You need to keep it together."

He was right. She drew a bracing breath, knew she had to do something or she'd implode. Wyatt had already been busy, making calls and talking to the men he worked with in Argentina who were due to arrive later today.

So she rose and walked to the refrigerator then busied herself preparing lunch. She stuffed thick tortillas with beans and cheese and chicken and tried not to let the fear take over.

"*Pupusas*," she explained, sliding a plate in front of Wyatt as she joined him at the island.

"Where's yours?"

She shook her head. The thought of food nauseated her. "I can't eat."

"Not an option." He reached for a knife from the thick wooden block at the far end of the black granite counter and cut his *pupusas* in half. "You need the protein."

"What I need is to get Lola back. What I need is for my daughter to feel safe. Look at her. She's hardly talked since this happened. Some bastard from the police department interrogated her and scared her to death. He even threatened her when she couldn't remember anything. Now I can't get her to eat, and I don't think she slept at all last night. She just stares. She doesn't even cry."

"She'll be okay," Wyatt assured her. "She's a kid. She's tough. She'll eventually remember something that will help us. With you in her corner, she will absolutely recover. In time. But right now, you need to set an example for her, darlin'. She's taking her cues from you. Now, eat."

He was right again, Sophie admitted, and forced herself to take a bite of the *pupusas*. "I feel so helpless."

"We're going to get Lola back," Wyatt insisted in that quiet, confident way he had.

"I want to believe you. God, I want to believe, but these monsters, whoever they are . . . there's no guarantee they won't kill her even if we do come up with the money, right? Wyatt, things go wrong. Victims get killed." She hugged herself to stall the chills that even the summer heat couldn't ward off.

"We'll get her back," he repeated.

She met his eyes and nodded, mostly because she knew he wanted her to. She glanced across the room at Hope, so quiet in front of the TV. "What happens when they figure out they don't have Hope?" She kept her voice low so Hope couldn't hear her. "The paper covered the story. There was no way to keep it under wraps. Not with so many witnesses."

"Yeah, I've been thinking about that," he said, matching her tone. "You should call the newspaper today. Maybe even the local TV news. Let them know that Lola is like a daughter to you, that you'll do anything to get her back unharmed. If the kidnappers understand that she's valuable to you, she'll remain valuable to them."

It made sense. Lola's abduction hadn't been front-page news—a sad commentary that another run-of-the-mill abduction wasn't worthy of the front page—but the media had been covering it.

A horrifying thought kept assaulting her. She couldn't keep it bottled up any longer. She glanced at Hope again, then back to Wyatt. "What if they come back for Hope?"

He gave her a hard look, and she knew she wasn't going to like what he had to say. "There's no way to soft-pedal this. It's a real possibility that they'll try. We need to get her out of El Salvador, Sophie. Tuck her away someplace safe where no one can get to her."

Sophie clamped her hands together in front of her on the counter. She stared at her mostly untouched *pupusas*. She knew he was right, but that didn't make it any easier to think about. "Where? Where can she go? I can't send her to my parents. I can't put them in the middle of this."

"I agree," he said. "I know a place where she'll be safe." He covered her hands and squeezed gently when her wary gaze shot to his. "You called me because you trust me," he added when tears threatened. "Trust me now."

Sophie looked at her vibrant daughter, who now possessed all the life of a statue. "She's so fragile."

"Yes," he agreed. "She is."

She met Wyatt's eyes again, saw the calm assurance there.

"Trust me now," he said again.

Trust him with the one thing she loved above all else in the world.

She closed her eyes and nodded. Then she prayed to God that her instincts were right.

Argentina. Wyatt wanted to send Hope to Argentina to stay with his friend Dr. Juliana Flores, and his boss, Nate Black, who would protect her. The idea flew in the face of every maternal instinct Sophie possessed. And yet what choice did she have?

She asked Carmen to take Hope with her for a little while. Then she called the newspapers and the TV station and asked them to spread the word that she considered Lola a daughter and would do anything to get her back. Now Wyatt was trying to reassure her that Hope would be fine. With strangers. Strangers to her, at any rate. But he'd asked her to trust him. And trust, after all, was the reason she'd called him in the first place.

"Tell me about Dr. Flores." She sat down on one end of the sofa. The thought of being separated from Hope, especially while she was so traumatized, broke her heart.

Wyatt eased down next to her. "Where do I start? Juliana is an amazing woman. She's a doctor, as you already know. In addition to her private practice, she runs a free clinic in Bahía Blanca that she and her husband, Armando, started together. Sadly, several years ago, Juliana lost both Armando and their daughter, Angelina."

"How horrible." She felt a deep, heart-wrenching pain for Dr. Flores. "What happened?"

Sophie read hesitation in Wyatt's eyes before he finally spoke. "The world is full of bad men, Sophie. Unfortunately even people as philanthropic and gentle as Juliana can't always escape the violence. Let's leave it at that."

Because the details are too horrifying, she surmised with a sick, sinking feeling in her stomach.

She shot up off the sofa, overcome by anger and fear and grief for a woman and a family she didn't even know but whose circumstances meshed with her own horrific situation. And she felt helpless and overwhelmed by the odds of getting Lola back alive.

"God, I hate this. I don't want this to be happening. I don't want—"

Wyatt walked up behind her; his big hands gripped her shoulders, steadying her.

"I'm sorry." She wiped at a tear, then bolstered herself with a deep breath. She was doing no one—especially Lola—any good by walking that road.

"The situation is what it is," she said with a weary acceptance. "It didn't start in my lifetime. It won't end in it, either. Even knowing what Hugh and his men, what you and your team, do every day, I just never expected such evil to come so close."

She turned around and faced him then. Saw the compassion and the understanding in his eyes and forced herself to smile. "And I didn't mean to sound ungrateful. Thank you for keeping my daughter safe."

"I want you to go with her, Sophie," he said after a long moment.

The sad and sorry truth was that she wanted that, too. It didn't make her proud, but she wanted to be with her daughter, leave the fight to Wyatt and his men, bury her head in the sand, and not pull it out until she was sure of a happy ending. But that was the coward's way. She would not let this turn her into someone she couldn't bear to be.

"I'm staying here," she said. "I need to do what I can to help you. And I *can* help you."

"You're not responsible for Lola's abduction," he said, reading her thoughts to the letter. "You can't carry that guilt."

"Doesn't matter. I'm not turning my back on her. Besides, the kidnappers have to know I got the note. They'll expect to deal with me."

When he opened his mouth to object, she cut off his protest with a hard shake of her head. "What if it *is* the Guerrilleros Nacionales? Then it *is* all on me. How many more of my students could be snatched if I were to leave?" she pointed out, trying another tack. "If I hide out and do nothing, I might not even have a school to come back to. The public outcry could close me down. This is about one lost child, yes, and if it is the GN, then it's also about hundreds of children who won't have a chance without my school.

"And if it's not the GN," she added, "it's still up to me to help find her."

Wyatt's continued look of skepticism prompted her final and strongest argument. "It was supposed to be my daughter. *My* daughter. Ramona and her family are grieving instead. You can't expect me to do nothing."

He searched her face, then turned and walked to the French doors leading out to the patio. He stood there, staring outside for the longest moment before turning back to her.

"All right." The hard look on his face showed his reluctance. "But no heroics. You will not go out on your own. You will—"

"Find her," she cut in. "You and I will find her. We have to find her. Alive," she insisted, swallowing hard. "There's no other acceptable outcome."

7

"How the hell could you fuck it up? Your bungling flunkies grabbed the wrong kid."

Vincente Bonilla held the cell phone loosely to his ear, choosing to extend benevolence toward the man screaming at him on the other end of the line. "You are lucky I'm in a forgiving mood, my friend, or you would die a slow and painful death for speaking to me this way."

Blame his good mood on the *ganja*. And the whore, Justina, on her knees between his legs.

And then there was the prospect of the money this latest venture—wrong girl or not—would net both him and his pissed-off silent partner.

Not too silent now.

"You watch TV. You see the news," Vincente stated. "The woman says she will still pay. No harm. No foul." Well, except for Joma. Sadly, mistakes like the one Joma made when he'd pinched the wrong kid could not go unpunished. Not if Vincente was to keep face with his soldiers as well as keep them in line. No, he could not be perceived as soft.

He would miss Joma, though. The boy had made him laugh. Now Joma made his mother cry, for her son, who was dead. But then, the crack whore always cried. Why should today be different?

"We proceed as planned." Vincente flipped the cell phone closed and tossed it onto the sofa cushion beside him. End of discussion. Although he had seen firsthand the brutality the man was capable of inflicting, he grew weary listening to his threats. Vincente could be every bit as vicious. And Vincente Bonilla was afraid of no man.

He drew deeply on the slow-burning joint, held it in his lungs, savored, and sank deeper into the plush leather sofa.

"Is good, my little *puta*," he murmured tenderly, petting Justina's hair as she worked him with her studded tongue—just the way he liked it—and rode on the sensations of her greedy little mouth.

Life was good, he thought through the haze of carnal pleasure and sweet, spiraling smoke as the Latino rap beat of Big Ceaze pounded in the background and Stevan Jos Batlle's latest porn flick filled the big-screen TV.

Yes, life in San Salvador was very, very good. Fuck L.A. Fuck the United States. Land of milk and honey? Land of maximum-security prisons. He had knowledge of one in particular in ways that no man should.

He had welcomed his deportation back to El Salvador four years ago. He had earned his many tattoos, his right to wear the blue and white colors, and his leadership position in Mara Salvatrucha several times over. Because of him, no one would forget May 13, 2006. Just like no one would forget that it was Vincente who had murdered Ernesto Miranda that day. To make his mark. To make a point that no man, not even a high-ranking soldier and one of the founders of Mara Salvatrucha, left the gang and lived.

Ernesto had been a friend. Now he was dead, and Vincente, who had proven his value and his ruthlessness to the gang, had the power, the wealth, and all the pussy and head he could handle.

His partner, too, was a powerful man. A wealthy man who lived in luxury. Vincente had his own form of luxury. His own territory. Soyopango was away from the prosperous populations in exclusive Colonia Escalón or a dozen other sections of the city, where his people worked like slaves to tend the lush gardens of the rich, to paint their security fences. Soyopango was rough, raw, impoverished. Vincente owned it. He protected it. He financed it. He decided who lived and who died.

And he reaped the rewards of his position.

His eyes rolled back when Justina lifted her head, licked her swollen lips, then squeezed his engorged cock between her magnificent breasts. Breasts he'd paid for, just like the meth he paid for to keep her high and happy and, most of all, grateful.

Life is very, very good.

The cries of a child tore him out of his swirling cocoon of pleasure.

"Silencio!" he roared in the general direction of the bedroom where she was bound on the bed.

"Mama . . . Mama . . ."

"*Silencio!*" he bellowed again, and took his frustration out on Justina by grabbing her hair and jerking her head back at a sharp angle. She cried out in pain.

"Go shut her up," he demanded, and shoved her away. She landed on her naked ass on the floor. "Then get back here and finish what you started."

Justina scrambled to her feet, rushed to the room, and disappeared behind the bedroom door. When she came back, the child was silent.

"*Bueno*," he said, and held out his hand.

She took it with a smile and straddled his lap like the good whore she was, taking him in with a low, humming moan when he gripped her hips and rammed her down hard onto his cock.

Life is good.

Wyatt had made his first call to Nate Black before he'd left the States the night before. He'd briefed his boss on what he knew of the situation and told him he would appreciate any bodies he could spare. He'd spoken to Nate again right after he'd convinced Sophie to send Hope to Argentina.

He'd known Nate would come through but hadn't understood why his boss had tagged one of BOI's best operatives, Johnny Duane Reed, to pull protection duty for Hope, along with Nate himself and Juliana in Argentina. At four in the afternoon, after Sophie had joined Hope next door at Carmen's, Wyatt answered the door, and there stood Reed, balancing on a pair of crutches; his right knee was trussed up in a brace. Now it made sense; the best Reed was up for was escorting Hope to Argentina, where they'd keep her under wraps.

Wyatt glanced from Reed's injured leg to his face. "And?"

"And even Superman can have a bad day." Reed grinned as his wife, Crystal, joined him at the door.

Wyatt could see Rafe Mendoza, Joe Green, Luke Colter, and Gabe Jones piling out of a Suburban that had pulled up in the drive behind the Reeds' rented SUV.

"What happened?" Wyatt asked Crystal, and stood back so the two of them could come inside out of the oppressive heat.

"Why are you asking her?" Reed thumped past him. "I'm the one on crutches."

"She'll tell me the truth," Wyatt said. "You'll just give me some bullshit story that will end with 'You should see the other guy.' "

"You wound me, bro." Reed hobbled to the closest chair, and even though he was putting on a good show to hide the pain, Wyatt noticed how carefully he sank down.

"He tore his ACL day before yesterday trying to do a stunt on a skateboard," Crystal said with a roll of her eyes that didn't quite hide the concern she felt for her husband.

"Mendoza dared him," Luke Colter—a.k.a. Doc Holliday, the team medic—put in, shaking Wyatt's hand as he entered the house.

Green, Jones, and Mendoza filed in behind Doc, shutting the door behind them.

"No one held a gun to the fool's head," Mendoza pointed out defensively.

Wyatt just looked at Reed and shook his head. Reed gave him a stupid grin, but Wyatt could see that he was embarrassed by the circumstances.

For all his Hollywood blond good looks and give-a-damn grin, Reed was one of the fiercest warriors on the Black Ops, Inc. team. And that was saying a lot, given the quality of the rest of the BOIs who had joined them. Reed had survived bloody firefights with little more than a scratch, and now a skateboard had put him on the disabled list. Had to be a helluva humble pill to swallow.

Hell, when Crystal had been abducted by the psycho head of an Indonesian human-trafficking ring, Reed had single-handedly rescued her from under the nose of one of the most ruthless thugs known to man. Of course, Wyatt and several other members of the BOI team had had to mop up after Reed—something they took great pleasure in reminding him of—but that didn't negate what the pretty boy had accomplished.

"So why isn't he on bed rest?" Wyatt crossed his arms over his chest and frowned at Reed.

Doc snorted. "He claims that anytime he gets horizontal, Crystal here sees it as in invitation to . . . you know. Says the woman can't keep her hands off him, and the knee can't stand the stress."

"The pain meds they gave him after the arthroscopic surgery are making him delirious," Crystal said with a smile generally reserved for the mentally challenged.

Wyatt adored Crystal. She was a tiny little redhead bombshell and the first girl to become a BOI when she'd joined the team several months ago as their commo, intel, and systems operator. She could also hold her own against any and all of the crap the BOIs tossed her way—the woman didn't take shit from any man.

"Reed was insistent that he be a part of this," Jones said, "so Nate figured the best place to keep him quiet until he heals up is in Argentina under Nate and Juliana's thumb."

"Just wait until Juliana gets a hold of him." Mendoza grinned. "Wish I could be there to hear him whimper when she starts his rehab exercises."

"You know, I'm right here," Reed grumbled as he gingerly lifted his leg and propped his foot on an ottoman. "I can talk for myself. I don't need you yahoos talking for me."

"Would you rather we talk about you behind your back?" Jones dropped his go bag by the door.

"*I'm* a yahoo?" Crystal narrowed her eyes at her husband.

Doc hooted. "Stepped in that one, pretty boy."

Reed encompassed the room at large with that give-a-damn grin. "Fuck you all very much," he said, then hastily added, "Not you, Tink, darlin'."

Crystal—a.k.a. Tinkerbell—pretty much made it clear that she thought her husband was hopeless. Still, Wyatt noticed that she couldn't stop herself from propping a pillow under his knee and laying the back of her hand on his forehead in concern. If the guys noticed

Reed fold her hand in his and bring it to his mouth, they chose to let it go. They must have figured they'd already ragged on him enough.

"So what have we got?" Gabe Jones asked, the line of his mouth hard, setting the tone as the lot of them put on their game faces.

They were here to do a job. And to a man, they knew it.

8

The old adage was true. The company a man keeps says a lot about the man. And Sophie's first impressions of Gabe "the Archangel" Jones, Raphael "Choirboy" Mendoza, Luke "Doc Holliday" Colter, and "Mean" Joe Green told Sophie a lot about Wyatt "Papa Bear" Savage. Then there was Reed, who was clearly in pain but had insisted on doing what he could to help. That kind of loyalty said even more about Wyatt.

She watched them from the kitchen as they huddled in her living room, their heads together, laying out their plan of action.

"Don't worry. They'll make this happen."

It was a little early for dinner, but Sophie had gotten them to admit that they hadn't eaten since morning. She glanced at Crystal, who was helping her throw a meal together. She nodded absently, wanting to believe that the diminutive, curvy younger woman with the brilliant red hair was right. As with her husband, Johnny Reed, there was clearly more to Crystal than met the eye, Sophie thought as Crystal got busy spreading mayo on bread.

"Tell me about them," Sophie urged, unable to hold back her fascination.

It wasn't that she wasn't used to being around men like these. Hugh had a huge payroll. Over the years she'd had occasion to meet many of the operatives who worked for him. Men who were just like Hugh. Focused, driven, and so hard around the edges she'd often wondered what had become of their souls or if they'd ever had souls to begin with.

"Sweethearts, every last one," Crystal smiled across the kitchen island at the lot of them. "Don't tell them I said that," she added with a conspiratorial grin.

Sweethearts? Sophie couldn't think of one man in Hugh's employ who merited the endearment. Cold-blooded killer. Ruthless. Soulless. Those descriptions fit.

She glanced at Crystal, who smiled and kept on working.

"That's all I'm getting from you?" The question was rhetorical. Sophie could clearly see where Crystal's loyalty lay—and that said a lot, too. Crystal knew these men, worked with them. She didn't know Sophie; therefore, she wasn't talking—which told Sophie that all the men of Black Ops, Inc. inspired loyalty.

"Do they always give each other this much grief?" she asked.

"Pretty much, yeah. Johnny told me once that it's all about checks and balances. Can't have anyone taking himself too seriously. They count on each other to keep things real. It's also a cross-check on their mental health. If someone's nose gets too far out of joint or if they don't react at all, then they figure there's something eating at him. They make sure they get him to unload, get it out of his system, you know?"

Yeah, Sophie knew. It used to be that way between Hugh and Wyatt. They covered each other's back, kept each other squared away.

"Like brothers," Sophie observed as she emptied a package of corn chips into a bowl.

"More than you'll ever know," Crystal agreed, opening up a jar of salsa.

And there was the difference between Hugh and Wyatt. Wyatt and these men were still the whole package. Driven. Focused. Capable. But still human. Somewhere along the way, Hugh seemed to have lost some of his humanity. She'd assumed it was a casualty of the profession, and while she understood it, she hadn't been able to live with it anymore.

She felt a hollow sadness for the loss of the man Hugh had once been, even wondered if he'd ever been that man or if she'd been so blinded by his light that she'd overlooked that something had been missing.

Wyatt glanced up and across the room, caught her eye. He gave her a reassuring nod. *We're on it*, his look said. *Trust me.*

I always have, she thought, realizing in that moment just how true it was. She had always trusted Wyatt Savage. To be who he was. To do the right thing. As she watched him now, she thought about one time in particular when he'd earned that trust a little too well . . .

Hampton, Virginia
Twelve years ago

"I'm not so sure I want to get on that thing."

"It's not like I'm taking you skydiving, sugar," Wyatt said in that Georgia drawl that was as soft as warm butter and as sexy as silk sheets. "It's just a little bike ride. Nothin' dangerous 'bout it."

Nothing dangerous but him, Sophie thought as he stood, his strong legs straddling the "little bike" that looked like a monster motorcycle to her. And it looked fast, just like he did, which was a surprise. Speed was more Hugh's style, but it was sure working for Wyatt today.

Lord, look at him. Faded blue jeans and black leather jacket. Aviator shades and pearly whites, both glinting under the warm noon sun. He was as tempting as the beautiful day and the promise of what was hidden inside an old-fashioned wicker picnic basket that he'd strapped onto the back of the bike.

"Thought we'd stop for a picnic somewhere along the way," he said when he caught her gaze drift to the basket and the blanket anchored beneath it.

The man knew how to entice.

"Now, quit scowling, Teach." He handed her a sleek silver helmet, then leaned toward her and helped her fas-

ten the chin strap. "It's Sunday. The weather is fine, and you could use a little fun. And some food," he added on a grin when her stomach growled.

She'd picked a bad day to skip breakfast. And he, apparently, had picked a perfect time to cruise up on this big black bike and infuse a little excitement into her life.

About one thing, he was right. She could use some fun, and if she'd learned anything having Wyatt in her class during the past month, it was that he knew how to have fun. He and his gorgeous friend.

Speaking of gorgeous, "So where's Hugh?"

"Tucked him under a rock," Wyatt said deadpan. "Where he belongs."

She rolled her eyes, took the hand he offered to help steady her, and swung a leg over the seat behind him. "I thought you two were connected at the hip."

"He thinks so, too. Guess he was wrong."

She didn't have any brothers, but she imagined that if she did, they couldn't be any closer than Wyatt and Hugh. Trash talk was the standard method of expressing that brotherhood.

He strapped on a sexy black helmet and glanced over his shoulder. "You ready, sugar?"

"Would it matter if I said no?"

He laughed and stomped down on the kick start. The big motor growled to life with a thundering roar. She couldn't stop a little squeal of alarm as he throttled forward. The quick takeoff had her wrapping her arms tightly around his waist and hanging on for her life.

"You did that on purpose," she yelled above the motor's rumble as he swung out into traffic.

"Yes, ma'am," he admitted without an ounce of repentance. "You just feel free to hang on to any little ol' thing that makes you feel safe," he added with a smile in his voice. Then he goosed the throttle and laughed when she squealed again and tightened her hold into a death grip.

"My God, that was amazing!" Sophie cried an hour later as she climbed off the bike and whipped off her helmet.

Soon after they'd hit the city limits, he'd pulled off the freeway and onto a winding blacktop road that led to the country and this spot, a few miles into the gently rolling hills of a wooded county park.

"First time on a bike? Seriously?" Wyatt eased off the bike.

"Seriously," she admitted as she got her legs beneath her again. "I know. My education is sadly lacking."

"I kinda like it that you made your virgin run with me."

Oh-ho. Now, there was a loaded statement if she'd ever heard one. A loaded look in those amused baby blues of his, too, as he searched her face for a long moment before turning back to the bike.

"Come on." He undid the straps on the picnic basket and tossed her the blanket. "It's just up over the rise."

"What's just over the rise?"

He took her hand and led her toward a narrow path cutting through the woods. "Let's talk about this little problem you have with trust. Anyone ever tell you you've got a highly suspicious nature, Miss Baylor?"

"Cautious does not necessarily translate to suspicious." She ducked under a low-hanging branch that he gallantly lifted out of her way.

"Okay, cautious, then," he conceded, helping her over a deadfall log. "And you feel the need to be cautious around me? After all the Spanish verbs we've conjugated together?"

Oh, he really was too charming, she thought, unable to stall a smile. She was considering telling him so just to see what his reaction would be, when they reached the top of the rise.

"Oh," she said, because it was all she could say when she saw the beautiful scene before her.

"Yeah." His voice was soft, satisfied. "I thought you'd like it."

She loved it. On the other side of the rise, the forest thinned out on a long, wide slope at the bottom of which was a tranquil, sylvan pond, mirror-still, surrounded by sweet tall grass and golden flowers bobbing on long, springy stems.

She grinned up at him. "You're just one surprise after another, aren't you?"

"I do try," he said with a cocky lift of his brow. "Come on, let's go pick out a spot before the butterflies hog all the best places."

And damn, if there weren't butterflies and songbirds and the sweetest breeze and the most perfect shade tree to spread the blanket beneath.

She laughed and shook her head in disbelief after they'd settled onto the blanket and he pulled a bottle of

Pinot Grigio out of the basket. "I figured you were more of a six-pack kind of guy."

He grinned, taking no offense, knowing she hadn't intended any. Hey, she liked an ice-cold beer on a hot day herself. After fishing around in the basket, he came up with a corkscrew and a pair of plastic wine glasses.

"To lazy Sundays," he said after expertly uncorking the wine and pouring them each a glass.

"To lazy Sundays," she agreed, and they clicked plastic to plastic.

"And to my good fortune of having a beautiful woman to spend one with."

"Thank you." She smiled over the rim of her glass. "For knowing I needed this."

He could have said a lot of things then. Could have gone for the gold and told her that whatever she needed, he had it. Could have flirted outrageously and turned the moment into something she hadn't wanted it to be. Not right then. Right then, she needed just what he gave her. A silent nod. A soft smile. And a clean, handsome profile that she found herself studying for a long time after he'd turned his head to gaze at the pond.

She liked him for that. In fact, she liked him for a lot of reasons. He was sweet and smart and intuitive enough to know that a picnic by a pond in a verdant glen would score an eleven out of ten on her "Just what I needed today" chart.

Yeah. He was one special guy.

Like Hugh Weber was special. Special in ways that too often made her heart flutter and her knees get a little weak.

She thought of Hugh now. Knew that she thought of him too much. Hugh was just such a . . . presence. Larger than life. Movie-star gorgeous. And as persistent as a bee after honey.

Hugh wanted her. He made no bones about letting her know it. Made no excuses for his outrageous flirting and flattering, and, well, she liked it. He excited her.

Maybe too much. He was a spooky boy, after all. And she knew, bone-deep, that nothing good could ever come from getting involved with a CIA operative.

"You are thinking waaaayyy too hard," Wyatt said, snapping her out of her musings.

She glanced at him and felt her face flush with embarrassment when she realized he must have been watching her for a while. "Guilty," she admitted. "I probably need more wine."

He grinned and lifted the open bottle out of the basket. "There may be hope for you yet, Teacher Lady."

"Oh, God, I hope so." She laughed and let him fill the glass to the brim.

An hour or so later, she was feeling full of his yummy lunch of delicious French bread, cheese, and grapes and drifting on a mellow little wine buzz.

"Bear," she said as they lay side by side on their backs, finding shapes in the fluffy white clouds. "See him? To the left. Right there." She lifted her hand and pointed when he squinted.

"All I see is a cloud."

"Do all Georgia boys lack imagination, or is it just you?" she teased, turning her head to find he'd rolled to his side and propped himself up on an elbow so he was looking down at her.

"Never had much problem in that department, nope." His eyes searched hers. "In fact, my imagination's going wild right now."

He wants to kiss me, she thought. It didn't take much imagination to figure that one out. Even less for her heart rate to pick up as she imagined what it would be like to kiss him back.

While Hugh had always been the aggressive one, she'd known that Wyatt was interested in her, too. And while it was Hugh who captivated her, there was something about this cute Southern boy that intrigued her.

He'd moved in closer. So close she could feel the heat of his big, hard body against her side. See the pulse beat at the base of this throat. Notice, and not for the first time, that his thick lashes were lightly tipped with gold, that there were the beginnings of smile lines around his eyes.

Yeah, she thought as his eyes searched hers. He really wants to kiss me. And in that perfect moment in time, she really wanted to let him.

"You okay with this?" he asked, because he was Wyatt, and he was a Southern gentleman.

"Would you accuse me of being cautious if I said no?" she asked, even as she lifted her hand and cupped his face in her palm.

"No, ma'am. I'd accuse you of lying." His blue eyes twinkled with an intoxicating mix of fun and teasing and arousal.

"Then yes." Her voice was barely a whisper as his big hand moved to cover her hip and he urged her gently toward him. "I'm very okay with this."

His eyes softened with desire as he lowered his mouth to hers, touched, pulled back, touched again, with a slow, deliberate seduction made all the more enticing for his calculated patience.

Just when she thought he would never truly, deeply kiss her, just when she thought she would burst into flames if she didn't get a richer, fuller taste of his wine-scented breath, he opened his mouth over hers and took the kiss to another level.

A level that sizzled and burned and awoke everything female and sexual and not cautious bone in her body. Heady and thorough and hot, and, holy God, did this man know how to kiss a woman.

"W . . . wow," she managed when he lifted his head and smiled down at her.

"In a word," he agreed, lowered his head, and kissed her again.

If possible, even deeper. Took her even higher, with gentle suction and luscious sweeps of his tongue and the exchange of breath that had become labored and heart-beats that had become frenzied.

She lost herself in honeyed sensation, clung to every nuance, sank into the incongruous reality of his soft, seductive lips and hard, hot body that had moved over hers and pressed her deep into the summer-sweet grass beneath the blanket.

Lost herself in pleasure as she ran her hands up under

his shirt, and wild for the feel of skin on skin, tugged frantically at the hem, moved restlessly against an erection that pressed against the relentless ache in her belly.

She was absorbed in him, in thrall with him . . . and then totally without him.

On a frustrated groan, her eyes snapped open to dappled sunlight and sky. She turned her head, and there he was. On his back beside her. One arm flung over his eyes. Breathing hard. The heel of his hand pressed against the bulge beneath his fly.

"Wya—"

"Don't. Say. A. Word," he ground out between labored breaths. "Give me a minute."

After several rough breaths, he sprang to his feet on an oath. Then, without a word, he walked off into the woods.

Sophie closed her eyes. Attempted to level her breathing and regulate her heartbeat. She'd only halfway succeeded when she heard Wyatt walk across the grass toward her again.

She took a page from his book and covered her eyes with her forearm, unable to look at him, wondering what the hell had just happened.

She didn't lose control like that. She didn't do things like strip naked under the sun and indulge in mad, passionate sex with men she barely knew.

But she would have, she admitted, trying to ignore the tug of the blanket that told her he'd sat back down beside her. She really, really would have, if he hadn't stopped it.

"Sophie." His voice was gentle. "You can open your eyes now."

"I don't think so," she said, beyond embarrassed.

His soft chuckle finally had her lifting her arm and chancing a glance at his face.

Oh, God. Would you look at him? His lips were swollen from their kisses. His eyes were so blue they could have been a flame. And he looked so kind she wanted to cry.

"I guess we can officially cross cautious off your list of character traits," he said with a grin.

Which finally made her smile. Then laugh. Then cover her eyes again with both hands.

"Hey," he said, touching a hand to her arm. "It's okay. Now come on. I'd better get you home."

"How did you meet Wyatt?"

The sound of Crystal's voice took Sophie away from that long-ago summer in Virginia and back to the kitchen in San Salvador. She glanced across the room at Wyatt, then back to the serving platter she'd filled with meats and cheese and bread. "I taught him Spanish."

"And what did he teach you?" Crystal asked with a cheeky grin.

Sophie wasn't feeling so cheeky. "He taught me about loyalty," she said, and thought about the look in Wyatt's eyes when, six weeks after that picnic, she'd married Hugh Weber, with Wyatt standing at his side as his best man.

9

It was so hard to let her baby go. Sophie held Hope tight and hugged her close one last time before she helped her settle into the backseat of the rented SUV. If only she could have sent someone with her, Carmen or Maris from school. But she couldn't ask that of either of them. They had their lives to live, and who knew how long Hope would be gone or if and when this nightmare would be over.

"Think of it as summer camp," she said with false brightness, leaning in through the open car door. "Crystal tells me that Dr. Flores's villa looks a lot like a castle."

"Got that right," Johnny Reed said from the shotgun seat. "And I fully expect to be treated like a king."

"More like court jester." Wyatt stood by, his gaze watchful and concerned.

"But *I* can be the queen." Crystal caught Hope's eye and smiled into the rearview mirror from the driver's seat. "Hope, you can be a princess."

When Hope had returned from Carmen's and seen the BOI crew in the living room, Crystal and Johnny had both made great efforts to draw her out of her silence. Reed had even teased a smile or two out of her. He'd become aces in both Hope and Sophie's deck from that point on.

"See?" Sophie hugged her daughter one last time. "It's going to be good, baby. And I'll get you back home as soon as I can, okay?"

Hope's arms tightened around Sophie's neck. She nodded uncertainly, and it broke Sophie's heart.

"Tell you what. I packed your jewelry kit. Why don't you make something special for Lola while you're there?"

"Like a welcome-home present?" A flicker of hope flared in her daughter's dark eyes.

"Yes. Exactly like that."

"I could make her a bracelet. Maybe I could make two," Hope added, her voice rising with excitement at the prospect of something that might please her friend. "One for each of us so we'll match."

"I think Lola would love that." Sophie touched a hand to Hope's hair, relieved to see even this little spark of life return.

"Sophie," Wyatt said quietly behind her, "we need to move on this."

She braced herself and, for Hope's sake, plastered on a smile. "Okay, baby. Let's get you buckled in so you don't miss your plane."

Her face felt as if it would freeze in forced-smile mode as she watched Hope fasten her seatbelt.

"Ready to go, *Princess*?" Johnny asked, shifting in the front seat and directing his dazzling smile at Hope.

Hope nodded, and Sophie could see that her daughter was just a little bit taken with the handsome Johnny Duane Reed. Unable to help herself, Sophie leaned into the car for one last kiss and hug.

"We'll take good care of her," Crystal promised when Sophie finally made herself shut the car door and back away.

"She'll be fine," Wyatt assured her, standing beside Sophie in the driveway, watching the SUV back out and pull onto the street. Jones, Colter, Green, and Mendoza followed them in the Suburban, providing escort.

Sophie hugged herself and finally let the tears trail down her cheeks, watching until the vehicle taking her daughter away drove out of sight.

"She'll be fine," Wyatt repeated, and pulled her into his arms.

She gave herself that moment—that one heart-wrenching moment of loss—and let herself lean into him. Let the tears fall. Let his warm, comforting strength surround her. Then she drew a bracing breath.

"You doing okay?" he asked after she'd taken a moment to compose herself. "Truth, now, darlin'."

"Okay. Truth. I'm more frightened now than ever. What happens when she remembers? How will she cope? I won't be there."

"But Juliana will be. She's a doctor, Sophe. She'll take good care of her. The key here is that Hope will be safe in Argentina."

That was the bottom line. Until these people were

caught, Hope remained in danger, especially once they realized they'd taken the wrong child.

"Okay." She made herself pull away. The clock was ticking for Lola. "Where do we start?"

He checked his watch and, with his arm still slung supportively around her shoulders, walked her toward the front door. "As soon as the guys see the Reeds and Hope off at the airport, they have a few purchases to make."

Sophie knew what purchases he was talking about. She'd heard them talking. They needed to buy weapons. Lots of them. Which told her they thought they were going to meet up with deadly resistance.

"Then they're going hunting."

"The guys are chameleons," Wyatt had told her earlier. "They can blend in and adapt to any situation. And it doesn't take long to figure out where the bottom feeders hang out. When enough money is involved, someone always talks. They'll work every angle. They'll get a lead. They'll pin it down."

"I need to help," she reminded him.

"You already have."

Earlier, they'd pored over city maps, and she'd pinpointed target areas for them to search—specifically Soyopango, the gangland on the east side of the city. She didn't know anything about their specific strongholds or the names of the lesser-known gang leaders, but the head bad guy was common street knowledge.

"Vincente Bonilla," she'd told Wyatt, "is a ruthless, soulless import from L.A. Hugh once told me that

Bonilla earned his top-dog status before migrating to El Salvador and muscling in as the Mara Salvatrucha kingpin.

"His specialties are execution, abduction, and prostitution. He sees himself as a real cocksman," she'd gone on. "Likes to use his knife to intimidate."

And because of what she knew of Bonilla, she was terrified for Lola. She'd also ID'd FMLN fringe groups and their headquarters as well as alleged GN strongholds—information she'd bullied out of the *policía* when she'd first spoken to them about Lola's abduction.

"I need to do more." Sophie turned to Wyatt. "I have this fund-raising event I'm supposed to attend tonight, but I'm going to cancel. I can go out on the streets with you and help you question people."

His head came up. "What kind of fund-raising event?"

She gave a dismissive shrug. "Doesn't matter."

"What kind of event?" he persisted.

"A cocktail party for renovations on the Teatro Nacional de El Salvador."

"Who's on the guest list?"

When she saw the contemplative look on his face, she realized he wasn't just making idle conversation. "I don't know specifically—doctors, lawyers, university types, school administrators, I would imagine. You know, the usual suspects with deep pockets who shell out for the arts."

"And political figures? Like maybe FMLN leaders? Other city officials?"

She nodded, finally seeing where he was going with this. "Them, too. Probably the police commissioner. Some foreign dignitaries as well as regional government officials. But Wyatt, it's not as if they're going to come out and talk to me about Lola. After my meeting with the police commissioner yesterday, he'd just as soon shoot me as help."

"Ticked him off, did you, sugar?"

She grimaced. "You could say that. He didn't particularly like my not-so-veiled opinions of his incompetency in the face of several other unsolved abductions," she explained. "But someone had to light a fire under him."

"So why not start a few more fires tonight? Sounds like there'll be a lot of likely candidates there. You get enough people riled, sometimes you get unexpected results. Maybe even a lead. And no matter how corrupt this government is, not everyone can be on the take. Someone might actually be looking for a chance to approach you without drawing any suspicion. The party will create a safe environment and an opportunity for that to happen."

He could be right, she realized. Fear bred silence, and there was a lot of fear among the ranks.

"What time is this shindig supposed to start?"

She checked her watch. "In a couple of hours. And this *shindig* isn't a backyard barbecue. It's black-tie all the way."

A resigned look came over his face. "I never thought I'd willingly ask this question, but where can I get a tux fast?"

10

Antonio Gutierrez, the director of the National Theater of El Salvador, droned on in Spanish from a podium erected in the theater's Great Hall. "As many of you already know, the Teatro Nacional de El Salvador is the oldest and one of the most beautiful theaters in all of Central America."

Yeah, yeah, yeah, Wyatt thought as Gutierrez continued his welcome address, which would no doubt end with an earnest and heartfelt plea to open up wallets for the ongoing restoration project. *Let's just get this over with and get back to the elbow rubbing.*

It was closing in on ten. They'd arrived unfashionably early at eight fifteen, and Sophie had been masterfully mingling and introducing him as her American friend from college ever since. The hope had been that someone would approach Sophie with information about Lola that might be of value. So far, it wasn't happening.

Sure, it had been a long shot, but Wyatt's experience had taught him never to discount even the slimmest possibility. As his buddy who worked homicide on the LAPD repeatedly said, it was the unexpected tip that generally broke the case and trumped all of the intricate forensic findings.

Wyatt figured there must be three hundred or so highbrows, lowbrows, famous, and infamous crowded into the theater's massive Great Hall, listening attentively to Gutierrez extol the building's virtues. As he scanned the crowd, he had to admit that the theater was an impressive piece of architecture—a mix, according to Gutierrez, of French Renaissance, rococo, art nouveau and Versailles style. What Wyatt knew about architecture could fit into an empty rifle shell casing, but he could still appreciate the stunning murals and frescoes covering the walls and ceilings. And the elaborate copper artwork fronting the doors to the theater boxes was pretty damn cool.

Not that he was a complete dolt, but this Georgia boy felt way out of his element. He had a college degree—his momma had seen to that—and yeah, his experience with the CIA could damn near qualify as a master's in political science. But he'd been manning the trenches with the BOIs for a while now and was out of touch with the high rollers of upper-crust society. Dressed in a hastily rented tux, he felt like a pair of scuffed brown shoes in a room full of shiny black patent leather.

Sophie, however, looked like the most brilliant jewel in the middle of a marquee full of dazzling lights.

"Master artisan Carlos Canas painted the cupola above us in 1977 with the magnificent fresco *El Mes-*

tazaja cultural. It reminds one of the great hall of Palais Garnier, decorated with Chagall, does it not?" Gutierrez continued.

Again, while Wyatt did have a certain appreciation for fine art, he'd be hard pressed to tell a Chagall from a Cézanne. And at the moment, he had absolutely no appreciation for the starched collar of his white dress shirt and neatly tied tie. Both felt like they were about to choke him, but he nodded and smiled along with the rest of the potential donors, who seemed to hang on Gutierrez's every word, Sophie among them.

She looked stunning. Knockout, gorgeous, stunning. Once he'd gotten his breath back, he'd said as much when she joined him in the living room before they left for the big doings.

"You don't look so bad yourself," she'd said with a smile as she walked over to him and set her pearl-encrusted clutch on the kitchen island. "Looks like you could use a little help with this tie, though."

"Thank God. Humanitarian aid. I won't turn it down. I'm all thumbs," he added with a helpless shrug, then fought a valiant fight not to look down the deep V of her gown while she took her time fussing with his tie.

Jesus God. The dress was floor-length and blue. A saturated, deep-water-blue silk that shimmered in the light and shifted to shades of jade and aquamarine in the shadows. It was also sleeveless and body-hugging and showed off slim hips, a narrow waist, and an amazing pair of breasts that he'd defy any straight male to ignore or fail to appreciate.

She'd done some female magic to her hair and piled it up on top of her head in what he suspected was a very intricate process. The shiny mass of it looked elegant and sophisticated with wispy little tendrils drifting around her face and trailing down her long, sleek neck. All he could think about was pulling out the pins and raking his fingers through all that sable silk until it tumbled to her shoulders, all bed-mussed and inviting.

". . . and so I urge you, distinguished ladies and gentlemen, open your hearts and your checkbooks, and help us continue our vigorous restoration of this magnificent theater for the benefit of all the people of El Salvador."

Yeah, Wyatt thought as Gutierrez wound down and polite applause broke out, Sophie looked stunning. As he stood beside her in the midst of a throng of custom-tailored tuxedos, designer gowns, and glittering jewels, he realized that while he felt like the proverbial bull in a china shop, she was utterly at home.

Seeing her so comfortable in this urbane setting forced him to see her for the high-powered member of the community that she was. She had status, prestige. Her accomplished elegance and natural poise also made him realize she might just be in her niche here with these people, many of whom he'd pegged for pompous blowhards whose desire to be seen in the right social circles far outweighed their philanthropic impulses.

He realized something else, too, tonight. The woman

was out of his league. So far out of his league that even with Hugh out of the picture and his own guilt aside, Wyatt didn't have a chance in hell with her.

Someone else apparently thought he did, though. A darkly attractive man approached her, pulled her into his arms, and kissed her once on each cheek. He kissed her as if he'd done it many times before and was confident that he'd do it many times in the future.

"*Mi amor.*" The man's smile was full of intimacy as he met her eyes, folded both of her hands in his, and brought them to his lips. "Your beauty eclipses all of the diamonds in the room."

Wyatt reined in a sharp twist of jealousy. Only years of practice in covert ops kept him from showing the slightest reaction while he contemplated the pain he could inflict by driving his knee full force into the Latin Casanova's *cojones.*

Sophie smiled for the bastard. "Diego, it's lovely to see you, as always."

"Always? If only that were so. Her definition of always," Diego said with a man-to-man glance at Wyatt, "is to *always* be busy when I call. To *always* have an excuse not to let me take her to dinner."

"You exaggerated about the diamonds, too," Sophie admonished him with a playful smile. "We had dinner just last week. And the week before that."

Dinner. Last week. And the week before.

Wyatt fought a jealousy he had no right to feel at the reminder that she had a life that didn't involve him.

"I never exaggerate when it comes to you, *cara*," Diego said, pouring it on.

"And I'm not usually this rude," Sophie segued with an apologetic smile for Wyatt. "Diego Montoya, this is Wyatt Savage. Wyatt's a very dear friend visiting from the States."

Wyatt couldn't help but wonder if Montoya's reaction to Sophie's choice of the word *friend* was as strong as his own. *Friend* could imply many things. Unfortunately, Wyatt knew the implication between him and Sophie. Friends. Buddies. What he didn't know was what kind of a "friend" she was to Montoya.

"Montoya." Wyatt extended his hand and forced himself to make nice. "I believe Sophie served Montoya coffee this afternoon. Any connection?"

Montoya returned Wyatt's handshake with a little too much enthusiasm.

Ah, Wyatt thought. *So he wants to play*.

The man was primed for a show of strength, which told Wyatt that he felt the right to demonstrate a claim on Sophie. He shouldn't, but Wyatt returned the favor with a squeeze just tight enough and just long enough to put the hurt on him.

Montoya's magazine-perfect smile transitioned to a pained grimace before Wyatt released his hand.

"I trust you enjoyed it," Montoya said through gritted teeth. He was talking about the coffee.

"I did. Very much." Wyatt was talking about the fact that he'd won their little power play.

"Diego is CEO of Montoya Coffee," Sophie broke in, apparently picking up on the undercurrents of the pissing match going on between them.

"Right." Wyatt manufactured a congenial smile. "El Salvador has a healthy and lucrative coffee-export industry."

"We do. And Montoya Coffee claims more than its fair share of the market," Montoya stated as he sized up Wyatt's rented tux in a subtle but pointed appraisal that implied he found both it and Wyatt lacking.

He was an elitist bastard, Wyatt decided then and there. It was also clear by the familiar way he looped an arm around Sophie's waist and by the possessive look in his eye that Montoya felt he had certain rights where she was concerned.

Hell, for all Wyatt knew, he did. Sophie had been divorced for two years. She was a beautiful, desirable woman. She had a life here. It made sense that she'd want to live it.

Apparently, she wasn't opposed to living it without him. That had been stinging ever since she'd told him about the divorce. If she'd wanted to contact him, she'd had plenty of time and opportunity. And yet she hadn't gone looking for him until she'd run into a situation that required his special skills.

Maybe Montoya was the reason. Maybe Montoya satisfied her . . . other needs. And maybe Wyatt would feel better if he could wipe that smug-ass smile off the coffee baron's face.

"How are you holding up, *mi amor*?" Montoya drew Sophie close to his side. "Have you received any word? Any progress finding the child?"

"I'm fine," she said, "but sadly, there's been no word on Lola."

"I am so sorry, *querida*. I know how painful this is for you." Montoya glanced from Sophie to Wyatt. "Please excuse us for a moment." Then he drew Sophie aside and out of earshot.

Sonofabitch was grandstanding. Didn't want to miss an opportunity to play the concerned suitor. Wyatt couldn't do anything but stand back and scowl as Diego had an intimate little moment with Sophie.

Montoya should have been an actor, Wyatt thought grimly. Not just because of his dark good looks and camera-ready smile but because he had the sincere, earnest look down pat as he brushed his fingertips along Sophie's cheek and gazed deeply into her eyes while he spoke to her.

Yeah, I'd really feel better if I could bring this bastard to his knees with a howl of pain.

Her life, her choice, he told himself again, and since plowing his fist into Montoya's pretty face wasn't an option, he stood by quietly and tolerated the man's intrusion. Reluctantly, he thought about everything Montoya could give Sophie that he couldn't. Social standing, money, a life she was suited for and deserved.

Wyatt could never give her those things. He could never be that man. So maybe coming here tonight and meeting Montoya was a good thing. As he stood there, on the outside looking in on a picture of a life he could never offer, he told himself that he was lucky to have gotten this glimpse into Sophie's world. Without it, he might have started thinking that he had a chance with her now and done something stupid. Like confess that he still loved her, that he'd always loved her.

"It's unfortunate that you picked such a difficult time in Sophie's life to visit San Salvador," Montoya said as he walked Sophie back to Wyatt's side, effectively reminding Wyatt of his outsider position.

"Wyatt's here because I asked him to come," Sophie explained, which told Wyatt that none of their private conversation had been about him. "He's helping me search for Lola."

That's right, asshole, Wyatt thought when a knowing look crawled across Montoya's face. *I'm the lowly hired muscle ready to take the heat so nancy boys like you don't have to worry about getting their hair messed up.*

"*Señora.*"

A uniformed waiter appeared at Sophie's side, surprising her. "*Sí?*"

He gave an apologetic bow of his head and extended a silver tray holding a sealed envelope bearing Sophie's name. "I am sorry to intrude, but my manager directed me to deliver this to you."

Puzzled, Sophie reached for the envelope. "*Gracias.*"

"Wait." Wyatt stopped the waiter when he started to walk away. "Who sent this?"

"I'm sorry, sir. I do not know. Apparently, it was left

on the reception table. As I told you, the manager asked
that I deliver it to Señora Weber. Now, if you will excuse me, I have other guests I must attend to."

Wyatt decided the waiter was either in the dark, as
he stated, or a damn fine actor. Either way, he couldn't
question him further without making a scene, so he let
him go as Sophie unfolded the note and scanned it. She
shot Wyatt a quick glance and slipped it back into the
envelope.

"From an admirer?" Montoya suggested with a teasing tone. "Tell me, *cara*, do I have competition?"

Wyatt had seen the swift flash of alarm in Sophie's
eyes. She recovered quickly with a smile that answered
Montoya's playful look as she tucked the envelope into
her small purse.

"As if anyone could compete with you. Someone
found a bracelet and recognized it as mine," she said.

Wyatt knew she was lying through her perfect white
teeth. She hadn't been wearing a bracelet when they'd
left the house. He would have noticed, because he had
noticed every minute detail of her appearance.

He found it interesting that she felt the necessity of
hiding the contents of the note from Montoya.

"The clasp must have broken," she continued
smoothly. "I can't believe I didn't miss it. Anyway,
they're holding it for me at the reception desk. I'm
afraid you'll have to excuse me for a moment, Diego."

"I'll accompany you," Montoya said.

"Thank you, but there's no need. I know you have
many hands to shake tonight. Wyatt will go with me."

Just try and stop me, Wyatt thought, directing a hard look Montoya's way.

Montoya got the message and conceded with a forced smile. "Save a dance for me, *querida*. I will find you later."

She gave him a brilliant smile. "Count on it."

"What?" Wyatt asked when they were out of earshot.

She glanced around, then pulled him into an empty alcove. "Looks like you were right about coming tonight."

Her eyes were wide with excitement as she dug the note out of her purse and handed it to him.

South side of the rear terrace. 10:45. Tell no one. Come alone. Make certain you're not followed.

"This *has* to be about Lola," she said, clutching his arm.

Wyatt figured it was, or there wouldn't be a need for all the cloak-and-dagger crap. It also explained why she hadn't wanted Montoya to know. The instructions were explicit that she tell no one.

He checked his watch. It was ten sixteen. "Come on, let's walk toward reception in case Montoya's tracking you. Tell me about the layout of the terrace."

"Let me think. It's . . . it's a big open area. No roof. Surrounded by palms and, I don't know, flowering shrubs and vines, if I remember right. It's been a while since I've been here, let alone wandered around the grounds. What are you thinking?"

"I'm thinking that I don't like the 'Come alone' part of this invitation."

She stopped walking. "What choice do we have? I can't take a chance that whoever sent this will bolt if you come with me."

"And I can't take a chance that it's a setup and you end up with a hood over your head, carried off, and thrown into the back of a van."

"So what do we do?"

"Hedge our bets," he said, and told her how it was going to go down.

11

It was ten forty-two by the time Sophie felt she could slip outside to the terrace without being noticed. She waited several beats to make sure no one had followed her, then set off across the empty expanse of marble tile. Her heels made clipped clicking sounds as she walked across the polished stone toward the far end of the walled terrace.

The night was warm and dark. A heavy cloud cover hung over the city. Bach's Suite No. 2 in B minor, performed by a string quartet, wafted through the open doors of the theater and blended incongruously with the distant roar and grind of traffic in a city that seemed to run on wheels twenty-four/seven.

She made a conscious effort not to glance toward the tall, lush foliage that surrounded the perimeter of the terrace and provided a privacy fence of sorts. Wyatt was out there somewhere in the dark. He'd insisted that she could not go out there alone, so he'd quickly left her and gotten into place outside.

At least, she hoped he was close by, because right

about now, as hopeful as she was that this secret meeting was about Lola, she was scared half out of her mind by all the possibilities she could be facing out here in the dark. She knew basic self-defense. Hugh had insisted she take classes. She knew how to fire several types of pistols and rifles, also at Hugh's insistence. She'd agreed because she wasn't stupid, and she'd never been one to bury her head in the sand. El Salvador was not a safe place under the best of circumstances. She needed to know how to defend herself.

But she carried no weapon tonight. Security for this function was tight. She'd never have made it inside if she'd been armed. With any luck, that meant no one else would be carrying a concealed weapon, either. That expectation gave her only a marginal sense of safety. Alone in the dark, away from the crowd gathered inside the theater, was not a safe place to be, no matter what.

And if, for some reason, Wyatt hadn't had time to get out ahead of her, she was totally on her own.

No one could see her. No one could hear her scream. She swallowed back the fear as she neared the designated meeting place.

She saw no one. Heard nothing.

So she waited and listened.

Night sounds.

Crickets.

Laughter and music drifted softly from inside the theater.

Traffic sounds were like white noise in the distance.

A hand touched her shoulder.

She gasped and whirled around, clutching a fist to her racing heart.

"My apologies. It was not my intention to frighten you."

It took a moment for her to catch her lost breath. Another to find her voice and the wherewithal not to point out exactly what he could do with his intentions.

Her heart was still pounding as she squinted into the dark. He was a small man, shorter than she was by a few inches. It was difficult to see his face in the shadows, but she could make out thick, dark eyebrows, a high forehead, a nose that appeared to have been broken.

"Señor Vega?" She couldn't hide her shock when she finally recognized the assistant to the director of San Salvador's Primary Education Board. She'd known Jorge Vega for years, had appreciated his levelheadedness whenever he had participated in board meetings. "*You* sent the note?"

"We must talk quickly," Vega said. "I know you are looking at the Guerrilleros Nacionales for the child's abduction."

Lola. This *was* about Lola!

"We are not responsible," he stated.

"We?" She couldn't hide her shock. "You're GN?"

"Not all of us are as radical as the extremist members of the organization, you must believe that. And we are trying desperately to get a handle on their activities and curtail the violence."

"Yet you say the GN is not involved in Lola Ramirez's

abduction?" She could have told him that the GN wasn't at the top of her suspect list, but she wanted to hear what he had to say.

"I do not want to believe so, no," he insisted. "Because of that belief, I am risking a great deal tonight. I have come by some information.'

"Come by how?"

"It does not matter how I received it. What matters is that it strongly suggests members of MS-13 are involved."

If it was true, then he wasn't exaggerating about the risk. No one crossed MS-13 and lived to tell about it.

He glanced nervously over his shoulder and lowered his voice. "There is a viable report that the Ramirez child is being held in an MS-13 stronghold."

She gripped Vega's arm, her heart jumping with the first flutter of hope since Lola had been taken. "Lola's alive?"

"Indications are that she is, yes."

"Where? Where is she?"

Again, he glanced around, clearly afraid of being caught talking with her. He reached for her hand, pressed a folded sheet of paper into her palm, and closed her fingers around it. "Don't look at it now. Wait until you're clear of here and certain no one followed you. Please, tell no one I spoke with you, and whatever you do, do not contact me. My life will be worth nothing if you do."

"I don't understand. Why are you doing this? Why are you taking such a chance?"

"I respect you, Mrs. Weber. I respect what you do. And I know the child's abduction has wounded you. I want to help. And I want you to know that the majority of the GN do not condone violence."

"Then what would you call the attack on the British contingent at the airport?"

"Deplorable," he said with a sincerity that made her believe him. "I have to go before we are seen together."

"Seen by whom? If someone here tonight is responsible for this—"

He shook his head. "I must go."

She grabbed his arm when he turned to leave. "Please, if you know who's responsible for abducting Lola, you must tell me."

A look of such stark guilt and regret came over his face that for a moment, she thought he would tell her.

A shot rang out in the distance.

She jumped away from him, then realized it was just a car backfiring. It hadn't only spooked her. Vega looked as if he'd been marched in front of a firing squad.

"Please," she pleaded again as her heart went haywire.

"I've already risked too much. God speed you on your search. I pray you will find her."

"Wait." She reached out to stop him again, but he'd already disappeared into the shadows.

She was alone with her pounding heart and fractured breath.

"Let's get out of here." Wyatt's voice startled another gasp out of her.

When she spun around, he was standing right behind her. "How do you *do* that?"

"Practice."

"Did you hear?"

"Yeah." He gripped her elbow. "We need to go."

"I'll have to make excuses."

"Plead a headache," he said, and steered her back to
the theater.

By the time they made their way through the crowd—
many of whom felt a need to express their concern over
her "ghastly situation"—and a valet showed up with
her car, she didn't have to fake the headache. A dull,
hard throb had settled deep at the base of her skull. Too
much adrenaline. Too much drama. She prayed that
it wasn't also too much to hope that Vega had actually
given them a lead on Lola.

"It's a map." Sophie studied the sheet of paper under
the dome light as Wyatt sped away from the theater.
"Looks like it was scribbled with a pencil, very crude.
Also looks like it's been through a war."

"Or drawn under duress," Wyatt said, glancing at the
paper.

Oh, God. She held it closer to the light. The paper
had been crumpled, sweated on, possibly bled on. "Tor-
ture? You think that whoever drew this was tortured into
cooperating?"

He glanced at her, then looked back to the road. "I
don't think they got results with 'pretty please.' "

Her stomach rolled. This was just too . . . real.

She couldn't let herself think about how Vega had come by the information. She had to think about Lola. "It's got to be a map to where they're holding Lola, right?"

"That would be the best-case scenario, yeah."

"And the worst?"

"It could be a setup."

She shook her head. "No. I believe Vega. I've worked with him. Jorge has always been a straight shooter. His own sister was abducted and murdered when they were both children. He was responding to that. I know it."

"Let's hope you're right."

She ignored the skepticism in Wyatt's voice, stared at the map for a moment then looked up at the windshield. "There's one thing I don't get. If Vega didn't want anyone to know he was talking to me, why didn't he simply mail the map to me? Even e-mail it? Or just give it to the waiter in the first place?"

He lifted a shoulder. "Mail or e-mail is easily intercepted. If Vega's GN, then he's no stranger to subterfuge. He'd never count on a waiter to deliver it. He'd rather take a chance that you wouldn't show up than risk someone intercepting the map. There also might have been some pride involved or possibly a need for retribution. Whatever his reasons, he definitely wanted you to think that he and his GN buddies aren't the bad guys in this."

"I believe him," she insisted, reflecting back on her conversation with Jorge. "He was scared to death."

"That just tells us he's a good actor.

"Okay," he conceded when she scowled at his continued skepticism, "it could tell us that he's not stupid. MS-13 takes no prisoners. If GN really isn't responsible for Lola's abduction, then Vega's wise to be afraid that whoever is may have been at the benefit or that someone who was there could have been reporting back.

"Think about it," he went on. "Everyone from the police commissioner to FMLN political heads to GN leadership was in attendance tonight. It was a who's who of the wealthy and corrupt."

"I can't believe that everyone is on the take," she said, feeling the need to defend. "Some of those people are my friends."

"Like Montoya?"

His face was mostly in shadows, but it wasn't necessary to see his expression to get his underlying message; the disdain in his tone pretty much told her what he thought about Diego. So had that little power play of a handshake.

Testosterone, meet my friend, Testosterone.

"You didn't like Diego," she surmised, shaking her head over the way the two of them had acted.

"I didn't like him," he agreed without a nanosecond of hesitation.

She was tired. And while she understood that it was his "job" to be suspicious, she was suddenly tired of his attitude about Diego. Especially after what Diego had offered to do tonight.

"So, because you don't like him, that automatically slots him into the wealthy and corrupt category," she said wearily.

"If the custom-made Italian loafers fit . . ."

"Come on, Wyatt. Diego's wealthy, yes. But corrupt? I don't see that."

He had nothing to say to that. He just shifted his grip on the steering wheel and kept his eyes on the street ahead.

She thought about her private conversation with Diego at the theater . . .

"*Querida, it pains me to see how hard this is on you. I am here if there is anything you need,*" he assured her kindly. "*There is sure to be a ransom demand.*"

She swallowed and nodded. "*We've already received one.*"

"*How much do they require?*"

She hesitated.

"*Tell me,* cara."

"*Half a million dollars,*" she said, overwhelmed all over again by the staggering sum of money.

"*I can help you with this.*"

"*Diego.*" Stunned by his generosity, she touched a hand to his chest. He quickly covered it with his own. "*I couldn't ask that of you. You don't even know Lola. For that matter, you and I . . .*"

"*Cara,*" he interrupted sternly, "*you did not ask. I offered. And now is not the time to stand on your principles or to question what does or does not matter between us. Now is the time for action.*"

He was right. Lola was all that mattered. "*I don't even know what to say. Thank you, Diego.*"

"There. See? There is no point in saying no to me. I always win."

And that, Sophie thought as headlights from an oncoming car flashed through the windshield, might be the crux of her problem with Diego Montoya. He was a man accustomed to getting his way. In fact, sometimes she wondered what kind of measures he would take to get what he wanted.

She glanced at Wyatt, considered telling him about Diego's offer to pay Lola's ransom, but decided that little secret could wait until it was absolutely necessary to divulge it. He would only question Diego's motives.

The truth was, she found herself questioning them herself. Was it really concern for Lola that prompted his generous offer, or was it another ploy in an endless volley of attempts to win her over?

She stared through the windshield. What did it matter? The fact was, she needed Diego's help. She would deal with his persistence later. Figure out why she couldn't shake the idea that he was just a little too smooth for her. Just a little too interested, a little too determined, and a little too inclined to believe he was irresistible.

Speaking of irresistible. She glanced at Wyatt, silent and steady behind the wheel. She couldn't fight the notion any longer that he could easily become irresistible to her. For many reasons. The most striking one was that he didn't know it. The last time she'd seen him in black tie and tux had been at her wedding. He'd worn both well then, but it had been Hugh who stood out. Hugh who captivated her.

Tonight, however, the man wearing the hastily rented and far from tailored tux had been the one to stand out in a crowd of polished dignitaries and politicians. Wyatt hadn't even been aware of how many heads had turned when he'd walked by, how many women had given him long, hungry looks and attempted to attract his attention.

She shifted in the seat so she could see his face when they stopped at a red light. A huge security lamp hung over the busy intersection, pouring light into the car.

His white shirt looked pristine and stark against the beginnings of a stubble on his cheek; the hard line of his jaw juxtaposed against the loosened shirt collar was yet another contrast. Both held her in rapt fascination.

He'd loosened the tie she'd so carefully knotted, and she wondered now if he had realized her hands had been shaking when she'd tied it, if he'd been aware of the effect he'd had on her earlier, in the tight confines of the guest bathroom, when she'd treated his cuts. All that blood. All that bare skin and honed muscle. Her lower abdomen clenched again at the memory of his skin beneath her fingertips. Smooth, taut, hot. Wholly, tantalizingly male.

It had been a long time since she'd felt a sexual reaction to a man. Longer still since she'd felt one this primitive. And no one since Hugh had made her want to act on it.

She gave herself a little latitude. She'd been strung

wire tight in those moments. So had Wyatt. If he'd had the same reaction, however, he hadn't shown it. He'd been quiet.

The realization dawned on her slowly. Yes, he'd been quiet. Quiet as he was quiet right now. And now, he definitely wasn't relaxed. In fact, the look on his face was exactly the same as when she'd tied his tie and cleaned his wounds. Then as now, he wasn't smiling, and it was the absence of his easy smile—a smile that diminished the hard edges of his face with laugh lines around his eyes and mouth—that gave away his tension.

Did that mean he felt the sexual tension, too? She thought of that wild, ravenous kiss they'd shared long ago one sultry Sunday and not for the first time regretted letting that moment get away. One of many choices she regretted making.

She thought of Hope and prayed she hadn't made another bad decision when she'd let the Reeds take her away. She checked her watch, wondering when she could expect a call from Johnny or Crystal, letting her know that they'd made it safely to Argentina. A sharp ache of loss seized her when she thought of her daughter. She didn't realize how deeply she was immersed in missing her until Wyatt cleared his throat.

"So. You and Montoya. Are you two—?" He let his words trail off, lifting a hand as if waiting for her to supply the rest of the question as well as the answer.

She should make it easy on him and say it flat out. She wasn't "with" Diego. But something stopped her. She didn't understand why, but she felt a little provoked. Not with Wyatt. At least, she didn't think so, but it looked as if he was going to bear the brunt of it.

Blame it on the day. The entire day had been a thousand-mile-per-hour assault on her senses, her emotions, her equilibrium. Seeing Wyatt again after all these years, the attack at the airport, coming home to a ransom note, meeting the BOIs, watching strangers take her daughter away, dressing to the nines, then playing not-so-super-spy with Jorge Vega. Maybe it was simply a case of adrenaline overload that got to her. Her fear and building sense of helplessness over Lola. Her worry about Hope. Her untimely and probably unwise attraction to this man.

It was all so crazy. She needed order; she had chaos. She craved control; yet in the last forty-eight hours, she'd lost power over everything important in her life. At least, it felt like she had.

But she could control this moment. At least she could try.

"If you have something to ask me about Diego, Wyatt, then ask."

If the edge of bitchiness in her tone surprised him, he didn't let it show. She was about to apologize for taking her foul mood out on him when he broke the silence.

"Forget it. It's none of my business."

Wrong. *Wrong, wrong, wrong* answer. That window for apology slammed shut.

"For God's sake, Wyatt. You're risking your life to help me save a child you don't even know, and you honestly think that you have no right to know my business?"

Another long, heavy silence followed before he turned to her. His eyes were hard. His jaw rigid.

"Two years." His deep voice was hardly recognizable for the total lack of soft, Southern charm. In fact, there was so much anger in those two words that she recoiled in shock.

He looked back to the street, dragged a hand over his face, and breathed deep. "You've been single for two years," he repeated, getting himself under control, "and you didn't bother to contact me. So no, Sophie, I honestly didn't think I had any right to know your business."

Her own disjointed anger deflated in the face of his and another sudden realization. He wasn't merely angry because she hadn't contacted him after the divorce. He was hurt.

A horn honked, startling them both. The light had changed. He hit the gas and drove into the relative darkness again. While she could no longer see his face, she could still remember every nuance of his expression. It was the same expression he'd worn on the day she'd married Hugh.

He'd been hurt then, too. She'd known it then. Had lived with it since.

She'd never intended to, but it seemed she was always hurting this man. And that was the real root of her anger. She was angry with herself.

She stared at her lap. "I'm sorry."

He tapped his thumbs on the steering wheel, an attempt to show an indifference she knew he wasn't feeling. "No need. It's just the way it is."

She could tell him. Maybe she *should* tell him. God knew, she'd wanted to tell him over the years. She'd wanted to run to him even before things went totally sour between her and Hugh and confess that she'd made a mistake. That she'd married the wrong man. That Hugh wasn't who she'd thought he was. That she'd lain in bed too many nights to count and thought about leaving Hugh and running to him.

She averted her gaze to the passenger-side window. Yeah, she could tell him all of that.

And accomplish exactly what?

Make herself feel better?

Make him feel worse?

Wyatt had loved Hugh. Just as Wyatt had loved her.

She'd always known that, too. Just as she'd always known that if she had gone to him again after that first time she'd cried on his shoulder, he would have let her cry again, told her everything would work out — again — and then, no matter how badly he wanted her himself, he would have sent her home to her husband. Again.

Because that was who he was. Loyal to the end to a man he called brother.

12

Juliana Flores stood back from the frilly four-poster bed with its pretty pink floral coverlet and lace-trimmed pillows and, for the first time in longer than she could remember, felt something other than sorrow.

She'd decorated this room for Angelina. For a daughter she had adored. She glanced at Angelina's portrait on the dresser, the last one she'd had taken, and felt pride to see so much of herself in her Angelina's brown eyes and dark, curling hair.

"She's a younger version of you, *mi amor*," Armando used to say. "However did I get so lucky to have two such beautiful women in my life?"

Lucky. *Sí.* They had all been lucky once. Lucky to have each other for as long as they had.

She drew a bracing breath, could not allow herself to go to that dark place where she missed them both so much her heart could not bear the pain.

"It's time for another pretty girl to enjoy this room," she told herself, running her hand along the bedspread to smooth it. "It's time there was life in this room again."

"She's going to love it."

Juliana turned to see Nate Black standing in the doorway, his arms full of extra pillows she'd asked him to fetch from the linen closet down the hall in preparation for Hope Weber's arrival. She suppressed a smile at the sight of this lean, rough-hewn protector, practically drowning in down.

Then again, it seemed she was always compelled to smile around Nate Black. Such a handsome man. A study in contradictions. His beautiful blue eyes were granite-hard and unyielding when he was deep in thought, yet when he smiled, they softened, and the most amazing dimple dented his left cheek. A tall man, more than six feet, both rugged and runner lean, he could easily be imposing, yet there was an innate kindness in his face that disguised the fact that inside his chest beat the heart of a warrior.

"Angelina loved it," she said with a soft smile, and relieved him of the pillows. "I think she was ten or twelve when we decorated it for her. I always thought she'd outgrow it when she got older, and I think perhaps she did, a little." She smiled, thinking of twenty-two-year-old Angelina sitting at the delicate Queen Anne dresser, surrounded by hair clips and makeup and perfume. "But she was always a bit of a princess in her heart, so she never redecorated it."

"I'm sorry I didn't know her." Nate wrapped a strong hand around a post at the foot of the bed and leaned casually against it.

He worries about me, Juliana thought. *He reads my*

*moods and worries. It just comes naturally to him. Just
as the way he carries himself with such understated confidence and ease, comes naturally.* Beneath that quiet
confidence, however, beat a warrior's heart. A protector's heart. That's why he was here tonight, after all. To
protect a child.

"I, too, am sorry you never met her. Angelina would
have liked you very much."

He nodded, his gaze searching hers in that way he
had of seeing deeper than she wanted him to see. That
was the thing about Nathan Black. He sometimes saw
too much.

"I'm fine with this. Really," she assured him, because
she knew he wanted to ask. "Angelina would approve.
She was always about helping the children."

"She's going to be scared," he said.

"I know. But we'll help her through it."

Just as Nate had helped her through some difficult
times. Had been helping her, in fact, for almost two
years, before she'd realized that he'd been watching
over her. He'd done it as a favor to Gabe Jones, who
had been deeply in love with Angelina and feared that
Juliana's life might also be in danger because of the
madman who had killed every living soul Juliana loved.

Despite her best efforts not to, Juliana let herself drift
back to that fateful night two years ago when her world
had changed again—only this time, for the better. If
it hadn't been for a break-in at Villa Flores, she might
still be in the dark about Nate Black's true identity. She
might never have found out that the unassuming expat

she'd known as David Gavin was, in fact, Nathan Black, the leader of the elite team of men, making up Black Ops, Inc.

As far as she'd known then, David Gavin lived quietly in a small flat in nearby Bahía Blanca and volunteered twice a week to balance the ledgers at her free clinic. But when David Gavin had shown up that horrible night after she'd dialed a phone number Gabe had told her to use if she ever felt threatened, the truth had come out.

And nothing had been the same between her and Nate since.

She'd been frightened and lonely and confused. He'd provided comfort and care and escape. He'd made love to her that next morning, and it had been wonderful. Lush. Intense. Caring. Because it had felt like a betrayal to Armando, she'd struggled with the guilt ever since.

Guilt, however, hadn't stopped the longing.

She glanced at Nate again, her gaze caressing the short black hair that showed a distinguished hint of gray at his temple, then busied herself storing the pillows in the closet because he had that look in his eyes again. The one that suggested he might be reading her thoughts.

And what she was thinking was that perhaps she'd made a mistake keeping him at arm's length, wondering if he thought it was a mistake, too.

Maybe he didn't feel the same tug and pull. Maybe she was the only one who sometimes regretted the course they'd taken. But he would get a look in his eyes sometimes, a look rife with pain and yearning, and when he did, it was all she could do to keep from reaching for him and taking him to her bed again.

"I hear the chopper." Nate walked across the room and looked out the window.

The lights of the Angelina Foundation helicopter, which Juliana had dispatched to Buenos Aires to meet the plane carrying the Reeds and Hope Weber, flashed through the bedroom window. "That'll be them."

Juliana didn't know if she felt disappointment or relief that she'd lost yet one more opportunity to confront Nate about his feelings for her. Once again, she had almost gathered the courage to open herself up to broaching the possibility of life, the possibility of love after all these years of being closed off in the dark.

"Juliana?" His dark eyes searched hers, expectant, questioning.

Suddenly self-conscious, she averted her gaze and hurried out of the room ahead of him. "Let's not keep them waiting."

"Hugh left these maps."

Wyatt turned away from the French doors that led to the patio when he heard Sophie return to the living room. Her arms were filled with rolled cylinders. The minute they'd arrived back at her house after leaving the theater, she'd made a beeline for her office. Apparently, she'd found what she was looking for.

"Maps of the surrounding area, each individual region, and an aerial map of El Salvador." She leaned over and dumped them on the coffee table.

A stray lock of hair tumbled over her forehead and fell across her left eye when she straightened. "We should be able to use them to pinpoint the drawing of the map Vega gave me," she said hopefully, tucking the hair hastily behind her ear.

Wyatt knew she had never been aware of the effect she had on him. If she had, she'd be running scared, because that simple action—so alluringly female, so unconsciously sensual—had his gut clenching and his mouth going bone-dry.

It had always been that way when he was around her. His senses viscerally alert, his emotions raw to the point of bleeding. He wanted to lunge across the room, yank that wet dream of a dress above her waist, and bury himself hard and deep inside her. No finesse. No romance. Just lust. He wanted to consume and overwhelm and possess. And then, only then, did he want to settle her, gentle her, and make her achingly aware of how much he loved her.

Instead, he did what he had always done. He swallowed back the need, didn't let on that he was boiling inside. He simply nodded in agreement, shrugged out of his black tuxedo jacket, and tossed it over the back of a chair. She turned to leave him there but stopped, slowly turned, and regarded him with serious eyes.

"I need you to be straight with me about this," she said abruptly. "Do you really think we can find her before . . . before it's too late?

Hope rode high on her question. He'd like to give her something solid to hang on to. The realist in him, however, wasn't onboard. Human life meant nothing to the barbarians who had abducted Lola. Money was their god, and yeah, there was a very good chance that if they didn't deliver the ransom by the Thursday deadline, Lola would become a casualty of greed and depravity.

But how could he look at those expectant brown eyes and tell her that?

"The biggest single thing in Lola's favor right now is that the kidnappers will be smart enough to keep her alive until they get their money. They understand that no one is going to hand over that much cash without proof of life."

She breathed deeply. "About the money . . ."

"Don't worry about the money," he said. "We're going to find her before the deadline. It's what we do. We find bad guys. Trust me on this, okay?"

He could see in her eyes that she wanted to believe him. She needed to believe him.

"Okay," she said on a bracing breath. "Give me a minute to change. Then I'll make a pot of coffee and help you with these maps. It could be a long night."

No shit, Wyatt thought. Long day. Long night.

Like the very long silence in the car after he'd done the emotional equivalent of puking up his guts.

Two years, and you didn't bother to contact me. So no, Sophie, I honestly didn't think I had any right to know your business.

Christ. Like she needed to deal with his emotional baggage in addition to everything else.

Disgusted with himself, he went to work on the cuff-links and rolled the shirtsleeves up to his elbows. He sat on the edge of the sofa and reached for one of the maps.

Twisted up, he thought absently as he unrolled it. He was twisted up ten ways from Sunday because a woman he hadn't seen in twelve years had been divorced for two of those years and hadn't bothered to tell him.

Get over it.

Well, shit, Sherlock, that was the problem, wasn't it? He flattened the map on the low table and used a set of coasters to pin down the curling edges. He'd never gotten over it. Never gotten over her.

He scrubbed his hands over his face and absently scanned the map. And he thought about anything but the way she'd looked tonight. Instead, he thought about the brave way she'd opened herself up to attack when she'd gone out on that terrace alone at the theater. The guilt in her voice when she'd told him she was sorry she hadn't contacted him.

Now, as then, it was crystal-clear that the apology translated to exactly what he'd always known.

She was sorry she hadn't loved him.

She was sorry she would never love him.

Knife to the heart. Gun to the head. Pick a pain. He felt it.

He shot up off the sofa and paced across the room. He really needed to get a grip. He wasn't a drinking man. The last time he'd gotten flat-ass wasted had been the night after Sophie and Hugh's wedding. He'd stayed that way for a week.

Maybe he was overdue for another bender. He added it to his to-do list, right after "Save the child, then get on with your life."

"Yeah, and maybe you ought to just suck it up and get it through your hard, thick skull you're not the man of her hour, and you never will be," he muttered.

In the meantime, the clock was ticking for Lola. It was a little after midnight, which meant twelve of their seventy-six hours were already gone. The kidnappers had given Sophie until noon on Thursday, at which time they would deliver their final instructions on where and when to drop the money. That gave him sixty-four hours to find a lost child before she became a dead child—a job that was much bigger than nursing his pathetic little wounded heart.

Wyatt's cell rang just as Sophie came back into the room. It was Nate.

"They made it," he said, and motioned Sophie over. "Hope wants to talk to you."

She reached for the phone with trembling hands. "Hey, baby, how you doing?"

She listened, her eyes glistening, before a laugh that was a mixture of nerves and relief bubbled out. "A helicopter? And you weren't scared?"

She was smiling now, a single tear rolling down her cheek as her daughter apparently filled her in on her big adventure.

"It turns out Juliana Flores *does* live in a castle," she said after hanging up a few minutes later.

"Told you she'd be fine."

"Yeah," she said, smiling her thanks and stirring up those feelings again that he didn't seem to be able to control. "You did."

"Should we be worried about the guys?"

Wyatt glanced at the clock. It was close to two a.m. He'd showered and changed into a T-shirt and cammo pants, and he and Sophie had been poring over the maps for damn near two hours. Side by side. Alone. In the night. The scent of her driving him crazy. The nearness of her testing his resolve.

"They're big boys. They can handle themselves," he said, hoping he didn't have to eat his words. "If there was a problem, they'd call."

At that precise moment, he was a lot less worried about them than he was concerned about how he could continue to handle himself around her. As the night grew deeper, his resolve grew weaker.

He glanced at her and realized, with surprise, that she was watching him. That she'd been watching him. She quickly looked away, her face flushing a pretty pink. And his pulse damn near went off the charts.

Beside him, she seemed to stop breathing. Beside him, she seemed to be as conscious as he was of the two of them, alone, together. The notion that she was on the same page, in the same place as he was, both stunned and scared the crap out of him.

They lapsed into an unsettling silence. The air surrounding them grew thick with an unexpected and acute awareness of each other.

Could it be? And did he really want to question it? Question that they'd been concentrating on pinpointing the coordinates on Vega's sketchy map when the earth moved beneath them? Question that her silence had shifted from concentration to raw sexual awareness that encroached like a fog, crowding into the room and encompassing them in a warm, sensual mist?

Consciousness shifted to the tactile awareness of their thighs almost touching as they sat side by side on the sofa, leaning over the low coffee table. Of the closeness of their hands, his left, her right, his large, hers so small, where they were planted on the scattered maps. Their fingers were within a hair's breadth of contact.

His heart, *Jesus*, his heart jumped so hard that she had to feel it. He had to get hold of this. He had to back away. But then she turned her head and met his eyes again. And he saw with staggering clarity that she was as caught up in whatever this was as he was.

Caught up in the heat.

Caught up in the need.

Caught up in the rush of insanity that was desire, her mind closed to the senselessness of acting on it.

And it *was* senseless. Senseless and stupid and . . . hell, it didn't matter what it was. In this intense and immediate moment, the world could come to an end, and they wouldn't notice. Just as they didn't care that what was about to happen had the potential to be life-altering in its magnitude.

He wasn't certain who made the first move. Who brushed whose thigh against whose. Who moved whose hand that microscopic degree until they were touching. Seeking. Connecting.

He was only aware of the astounding electric shock when their fingers linked, held, tightened. He lifted her hand to his mouth, tasted the silk of her skin, and felt a heat beyond fire. A need so strong it would have dropped him to his knees if he'd been standing.

And over it all, he felt a love so pure it demanded that he try to infuse reason.

God damn, he didn't want to stop it, but someone had to.

"Sophie."

"Shh . . ." She pressed her fingertips to his lips, hearing the denial in the way he had spoken her name. "Don't talk. Don't think."

He swallowed hard. "One of us needs to."

"No doubt both of us will," she whispered, moving into his arms. "No doubt we'll think it to death. Later. Please. Let's save the second guesses for later."

He closed his eyes, pressed his forehead to hers, and somehow assembled the will to shake his head.

She wasn't having any of it. "I need you now," she murmured, pulling away far enough to cup his face in her palms. Her beautiful brown eyes met his with soulful longing and unleashed a hunger inside him that had gone too many years without being fed.

"Don't make me beg, Wyatt. Don't make me analyze. Just help me feel something that doesn't start and end with anger or hopelessness or fear."

She kissed him then. Softly parted lips. Sweet, quivering breath. Her determined hesitance was heartbreaking in its vulnerability. He didn't want her vulnerable. He wanted her strong.

Hell, he just wanted her. It didn't matter that she'd never loved him. It didn't matter that she didn't love him now or that she needed him for all the wrong reasons. Didn't matter when she walked him to the bedroom that the condoms she pulled out of the nightstand drawer had been purchased with another man's use in mind.

Knife to the heart. Gun to the head.

Yeah. He'd feel the pain later, all right. But now, *right now*, he was going to let her use him to numb her own pain. Maybe in the process, he'd take the edge off some of his own.

Use me, he thought as he covered her mouth with his and kissed her until he couldn't breathe or taste or feel anything but her. *Use me up.*

13

Wyatt had spent the better part of a lifetime fantasizing about this woman. He'd spent a damn lot of lonely nights in other women's arms trying to find something with them that he knew he'd never find. And in all those years, in all those nights, he'd always known that Sophie would never be his. Not even once.

Yet here he was. Here she was. And in his wildest dreams, she'd never been this beautiful.

Jesus, God, look at her, he thought as he stood above her where he'd laid her on the bed. Reality bucked the odds and beat out the fantasy. A diluted slice of light from the hallway washed over her as her trembling fingers gripped the hem of her shirt, lifted it over her head, let it drop to the floor. She was so fucking beautiful. Her thick dark hair spread across the bedding; pale smooth skin and lean soft curves sank gently into the mattress. The waistband of her jeans rode low on her hips, her navel just peeking above the snap and zipper.

"You have no idea how long I've wanted to see you

this way," he confessed as he worked the zipper on his jeans and watched her do the same.

"I do. I do know," she said breathlessly. Lifting her hips, she shimmied out of soft denim and kicked it impatiently away. She lay before him in nothing but her bra and panties. Both were black and lacy and silk . . . and just transparent enough that he could see the dark tips of her nipples jutting against the fine fabric of the cups, the tight triangle of dark pubic hair between her thighs.

She reached between her breasts, her unsteady fingers struggling with the clasp of her bra.

"No." He stopped her with a look and shrugged out of his shirt. Pressing a knee into the mattress, he leaned over her. "Leave it. I want to taste you like this."

Her eyes darkened as he bent over her left breast and sucked her into his mouth, silk and all. She arched into him with a shivery sigh, then gasped in pleasure when he bit her lightly, wetting her flesh through the bra cup, tugging at both it and her with his teeth.

She seemed to come apart then, came to him with open abandon as she gripped his head in her hands and pressed him harder against her, inviting him to do anything, everything he wanted. And everything was exactly what he was going to do, he thought through a haze of pure carnal lust as he moved to her other breast, sucking with greed, then shoving the cup roughly aside and baring her breast to his seeking hand and hungry mouth.

She cried out. For a moment, he thought he'd hurt

her, until her urgent demand of "More" and the frantic way she reached for him assured him it was a cry of pleasure. "More," she demanded again, groaning in frustration when she couldn't shove the pants down his hips fast enough to suit her.

"Easy," he murmured against her breast, knowing that if they didn't slow things down, this was going to be over long before he'd had his fill of touching and tasting and possessing. It was an illusion, yes, but tonight, she *was* his to possess.

"Easy," he repeated, pulling away slowly, using gentle suction to extend the contact with her nipple and intensify her pleasure and his.

"Oh, God, Wyatt. I need you naked. You're killing me here."

He smiled against her skin. "Killing is not what I had in mind, sugar."

Desperation transitioned to an embarrassed groan, then she was smiling, too, as she lifted a hand to his face and caressed his cheek. "Naked," she repeated, then held her breath when he rose above her again and gave her what she wanted. Him. Naked. Jutting. Engorged.

Her gaze held his before lowering and roaming his body. "Beautiful," she managed after swallowing hard. This time, her index finger roamed as her eyes held his. "Beautiful," she repeated in barely a whisper as that wandering finger skimmed down his chest, lingered over his abs, then slowly descended into the thatch of coarse hair at the root of his erection.

He sucked in a harsh breath when, with the lightness

of a whisper, she measured the length of him, then the girth of him, then invited him home with a willing sigh and parted thighs.

His heart rumbled like rifle recoil. Thundering and thumping and banging the hell out of his ribs as she waited, suppliant and needy and almost to the end of her wire.

But just as he wasn't done touching, he wasn't nearly done looking at her, either. Wasn't nearly done exploring, indulging, discovering. He leaned over, switched on the bedside lamp, and knelt between her parted thighs to look his fill.

"I've wanted this," he said, watching her face as his fingers spread over her flat stomach, gently kneading her mons with the heel of his hand. "I've wanted to have the right to do this," he whispered, moving his hand lower, watching his fingers now as he parted delicate flesh that was damp and slick and scented with the heat of her desire.

She moaned and closed her eyes when he caressed her clitoris, felt it grow hard beneath the pad of his thumb as he delved inside her with two fingers.

"I've wanted . . . I've imagined how you'd feel, all silky and wet and hot. God, you're so wet," he grated out as she moved against him, reaching for his hand with both of hers, pressing him harder against her and into her.

"I've wanted to taste you here, Sophie. Let me. Let me," he murmured as he lowered his head and opened his mouth over that part of her he constantly craved. He breathed deep of her arousal, growled low in his throat in pure, primal pleasure at the taste of her.

Sex and heat and woman. Power and lust and love. He was consumed by it and by her and her lusty cries as she came, pouring into his mouth like honey.

She was weeping softly, alternately begging him to stop, to never stop, as he crawled up her body, fit the head of his penis between the lips of her vulva, and slowly pushed his way home.

More . . . more . . . more. His head and his heart and his cock chanted in unison as he pushed in and out of her, as her legs wrapped around his hips and squeezed. Her hands blindly sought his face, and she guided his mouth to hers for a kiss as deep as space, as yearning as time.

Perfect. She was perfect and tight and giving, and he wanted . . . *Jesus,* he wanted to move inside her like this forever, because it was so good, so damn good . . .

But forever wasn't in the cards. He tried to hold back. Couldn't. Attempted to rein himself in. Failed. It was too intense, too strong, too fine to delay. He groaned her name against her throat, swore it through clenched teeth, and gave up the fight in favor of the fall into exquisite, inconceivable pleasure. Her fingers dug into his back as she cried out and rose to meet his final thrust. The uncontrollable rush burned through his belly, molten and thick, heat building and rising and finally shooting out of him and into her with a sharp, powerful orgasm that had him gasping and grinding as close as humanly possible.

Jesus. Jesus.

When he could breathe without gasping, when he could focus his eyes, he glanced at the clock by the bed.

And groaned in disgust. *Hail the five-minute wonder.*

"I'm sorry." He lifted his head and touched his lips to her forehead.

She sighed deeply. "Sorry?"

"For the sprint. I'd hoped for a marathon."

She laughed and made him shiver when she ran her palms from his bare shoulders down to his waist and lightly squeezed his buttocks. "You may not have noticed, but I won that race. Twice, in fact." She smiled into his eyes. "So, sorry's not on the table. But thank you definitely is."

Contentment. Profound and sweet. It clouded her eyes and made him believe that he hadn't disappointed her.

"In that case, you're very welcome." He kissed her then. Softly. Lingered there, over her swollen lips, wondering if once would ever be enough. Knowing it might just have to be.

For the moment, however, he wasn't going anywhere. Careful to make certain he wasn't crushing her with his weight, he lowered his head to the crook of her shoulder. Then he closed his eyes, breathed her in, and held her . . . just held her.

She'd always known he would be like this, Sophie thought with a sigh of pure and achy satisfaction as Wyatt pinned her to the bed with his delicious weight and they both eased down from the high of amazing, mind-blowing sex. Hot and sweet, reckless yet gentle, possessive yet giving. Yeah. Great sex.

She should leave it at that. The past twenty-four hours had been a nonstop race against kidnappers, bullets, loss, and despair, and yeah, she'd needed something to break the cycle. But it wasn't just about escape and great sex. Not for her and not, she suspected, for him.

She breathed deep of the sweaty, aroused scent of him, clung to contentment just as she clung to his weight. She didn't want to think about what this meant right now. She just wanted to think about . . . now. Now was what she wanted. Now was what she needed. Just this moment, just this man, whom she trusted completely to take care of her in ways that transcended physical needs. So she enjoyed the cadence of his breathing as it settled and the easing of his heart rate.

His body was a miracle. She wanted a lifetime to explore the wonder of it, at least an eternity to feel the worshipful and urgent glide of him pumping in and out of her.

Unfortunately, they had neither, and Wyatt was as aware of that fact as she was.

"We'd better get dressed," he said, reluctantly lifting his head and meeting her eyes. "The guys will be rollin' in anytime now."

When she nodded, he moved to pull away.

She stopped him with a hand on his arm. She wanted to say something. Something to answer the question in his eyes. Something to keep him with her just a little while longer.

But she didn't have to say a word.

"I know." He leaned back down to kiss her. "Timing is everything," he whispered against her lips, then dutifully left her bed.

She lay there for a while, her mind spinning through her choices, her life, a hundred different ways, to a hundred different ends. And she wondered, as she'd wondered so many times since she agreed to marry Hugh, how she could have been so wrong about so many things.

She drifted off to sleep thinking about the look in Wyatt's eyes the night she'd told him she was marrying Hugh . . .

Hampton, Virginia
Twelve years ago

Class had run over because of finals, so it was already dark outside as Sophie leaned against the corner of her desk, staring at the closed classroom door. Yeah, it was dark outside, but she felt lit up like the Fourth of July.

Hugh had waited after class until he could get her alone to drop his bombshell. She'd known Hugh Weber a sum total of three months—a wild and intense three months—and not more than five minutes ago, he'd asked her to marry him. Just like that. Then he'd kissed her until her knees melted, left her literally speechless, and, with his cocksure grin, told her he wanted an answer by oh-eight-hundred tomorrow morning.

"Well, no pressure there," she'd managed as he backed away, looking gorgeous and pleased with himself and pretty damn sure what her answer would be.

"No pressure," he'd agreed with a flirty lift of his brow and tapped his watch. "Oh-eight-hundred."

Then he was gone.

She was still leaning back against the edge of her desk where he'd left her, her hands gripping the metal on either side of her hips, when she'd realized she wasn't alone.

"Wyatt." When she saw him standing in the open doorway, she stood and ran a shaky hand through her hair, hoping she didn't look as frazzled as she felt. She glanced at the clock and made an attempt to pull herself together as he stepped hesitantly into the classroom. As hesitant as she'd ever seen him.

"Did you forget something?" she asked.

"I don't know," he said, watching her face carefully. "Maybe."

She wasn't sure what to make of him . . . or the look in his eyes, as if he wanted to ask her something but couldn't quite make himself do it.

She'd been in trouble with both Wyatt and Hugh from the first day of class. They'd never run out of ways to make her smile, make her laugh, make her marvel at the lengths they would go to to ensure that there was no possible way she could ignore them. Yeah, they were both trouble.

Picnic-by-a-pond trouble. Sweep-her-off-her-feet trouble. It was so not like her to be so taken by a man—in this case, by two men. And it was against her personal policy to get involved with any of her students.

These two, however, had made it impossible to resist them. They were so different from each other—Hugh with his breathtaking good looks and wildness and Wyatt with his Southern-boy charm and level head—and yet they were completely in tune with each other.

She realized she was wool gathering and smiled at Wyatt. And wished with all her heart that she had fallen in love with him. Why did she have to lose her heart to a wild man?

"Are you okay?" Wyatt finally asked, walking toward her.

"Honestly? I'm not sure."

"What's bothering you, sugar?" he asked in his slow, sweet drawl as he took her hands in his. "Tell Papa Bear all about it."

This was going to be hard. She breathed deep. Took the plunge. "Hugh just asked me to marry him."

His smile never faltered, but she swore she saw the light in his eyes dim in the moment of stunned silence that followed.

"Smart man, that Hugh. Lucky man." He squeezed her hands, then let them go. "So when's the big day?"

"Big day? Lord, Wyatt, I haven't even given him an answer yet. It's just so . . . sudden." She wished she didn't feel as breathless as she sounded.

"That's Hugh," Wyatt said. "Shock and awe."

"Yeah. You've got that right."

She smiled at him then, gently prodded. "Are you . . . are you okay with this?"

"With you and Hugh? You're two of my favorite people. What's not to be okay?"

She wanted to believe him. She wanted it to be okay. But she was still so staggered by Hugh's proposal that she couldn't think her way through Wyatt's reaction. She checked her watch. "Oh, man. I've got to head for home."

"I'll walk you to your car."

She'd parked her little white compact under a security light in the almost empty parking lot. When they reached it, she hit the keyless remote and looked up at him. "You never did say why you came back to the classroom."

"Not important," he told her with a shrug of his shoulder. He searched her face for the longest time, and a sixth sense told her that he was lying. It had been very important. That kiss he'd kept from getting out of control several weeks ago had meant more to him than a Sunday flirtation.

He lifted his hand and touched her hair, letting it sift through his fingers before caressing her cheek. His eyes were so blue and so sincere and so . . . sad, she decided finally.

She covered his hand with hers, not knowing what to say, not knowing what to do, and for a moment as they stood so close, alone in the night, she thought he was going to kiss her. For a wild part of that moment, she wanted him to.

Then he dropped his hand, leaving her wondering, leaving her breathless again, but this time with a confusing mix of wanting and regret.

"You'll make a beautiful bride." Then he tucked his fingers in the front pockets of his jeans, turned, and walked away.

14

Wyatt hadn't wanted to admit that he'd been worried about the guys, but he breathed a sigh of relief fifteen minutes later when they filed through the door and into the house, tired, dirty and hungry at a little after three a.m.

He'd known their plan had been to score some weapons, then spend most of their time canvassing gangland territory in Soyopango. Not exactly a day at Disney World. No matter how well they "adapted" to their surroundings, three Anglos—as big as box cars—were not going to blend in. Mendoza was the only one with a chance of doing that. And apparently, things hadn't gone so well for the Choirboy.

"He's hurt." Sophie gasped when she walked out of the bedroom and saw the shiner Mendoza was sporting on his right eye.

"What happened?" Wyatt looked away from her kiss-swollen lips and gloriously untidy hair and prayed to God that the guys would think she'd been catching a cat nap.

"I keep telling him he needs glasses," Doc said, feeling the needed to intervene on Mendoza's behalf.

"I do not need glasses," Mendoza grumbled, reluctantly allowing Sophie to lead him into the kitchen.

Doc grunted. "Then why did you run headlong into that asshole's fist?"

Mendoza expelled a breath of annoyance, while Sophie hurriedly gathered ice from the freezer and dumped it into a zip-lock bag. "Because I didn't see it coming."

Triumphant, Doc lifted his hands. "I rest my case."

"Will somebody please shut him up?"

Doc grinned and, now that he had decent lighting, shifted from tormentor to medic. He checked the wound, checked his pupils, and grinned again when Mendoza winced and swore at him.

"Garden-variety black eye." Doc finally pronounced him bruised but not broken. "You'll live."

"Thank you, Dr. Kevorkian."

Gabe and Green dragged bar stools away from the counter and sank down, too tired to pay much attention to either of them or to the subtle tension between Wyatt and Sophie.

"Is there a short story here?" Wyatt asked while Sophie folded the ice bag into a dish towel and handed it to Mendoza.

"Yeah." Rafe pressed the ice gingerly against his eye. "We busted a lot of chops, asked a lot of questions. Guess the sucker who threw the punch didn't like my smile."

"Or your lack of tattoos," Green interjected.

Green was probably right. MS-13 members typically covered themselves in body and facial tattoos—all of them had a meaning. "MS," "13," dice, crossbones, and daggers were among their favorites. Unless, of course, the gang member had a specialty. Wyatt had once seen a grenade tattooed on a dead MS-13 member's back in Honduras. Seemed he'd been that cell's explosives expert.

"Any luck at all?" Wyatt asked.

"With weaponry, yeah. We should be good. But we struck out for leads on the girl." Gabe yawned and nodded his thanks when Sophie set a mug of coffee in front of him. "What about you?"

Wyatt told them about Sophie's unexpected meeting with Jorge Vega and the map he'd slipped her.

"So far, we haven't pinpointed the location."

"Well the A-team's here now," Doc said, earning a head shake from Wyatt. "Let's get 'er done."

"Wait," Sophie said. "You guys are beat. You've got to be hungry, and I'm guessing a shower would feel darn good about now."

Same old Sophie, Wyatt thought with bittersweet affection. She'd always worried about him and Hugh getting enough to eat and enough rest. Hugh used to call her Mother Henrietta just to get a rise out of her.

And he'd just made love to her. Finally. After all these years of wondering, he finally knew how she tasted, how she smelled when she was aroused, the soft sexy sounds she made when she came.

Yeah. Finally. And now she didn't seem capable of looking him in the eye.

"I wouldn't turn either one down." Gabe gave Sophie a grateful smile.

"I've got two bathrooms. Who's first?"

"Injured first, then the knuckle draggers." Mendoza followed her toward the hallway. "I guess that means Doc gets the cold water."

"What do you think?" Gabe leaned back from the table, rolling the stiffness out of his neck.

Wyatt checked his watch. It was closing in on four a.m. They were all used to functioning on very little sleep, but at Sophie's insistence, they'd all showered and refueled on calories and caffeine. For the last forty-five minutes, they'd set their collective efforts to the task of pinpointing the location that matched Vega's map. All except Sophie. She'd been weaving-on-her-feet tired. Wyatt felt partly responsible for that. Not just because of the physical workout they'd had in bed but because of the emotional toll on her.

He was certain she regretted what they'd done. The heat of the moment had cooled to the icy starkness of common sense. In any event, he'd insisted she lie down—by herself this time—and catch a few winks. The fact that she hadn't fought him on it was telling. She needed the distance.

"I think," Wyatt said after pushing back from the table, "that I wish we had access to a spy satellite that could give us an aerial view of this jungle-ridden country. Maybe some infrared technology that could hone in on the target. Without either, this map of Vega's could lead to a dozen different locations we pinpointed as potential places to search."

"Too bad one of us doesn't have a close contact at the NSA. Someone who might be able to pull a few strings, get access to the National Reconnaissance Office." Mendoza gave Green a pointed look.

Joe Green was already reaching for his cell phone. "On it," he said with a nod.

"Tell Stephanie we say hi," Doc added with a grin.

"I'm sure she'll be tickled as hell to know you were all thinking about her before sunrise." With his cell pressed to his ear, Joe lowered his voice to a soft caress, making it clear to all that Steph had answered.

"Hey, babe, wake up. It's me," he said, and walked out of earshot.

Stephanie and Joe. Wyatt was still getting used to it. For as long as he'd known Joe Green, Wyatt had never seen him with a woman. That didn't mean he hadn't ever been involved, it was just that Joe was a very private kind of man. The big guy was the silent, stoic type, professional to a fault, and pretty much dedicated to the job to the exclusion of having a personal life. In combat situations, he was a machine: cold, hard steel. The BOIs didn't call him Mean Joe Green for nothing.

But a little more than six months ago, Joe had been assigned protection duty for Stephanie Tompkins. And something major had happened between them.

Steph was the daughter of Ann Tompkins—who just happened to be a deputy attorney general in the Justice Department—and Robert Tompkins, former adviser to President Billings. The Tompkinses, in turn, just happened to be a second family to each and every one of the BOIs.

Wyatt thought of their son, Bryan Tompkins, as his brother in arms. Hell, Bry had been like family to all of the BOIs, and he sure as hell shouldn't have died on a mission gone wrong in God-forsaken Sierra Leone. He'd been too young, too good, and, like the others, Wyatt knew he would miss Bry until the day he died.

Yeah, Bry had been their brother, and since he'd been gone, the Tompkinses had treated the BOIs like adopted sons. Sam Lang had even named his own son after Bryan.

"Come home anytime," Robert and Anne Tompkins had told them at Bryan's memorial service. "You'll always be welcome. Always have a safe place to land."

That had been a lot of years ago. Time enough for all of them to part ways with the military and regroup again with Nate Black at Black Ops, Inc. Time enough for some of them, like Gabe and Sam and Reed and Mendoza, to meet and marry some of the most amazing women Wyatt had ever known.

Time enough, maybe, for Joe to realize that there was a woman worth loving. That woman was Stephanie, and damn if it didn't look like Green might actually become a true member of the Tompkins family someday.

It had been apparent ever since the conclusion of that op—which had also sent Rafe Mendoza undercover to infiltrate a drug cartel in Colombia—that Stephanie and Joe had shared more than warding off the hired guns of a corrupt U.S. senator who had sent a detail to eliminate her.

Unfortunately for the senator, Stephanie, an NSA cryptologist, had ferreted out a security breach that led directly back to the senator. Consequently, Steph had become a regrettable "loose end" in an international plot to destroy the U.S. electrical power infrastructure and in the process drop the already ailing economy to its knees.

Thanks to the BOIs—specifically, Rafe and a tough-as-nails DIA officer by the name of B. J. Chase—now B. J. Mendoza—the senator and the Russian mafia and the Colombian drug cartel which were all in league with an al-Qaeda operative had been thwarted. A catastrophic event had been averted.

The U.S. government remained eternally grateful to the BOIs. Joe and Stephanie remained tight. And now Stephanie and her NSA connections were going to return the favor and help the team pinpoint the Mara Salvatrucha stronghold.

At least, that was the hope.

"She's on it." Green rejoined the guys at the table that was covered with maps and charts. "She put a shout-out to a buddy at the NRO, but he's in a marathon closed-door meeting. Something very top-top. Could be ten, possibly twelve hours before he gets back to her, but she has hopes she can find out who's tasking the spy birds and get us what we need."

"So what's the interim plan?" Doc asked.

Wyatt used a black felt marker to circle a dozen different locations on two different maps. "Looks like we get to play jungle boogie."

The areas they'd pinpointed were a couple of hours south of San Salvador, deep in a triple-canopy rain forest. It was not only off-road, but the last several clicks appeared to be no road.

"We hit them one by one, pray we get lucky, and, if not, hope Steph gets back to us with an exact location before we run out of potential targets."

Mendoza crossed his arms over his chest, his expression thoughtful.

"Something on your mind?" Wyatt asked.

Mendoza's eye was transitioning from red to purple, but the ice was keeping the swelling down. "What if this Vega guy's info is bogus? Are we seriously putting all of our eggs in his basket?"

"Yeah, that's the money question," Wyatt agreed, rubbing the back of his neck.

"What do we know about him?" Doc stood and stretched, then walked to the coffee pot for another refill.

"Only that Sophie says he's solid." He thought of her sleeping in the bed where he'd held her, naked and spent, her heart beating wildly against his.

"And what does Papa Bear say?" Gabe asked around another yawn.

"I say I'd like to have a little talk with Jorge Vega," Wyatt responded, jerking his thoughts back to the moment, "before we head off on a wild-goose chase."

"Or an ambush."

Gabe had pretty much put the hammer to the nail,

and, judging by the looks on the other faces surrounding him, the rest of the guys were thinking the same thing.

"Clock's ticking, but I think I need to make time for a little up-close-and-personal with Vega," Wyatt said. "See if I can figure out his angle. Maybe even get a little more intel out of him. If he knows this much, he could know more."

Wyatt walked to Sophie's desk. He would feel guilty for rifling through it for her address book if so much wasn't at stake. When he found what he was looking for, he scribbled down Vega's address and located it on the city map.

Doc looked over his shoulder. "At this time of the morning, with traffic at a minimum, it shouldn't take more than half an hour to get there."

"I'll need a weapon."

"Got you covered." Gabe hitched his head toward the door. "H&K in the Suburban."

"I'll go along for the ride." Colter pushed away from the table.

"We'll all go," Green said.

Wyatt shook his head. "You three stay here with Sophie. I don't want to leave her vulnerable. Doc and I can handle this. Oh, and call Crystal."

He stopped on his way to the door, checked his watch, and realized that, like Stephanie back in Virginia, Crystal, along with Reed, Nate, and everyone else at Juliana's Bahía Blanca estate in Argentina, would most likely be sleeping. "Check that. Let's not mess with the redhead at this hour. Text her so you don't wake up the entire house. Tell her we need anything she can scare up on Diego Montoya."

Doc frowned. "Montoya? Should we know that name?"

"He's a big-money coffee baron here in San Salvador. He's also a big question mark. Met him last night at the charity event."

"You're thinking this Montoya has something to do with the abduction?" Gabe asked.

What Wyatt was thinking was that he didn't like the creep, and it was quite possible that the only reason he didn't like him was his blatant interest in Sophie. Then again, there was something about the guy, something underlying his arrogance, that didn't set right.

"I don't know," he finally admitted, stopping with one hand on the door. "Gut feeling. Just see if Crystal can find any connection to Montoya and organized crime, any shady dealings, whatever. Have her check on Vega, too. And while they're at it, see if they can find Hugh Weber. Sophie's ex," he explained, not going into details. "He's got his own security firm that he operates out of San Salvador. Has a history with kidnap recoveries. Right now, he's out of country on an op and out of touch. We could use his help if we could find him."

"Will do," Gabe said.

"If we're not back in three hours," he added as Doc walked out the door ahead of him, "call Nate, then get Sophie the hell out of here."

15

_____

Even though their past joint kidnapping ventures had been highly profitable, Vincente had begun to consider that it might be time to break the partnership. Now, in the middle of the night, was one of those times.

He did not like complications. The news that had reached him today had been disturbing. So he'd lulled himself to sleep on tequila, sex, and a slow-simmering rage.

Now he was forced awake again, opening bleary eyes to pitch dark except for the crack of light seeping in through the door Juan had dared to open.

He breathed in the scent of stale sex and sweet weed. The light from the hallway sliced across the tangled sheets, illuminating the rose and skull tattoo burned into Esmeralda's naked back where she lay beside him. He hadn't wanted Justina tonight. He'd wanted to wound someone. Esmeralda was younger, sweeter, cried so pretty when he hurt her.

"What?" he demanded on a hoarse growl as Juan entered the room.

Juan held out a cell phone. "He says it's important."

Complications, he thought again as he leaned up on an elbow, reached for the phone, and pressed it to his ear. Only one man brought him complications these days. "Speak."

"We've got a problem."

He grunted out a laugh. "No, *you've* got a problem. There are men in my territory. Three Americans. One Latino. All of them asking about the girl. You said this would be easy money."

A quick $250K, his half of the ransom for the girl. After expenses, of course. Payoff for the *policía* would take a substantial chunk of cash.

"No resistance, you said," he continued, reckless with his anger. "And yet who are these men? And how do you intend to make them go away?"

"I'll take care of them," his partner said. "In my own way. Right now, there's an issue that needs your immediate attention."

Vincente seethed with rage when he hung up the phone a few minutes later. Only the day before, this man had dared to call him out for taking the wrong child? Now Vincente had to fix a problem of his creation.

So be it. He would give this matter immediate attention. And tomorrow, he would remind his late-night caller who owned this city. Inform him that there would be no more complications. No more interlopers on his turf.

"Juan!"

His lieutenant appeared at the door.

"Tito and Benito. Get them here now."

Five minutes later, his two soldiers had been dispatched to clean up the "big" man's mess. Vincente would cover his ass. No matter that he was pissed. No matter that tomorrow, they would meet, and there would be new terms dictated for their partnership.

He lay back on the bed, rolled to his side, and slapped Esmeralda hard on her tight bare ass. She awoke with a start and shot to her knees beside him.

He smiled, reached out, and tweaked a tight pink nipple until she cried out. "Blow my head off, baby," he whispered, and forced her head down to his jutting cock. "Yeah. That's sweet. Very sweet . . .

"Tomorrow," he grated out between clenched teeth as she labored over him. "Tomorrow, I think we will get your tongue pierced. A gold stud, yes?" He fisted his hands in her hair and guided her head to take him deeper into her mouth. "A gold stud to please your big gold stud."

"The U.S. could take a cue from El Salvador's street-numbering systems," Doc said as he directed Wyatt toward Vega's residence, then went on to explain that every city had a *parque central*—central park—at the intersection of the main street and the main avenue. The *avenidas*—avenues—always ran north and south, and those west of the main avenue bore odd numbers while those east of the main avenue bore even numbers. Same process went for the *calles*—streets.

"Makes getting around a snap, even in the dark," Doc said after directing Wyatt to take a right turn.

It wouldn't be dark much longer. They were pushing sunrise. Not a good thing, considering they didn't want to be seen.

"Okay, slow down. There. That would be Vega's house up on the left."

He reached between his legs to retrieve a mini Uzi from the floor beneath the passenger seat while Wyatt circled the block. Other than a car parked by the curb two blocks down, all was quiet. Wyatt doubled back, then parked on a side street a block away. As soon as he killed the motor, Doc handed him a loaded H&K P10 9mm pistol and an extra magazine.

They slipped soundlessly out of the vehicle and tucked into their Kevlar vests. Keeping their profiles low, they cut across two backyards until they reached Vega's house. It was a single-story rectangular structure in an upscale neighborhood. The backyard was enclosed in a six-foot-tall wooden privacy fence. Wyatt could hear a pool filter humming away inside the fence.

"You're sure this is the right place?" he whispered as they scoped it out for the best method of entry. This wasn't going to be a "friendly" visit. They didn't have time to play nice. Wyatt wanted to scare the piss out of Vega before he made it clear that the truth, like Vega's life, was on the line. They had no intention of hurting him, but it would be nice if they had the right guy.

"Guess we'll soon find out," Doc said. "Yes," he quickly amended when Wyatt glared at him. "I'm sure."

They had their heads together conferring about whether to simply walk up and pound the hell out of the front door or scale the backyard fence and break in, when three distinct pops shattered the night silence.

"That came from inside." Doc hunkered down, taking cover. "Jesus. Sounded like a fucking cannon."

A .45-cal, Wyatt figured. A subsonic round without the distinctive sonic crack of his 9mm.

"Someone else had a need to question Vega?" Doc speculated.

"Or shut him up."

When another shot rang out, Wyatt took off for the front of the house. With Doc right on his heels, he rushed toward the front door, trampling flowers and bushes on the way, hugging the exterior stucco wall that still held the heat from yesterday's scorching sun.

The door stood open a crack. With a quick nod that told Doc he'd go left and high, Wyatt burst inside, leading with his H&K. Doc came in low with the Uzi.

The foyer was empty. So were the living area and the kitchen. Wyatt touched a finger to his lips when he heard voices, then hitched his head in the direction of a hallway. A narrow sliver of light arrowed across the tile floor. He followed the light to where it ended at a door that stood slightly ajar.

He could hear mean laughter on the other side, interspersed with rapid-fire Spanish. They were gloating over the kill. High on adrenaline and blood lust.

Doc held up two fingers.

Wyatt nodded. Yeah, he heard two distinct voices,

which meant there were two guns to contend with. With another nod from Wyatt toward Doc, they took positions on either side of the doorway. They'd made these kinds of entries so many times their actions were as automatic as breathing: move and shoot, get off the X and out of the fatal funnel of the doorway.

On Wyatt's signal, they charged into the room.

Both men inside swung around to face them, automatically lifting their weapons.

Wyatt rolled left, and Doc rolled right, both leaning on their triggers. Wyatt popped at least three rounds into one man's chest with his H&K before the shooter ever fired a round from his handgun. Doc's aim was just as deadly. The second shooter dropped like a stone, blood trickling out of a dime-sized hole right below his eye socket.

Wyatt's ears rang like church bells; the scent of gunsmoke and blood filled his nostrils as he rose quickly to his feet, rushed to the downed men, and kicked the weapons out of their reach. Not that it mattered. They were both dead. Lifeless eyes stared up from faces covered in tattoos typical of MS-13 gang members.

He slowly turned to the other man lying spread-eagled on his back on the floor. Doc had already reloaded and was quickly clearing the rest of the house.

"Vega?" Doc asked when he returned to the blood-splattered room.

Wyatt nodded. "Bastards tortured him," he said. Vega had been shot at least half a dozen times. "They shot holes through his hands, into both feet and knees."

"Figure they found out he ratted them out to Sophie?"

"Either that, or they wanted to find out what he knew."

For one split second, as he stood there, the sound of gunfire still ringing in his head, the scent of blood and death permeating his senses, and Vega's dead eyes staring up at the ceiling, Wyatt felt a hatred so strong it was dizzying. Hatred for the corruption that lowered men to such inhuman levels. Hatred for all the similar scenes he'd either come upon or been the cause of during the course of his life.

Hatred for himself.

Yeah, he was supposed to be one of the good guys. Yet here he stood. Playing in the very same sandbox with the very same toys, right along with bottom feeders like MS-13.

Good guy. Bad guy. In the end, there was a very fine line that separated them.

"Savage?"

He stared another moment at the poor bastard, Vega, a man who had been trying to do the right thing and was dead because of it. Then he headed back out into the night. "There's nothing we can do here."

If Doc wondered about Wyatt's silence on the ride back, he was wise enough to keep his questions to himself. They rolled back into Sophie's drive a little before six a.m., fifteen minutes after a sunrise Jorge Vega would never see.

Gabe looked up when the front door swung open. "That was fast."

Doc responded to the guys' curious looks when Wyatt shouldered on into the house without a word. "Doesn't take much time to question a dead man."

"Dead man?"

Wyatt stopped cold.

Sophie.

He turned and saw her standing in the hallway. Clearly, she'd overheard Doc's remark. He hadn't wanted her to find out about Vega's execution. He glanced at Gabe and saw by the look on his face that someone had filled Sophie in on where they'd gone.

Her face paled when she saw the grim looks the men exchanged. "Oh, God. Not Jorge."

"I'm sorry, Sophie." Wyatt steadied her with a hand on her shoulder. "They got to him before we did."

The rest of the blood drained from her face, but she held it together. "Who?"

"MS-13 thugs," Doc said. "High-level gang members, judging by their tattoos."

She swallowed hard. "Tell me what happened."

When Doc looked at Wyatt, clearly wondering how much information to share, Wyatt shook his head. He didn't want her to know the details.

God damn it, he didn't want any more of this violence to touch her. He hated that she had to be a party to any of it. Lola's abduction was tough enough for her to deal with. The hollow look in her eyes told him what sending Hope away was doing to her. And now she had to come to terms with Jorge Vega's brutal death.

"Tell me," she insisted, bypassing Wyatt and looking directly at Doc for answers. "Was he . . . was he tortured?"

Doc looked away, then finally nodded, unable to lie to her.

Her eyes glazed over with grief and guilt.

Wyatt never should have agreed to let her stay. And the danger for her personally because of her association with Vega had just ratcheted up several degrees.

"It's small consolation," Doc said, "but they won't be hurting anyone else."

Her gaze shot to Wyatt's. "You killed them?"

He worked his jaw, hated what he saw in her eyes. Accusation threaded with satisfaction. She was struggling to come to grips with both her horror and her desire for retribution. "They didn't give us much choice."

The silence was as brutal as the scene they'd left behind. The *policía* should be at Vega's by now. Wyatt had made an anonymous call just before they beat it out of there.

"Gotta figure Vega talked," Green said with a glance at Wyatt, who had pretty much decided the same thing. "So the question is, did they have a chance to share his confession with whoever sent them to do the dirty work?"

That was the big question, all right.

"They both had cell phones on them," Doc said, while Wyatt continued to watch Sophie's face. "I was able to check one—there were no recent outgoing calls on the call record. The other phone was shot up too badly to tell. So I'm thinking no, but it's still possible they had time to call someone before we got there."

"And if they did," Gabe added, "our odds of tracking the child to the location on Vega's map just sailed beyond long shot to nonexistent. They're sure to move her."

"My money's still on them not getting a chance to relay the info," Doc reminded them. "In which case, we still have a chance of finding her there."

"I say we go for it," Green said. "Now, before we lose any advantage we might have."

Joe was right. And Wyatt was more certain than ever that he had been dead wrong in not insisting that Sophie go to Argentina with Hope. She didn't belong in the middle of all this evil.

"Sophie," he said, turning to her, "it's not safe for you here. I want you in Argentina with Nate and Reed."

"We already discussed this." A new resolve came over her as she pulled herself back together. "We're not going to discuss it again. A child is in danger, a child who was mistaken for my child. Now a man is dead because he tried to help me find her." She met his eyes then, and the hardened determination he saw there made his heart ache. "You don't know me . . . you don't know me at all if you think I would turn my back on either of them."

She might just be right. Maybe he *didn't* know this woman. *This* woman had been forced by brutal and vicious predators to become someone she should never have to be. This kind of evil should never have invaded a kind and gentle heart and turned her into someone driven by fear, outrage, and desperation.

Long moments passed as their locked gazes held and he came to terms with this new Sophie. She wasn't backing away. "If anything happens to you," he said, so low that only she could hear him, "I'll—"

"Nothing's going to happen." Her eyes were clear and sharp when she cut him off.

He breathed deep, gave in to her with a nod, and prayed he wouldn't regret his decision for the rest of his life.

"We need to get a move on," Gabe reminded him quietly.

"Throw some essentials into a bag, and dress for rough country," Wyatt told Sophie. "We roll in five."

They had to leave before the puppet master decided to dispatch more thugs to "chat" with Sophie. Before what little time Lola had left—sixty hours and counting—ran out.

16

⟞

"How's she doing?"

Nate glanced away from Hope when Juliana joined him outside under Villa Flores's massive covered patio. He'd been watching over the sad and solemn girl, who had touched very little of the breakfast Juliana had served them a little while ago.

Hope sat in the grass, staring out toward the cliff line where, far below, the azure waters of the Pacific slammed against the west coast of Bahía Blanca, Argentina.

"She's very quiet," he said. "It seems even her excitement over the chopper ride and a case of puppy love over Reed can't snap her out of this funk."

When Juliana smiled, Nate looked away before she could see the effect she had on him. There wasn't one thing about her that didn't mesmerize him. The way she moved. The way she worked. Fluidly. Effortlessly. Always with an economy of motion and vibrant energy. He sometimes wondered if she had any idea what a beautiful woman she was, both maternal and sexual, with her long chestnut hair and lush figure.

Her face fascinated him. The warmth from her dark, intelligent eyes, the honey and gold of her complexion, the pillow-soft lips that, to this day, he swore he could taste on his tongue. But over it all, what had drawn him to her like a tether nearly four years ago was her valiant spirit, her sense of purpose.

He'd loved her on sight. Had never stopped loving her.

"Let me see if I can take her mind off things," she said with a soft smile, and walked to the girl.

How the hell did a grown man—a mature man who'd been through the wars and beyond and who commanded the respect of not only his country's top military leaders but a team of deadly, stand—up fighting men—turn into a marshmallow when this woman did nothing more than smile? Or walk into a room. Or approach a child, as she was doing now.

Transfixed, and hoping to hell it didn't show, he watched as Juliana knelt down beside Hope on the grass and murmured soothing words while touching the girl's hair. Then she lowered her head close to Hope's, and, as if by magic, the child reached far enough out of herself to take Juliana's hand, stand, and walk with her toward the lush gardens in back of the villa.

Nate knew what Hope would find there. Nestled on more than half an acre of riotous blooms, miniature fruit trees, and whimsical topiaries was a wonderland right out of a fairy tale. Enchanted castles made of moss-covered pebbles and alabaster and coral seashells were hidden in secret glens. Intricate winding paths all led to a vine-covered white gazebo that hosted a half-dozen glittering, melodious wind chimes made of moons and stars, brilliantly colored butterflies, and iridescent dragonflies. Even a twelve-year-old's imagination could run wild in this tiny paradise as she envisioned tree spirits and forest nymphs and maybe even herself as princess of the realm.

He watched them walk hand in hand down a cobblestone path in the sparkling morning sunlight—a mother missing a child she'd lost, a child missing her mother—and he remembered the first time Juliana had shown him the garden.

"Angelina would spend hours out here," she'd told him, and he'd seen in her eyes that she could still picture her own daughter there. A bittersweet sadness that she tried in vain to hide would always engulf her when she spoke of the daughter she'd lost at the brutal hands of the same madman who had also taken her husband's life.

As he watched Juliana's and Hope's dark heads together, he couldn't help but wonder what it would have been like to have made a child with this woman. To have had the right. To have been that young man who had wooed her and won her and taken her as a virgin to his bed.

There was something about this place, this fortress of stone, light, and sea breeze, of towering windows and sheer, billowing curtains, of gleaming cypress floors and what Gabe referred to as dead king's furniture, that made a man yearn for many things that could not be.

He could not be Juliana's first love. And during the

course of the few years he'd known her, he'd come to accept that he could not be her last. Not that there were any other men in her life, but Nate had shared her bed only once—she'd turned to him for relief of both loneliness and pain. She'd never said as much, but he knew she'd always regretted what they'd done.

He, on the other hand, had only regretted her guilt. And sometimes his own stubborn pride, which kept him from telling her that he loved her. Just his luck, he thought, as he watched Juliana and Hope, that he'd finally met a woman who could make him think about wrapping up his career and spending the rest of his life devoted to her, and she—well, she was still in love with her dead husband.

He couldn't compete with a dead man's memory, especially a man as revered as Armando Flores.

There were times when he wished he'd never met her. For many years, he'd been happily oblivious to anything but his work. He'd married the military, and she'd been a demanding and rewarding bride. But after a twenty-year union, he'd had enough of her difficult ways and called it quits. That's when Black Ops, Inc. was born, and he'd recruited his team of merry men to put the screws to the bad guys—still under orders from Uncle Sam but without the government restrictions and colossal reels of red tape.

Speaking of merry men. Reed thumped up behind him on his crutches.

"What?" Nate demanded when Reed just stood there and glared at him.

"Are you ever going to tell that woman how you feel about her? Oh, wait," Reed muttered after Nate pinned him with a warning scowl, "I forgot who I was talking to. You haven't even admitted it to yourself yet."

Only Reed, reckless, irreverent, and pretty damn secure in the knowledge that Nate wouldn't hurt an injured man, would dare goad his former Task Force Mercy CO and current employer at Black Ops, Inc.

"Something give you the impression that I wanted your input on my personal business, Reed?"

The good-looking Texan only grinned and opened the door that Nate had just slammed in his face. "Bigger men than you have taken the plunge, boss. Take me for example."

"I'll pass, thanks just the same. And in case you missed the message, let me repeat: Butt out."

"You think I wanted to admit that a little redheaded pixie had the power to bring me to my knees?" Reed continued, unfazed by Nate's glare. "I didn't want any part of that. But there came a time when I finally got it through my head that there wasn't a damn thing I could do to fight it. Life got a whole helluva lot easier after that. A lot sweeter, too," he added, grinning like a goon.

Nate knew he should be pissed at the younger man for butting in, but he'd learned over the years that Johnny Duane Reed was a hard man to get pissed at. He was also a hard man to ignore, because behind that pretty-boy façade was one of the most stand-up fighting men and team players Nate had ever had the good fortune to command.

"Not every story ends with 'They all lived happily ever after,' " Nate pointed out.

"Well, yours sure as hell won't if you keep up the invisible-man act with the pretty doc."

"D'you ever think she just might not be interested?"

Damn. Nate hadn't meant to give Reed even that much of an admission that he cared.

"Well, hell, boss, all you have to do is watch the woman's face when she looks at you to know she's got it bad."

Nate jerked his gaze toward Reed. He was serious. *Christ.* He hadn't thought Reed was capable of surprising him anymore.

Reed shot him an incredulous look. "You didn't know? Shit, boss, for a smart man, you don't know jack about women."

"And you're the supreme oracle on the subject."

"Apparently, I know more than you do," Reed pointed out.

Nate squinted at him. "Aren't you up for a performance review with a raise hinging on the results? And correct me if I'm wrong, but didn't I approve full salary while you nurse a torn ACL that you managed to injure while performing a stunt on a skateboard? *Off* duty?"

"Okay, fine. You don't want my advice. I got it. But for God's sake, man—"

"Zip it," Nate cut in with a no-nonsense glare.

Far from looking threatened, Reed just rolled his eyes. "Zipping it, boss. I'll just go soak my knee."

Nate added, "And check with Crystal. Let me know if she found anything of interest on either Vega or Montoya."

Something had to break on the abduction case, and Nate knew that Crystal had been busy on her computer ever since she'd picked up a text this morning from Green.

They hadn't heard from Wyatt or any of the other guys since the night before. He checked his watch. It was close to ten a.m. in El Salvador. By his calculation, that left the BOIs a little more than forty-eight hours, give or take, before the Thursday deadline imposed by the kidnappers.

If he had a child and that child's life came down to a matter of two days, there wasn't anyone he'd rather have on the case than the men he'd left in El Salvador.

If he had a child, he thought again, for the first time in his life regretting that he'd never taken that monumentally life-changing step, he would have wanted it to be with Juliana.

Maybe Reed was right. Maybe . . . hell, maybe he should let her know how he felt.

He saw her now, shepherding Hope back from the garden. She looked guardedly hopeful.

"What's up?" he asked.

"Hope remembered something, didn't you, *cara*?"

Hope nodded.

"You can tell Nate," Juliana assured her, her tone patient and gentle. "Go ahead, *querida*, tell him what you told me."

"I saw them," Hope said hesitantly. "I saw the men who took Lola."

"Do you remember what they looked like?" Nate asked carefully.

She looked down and shook her head.

"It's okay, *cara*." Juliana sat down at a patio table and urged Hope to sit beside her. "It doesn't matter that you can't remember everything. Just tell Nate what you do recall. And maybe when you tell it again, you'll remember something else that will help us find Lola."

Very slowly, Hope began telling him what she remembered, relating with a chilling clarity the feel of the sun burning on her skin, the squeal of the tires as the van skidded to a stop. The door opening, the sound of metal rolling on a track, a glimpse of the inside of the van littered with fast-food wrappers and dirty blankets. The scent of the white coffee-bean blossoms in the air.

"He . . . the driver. He wore a hat. It said Los Cuscatlecos on it."

"Good. That's good," Nate encouraged, even though Los Cuscatlecos was the name of El Salvador's national soccer team and half the male population wore caps with its logo.

"He . . . the man . . . he had a big gun. The man pointed it at Lola, and he . . . he pulled her into the van."

She started crying then. Juliana wrapped her in her arms, murmuring praise and reassurance into her hair. "Come on, *cara*, that's enough for now. You've done well. Very, very well. Now, let's go see what Johnny's up to, okay?"

A few minutes later Juliana joined him on the patio again. "How's she doing?"

"She's okay," Juliana said. "Johnny talked her into a game of Scrabble.

"It will come to her," Nate assured Juliana. "She'll eventually remember, and then we'll be able to put faces to these guys, get a line on them."

"It's so hard on her."

"Yes," he agreed. "But it's also good for her to get it out."

"She's suffering from posttraumatic stress," Juliana said, her dark eyes concerned.

"That's all going to get better," Nate assured her, "once Wyatt and the guys get Lola back."

The sun prodded noon in the ass with a burning torch. But not as hard as Wyatt and the guys had been pushing for answers. They'd already visited three of the twelve potential locations of the MS-13 stronghold where Lola might be held, when Wyatt turned off the main highway following Green, Mendoza, Gabe, and Doc, who led the way in the Suburban.

Sophie sat beside him in the passenger seat, dozing on and off. She was dead tired. Hell, they were all running on adrenaline and fumes and powering through on the few hours of sleep they'd managed to grab in the two days since Lola had been abducted. By unspoken agreement, neither had said word one about what had happened in her bed the night before.

He sure as hell thought about it, though, and he suspected that she was thinking about it, too. And yeah, sooner or later, they would talk, but now was neither the time nor the place. This next stop would be their fourth foray into some backwater hamlet where they hoped to get lucky and get a lead on the MS-13 camp and Lola.

So far, they'd struck out in spades. It would be at least another two, possibly four, hours before Stephanie could report on the satellite photos. Until they heard from her, the plan of attack hadn't changed: try to find a needle in the proverbial haystack. Or in this case, locate a particular clew of worms in a jungle teeming with creepy crawlies.

He glanced at Sophie after maneuvering over a hole in the road that was big enough to swallow a small steer. She was buckled into the passenger seat of her SUV. She looked exhausted, but she was holding up without a word of complaint about the insufferable heat or the teeth-jarring ride as the SUV labored over the rutted dirt road. Neither had she complained about the disappointment over the three times they'd come up empty-handed.

She was a lot damn tougher than she looked, and even though he had no ownership, he couldn't help but feel a swell of pride that she was holding her own in a grueling back country capable of beating the most seasoned off-road warrior bloody. Hell, Wyatt was a Southern boy; he knew about insufferable, sweltering heat. And yeah, he'd run as many ops in the roasting furnaces of places like Honduras, Colombia, Sri Lanka, or Indonesia as he had in the bitter cold and barren mountains of Afghanistan. But El Salvador lent a whole different meaning to the term *hell hole*.

The closest comparison he could make was Panama, when he'd gone to snake eater school and learned how to be a good little operative for Uncle. He'd been a hell of a lot younger then. And this 130-degree heat and 100-percent humidity coupled with a mountainous jungle terrain that made Vietnam look like a spa retreat wasn't as easy to hack as it had been back then.

If the rough, mountainous country and the dirt roads carved along the sides of mountains weren't enough, the oppressive stench of despair in the scattered villages they'd driven through could make a person appreciate the good fortune of being born in the US of A, where a child could at least aspire to something better and stand a chance of making that dream a reality. Here, there was nothing to aspire to but survival.

They drove by a row of corrugated tin shacks, the structures barely managing to hold back the relentlessly encroaching jungle. Thin, ragged children played listlessly along the dirt road and barely took note of their passing; a feral dog slinked around a corner. This was only one of many desperate and depressing scenes they'd witnessed, and Wyatt knew without asking that the abject poverty was taking as much of a toll on Sophie's strength as the heat.

"Hugh found Hope in a village like this one," Sophie said, surprising him that she was awake.

She brushed her hair away from her face—a face that was damp with perspiration, hair that was wet with sweat even though the air conditioner in her SUV was working overtime to cut the oppressive heat.

He'd wondered about that. Didn't surprise him at all that Sophie had rescued a child.

"Her parents were dead. Her older brother tried to sell her to Hugh for sex. She was seven years old."

Jesus.

"When Hugh wouldn't fork over the money, the boy—Hugh said he couldn't have been much over ten or twelve himself—just left her and took off running. He disappeared into the jungle, and they never saw him again."

"So Hugh brought her home to you," Wyatt concluded.

"He knew I had connections with the child-welfare system because of the Baylor School. He wanted me to use my contacts to get her into an orphanage."

"But you didn't."

"No. I couldn't. She was barefoot, half starved, and dehydrated from dysentery. I took one look at those sad, soulful, and hopeless brown eyes, and I was as lost as she was. I fell in love, deeply, irrevocably. I knew I had to save this child—she was mine from the moment I saw her."

Wyatt had always seen Sophie as a mother. Her patience, her easy, gentle way. Sometimes he'd even seen himself at her side with a child they'd made together before he'd gotten a grip. And then she'd married Hugh.

"I always hoped Hugh would grow to love her, too."

"He wasn't in favor of the adoption?"

She averted her gaze out the passenger window. "It was a difficult adjustment for him. He tried, for my sake, maybe even for Hope's. He liked Hope, I think he wanted to be a good father to her, but he never got around to making time for her. The connection . . . it just never developed, you know? To this day, I'll never understand why he fought for joint custody during the divorce proceedings."

"You never thought about . . . having your own kids? Together?" *Christ.* Had he really asked that out loud? Apparently, he had, because she shook her head.

"Hugh didn't want children. Something he didn't level with me about until after we got married. Only later, when I started making noises about wanting to start a family, did he admit it. His stock answer was that the world was too dangerous."

"Too dangerous to bring a child into," Wyatt concluded. To a degree, he could understand Hugh's reasoning. In their line of work, they saw the worst the human race had to offer. Sometimes it was difficult to believe that they could save the world for future generations—especially when pitted against the brutality inherent in certain cultures and religions that placed so little value on human life.

Wyatt had even felt that way himself for a while. But then Sam and Abbie had had little Bryan. And he'd met Will Cooper, with his sister's fly-away blond hair and robust little body, and he knew exactly why children were the saviors of this world.

"It would be generous to think that was behind his

decision." Sophie's voice relayed more weariness than anger as it cut into his thoughts. "But the truth was, a child would have taken Hugh away from his work. His life's work—which revolved around bad guys."

Okay. That still sounded like Hugh. The Caped Crusader. At least, it sounded like the Hugh he had worked with and trusted and considered his best friend.

"So what happened, Sophie?" He didn't have to clarify. *What happened to your marriage? What happened to Hugh that made him stupid enough to let you go?*

"I don't know." She actually looked bewildered. "I can't pinpoint a day or even a moment when everything changed. But he got so secretive. Hardened. Entrenched, night and day, in his business." She glanced out the window again and shook her head. "I tried to understand. I tried to go with it."

"What exactly was he into?"

She lifted a shoulder. "At first? It was all about providing armed security. Mostly for corporations. You know what it's like down here. U.S. and foreign companies—the top brass are always targets for abductions."

Wyatt knew exactly how it was. A big portion of the Black Ops, Inc., revenue came from executive protection. CEOs flew down dressed in their Armani suits, ready for cocktails at eight. The only problem was getting them from the airport to their high-dollar company digs or to the factory or the supplier or whatever without catching several ounces of lead or an RPG or two. It took an armada of armored cars and a skilled, smart team to run interference and provide protection.

RISK NO SECRETS 199

"Hugh has also been instrumental in recovering several abductees over the years. More than several," she added after thinking about it for a moment. "A lot lately, in fact. Just last month, he recovered the son of a Brazilian diplomat after negotiating a two-million-dollar ransom and the safe return of the child."

So Hugh rescued children, and yet Sophie needed him now to help her with the very same problem, and he was nowhere on the landscape, had yet to be heard from.

"He's actually thought of as a bit of a hero in the country."

"But not *your* hero," Wyatt said with equal measures of concern and curiosity.

"Not anymore, no," she said, regret heavy in her voice. "Not after it started to be all about the money to him," she said with a weariness that suggested she no longer had the strength to work up any anger. "He became obsessed with it. With the jobs that paid him the high dollars and gave him more money than we needed. It reached a point where it didn't matter anymore who he worked for. Good guy, bad guy—I swear, he would have contracted with bin Laden. Just show him the money, and he was your man."

So Hugh had gone mercenary. No wonder she sounded so disillusioned. There was a huge difference between going private contractor and hiring out to any Tom, Dick, or Ahmadinejad and working for Uncle as Wyatt and the guys did for Nate at Black Ops, Inc. A mercenary worked for the highest bidder. God and country flew out the window.

"I'm sorry to hear that," he said after a long moment. In truth, he was bewildered and disappointed that Hugh, a man he'd respected, admired, and even loved enough to think of as a brother, had traded integrity for the almighty buck.

He wanted to believe there was a good reason, but there was never a reason good enough for that kind of sell-out. Yeah, a man in this line of work laid his life on the line damn near every day, and no, it wasn't easy. And hell no, it wasn't all about altruism, but fuck. It should never be about aiding and abetting a potential enemy, either.

"I wish I knew what to say," he said after several moments passed.

"Just tell me that you're still who I think you are," she said, looking his way. "Just tell me you're still one of the good guys."

Was he still a good guy? That question had been plaguing Wyatt too often and for too long. He thought of Jorge Vega, whom he hadn't been able to help, of the two men he and Doc had killed defending themselves, of the many men he had killed over the course of his career. And he honestly couldn't decide if he was a good guy anymore, much less try to convince her that he was who she wanted him to be.

"I work for the good guys," he said, hoping she didn't realize that he hadn't exactly answered her question.

17

Stretched out on a pale blue velvet sofa that had probably once graced some princess's or queen's sitting room, Johnny Reed watched his wife as she stared out the window of Juliana's office.

He knew what she was looking at. Outside on the terrace, Juliana and Nate were sharing high tea in delicate, flowery china cups with a little girl who needed a bit of fantasy in her life.

"It's great that they've managed to make her smile." Crystal looked relieved as she turned back to the computer and continued her search on Diego Montoya and Jorge Vega.

"I know a way that you could make *me* smile." He tilted his head and grinned his best come-hither grin.

Her fingers continued to fly over the computer keys. "That's because you're easy."

"You say that like it's a bad thing."

She turned to look at him then, graced him with an indulgent smile. "Darling man, right time, right place, it's a wonderful thing." She kissed the air in his direction. "But for now, put it on ice, lover boy. Speaking of ice, shouldn't you be icing that knee?"

"From lover to nursemaid in the blink of an eye. How did I let this happen?"

"Just behave yourself—foreign concept, I know— and read this, would you?" She pushed back in the chair and stretched to hand him several pages that she'd printed concerning Montoya. "See if you spot something I didn't, but for my money, Montoya looks clean."

"The best bad guys usually do," he said on a grunt as he started scanning the sheets. "What about Vega? Anything on him?"

She shook her head and went back to the screen. "Average Joe. Whistle-clean, except for his association with the GN, all public, all aboveboard. I'm thinking he was just a good guy trying to do a good thing and got killed for his kindness."

"Damn bad break." What else was there to say? He felt bad about Vega, yeah, but no one could help him now. "I don't like this Montoya," he said after giving the printouts a thorough once-over.

"You don't like him for the kidnapping?"

"I just don't like him. Period."

"Because he's richer than God?"

"No one should have that much money. Just like no one generally acquires that much money on the straight and narrow. Dig a little deeper, okay, babe?"

"Right after I get you an ice pack." She rose, dropped a kiss on his forehead, and walked out of the room.

"I'm the luckiest sonofabitch alive," he announced

to the empty room as he watched his little redheaded Tinkerbell walk through the doorway. Smart, sexy, funny, and, God help her, he thought on a contented sigh, she loved him in spite of what he'd come from, who he was, and who he'd never be.

He'd never be Montoya, that's for damn sure. He'd never be rich. But he would, by God, love that woman until the day he died.

Lucky man. Lucky, lucky man, he thought, hitching himself up a little straighter on the sofa, keeping the groan to a low moan when pain speared through his knee. *Stupid man,* he admitted, propping a pillow under the knee and settling back to wait out the pain.

Stupid damn stunt. The BOIs were never going to let him hear the end of a skateboard getting the best of him. He glanced out the window again. Talk about stupid men.

Nate just didn't get it. For that matter, neither did Juliana. For two intelligent people, they sure were ignorant of not only the chemistry but the bond that had grown between them over the past year or so.

Or maybe not, he thought, watching them a little closer, thinking that he might detect an earthy awareness in the way they moved around each other that he hadn't noticed yesterday.

"What's so interesting?"

He glanced toward Tink when she walked back into the office, ice pack in hand.

"Those two," he said with a nod toward the window. "It's like watching a train wreck."

She busied herself placing the ice just so over his knee. "I hear you. Kind of hard to look away from them, because you just know that one of these days, they're going to wise up, and then, Katie, bar the door. They're going to be all over each other."

He turned his attention back to his wife and smiled. "So, when did *you* wise up?" He ran a hand up the length of her slender thigh.

"About *you*? Darlin'." She eased a hip onto the sofa, then leaned in and kissed him. "I knew the first time I saw you that you were the best kind of trouble I'd ever get into."

"Yeah?" He flashed her a smug grin. "So why did you constantly brush me off?"

"Because I knew you were the best kind of trouble I'd ever get into."

Her soft smile stole his breath. Always had. Always would.

"I didn't know if I had what it took to survive the ride," she admitted. "But then I decided, what the heck. Live dangerously. What about you? When did you wise up?"

"I think it was the first time you told me to get lost." He cupped a hand around her nape and pulled her toward him for a long, deep kiss. "I thought, man, the girl's got spunk."

She grunted. "Bruised your ego good, did I?"

"Nailed it with a hammer. Now, come 'ere. I want some more of that mouth."

"Reel it in, Reed."

Johnny made a big production out of a sigh when

Nate walked into the room. "He *is* the boss of me, you know," he told Crystal, who just grinned as he shifted his attention to Nate. "What's up?"

"Hope remembered the rest of it. She remembers what both the driver and the grab man looked like."

Crystal sprang up off the settee. "Do you think she's ready to talk about it?"

Johnny understood why Crystal was concerned. Since Crystal herself had been the victim of a Jakarta-based human-trafficking ring, she had been assisting Juliana in the Angelina Foundation, an organization that helped children and adults who were caught up in the horrendous web of the slave trade.

"She's a tough kid," Nate said. "Juliana thinks she's up to it. And then there's the fact that Hope wants to get her friend back."

Hope wanted Lola back so badly, in fact, that an hour later, she fed Juliana—who could have been an artist had she not gone into medicine—enough information that they now had two viable sketches to share with Wyatt and the guys to help them narrow their search.

"How about this guy? Ever seen him before?" Wyatt asked in Spanish. He didn't expect much as he showed his cell-phone screen to a guy who could loosely be called a bartender in a dive that could loosely be called a *cantina*. Business was good, even at two in the afternoon. The tables around the perimeter of the bar were cloaked in smoke and shadows and populated by the type of bottom feeders who liked both just fine. Every foray into every dive since Reed had sent images two hours ago via e-mail to all the BOIs' cell phones had been pretty much the same story.

Juliana had sketched two men based on Hope's description, then snapped photos of the drawings. Armed with the images, concealed sidearms, and KA-Bars—with the exception of Gabe, who always carried his Archangel butterfly knife—the lot of them had paid visits to three other hamlets. They'd split up; Mendoza and Gabe, Doc and Green were currently working the other side of the street several blocks away, while Wyatt and Sophie flashed around the sketches in this dive along with a promise of cash to anyone who could send them in the right direction.

They'd repeated the same drill all day, and Wyatt hadn't met with as much as a flicker of interest, let alone acknowledgment. Until now. This guy knew something, Wyatt was sure of it. When he'd shown him the sketch just now, Wyatt saw something that looked a helluva lot like recognition in the bartender's eyes, even though he'd just given Wyatt a head shake and a mumbled "No."

Wyatt leaned an elbow on the bar and studied the guy. He was a derelict in a room full of derelicts. Wyatt guessed the age of the short, swarthy man to be somewhere between forty and eighty. His pocked face sported several days' growth of salt-and-pepper stubble; his black eyes were narrow slits above hollow sockets that framed a badly misshapen brawler's nose. A sloppy wife-beater in a grungy shade of dishwater sludge marginally covered his pigeon chest. Except for an artless bloodied-heart tattoo on his left bicep, his arms were scrawny and bare. The ink was faded, the drawing crude, but the "MS-13" inked into the center of the heart was unmistakable.

"You sure you've never seen him?" Wyatt asked again, watching the guy's face.

The man's gaze flicked from the photo to beyond the bar and briefly connected with someone across the dark, smoky room, before he went back to wiping the scarred wooden counter with his grimy rag. His answer was the same this time. But the atmosphere inside the *cantina* now hummed with tension.

"You go on outside," Wyatt told Sophie, who, until that moment, he'd wanted stuck to his side like a tack on a cork board. But given the sudden climate change, he wanted her out of here now. "Give Jones a shout-out, okay, sugar?" he added, not giving away that he'd shifted into combat mode. "I'll be out in a minute."

She caught the signal, instantly tuned in to the fact that something had changed. Still, she touched a hand to his arm in concern. She didn't want to leave him in here.

"Just go," he said. He didn't want her anywhere near the action that he was ninety-nine-point-nine percent certain was about to break out. He also wanted backup and needed her to get clear of the *cantina* so she could call the guys and get them over here.

She hadn't taken two steps toward the door when Wyatt heard the ominous scrape of a chair leg on the stained wooden floor. From the corner of his eye, he saw a big guy who'd been nursing a beer at a table in the back rise to his feet. Even at this distance, Wyatt could make out the MS-13 tattoo inked on the side of his beefy neck and the gunmetal-gray barrel of the Beretta he slipped out of his belt.

At the same time, two other men rose and blocked the exit door; the bartender replaced his counter rag with a Saturday-night special and laid it on the bar, his scarred fingers wrapped tight around the grip.

"Something I said?" Wyatt reached for Sophie. He pulled her behind him and out of the line of fire, angling his body so his left hip connected with the bar and Sophie's back was to a wall lined with shelving approximately ten feet away from the bad guys.

Beef Boy stood, shoved a chair aside, and shuffled across the room toward Wyatt. One by one, his buddies rose and adopted menacing poses, intended, no doubt, to deliver the fear of God from the godless.

"Time to move on, *gringo*."

Wyatt sized up the big guy, pegging him as the ringleader of this motley crew of miscreants, all the while keeping track of the cannon in his hand and his fat, stained trigger finger just itching to do some dirty work. The guy was around five-ten and 280, maybe 300, pounds of sweaty blubber, mean and stupid. And it was clear that every man in the bar—Wyatt being the notable exception—danced to the fat man's tune.

Wyatt had been CIA, not military, before hooking up with Task Force Mercy and then teaming up with BOIs,

but he'd always been a student of Colonel John Boyd
and a believer in Boyd's combat-operations process:
Observe. Orient. Decide. Act. Wyatt had employed
the OODA loop in more than one dicey situation. He
knew from experience that in order to win—in this
case, *live*—in a situation where he was outgunned and
outnumbered, he needed to operate at a faster tempo
than the MS-13 thugs populating the bar. Better yet, he
needed to get inside those guys' OODA loop, figure out
how they would think, how they would react.

It didn't take much to get a bead on that one. They
wanted Sophie for fun and games and him for landfill.
He saw how it would come down: the fat guy does a
little strutting and posturing to show his boys how tough
he is, then he shoots Wyatt, and they line up to gang-
rape Sophie.

The plan was neat, simple, and done—unless Wyatt
could stall them long enough for his guys to come
charging in and save the day.

"Now, I heard this was a real friendly bar," Wyatt
said, flashing a tight smile, wishing to hell he hadn't
brought Sophie in here with him. Then again, she was
an extremely resourceful woman. He felt her hand
slide stealthily into his hip pocket where it was pressed
against the bar, making certain no one saw what she
was doing.

Resourceful and smart, and *Jesus God*, given the fix
they were in, it took a lot more concentration than it
should have not to react when her warm fingers connected with his thigh as she searched for and finally

found his cell phone. They'd coordinated signals with the other guys before they'd ever started this little manhunt, so she knew to punch one to alert Gabe, who would in turn contact the other BOIs. All she had to do was keep the phone on, and the guys could lock in on their coordinates via the phone's GPS. This rathole village wasn't much more than a few streets lined with bars, a lone gas station, and a handful of run-down shacks. The guys couldn't be that far away.

"You heard wrong," Beef Boy said with a pig-eyed smirk.

"Well, now, surely there's something I can do to change that," Wyatt drawled. He lifted his hands to show he had nothing threatening and slowly reached into his breast pocket for the cash he'd stuffed inside. All the while marking the positions of the other eleven men who were circling this one who was as big as a wagon wheel, Wyatt peeled off several bills. "Where I come from, a man could always use more friends."

"I don't need to be your friend to take your money," the fat man said. He held out his hand, making impatient "come on" motions with his fingers. "Hand it over, the pouch on your belt, too—and I might let the woman live after she and me get real tight."

He smiled then, oily and cocksure and mean, and it was all Wyatt could do to keep from lunging at him, plowing his fist through the dirt bag's face, and jamming a knee so hard into his balls he'd be eating them for a late lunch. He could take him out in a heartbeat—and he would when the time was right, but in the meantime, he had to get a read on how the other men backing him up would react when their lardy leader went down. Right now, all of them were itching for some action to kill the boredom, but they would wait for the head cheese's cue before they kicked their adrenaline into high gear.

Small men. Small town. If they had any standing in MS-13, they'd be deployed in the city, not exiled out here in no-man's-land, swatting mosquitoes, sweating in the jungle heat, and bored out of their gnat-sized brains. No, the real threat was Beef Boy, and only then because he needed to keep up appearances for his soldiers' sake.

Wyatt focused his attention on him, honed in on his deep set eyes, decided that the sweat dripping off his forehead wasn't caused entirely by his obese frame and the insufferable heat and humidity. The bastard talked tough, but Wyatt could tell that he wasn't as cocksure as he wanted Wyatt and his wormy army to think he was. All of that was going to work to Wyatt's advantage.

"Okay," Wyatt said on a conciliatory sigh. "I'm thinking that what we've got here is a communication problem. So let's clear that up, all right? First off, the lady is *tight* with me. She doesn't need any more friends. Second, y'all don't really want to kill me for this little bit of cash—not when I can get you a lot more if you help me out."

The big guy smiled, revealing stained and rotted teeth and not even the slightest hint of humor. "Me, I figure talk's cheap. 'Specially from a man who knows he's gonna die. You say you got more money?" He lifted a thick shoulder. "Maybe yes. Maybe no. I'll bet on a sure thing and take what I can see. That includes the cash and the woman."

He moved a step closer. Close enough that Wyatt could smell the rotgut he'd been swilling. Close enough that he'd just made a huge mistake. His second one in as many minutes. Mistake number one: not checking Wyatt for weapons. Mistake number two: moving within striking distance.

"The money, *gringo*," the fat man repeated.

Mistake number three: underestimating his opponent.

Wyatt made a gesture of submission, reached for the money pouch on his belt, and, *whoops*, came up with his H&K. At the same time, he yelled "Duck!" at Sophie, and slammed his booted foot into the side of Beef Boy's knee. The stomp kick broke at least two bones on contact.

Beside him, the bartender had lifted his pistol, but before the big guy could even scream in pain and crumple to the floor, Wyatt pumped a round into the bartender's face and blew him back into the wall. The impact sent half the bottles lined up behind the bar flying and the bartender to a special spot in hell reserved for MS-13 scum.

Wyatt didn't wait to see if anyone got up. He dove for the floor and for Sophie. Together, they rolled and skittered behind the bar, using it for cover as bullets from ten guns flew in as many different directions and Beef

Boy's screams of pain and gasped obscenities ripped through the air like a storm siren.

"Now what?" Sophie asked as she huddled beside him on her haunches, covering her head to protect herself from flying glass.

"Now we get the fuck out of here."

18

"Hang on to my belt." Wyatt wanted Sophie staying close.

Holding the H&K in front of him and satisfied that she was right behind him, he crab-walked behind the bar, stepping over broken glass and cheap booze. The dead bartender was still twitching and bleeding on the floor. Wyatt stepped over the body, then continued until they reached the far end of the bar, which was four very long feet from the door.

"Hold fire!" Beef Boy yelled above the barrage. "Hold your fucking fire!" he screamed as more bar glasses shattered, wood splintered, and another row of whiskey bottles came crashing down behind them. "I want to kill that motherfucker myself!"

A few more stray rounds popped off before the shooting stopped. Then the only sound in the *cantina* was that of dripping liquor, heavy breathing, grunts of pain, and the ringing in Wyatt's ears.

"You hear me, you sack of shit? I'm going to kill you, asshole! You broke my fucking knee! Help me up!" he roared, and the sound of scraping chair legs and scrambling boots competed with the swearing and the grunting and the strangling pain.

"I'll cut your fucking heart out!" he bellowed like a wounded bull. "Then I'm going to feed it to your whore while I fuck her, you hear me? Do you hear me!" The words surged out on a pain-wracked roar as his big body connected with a chair that his minions had dragged around for him.

"I guess this means we're not gonna be buddies," Wyatt drawled, hearing the hysteria in the guy's voice and working it while he assessed the best avenue of escape. Given that the back door was ten feet to the left of the bar with those same ten feet fully exposed to a shitload of unfriendly fire, and the front door was only four feet away but blocked by the bad guys, there *wasn't* a best avenue of escape. Which meant he had to increase the odds in favor of the good guys.

He spotted a bottle of rum and quickly grabbed it. The top had been blown off, but the bottom was still intact and half full.

"Gimme one of those," he told Sophie, who followed his line of sight and spotted the stack of dry bar rags. "The matches, too. Be careful of the glass," he warned as she scrambled on all fours, grabbed a rag, and tossed it to him.

Wyatt quickly stuffed the rag into the broken bottle neck, flipped it upside down to soak the trailing ends like a wick, and shoved it toward Sophie.

"On my go, light it and get rid of it," he whispered just as Beef Boy roared again.

"What are you waiting for? Go get him! Get the fuck behind that bar and get him!"

Wyatt had been expecting this. But he also knew that in the moment after the order was given, there would be hesitation. He took immediate advantage of the fact that bullies don't know how to deal with someone who was willing to shoot from zero mph to the speed of light on the violence scale in a microsecond. Just as he knew what brutal, sudden, and extraordinary violence did to the human psyche. Even the psyche of a clew of bad asses.

He shot to his feet, leading with his H&K, and popped off two rounds. Both connected. Crimson stains spread across dirty shirts as two more gang members howled in pain and slumped to the floor.

Dropping back to one knee behind the cover of the bar, Wyatt rolled left five feet, knowing they'd expect him to pop up in the same spot.

"Now!" he yelled at Sophie, who was holding the makeshift Molotov cocktail.

She lit the rag, held it until it was fully ignited, then let it fly. The improvised bomb landed on the floor on the other side of the bar and blew like a land mine.

Wyatt waited two beats, just enough time for the thugs to scatter, then popped up again, fired two more shots, and dropped two more men.

Four down. Eight to go, and some of them were

screaming in pain and slapping at flames that had
jumped from the exploding cocktail onto their clothes.
Even though he still had eight rounds left in his magazine, he ejected it and rapid reloaded his extra clip.
Twelve rounds trumped eight any day of the week.

"Do you want to make nice yet?" Wyatt asked, aware
that Sophie had pulled out her handgun.

Okay. Make that twenty-four rounds. She'd told him
she could shoot, assured him that Hugh had taught her
how. He didn't have any reason to question her ability,
especially after she expertly pulled back on the slide on
the Glock 19 and quickly checked for brass to make
certain she had a round chambered.

What he did have reason to doubt was whether she
could actually fire at another living, breathing human
being. It was a helluva a lot different from pumping lead
into paper targets.

But then, given the fact that paper targets didn't
shoot back or threaten rape, he'd lay odds on her coming through, although, God in heaven, he hoped it
didn't come to that.

"You know, no one else has to die here!" he shouted
in Spanish, knowing that the moans of their fallen
brothers were laying a real psychological trip on the
remaining men. "Only one man here has a legitimate
beef with me. The rest of you could be tappin' another
bottle down the street. All you've gotta do is walk out
that door and leave me and Captain Blubber to come
to a friendly agreement."

"You sonsabitches leave me, and I'll shoot you myself!" Even though the fat man was panting, he managed to put his full weight behind his threat.

"You know what he's doing, right?" Wyatt asked the room at large, still crouching behind the bar. "He's asking y'all to take *his* bullet. Now, I'd understand if I was here to rob you or move in on your turf, but, Christ, all I want is an ID on a picture. You really wanna die for that? You wanna die for that pussy sack of shit?"

His answer was the distinctive *snick-click* of the safety being taken off an AK-47.

Fuck. His bad. He hadn't spotted the big gun. And it could just cost them their lives.

He jerked Sophie beneath him and covered her with his body. Then he made like a floor and prayed.

The rattle of the Kalashnikov was deafening. The asshole had set it to full auto and pumped a rapid succession of three-round bursts into the bar. He pressed them tighter to the floor as wood cracked and splintered and bullets skimmed above their heads as the hammer of the rifle rounds strafed the bar in front of them.

His ears rang like bells when the AK fell silent, and he thanked the fool for dumping the entire magazine in about three seconds. An experienced operator can pull off three-round bursts. Amateurs like this guy just dump the magazine, most of it into the ceiling. Not that knowing they were dealing with amateurs meant squat. The bastards still had the superior firepower. And the next words out of the fat man's mouth proved he wasn't going to be shy about using it.

"Next rounds go six inches lower," he growled to the

distinct sound of the empty mag hitting the floor and a fresh, full clip slamming into place on the AK. "You've got ten seconds to get the fuck out from behind that bar, or you're both hamburger. *Uno . . . dos . . .*"

Sophie's fingers dug into Wyatt's arm. He covered her hand with his, gave her an encouraging nod, and held up five fingers on his right hand and three on his left.

She looked scared to death but kept it together and gave him a determined nod, telling him she understood that he'd go for the five on the right and she was to shoot left.

"We run for the door on eight. *Ocho,*" he whispered as Fat Bastard jumped *cuatro* and *cinco* and cut straight to *seis.*

Sophie's eyes were huge and round, and Wyatt could have stopped a train before he could have stopped himself from reaching for her and kissing her hard.

"Ready?" he whispered, pulling away.

She swallowed and nodded.

"Okay," he said, and gathered himself. "Now!"

They shot to their feet, guns raised in two-handed grips, fingers leaning on the triggers—and *gawddamn*, the *cantina* door burst open before they reached it, hitting the poor bastard guarding it in the back of the head and knocking him face-first to the floor.

Then in charged the cavalry, with Green leading the way, an AR-15 assault rifle rammed against his shoulder, his finger jammin' on the trigger.

Joe dropped to his knee, clearing the path for Mendoza, Jones and Doc to burst in behind him, firing a couple of M-4s and a lone AK.

Jesus! They were a sight.

"Hold fire!" Wyatt yelled as the fat man's body jerked and jumped, then fell sideways off the chair into a doughy heap on the floor. Four more men had gone down; the remaining four had dropped their weapons and fallen to their knees, covering their heads with their hands.

The BOIs' rifles immediately fell silent.

Gunsmoke drifted as heavy and thick as the blood running across the floor. The ringing in his ears rivaled the groans of the dying and the cries of those pleading for their lives.

"I ever tell you guys how pretty y'all are?" he asked with a tight grin as the tension started to uncoil from his chest by slow turns.

"Only every time we save your sorry ass." Rafe's face was hard, his eyes watchful, as Doc and Green walked among the bodies, kicking weapons out of reach just in case one of the men sprawled on the floor was still alive.

"You okay?" Wyatt turned back to Sophie, who stood wild-eyed and very quiet beside him.

"Yeah. Yeah. I'm . . . I'm fine."

The hell she was. She was shaking from the adrenaline rush, her mind recoiling against the blood and the carnage and the very close brush with death she'd just managed to survive. This entire episode hadn't lasted more than two minutes—maybe three, tops—but to her, it had to have felt like a lifetime.

He wanted to wrap her in his arms and press her face against his chest so she wouldn't have to see it, wouldn't have to breathe it. And he would. Later. Right now, they had to strike while fear was still alive in the four survivors.

He walked out from behind the bar while Gabe rounded up those who were mobile and lined them up against a wall, hands on top of their heads, their eyes wide and scared. Wyatt had the numbers now—not to mention an arsenal of state-of-the-art weapons—and the bad boys had given up all pretense of acting tough.

"You know," he said, walking toward them, "we can just kill the rest of you now and let God sort it out." He paused for effect as two of the men started praying. "Or you can answer one simple fucking question, which is all I wanted in the first place, and be on your merry way."

Four pairs of eyes, now hopeful that they might still escape with their lives, turned his way.

Wyatt whipped out his cell phone and pulled up the sketch Reed had sent. "Do any of you know this man? And I'll warn you to consider carefully before you belch out a knee-jerk *no*."

"*Sí*," a small man said, though the others remained silent.

"Who is he?"

He swallowed hard, then spoke in low, hesitant Spanish.

"He's a lieutenant in the gang," Sophie translated from behind them, even though Wyatt had understood.

"He abducted a child," Wyatt told him in Spanish. "We want her back. Tell me where we can find her."

The man shook his head. "*Yo no sé!*"

Wyatt got right in his face, then pressed the business end of the H&K hard up under his chin. "Then what *do* you know?"

More rapid-fire Spanish spilled out, with a good measure of desperation.

"Anybody catch that?" Wyatt couldn't sort out the tumbling jumble of words.

"Between begging for his life and praying to the patron saint of street thugs and criminals," Rafe translated, "he still claims he doesn't know anything about this child. But he says that in the past, they've held hostages at a camp near here."

"Where is the camp?" Wyatt pressed the gun harder, lifting the man up onto his toes until he struggled to keep his balance.

"Puerta del Diabló."

Doc reached into his pocket and pulled out a map. He laid it out on the bullet-ridden bar. "It's a good two hours from here."

"What do you think?" Wyatt asked his men.

Gabe shrugged. "Could be another wild-goose chase, but what else have we got?"

Wyatt rubbed his brow and honed in on his reluctant informant. "If you're lying to me, I'll find you and make you wish I'd killed you now, quick and painless."

The man shook his head. "True. I speak true."

Green's phone rang just then. "Stephanie," he informed them, and answered. He moved to the map Doc had spread out on the bar, listened, talked, traced longitude and latitude lines with his index finger, then hung up. "SAT coordinates match what the guy says. Looks like we've got good intel."

Doc folded up the map. "Let's boogie."

"So what do we do with these cretins?" Rafe asked.

"If we leave them alive, we're going to have problems," Gabe said.

Wyatt backed away and lowered his gun. "We've already got problems. These bastards are like roaches; kill a nest, and more crawl out of the shadows. What's four more in the overall scheme of things?"

He glared at them. "You tell your buddies that if they want trouble, they'll find it if you follow us. *Comprende?*"

Four heads nodded like bobble-heads.

"Get the fuck out of here."

He didn't have to tell them twice. They cleared the *cantina* in ten seconds flat, stumbling unceremoniously over the bodies of their fallen gang mates.

"Like rats leaving a sinking ship," Gabe said on a grunt. "Guess they don't subscribe to the leave-no-man-behind doctrine."

"Not these belly-crawlers, no," Rafe agreed.

"We're burning daylight," Green reminded them. "Let's move out."

Only then did Wyatt turn back to see how Sophie was holding up.

She was frozen in the exact same position she was in

when he'd left her behind the bar. Her face was ghost-white, her eyes glassy and vacant. *Fuck.* He'd have given his left nut to avoid putting her through the bloodbath she'd just witnessed. No matter how many books a person read, how many movies they saw, how many stories they heard, nothing could prepare a sane, rational human being for the violent and stomach-clenching gore of reality.

And nothing could contribute to the loss of that sanity, that faltering faith in rationality, more than seeing a man die—even a man hell-bent on killing you—and knowing that you were the one who pulled the plug on his life.

Sophie might not have fired a shot, but he could see the weight of guilt pressing on her slim shoulders like a battleship.

"Shake it off," he said, more sternly than he'd have liked but knowing she needed a hard jolt of authority to nudge her out of the place she was in. And the place she was in was a very, very bad place. He knew. A long time ago, as a green-as-grass operative, he'd been there. "Sophie," he said with some bite in his tone when she didn't react.

She finally turned her head and looked at him as if he was a stranger and she couldn't figure out where he'd come from or why he was there.

He knew why. He knew exactly why. "Shake it off, damn it!" he repeated, reading the confusion in her eyes when she took his harshness for anger, as he'd intended.

He'd revert to military discipline if he had to—frog-march her the hell out of there, screaming in her ear in his best drill-sergeant voice—to keep her from going catatonic on him.

Later, he'd let her fall apart. Later, he'd hold her when she did. Right now, he needed her pissed off enough to hold herself together.

"I'm fine," she said, the two words clipped tight with her own anger. At him.

Yeah, that's right, sugar. You think about me being an asshole. That way, you won't be thinking about dead men with hollow eyes.

19

The good news was that three hours later, Sophie had definitely shaken it off. The bad news was, she was still pissed at him.

"Not after coming this far," she informed Wyatt with steely-eyed determination when he begged her to stay behind with the SUV after they'd gone as far as they could go in the vehicles. The last few clicks would have to be on foot.

"If Lola's out there," she said, "she's going to need to see a familiar face. She's going to need me."

"She's going to need you *alive*," Wyatt argued. He needed her alive, too, but he knew she didn't want to hear that right now.

God, she was something. Fire flared in her eyes. The set of her jaw was nothing short of militant.

"Then you'd better keep me that way," was her response as she gathered her hair and twisted it up under a ball cap. "If you leave me behind," she promised, smearing face black on her cheeks as the rest of them had, "I'll follow you. Deal with it."

She had him by the short hairs, and she knew it. Short of tying her to the steering wheel, which would leave her defenseless if one of the gang members stumbled onto her, Wyatt was out of options.

"Just tell me what to do," she said, loading the extra magazine for her pistol.

She was already doing it. She was toughing up. Leaving the nasty scene at the *cantina* behind. It's what he'd wanted. Only his "tough love" had worked a little too well, because she was beside him now, dodging tree branches and palm fronds and trying to avoid tripping over roots, and he was wondering if he'd ever truly understand the depth of this woman's character.

The jungle they hacked through smelled of green life and black death and layers upon layers of decay. As he trudged through the nearly impenetrable growth, all around him creepy crawlies bred and died and cannibalized each other under a triple-canopy forest so dense he couldn't see blue sky above or much of the sunlight that came with it.

He wiped the sweat off his forehead with the back of his arm. He remembered that years ago, a Special Forces buddy had told him that the El Salvadoran jungle was among the thickest he'd ever seen. "Whole damn place should be nuked to glass then cleaned with Windex," the crusty old vet had proclaimed.

Wyatt hadn't known exactly what he'd meant until years later, when he'd fought there himself, and still he'd forgotten. The jungle was so aggressively alive that any piece of cleared land left alone for any time would soon be taken over by vegetation again.

The growth was so thick, in fact, that combat was generally done at spitting distance. Full battalions could march within a hundred yards of each other, and neither would have a clue that the other one was there.

Wyatt didn't have a full battalion. He had himself, four highly skilled but exhausted men, and a woman on a mission. All of them were beaten down by the oppressive heat and humidity and a damn lot of hours without quality sleep. And they had no idea what they were going to come up against when they found the God-forsaken camp.

Doc's estimate of a two-hour drive to get there had been great—in theory. But it had taken them closer to three, because the freaking roads were made for mountain goats and tanks. So it was bordering on five p.m. by the time they'd arrived within half a mile of Steph's coordinates and, they hoped, the camp where Lola was being held.

They'd left the vehicles near a shrouded embankment and had been slogging through the jungle on foot ever since, exposed skin streaked with face black, weighed down by Kevlar vests, weapons, ordinance, and, in Wyatt's case, also a heavy coat of guilt over his inability to persuade Sophie to wait in her SUV.

Beside him, Gabe stumbled, almost went down, but righted himself again and pressed on. Wyatt didn't care how tough Gabe was or how state-of-the-art his prosthesis was, it had to be hell for him maneuvering through this shit on one good leg.

Rafe, who was leading the way, held up a hand, a signal for them to stop and hold their positions. Everyone—including Sophie—stopped, assumed a loose, back-to-back circle formation, and dropped to a knee, scanning the sectors around them for bad guys. Rafe pulled his binoculars out of a pocket, then, using hand signals again, indicated that he was going to take a closer look and that they should wait there. He disappeared into the foliage.

Wyatt glanced at Sophie, who had shifted to a sitting position and was wearily unscrewing the lid on her water bottle. It wasn't the first time they'd stopped and Rafe had gone ahead to scout. Each time, he'd come back empty. They needed a break. So did Lola. He hoped to God that they found her there.

Wyatt assigned Gabe and Doc watch positions, and the rest of them took turns hydrating and resting.

"Close your eyes." He gripped Sophie's shoulders and turned her so she was leaning back against his chest. "A quick five will do you good."

"I'm afraid that if I close them, I'll never open them again."

That idea worked fine for him. He'd like nothing better than for her to sleep through the confrontation to come. In a perfect world, she would. A little fairy dust, the wave of a magic wand, and he'd cast a spell to make her sleep until this debacle was over. But he'd never believed in fairy dust, magic, or spells—except maybe the one she cast over him as she gave in to exhaustion and closed her eyes.

No more than a few seconds later, her body slumped against his; her breathing grew heavy and deep. He rested his head against the top of hers, too aware of her softness covering a core of steel. Aware that he was being watched.

He glanced to the right. Gabe looked away but not before a small smile lifted one corner of his mouth.

Fine, Wyatt thought with a weary breath. He didn't care if Gabe had figured out that Wyatt had a thing for Sophie. It was pretty rare that he'd ever been able to hide anything from the Archangel, or any of the other BOIs, for that matter.

"Incoming," Green whispered, lifting his AR-15 to his shoulder and sighting down the scope.

"Friendly," Rafe said, appearing out of the brush a few feet away. "We've got game," he added, moving up in front of Wyatt.

Sophie instantly woke up. "What's happening?"

Rafe motioned for everyone to gather around.

"About thirty yards due south. Two shacks." He brushed aside leaves and jungle decay and cleared a spot of damp earth to use as a crude drawing board. "Here and here." He made a large X and a smaller one representing the two buildings.

"Any sign of Lola?" Sophie asked.

Her hopeful look broke Wyatt's heart.

Rafe shook his head. "They're holding someone there, though. No movement in or out, but there are a couple of guys who appear to be pulling guard duty on the smaller hut. Mostly, they're napping or strung out on *ganja* or crack."

"How many men?"

"Counted fifteen, but there could be more. Tattoos up the wazoo. Most of 'em teens, by the looks of them. Most of 'em high on something, by the way they're sprawled around the campsite."

"Ordinance?" Green asked.

"A shitload. Mostly AKs, but they're lying all over the place. Only a couple actually carrying."

Wyatt grunted. "Running a tight ship, huh?"

"No apparent leader and clearly no discipline. They sure as hell aren't expecting anybody—friend or foe."

"So, what? We wait 'til dark and take 'em out one by one?" Green suggested. "We've got a good three hours 'til dusk."

Wyatt read the worry on Sophie's face. She didn't want to wait. She wanted to get to Lola now. He was inclined to agree with her.

Rafe lifted a shoulder. "We could. Or we could just march in there, shoot the shit out of the sky, and they'll probably cry like little girls and ask for momma."

It could work. Had worked, in fact, many times for the team. The idea was to stage the attack so it appeared to their adversaries that they were up against overwhelming force. Shock and awe the hell out of them. There was bound to be a hero among them. The trick would be to make sure he died first and fast. The others would fold like tents.

They glanced at one another, nodded in agreement. "Plan B, then."

"Take out the guards at the shack first?" Doc suggested.

"Rafe, that'll be you," Wyatt said with a nod. They could all speak Spanish, but Wyatt wanted to take advantage of first-language arts, and Mendoza was from Colombia. If Lola was being held in that shack, Rafe could calm her, convince her she was safe.

"We'll deal with the remainders," he went on, studying the crude diagram and making a circle in the dirt with the tip of a stick. "Gabe, south perimeter. Green, north. Doc, you come in from the east, and I'll take west. Questions?"

They all shook their heads.

"Then let's lock and load. We get in position, then go in on my bang. And if you sense any resistance at all—" He met each guy's eyes with dead-level intent. "Light 'em up. And may the bastards burn in hell."

"Sophie—you hang back, you hear me? No heroics. You stay the hell out of the action. I don't want to have to worry about something happening to you. Make sure you've got a round chambered, keep your head down, and shoot only if you have to."

She gave him a quick, clipped nod.

"Okay," he said, looking at each man's face as they prepared to risk their lives—once again. "Let's do this."

Sophie tucked in on her stomach at the edge of the clearing where Wyatt had positioned her, her Glock gripped in both hands, her elbows dug into the dirt, wrists resting on a deadfall log. As exhausted as she was, her heart rate was off the charts; all senses hummed on overdrive.

After the narrow escape at the *cantina*, she hadn't thought her body capable of producing more adrenaline. She'd shaken until her teeth rattled for a good hour after Wyatt settled her into the passenger seat of her SUV.

She'd wanted to ask him if he ever got used to it as they rumbled over terrain so rough she held her breath waiting for a tire to blow.

But she couldn't compartmentalize the *it* part of the equation. Used to *it*? Used to the violence? The blood? The gore? The certain knowledge that you were going to die any second? A bullet? A knife blade? A coronary because you were so freaking scared it felt like your heart would explode like a bald tire in your chest?

It. Used to it.

Hugh had become used to it. Hugh had lost that part of himself that made life or death—his or someone else's—worth the cost of a second thought.

"Shake it off," she whispered, repeating Wyatt's order. He was right. She had to shake it off, because, like it or not, she was on the high side of another adrenaline rush while she waited to see who walked away from this alive.

She'd lost sight of the guys five minutes ago. Knew they were creeping stealthily into position. Knew that if anyone could pull this off, they could. Just as she knew that Wyatt was right in telling her to stay put. She understood that the BOIs worked like a machine. They were bonded through years of combat and worked together much like muscle memory and on instinct. Her intervention would be interference and could jeopardize the op.

Quiet. Except for the skittering and slithering of jungle creatures and the occasional call of a bird, it was as quiet as a tomb. She closed her eyes . . . and saw the faces of the men who were risking their lives.

She'd never forget the looks on those faces when they'd gathered for one final coordinate check. In the past wild several hours, she'd seen them laugh, seen them smile and give each other grief, seen them concentrate over maps and strategize. But she'd never seen them in premeditated combat mode. Face black smeared on their skin, weapons at the ready, eyes blank and already looking ahead to battle.

It wasn't a pretty sight. But it was powerful. And it was frightening to realize how often they'd had to dig this deep to find the guts and the determination and the will to charge head-on into battle. And humbling to know they were doing this for a child they didn't know. And for Wyatt.

Wyatt.

Fatigue let her mind drift to a memory she'd been avoiding all day: the early hours of the morning, when he'd been naked. Needing her. In her bed. In her body. Unbelievably tender and giving and—

A single crack of gunfire ripped through the silence.

Her eyes snapped open.

An unforgiving volley of rifle fire quickly followed that initial shot.

Oh, God. Don't let him die. Don't let any of them die.

Wyatt fired the first shot, taking out the man he'd tagged as the leader of the motley crew. On cue, the rest of the BOIs converged on the camp of miscreants. As he'd hoped, the sight of the five of them descending out of the blue like a team of vengeful angels, had the younger MS-13 gang members scattering in confusion and panic.

"Drop and spread and you live!" Wyatt shouted in Spanish after they fired off their initial salvo. "Fight back and you die."

They dropped. Like stones. Every last one of them. It was over in less time than it took to make a phone call.

Once he was certain that Doc, Gabe, and Green had the fifteen *ganja*-smoking, cracked-out "bad boys" secure, he walked to the smaller hut, where Rafe had swung open the door and stepped inside.

He could hear Rafe murmuring in Spanish, "You're safe now, little one. We've come to take you home."

Wyatt ducked through the door and joined him inside.

Jesus.

The stench nearly knocked him over. And when he saw the filthy little girl, her hair matted and tangled, her clothes soiled by her own waste, curled up in Rafe's arms, he wrestled back a vicious urge to march outside and empty a full mag into the bastards who had done this to her.

Instead, he got a grip, stood aside, and let Rafe carry the child out into the fresh air.

He turned to yell for Sophie, to let her know they'd found the girl, but she was already running out of the thicket toward them. She'd spotted Rafe with the child in his arms and raced toward them, tears in her eyes.

"Baby. Oh, sweet baby," she whispered as the girl burrowed her face into Rafe's chest. "What have they done to you?"

"It's okay," Wyatt told her as Rafe sat down on the ground, still cradling the child, and Sophie got down on her knees beside them. "She's okay now. We'll take care of her."

She touched a hand to the tangled hair, then drew her hands back to her thighs, knotted them into fists. "How could they treat a child this way?"

He didn't have an answer for her. Neither did she expect one. Wyatt had long ago stopped asking about the reasons for the atrocities man committed against his fellow man, the total lack of moral compass or humanity in a man's soul that led him to abuse the most innocent among them. Yeah, he'd given up. It just was. Accepting it didn't make it any easier to sleep at night, but it did make it easier to pull a trigger when he had to.

He handed Sophie his water. "Try to get her to drink."

"Not too much, now," Rafe warned as the girl grabbed for the water bottle with greedy, trembling hands. "Easy there, *cara*. Not too much," he warned with a tenderness Wyatt had never seen in the combat veteran, not even when he addressed, B.J., his wife.

"Oh, God." Sophie sat back on her heels, staring, when she finally got a look at the child's face.

"What? What's wrong?" Wyatt dropped down on one knee beside her, his gut telling him even before she answered.

"This . . . this poor, tortured child." Her emotions— anguish, sympathy, and despair—washed across her face and drained her of color. "Oh, God, Wyatt. This child . . . she isn't Lola."

"You look uncomfortable," Vincente observed with a deep sense of satisfaction. He leaned away from the table, hooked an arm over the back of the spindled chair, liking it that his "partner" felt uncomfortable and out of place. He caressed the blade he always kept with him, absently flipping it over and over in his palm. "My apologies if the surroundings aren't up to your standards."

And fuck him if he didn't like it, he thought, watching the man. Vincente had taken pains with his appearance, to make a statement about the differences between them. His pants were battle camouflage. His upper body was bare except for the bandoliers crisscrossing his tattooed chest and the white and blue colors of Mara Salvatrucha in a scarf knotted around his bulging bicep.

Felipe and Emilio stood at his right and left shoulders, their AK-47s in hand, their colors worn on the scarves tied around their foreheads.

Vincente had insisted on meeting the man here, in Soyopango. He wanted the face-to-face on his turf, where *he* was king. And he wanted to see him sweat. The way Vincente had sweated when he received the news that he had lost not only Tito and Benito on the Vega hit but that several of his outlying soldiers had been killed or arrested south of the city yesterday.

The worst, however, the very worst, was that a very valuable piece of goods had been stolen from him. The Hernandez kid had been certain to net him a fat ransom.

"Look, I know you're annoyed by the turn of events."

Vincente laughed at the understatement and glanced at his blade. "Annoyed? Because the very men you had guaranteed me would not be a problem have cut deeply into my operation? You think that would *annoy* me?" He lifted a hand as if brushing it off. "No, my *friend*. What *annoys* me is that you are not a man of your word. What *annoys* me is that you assume that what is mine is dispensable.

"What *annoys* me," he continued, mocking the choice of words, until the eyes that stared back at him finally showed signs of apprehension, "is that I did not listen to my instincts and tell you to fuck off when you first proposed this joint business venture."

"I could not have known she would bring outside resources into this."

Vincente reared forward, flipped open the razor-sharp blade, and buried its tip in the wooden table, all pretense of civility gone. "And yet you should have! Your oversight has cost me."

While he flinched, he did not retreat. "You'll recover the loss."

"No, my friend, *you* will recover my monetary losses. But I have also lost face among my men for trusting you. How do you intend to recover that for me?"

He said nothing.

Vincente stared at him hard, accepted that he had little choice but to see this through to the end.

"You will fix this," he said with deadly intent. "You will fix this fast, or I will. And trust me, my *friend*, you will not like the solution if it is left up to me."

20

"We're not going to get her back, are we?"

Wyatt leaned against the door frame that opened into Sophie's bedroom. They'd filed into her house around midnight, a little more than an hour ago, loaded down with takeout food and reeking of the stench of the day. She'd been the last one to shower—she'd insisted they all go first—and now, wrapped in a white bathrobe, she towel-dried her hair.

It was almost painful to watch her; she looked so exhausted and defeated. Even the tempered high of returning a lost child to her parents couldn't bolster her spirits.

It had been six grueling hours since they'd rescued the little girl who was not Lola. The child's name was Carmen Hernandez. This they'd found out when they returned to San Salvador and delivered her to the police station. Carmen was now being treated for dehydration and dysentery in a hospital and, Wyatt assumed, in the loving arms of her parents, who had given up on her being found alive. She'd been abducted six months ago.

That little girl was safe. Lola, however, was still out there.

"It's not over yet," Wyatt said, although he had to dig deep to interject some semblance of assurance into his voice. Before they'd left the thugs who'd been holding Carmen Hernandez captive like a caged animal, they'd questioned them. He'd known even before they resorted to threats that they weren't going to get any information from the bastards. They were low-level flunkies and knew nothing. They were the bottom of the MS-13 food chain, who took their pay in *ganja* and fed their egos by toting AK-47s and telling themselves they were bad.

Unfortunately for poor little Carmen, they were bad enough. Wyatt hoped they rotted out there in the jungle where he and the BOIs had left them tied together without food or water—just the way they'd tied that child.

Wyatt had taken his time pinpointing their location for the police. Let them sit out there in the heat of the night and the bugs and the creepy crawlies for a while. Might put the fear of something greater than their gang leader into them.

"We're running out of time." Sophie sat down heavily on the edge of her bed, holding a towel in one hand, a hairbrush loosely in the other.

He couldn't argue with that. They were down to a little less than forty hours by his calculations. And Sophie was down to the last of her reserve of strength.

He pushed away from the door and walked to her side. He hesitated only a moment before he sat down beside her and removed the brush from her limp hand.

"No, sugar. Let me," he said when she made a sound of protest. "You've been strong long enough. Just let me do this for you."

She closed her eyes on a sigh, and though he knew she wanted to tell him no, she just didn't have the strength—of body or of will—to do it.

Her hair was heavy and fragrant as he worked the brush through the damp strands, all the while quelling those voices that told him that one night with her in this bed didn't give him the right to be here with her like this.

He no longer cared about his rights. But he did care about this woman.

"I'm sorry," she said, then groaned, letting him know that what he was doing felt good.

"Sorry?" He gathered the heavy weight of her hair in one hand and continued stroking with the brush.

"That I fell apart . . . in the *cantina* . . . after—"

"You didn't fall apart," he interrupted. "You reacted like any sane person would react to the violence. I'm sorry you got caught up in it. And I'm sorry I got tough with you after."

"I needed it. It ticked me off. Made me concentrate on what a bully you were and forget about the blood. Thanks."

"We aim to please," he said with a soft smile. "You need to get some sleep." He swallowed back the words he really wanted to say and the questions he wanted to ask. Words like *I love you*. Questions like *Is there a remote chance for us to be together?*

Christ, he was tired. Damn tired, or he wouldn't have gotten within a Georgia mile of those thoughts.

"Stay with me." Her eyes were liquid and hopeful and, because he was weak where she was concerned, too much for him to resist.

He closed his eyes and drew a breath. Then he stood, walked across the room, and shut the door. The guys were catching a few wherever they could—Gabe had claimed Hope's bed, Rafe was snoring on one sofa, and Doc was sacked out on the other. Green had commandeered the hammock out on the lanai.

When Wyatt turned back to the bed, Sophie had turned down the covers. A not-so-subtle invitation. She'd slipped out of her robe and, wearing only a delicate white sleep gown, slid over to the middle of the mattress and made room for him.

Her eyes were filled with something other than gratitude. Something that made his breath catch, his heart stall, and his hand stop in midair.

And God, he wasn't sure he had the strength to say no to the blatant invitation. She wasn't the only one who was beat. She wasn't the only one who felt raw and open to possibilities that would not be wise to explore tonight—or what was left of it.

His muscles clenched with the desire to peel off his cammo T-shirt and fatigues, gather her in his arms, and indulge in all the warm woman sleekness of her against his naked skin. His heart slammed with the desire to explore, all over again, the places she loved to be touched, places she'd begged him to touch. Soft places. Wet, warm places that he'd remember until the day he died.

Hell yeah, he wanted to strip down to skin and take her everywhere he knew she'd love to go. But he kept his clothes on, because he wanted it too much and because he knew, gut-deep, bone-strong, that whatever need she felt for him in this moment came from all the wrong places. It was need that came from tension and stress and fear. Need that started with gratitude but would eventually end with good-bye.

He had a need, too, damn it—for something richer and deeper that would sustain them both. It was because of that need that he set his H&K within reach on the bedside table and lay down fully dressed. He steeled himself when she snuggled up tight against his side.

"Sleep," he whispered when she splayed her fingers across his chest. "Sleep," he repeated on a gruff command, because, *Jesus God*, she was killing him as her small hand began wandering slowly south.

He had a choice here. He could either go up in flames or go down in glory. Either way, it played out the same way in the end. He lost.

He stilled her hand against his beating heart. Breathed deep.

Turning her down had nothing to do with heroics. Nothing to do with self-sacrifice. It had to do with self-preservation. He was already in too deep with this woman, and he knew that the physical relief that mindless sex would bring could in no way offset the crippling sense of loss that would follow.

That was because he wanted more than sex from her. Okay, yeah, what they had was more than sex. They liked each other, respected each other, but that's where it ended for her. He needed commitment and all the goddamn bells and whistles, and yeah, damn it, the love and tender moments that went with it.

But even if she might want that, too, he'd already figured out that she wouldn't let herself go there. She'd committed to a warrior once before; she still wore the scars. She'd told Wyatt about some of them today. And even though she hadn't said it outright, he'd heard, loud and clear, that she wasn't about to subject herself to that kind of pain again.

Christ, he was tired. So tired he was lying there, letting his head get screwed up over something that could never be a part of his game plan anyway. She was a woman who wanted and deserved babies. Deserved a man like Diego Montoya, who could give her respect and social standing and money. He wasn't Montoya. He was what he'd always been. He killed bad guys and prayed to God he wouldn't become one himself

Finally, he felt the tension and the trauma ease from her soft body with her deep breaths. Felt the moment she let go completely and slid, all liquid and achingly easy, into sleep.

Dodged that bullet.

So why did he feel like he'd been gut-shot?

It felt like he'd just fallen asleep when a rap on the door shot Wyatt to instant consciousness. He checked to

make sure Sophie was still sleeping, then eased carefully out of bed so as not to wake her.

Gabe stood on the other side of the door when he
opened it.

"Time is it?" Wyatt asked around a yawn as he
stepped out into the hallway and closed the door quietly behind him.

"Four-fifteen," Gabe said. "We caught a few hours.
We're thinking we need to hit it again while the rats are
still tucked away in their holes. Word about our little
visit to that backwater *cantina* and the impromptu party
in the jungle has to have reached the streets by now."

Wyatt scrubbed a hand over his face. Yeah, they'd
been dealing with the MS-13 flunkies until this point.
The bigger players in San Salvador couldn't be too
happy. And the marginal members—the ones who held
a grudge because they'd been passed over for promotion
in the ranks or shit on one too many times by the upper
echelon—might be having second thoughts about gang
loyalty. Someone might be ready to talk, either for the
promise of cash or the prospect of taking out a rival
gang member. Long shots, but it was all they had. The
ransom deadline was noon Thursday. Thirty-two hours
and closing fast.

"I'll take the guys," Wyatt said. "You stay here with
Sophie."

"Yeah, that's not going to happen," Gabe said. "We're
geared up and ready to rock. Besides, Sophie needs you,
not us."

Because there was a modicum of truth in Gabe's

statement, Wyatt didn't argue. Dawn was still a couple of hours away when Wyatt locked up behind them after warning them to watch their backs.

For all of ten seconds, he told himself he'd catch a few more Zs on the sofa. Yeah, that thought held for all of ten seconds before he turned and walked back down the hall.

He eased Sophie's bedroom door open, slipped silently back into the room, double-checked the safety on the H&K, and set it quietly back on the nightstand. The only light in the room was a sliver of moonlight that leaked in through a window. Sophie was little more than a shadow on white sheets, the thin straps of her gown barely visible against her skin.

He didn't need light to know that beneath that gown, she was warm and fragrant and lush. Even in the dark, he could remember the smooth perfection of her skin, the generous curves of her breasts, the rosy pink hue of her nipples. And he sure as hell didn't need light to envision the whisper-soft moans of pleasure that had devastated him when she'd come in his mouth and then again when he'd come inside her.

Indulgence was a memory of the ebb and flow of their bodies, how she'd cried out and clung to him. Yeah, indulgence was a memory, but it was necessity and a whopping dose of stupidity that had him tossing his hard-won control to the wind.

Fuck his reason and good intentions, and damn him for a glutton for punishment. In this moment, in this room, with this woman, he no longer cared what happened tomorrow. He cared only what happened right now.

He whipped his shirt up and over his head and stepped out of his cammos and boxers. Then he slid back into bed beside her. He needed to feel her against him with nothing between them but skin. He needed to sink into something wholesome and giving and distant from the violence his life had become.

She stirred when the bed shifted with his weight, made a soft kitten sound of contentment when he eased back down beside her. She snuggled up against his side with a sigh, like she'd been doing this for years. Like she was coming home. Like he was the home she needed and loved and missed when he was gone.

Easy, he thought, wrapping his arms around her and losing himself in the soft, warm lushness of her body, her tender sighs, and unquestioning trust. *Easy*, he thought again, pressing her cheek to his chest, where the warmth of her breath feathered across his heated skin. It would be so easy to fuel himself on both her serenity and her fire. To ground himself in her giving. To believe — just for the moment — that he could be the man she needed, maybe even loved.

"I thought you'd left me." Her breath was whisper-soft against his jaw.

"Not a chance," he promised on a groan when her slender leg slid between his and her hand, soft and sensual and on a mission, drifted down his chest, across his abdomen, then lower. He didn't stop her this time when she cupped him in a loose, velvety caress.

When one silky leg started moving over his, a niggling voice of reason rose above the madness, reminding him that he should stop.

It would have been easier to stop the sunrise.

"I need you," she mouthed against his skin.

She needed *him*? *Christ.* He was the one in need. Deep need. Dark need. Insatiable need of everything about her that made her woman, and wanton and willing in his arms.

He groaned when her warm mouth opened against his throat trailing long, lingering kisses that were as much suction as consumption, as much greed as giving.

Lord God above, she was eating him by inches, and he was powerless to do anything but lie there and let her feed until there was nothing left of him but memory.

"Sophie," he murmured on a ragged breath when her lips brushed across his nipple.

"I need you," she whispered again, more plea than proclamation, more promise than prophecy.

She rose to her knees and, watching his eyes in the dark, peeled her gown over her head.

"Need you . . ." Then she bent over him and took him in her soft, soft hands. Took him in her warm, giving mouth.

He knotted his hands in her hair on a deep groan. Sank into the sensation of her tongue on his flesh and the selfless seduction of suction. *Christ, oh Christ,* this didn't feel like anything as simple as desire. This felt much more complex, much more intense, as she lost all inhibition and gave all-consuming pleasure.

Heaven. Hell. She took him there and all parts in between, her desire tempered with desperation and — he groaned when she sucked him hard and deep — and something he couldn't name. Something that transcended physical and brushed up against the realm of spiritual.

"Sophie . . ." He sighed her name on a harsh breath, buried his hands deeper in her hair, and guided her head, helping her set a rhythm that enhanced a pleasure that built to rich, rare heights he'd never known he could reach and not explode in the process.

It wasn't that she was experienced. It wasn't that she was practiced or perfect or even skilled. It wasn't just that she was willing to do this for him. She *wanted* to do this for him, wanted it with an urgency and ardor that robbed him of all reason and control and regret.

With a ragged groan, he stilled her, knowing he was a deep breath away from coming in her mouth. "Sophie — I can't — I can't hold back much longer."

She lifted her head, letting him go with a long lick, an enticing whisper of warm breath on wet flesh. Her tangled hair fell like a curtain of silk across his hands. Her eyes were dark and deep, her expression lost somewhere between passion and an unwavering longing to finish the work she'd started.

"Don't. Don't hold back," she murmured, her eyes pleading, before she lowered her mouth and took him in again.

He sucked in his breath and hooking, his hands under her arm, dragged her off him. "I want to be inside you when I come. I want you coming with me."

He was beyond finesse now, beyond anything tender or gentle, when he flipped her onto her back, moved between her thighs, and entered her in one hard, deep stroke.

She gasped, then moaned, then wrapped her ankles around his hips and urged him home.

21

Sophie didn't want to think. Not about Lola or Hope or the day's violence or the consequences of this moment. She just wanted to feel. To escape in the riot of sensations Wyatt brought to life in her body as he pounded into her again and again and again.

His fervor took her breath away. No tender love this time. No patient, giving tempo to ease her into pleasure. He wanted her like breath. He wanted her mindlessly. And he needed her like life blood and made no excuses as he staked a claim that made her feel both lost as she'd never felt lost yet found as she'd never been found.

"Harder," she demanded, wanting all he had to give her, wanting him the way he wanted her, needing him the way he needed her. Hard and rough and deep. She met him stroke for stroke as he wedged his hands beneath her hips and tilted her tighter against him, then pounded into her again.

And again and again, burying himself deep, with a

reckless abandon that made her lightheaded and frantic for a release that danced just beyond her reach.

She was fire. Burning, licking heat. He was steel. Forged, unyielding strength. Together they were hot, molten, unappeasable.

She didn't know when it had happened, but he'd become a craving for her. His tough body. His wounded, heroic soul. Somewhere in the course of that night, he'd become like a drug she couldn't get enough of. Like air that she'd die without breathing.

The friction of his hot body gliding in and out of her was at once unbearably stimulating and luxuriously sensual. She wanted everything he had to give her . . . but didn't know how she could possibly take any more.

And then it was out of her hands. A blinding orgasm ripped through her, frightening, stunning, breath-stealing. A lightning strike of pleasure, blade-sharp and perfect and pure. She cried his name, dug her nails into his back, and convulsed involuntarily around him.

"Please, please," she begged, crying now, for the sheer joy and consuming power of her release. "Come with me, please, please, come with me."

Through a haze of exquisite sensation, she felt his big body stiffen and knew he was already there. Already gone. Her orgasm was the final push that shoved him over the edge. He pumped once more, and she felt him soul-deep inside as he shot into her, riding on the wave of her release.

Both sweat and tears dampened her cheeks when he

pressed his face to hers and held her while she clung to him to keep from shattering into a million pieces, held her as if *he* was the one in danger of falling apart.

Rich, lush, devastating, the sensations rolled through her in gently surging currents. She savored every one, tried to make it last forever . . . and still, it didn't last nearly long enough.

His heart slammed against her breasts as he struggled for breath, and she made a feeble attempt to get her bearings. But there was no way to orient herself to an experience like this. No analyzing, no quantifying.

So she just let herself ride. She closed her eyes. Gave herself permission to drift on the amazing down side of their passion and let the tactile sensations wash over her like warm water.

The softness of his skin.

The steely bulk of muscle and bone beneath it.

The glorious, wonderful weight of him.

The way his breath gradually leveled when it fell soft and hot against her shoulder.

The dampness of his skin beneath her palms.

The heavy beat of his strong, giving heart.

Right now, it was all hers to value and indulge in. Right now, it was enough.

Later, she'd sort it all out. Later, she would question her sanity, ask herself where they could possibly go from here.

Yes, she told herself as she drifted off to sleep again, later would be soon enough.

* * *

Sophie was still sleeping when Wyatt woke up to sunlight shining bright through the bedroom window. He lifted his arm, checked his wrist watch. Six-oh-eight a.m.

Tick-tock. Thirty hours and counting.

He threw his forearm over his forehead, closed his eyes, and lay there for a moment, waking up by slow degrees, still shaken in the aftermath of the most intense sexual experience of his life.

Sexual. Soulful. Meaningful. He refused to believe it wasn't all of that. Emotions that raw and powerful and primal had to mean something to her. Something more than physical release. Something more than escape from the brutality of her current reality.

She stirred beside him. Soft and slumberous and—

A sound from the doorway yanked him to full alert.

Muscle memory kicked in like a bullet.

He shot to a sitting position and grabbed the H&K in one motion, leveling it at the bedroom door—and dead center in the middle of Hugh Weber's heart.

Hugh. An older, harder, angry Hugh.

Jesus.

Wyatt lowered the gun with a shaking hand. He'd almost shot him.

"Well. Hell. *This* is awkward." Hugh's tone was smartass and glib as his gaze flicked from Wyatt to Sophie before zeroing back in on Wyatt again. "Guess it would be an understatement to say you weren't expecting me."

Fuck.

Wyatt dragged a hand over his face, then glanced at Sophie who was wide awake now, her face awash with emotions that ranged from shock to rage to mortification.

"Give me a minute," Wyatt said, his tone making it clear that he wanted Hugh to leave and shut the door on his way out.

"Take your time." Hugh's voice was deceptively magnanimous, considering the venom in his eyes. He glanced back at Sophie, the corners of his mouth turning up in an ugly smile. "I always did."

"Get out," Sophie demanded, her eyes wounded and hard.

Hugh left, closing the door behind him—but not before Wyatt saw the flash of both anger and pain he'd tried to cover with a "who gives a shit" grin.

He still loves her.

The truth of it hit Wyatt like a sledge powered by guilt.

Christ. Jesus H. Christ.

Hugh still loves Sophie.

Wyatt shot out of her bed, never more aware that it was the same bed Sophie had once shared with Hugh. He stepped into his pants and zipped them before the sound of Hugh's footsteps faded away down the hall.

"He's angry," Sophie warned as she gathered the covers to her bare breasts and watched him with nervous eyes.

"I got that part." Expression grim, he bent over and picked up his shirt from the floor. "I'd be pissed, too, if I were him."

Sophie dragged her hair away from her face with a trembling hand. "He's dangerous when he's angry."

Yeah, Wyatt got that part, too. And he didn't need Sophie to tell him. He'd known Hugh longer than she had.

"I hate this." Her voice was low, shaken.

That made two of them. He just wondered if she hated it for the same reasons he did. Maybe she just hated that it hadn't been Hugh in bed with her.

"He lost his right to be angry a long time ago," she said, stopping Wyatt when he wrapped his hand around the doorknob.

He turned back to look at her.

"He lost his right," she repeated with a sincerity that had Wyatt wishing he could bank on the words she *hadn't* said.

Hugh lost his right, not just because they were no longer married but because she no longer cared.

But she didn't say that, and as much as he wanted to find out exactly where the two of them stood, he had some fences to mend.

So he left the woman he loved and went in search of the man who had once been his best friend.

Hugh was in the kitchen, loading the coffee pot, when Wyatt found him. His broad shoulders were squared, his motions routine and familiar in the house that had once been his home, in the kitchen where his wife had once cooked for him.

There was no easy way to do this. Wyatt scrubbed a hand over his jaw, then pulled out a bar stool and sat down, with the counter separating them. "Can't say this is how I saw things going down between us."

When Hugh turned, he was wearing that amiable grin Wyatt remembered. An underlying edge of anger sliced through it like the blade of a KA-Bar.

"What?" Hugh's smile was tight and forced. "No 'It's not what it looks like, buddy'? Christ, Savage. Couldn't you at least make the effort to *look* guilty?"

Yeah, there was guilt. No matter how many times Wyatt told himself that what he and Sophie had was righteous and pure, it still felt like he'd cheated on a brother.

He folded his hands together on the countertop and met Hugh's dark look. He saw that the years of living on the back side of danger and death had taken a toll on him physically as well as emotionally. Hell, it had taken a toll on both of them. "What is it that you want me to say?"

"Oh, I don't know. Maybe that you're sorry you screwed my wife?"

Nothing would feel better right then than flying across the counter, grabbing Hugh by the throat, and warning him to watch what he said about Sophie.

Because Hugh had been his friend, because threats wouldn't fix a damn thing, Wyatt stayed the hell put. "You really want to do this? Here? Now?"

Hugh held his gaze with a long, searching look. "No," he finally said, his tone more weary now than pissed. "No, I really don't." He worked his jaw, clearly struggling to keep his anger in check. "I shouldn't have barged in. I don't have that right anymore. And what Sophie does now is Sophie's business. It was just a shock, okay? I'll get over it."

Not likely, Wyatt thought. No, a man was not likely to get over seeing an old friend in bed with his ex-wife. He felt regret that it wasn't just the years that had gone by that had separated them as friends. Years ago, even when Wyatt had backed away and let Hugh have a clear path, Sophie had always been there between them. Just as she was between them now.

He studied Hugh's face, a face that looked older, harder, tougher. And he respected him for his restraint. "For what it's worth," he said, "I came here to help. Period. I didn't know about the divorce. I didn't expect—"

"I know." Hugh lifted a hand, cutting him off. For the first time, he met Wyatt's eyes without malice. "I know," he repeated, and shot Wyatt a tight, forced smile. "You were always a Boy Scout, Bear. No reason to believe that would change over the years." When Wyatt remained silent, Hugh shrugged. "Shit happens. I'll deal with it. Now, why don't you fill me in on what's happening with Lola?" He shoved a mug of coffee across the counter. A peace offering.

Wyatt wrapped his hand around the mug, nodded in silent concession that, yes, there needed to be peace if they were going to move on. *Move on* being the operative phrase. They could never be what they'd once been to each other, but for the sake of a child, they'd move forward.

That didn't mean this was over. Didn't mean this was anything more than a temporary truce. Hugh always settled scores. And right about now, Wyatt knew his former combat buddy figured he had a damn big score to settle.

Later. There was no doubt in Wyatt's mind that this would come to a roaring, raging head.

In the meantime, they had a job to do. The only way to get it done was by working together. So he hunkered down and told him everything he knew about Lola's abduction, all the while feeling a weary regret that this man, who had once guarded his back, saved his ass, and given him some of the best laughs of his life, would never be his friend again.

Sophie didn't know what she expected to find when she walked out of the bedroom five minutes later. Anger, for certain. Hugh had always had a temper. Sullen silence, possibly. She'd been the recipient of his brooding wrath more than once.

Divorce court had been a rabid, ugly humiliation for both of them. He'd screamed. He'd sworn. He'd threatened. She'd rather face a firing squad than the rapier edge of Hugh's rage again. But the fact was, she had no choice. Everything might have changed for her and Wyatt and Hugh, but nothing had changed for Lola.

Lola was still out there. Scared and alone. And Sophie refused to let herself think about what else might have happened to her.

On a bracing breath, she smoothed a hand over her hair and walked out of her bedroom, primed for anything but what greeted her.

The two men stood across from each other, drink-

ing coffee at her kitchen counter. Just standing there,
quietly talking like they met like this every day. Like no
years, no distance, no anger had passed between them.
Like her ex-husband hadn't just found her in bed with
a man who'd once been his best friend.

She wasn't prepared for the tug of nostalgia that
pulled at her heart, either, as she watched them together, both unaware that they had an audience. Hugh's
dark head nodded as Wyatt outlined the situation and
everything Wyatt and his team had done to date.

And Wyatt—while his broad shoulders weren't exactly relaxed, they weren't knotted tight with tension,
either. They seemed to have called a tentative truce,
put aside whatever residual backlash they felt, for the
sake of saving a child.

Warriors, she thought, and felt her heart swell with
pride. Pride for the man Wyatt was. Pride, even, in
Hugh, because he'd apparently dug deep and found
that part of himself she'd once respected and admired,
even loved. Yes, at their core, both were still warriors,
even though Hugh's motives had run amok somewhere
along the way.

For a moment, she forgot about the present and simply watched them together, let the look of them take
her back to a time when they'd all been young and
naïve and full of hope and idealism. It was a moment
that passed in a single heartbeat, when the pain of their
current circumstances eclipsed it.

These men had been friends once. Brothers. And no
matter that she and Hugh had gone separate ways, she

had never wanted to come between them. Not twelve years ago. Not now. And yet she had.

Since there wasn't a damn thing she could do to make it go away, she sucked it up and joined them in the kitchen. Hugh was the first to spot her.

His eyes were hard when he met hers, but whatever anger he was feeling, he kept it under control. "Sorry I didn't get here sooner," he said without preamble. "It took a while for your message to reach me. Longer still to make connections home."

"Thank you," she said, uncomfortable facing him but determined to get through it. "Thank you for coming."

His passive expression tightened. "You didn't think I would?"

No. She hadn't thought he would come. She didn't say as much, but her face must have telegraphed her thoughts.

"Jesus, Sophie." His rage snapped like a whip crack. "Hope's my daughter, too."

A flip switched inside her then. Like Pavlov's dog, she fell back on the anger she'd used for too many years to combat Hugh's mercurial mood swings. All of the old hurts he'd inflicted, all of the old scars that had never fully healed, resurfaced with a vengeance.

"*Your* daughter? You never wanted Hope. You never loved her."

Hugh threw up a hand. "It always comes back to that, doesn't it?"

"I'm just stating the truth."

"Right. The truth according to *Saint* Sophie."

"You haven't even asked about her," she threw back, to prove her point.

He dropped his chin to his chest and clenched his jaw. When he looked at her again, his guilt was undercut by impatience. "How is she? *Where* is she?"

"She's traumatized. And terrorized. And she's somewhere safe. Wyatt saw to that."

"I told you I got here as soon as I could," he reminded her, his anger rising because she'd pointed out the obvious. Wyatt had taken care of things because Hugh wasn't there. Hugh had never been there. "You know what?" He lifted a hand. "Fuck it. I'm not apologizing again. You want to blame every bad thing that happened in our marriage on me? Fine. But know this. It was *you* who changed when we adopted her. You never saw *me* anymore."

"That's because you were never here," she fired back. "I don't need you here now, either."

"Because you've got good old stand-up Wyatt to help you with every little thing?" His tone was full of ugly innuendo as he took a menacing step toward her.

Wyatt quickly blocked his way. "This isn't solving anything." His quiet strength interjected both a warning for Hugh to back off and a buffer that settled them both down.

Hugh glared at Wyatt, his fists curled at his sides, and for a moment, Sophie thought Hugh would hit him.

"Stand down, man." Wyatt's voice was soft, but his tone made it clear that he'd do what he had to do to keep the peace. "You don't want to mix it up. Not here. Not now. Let's focus on the real problem."

Hugh cut his gaze to Wyatt, his eyes narrowed in anger. "Fine," he said after a long moment, then held up both hands as if to say, *Okay, standing down now.*

He looked past Wyatt's shoulder to Sophie. "You're going to have to suck it up, Sophe, and deal with it. I'm not leaving. You're not gonna make me the bad guy by cutting me out of this. Hope is still my child. It could be her fighting for her life instead of Lola. I'm going to help find that girl. I'm going to get her back safe. You know I can do that."

On that point, Sophie couldn't argue, not without coming off as more of a shrew than she already had. She hated that she'd lost control, hated that Wyatt had seen a side of her she wasn't proud of but that Hugh always managed to bring out of her.

"I'm sorry." For Lola's sake, she swallowed back both pride and humiliation. They needed his help. "I appreciate that you came. I do. It's . . . it's been a rough few days," she added, because it was the best excuse she had for losing it.

She glanced at Wyatt. For approval? For understanding? Whatever she expected, she didn't see it. He was watching her with quiet eyes, so totally devoid of emotion it felt as if he'd physically left the building. Left her. The man who had come apart in her arms only hours ago was gone. The loss she felt was so acute tears burned her eyes.

She fought them back. Her tears weren't important now. What she felt didn't matter. What mattered was that Wyatt had just seen a side of her she wasn't proud of. What mattered was that Hugh was now in the mix, and Wyatt was the kind of man who would shoulder guilt where none was warranted. She knew without him saying a word that he was in pain, struggling with his feelings for her and with his guilt over what he perceived as a wrong he'd done to Hugh.

There was nothing she could do about it. He had to work through this miserable situation in his own way. Just as she had to work through the truth that last night, in Wyatt's arms, everything had been uncomplicated and perfect.

Yeah, last night, everything, including love—most especially love—had been crystal-clear. Today it was as muddy as the Río Lempa, churned up after a monsoon rain.

22

Sophie stared at the phone for a long moment after she'd ended the conversation with Ramona's brother Hector. She needed the time to pull herself together, well aware that the four men in her living room all had their eyes on her. Besides Wyatt and Hugh, Mendoza and Jones had arrived at the house about fifteen minutes ago. Wyatt had introduced them to Hugh, then they'd made a quick report.

"Shook a lot of trees," Mendoza said. "Not a single bad ass fell out."

"Doc and Green should be back within the hour," Gabe added as he sank down on the sofa, absently rubbing his leg when he thought no one was watching.

Until she'd spoken with Hector, Sophie hadn't thought her heart could hurt any worse. And now, after talking with Hector on the phone, the pain had multiplied by limitless degrees.

"Have they heard anything?"

She glanced at Wyatt, then away. "No. No one's contacted Ramona. Even the press has stopped bothering the family."

Hugging her arms tightly around herself, feeling all the more adrift and alone because it wasn't Wyatt's arms offering comfort, she walked to the patio doors. It was a little after seven a.m. The sun glinted brightly on the clean glass window panes of the colorful little *casita* where Ramona and Lola had spent so many peaceful, happy days.

"How's Ramona holding up?"

Sophie wished she could be magnanimous enough to trust Hugh's concern. She turned away from the door. It was too hard to see the little guest house empty and wonder if she'd ever see Lola playing in the backyard with Hope again. Or if she'd ever look into Ramona's eyes and not see haunting despair eclipsed only by grief.

"She's not," she said. "She's not holding up. She's in a daze. Not eating. Not sleeping. Not even crying anymore." A harsh, incredulous laugh burst out before she could stop it. "The neighbors have taken it upon themselves to collect money for the ransom. Two hundred sixty-eight dollars." She wiped back a tear. "Two hundred sixty-eight dollars," she repeated, overcome by the generosity and utter futility of the gesture. "To them, it's everything. How sad is that? How sad is it that they've given all they have to help, and it's so far away from what we need, they'd just as well have donated dirt."

The room fell into dead silence. Only then did she look at the faces of the men who had risked so much.

"Oh, God." Too late, she realized what her self-indulgent slide into anger had done. "Don't look like that. This isn't on your heads. You've done everything you could. Damn it," she swore when she felt tears well up again. "It's not your fault," she repeated. "But we have to face facts. Without the ransom, Lola's as good as gone."

When they said nothing, she realized that they, too, had lost confidence that they were going to find her.

"I agree. You need to pay the ransom, Sophie," Hugh said, earning a narrowed gaze from Wyatt.

"And take a chance on losing both the child and the money?" Wyatt shook his head. "I thought we'd agreed on this. We continue to work the MS-13 strongholds. Besides, we've still got the issue of money. Sophie doesn't have it."

Hugh made a concentrated attempt to hide his anger at Wyatt's challenge. "In the first place, I didn't agree to anything. I listened to what you've done so far. None of it's netting results.

"Look," Hugh went on when Wyatt said nothing. "You're in my backyard now. I know how it's going to come down. You can turn the city upside down, but you're not going to find Lola. What you *do* is come up with the money. These guys read the newspapers, watch TV. When they call to arrange the drop, I'll talk to them. They'll know who I am. They'll know they can trust me to get them what they want, and we'll get the child back alive. Shit, it's part of business as usual in this country. But you try to undercut them, she's going to end up dead."

He was right, Sophie realized with sudden, ringing clarity. Hugh had brokered successful deals with kidnappers before. He had brought children home safe. He was legendary in that area, a hero in some circles. That was why she'd tried to contact him in the first place. She'd been sure Hugh would know how to get Lola back.

Only when she hadn't been able to get hold of him had she contacted Wyatt. She'd been desperate. And she'd known that Wyatt would do anything to help her. Known, in fact, that he might even die trying.

That very real possibility had been hammering away at her conscience ever since she'd called him in Georgia. She couldn't let that happen.

"As for the money," Hugh continued, "what about your parents? They've got the coin."

"They *had* the coin," she said after a long moment.

"What are you talking about?"

"I'm talking about Bernie Madoff." She hated it but felt forced to reveal the private and personal hell her parents had suffered. It was still hard to believe that they had been among the thousands of victims Madoff had forced into bankruptcy with his Ponzi scheme.

Hugh's eyes grew dark with understanding. "Fuck."

"I'm going to be real generous and consider that an expression of your sympathy." Hugh had never liked her parents. She hadn't known until after the divorce that the feeling had been mutual.

Avoiding Wyatt's gaze, she rushed back to her desk, opened the center drawer, and pulled out her address book. She knew Wyatt would see what she was about to do as a betrayal of her trust in him. It wasn't about betrayal. It was about necessity. It was about keeping him alive, too.

"I'm going to contact Diego," she said abruptly.

"Wait. Diego? Diego Montoya?" Hugh's eyes narrowed.

She'd been dreading this. Hated that she'd kept it secret from Wyatt.

"At the theater," Wyatt said, thinking back and putting it together. "That's what that private conversation was about?"

"He offered to pay the ransom," she said, wishing she didn't feel as though she'd betrayed his trust.

Hugh snorted. "Jesus, Sophe. That's damn generous. Makes a man wonder. You fucking Montoya, too?"

Before Sophie even saw him move, Wyatt shot to his feet, clutched a handful of Hugh's shirt in his fist, and got right in his face. "You sonofabitch."

"Stop it!" she demanded, aware that all of the BOIs had adopted battle stances, ready to move on Hugh if Wyatt needed help.

"Just stop it," she repeated on a weary breath. "Let him go, Wyatt."

The two men remained locked in a feral stare-down. As much as it hurt her to see them at each other's throat, as much as Hugh's crude accusation angered her, there were bigger things at stake here than egos.

"This isn't the time or place for a pissing contest," she said, surprising them both with her bluntness.

Very slowly, Wyatt uncurled his fist and released Hugh's shirt. Slower still, he took a step out of Hugh's personal space.

"Diego offered to help, and right now, he's my only option," she said, relieved when they both backed away. "So, unless you've got a better idea . . ." She let the sentence trail off, looking pointedly at Hugh.

Silence from all quarters. As far as she was concerned, though, it was Hugh's silence that held more weight.

"I don't have that much in liquid assets," Hugh said, immediately defensive when he read her mind. "Every cent I've got is tied up in the business."

"Then what choice do we really have?" Sophie asked. "Where else am I going to get that kind of money?"

When Hugh just blinked at her, she looked up Diego's number in her address book.

"Where do we stand on the ransom timeline?" Hugh asked, his jaw hard.

She glanced at the wall clock. Felt her heart lurch. "At noon, Lola will be down to twenty-four hours."

"It could take Montoya that long to come up with that much cash," Doc said, giving Sophie her first indication that they knew as well as she did that the chances of finding Lola this close to the deadline were dwindling.

Sophie met Wyatt's gaze and silently appealed to him for understanding.

"Make the call," he said with a grim nod.

* * *

Wyatt heard only bits and pieces of Sophie's end of the phone conversation with Montoya, because Mendoza was banging around in the kitchen. Rafe's way of letting off steam was to sing and cook—in this case, he was whipping up a concoction of sausage, eggs, peppers, and cheese that he called Mexican breakfast tacos.

Hugh stood facing the sliders, his back to the room adding to the background noise as he talked on his cell phone. Wyatt gathered that he was checking in with his teams, which he'd told Wyatt were scattered across the globe.

Even though he hadn't heard the conversation, Wyatt figured he knew Montoya's response from Sophie's body language as she hung up the phone. She remained seated at her desk. One hand still gripped the cradled receiver. She'd lowered her head to her other hand. While there were too many factors weighing on her for her to feel much relief, it was apparent from the slight relaxing of her shoulders that Montoya had agreed to front the ransom money.

Hugh disconnected his own call and nodded toward Sophie. "Montoya come through like he promised?" he asked Wyatt.

"Looks like." Wyatt tabled his anger at Hugh and stared at Sophie's silent profile. He wished he'd been the one to offer her even this small amount of solace. Not just because he hated that it was Montoya she had turned to. Not even because he wanted to be her hero. Hell, he didn't care what it took to get the child home, he just wanted her back.

No, he hated it because the promise of Montoya's money had changed nothing and had given Sophie false hope. He didn't care what Hugh said. The bastards who had grabbed Lola would take the cash and run. And they could still kill her just because they could. Just because Lola's life ceased to be of consequence or value to them once they got what they wanted.

"So, is the gentleman coffee baron going to fork over the dough?" Hugh asked Sophie directly when she just sat there, staring into space.

His question startled her. She turned her attention to him, as if she'd forgotten he was even here. "Yeah. Yeah, he is. But it's going to take him a while to get the cash together."

"How long a while?" Hugh asked.

She let out a long breath. "He hopes to have it to us by nine-thirty tomorrow morning. Ten at the latest. What if . . . what if that's too late?" She turned to Wyatt, her temporary relief outdistanced by worry. "What if the drop location is more than two hours from here?"

"Don't borrow trouble," Hugh said before Wyatt could answer. "We wait until they give us the location, and if time is a problem, you explain what we're up against. They aren't going to walk away from five hundred grand over a few minutes' or even a few hours' delay."

"In the meantime, we're not giving up the search," Wyatt reminded her. "We could still find her before the deadline. Doc called in a few minutes ago. He and Green should be here anytime. They've got a lead."

She wanted to believe this was good news. Her eyes made that clear, but her bearing said she didn't hold out much hope.

"A lead on who?" Hugh didn't even attempt to hide his cynicism. "Another MS-13 tie-in? You're wasting your time. Even if Mara Salvatrucha took her, you're never going to pin them down. And why are you so sure it *is* MS-13? Why are you restricting your search to them? Why not look at GN or FMLN? Ransom is big money for their organizations. That Vega guy, the one you told me about who sent you chasing your tail down south. He was GN, right?"

"He's also dead," Wyatt reminded him. "Killed by Mara Salvatrucha gang members because he'd given us information about the camp where we found Carmen Hernandez."

Hugh glared at him.

"All you have to do is play the odds. MS-13 is running nine to one as our odds-on favorite."

"Okay, for the sake of argument, let's say it is MS-13," Hugh said, his patience waning. "You just add to the mix by pissing them off with this manhunt. You're making the problem worse, not solving it. Piss off their head banger, Vincente Bonilla, and you could be signing Lola's death warrant. Think about it, man. You and your men need to just back off. Let me work out the exchange with the kidnappers. Keep it simple. I'll get her back."

"While we sit here and knit sweaters? I don't think so." On that, Wyatt felt strong. They couldn't afford to stop their search for Lola.

Hugh worked his jaw. Wyatt knew there was a lot more he wanted to say on the subject. What he didn't know was why Hugh had dug in so deep on this.

"Fine," Hugh said finally. "But you're risking your necks for no good reason."

"Our necks, our call," Wyatt said, making it crystal-clear that he was not backing away.

Hugh finally shrugged. "And your funeral."

"Soup's on." Mendoza's announcement ended the discussion. "Sophie," he added, glancing across the room at her as he scooped a layer of the egg mixture onto a soft taco shell, then dressed it with salsa. "Ladies first."

"Thanks, but I'll pass." She offered him an apologetic smile. "I'm not really hungry."

"Oh, no, no." Rafe wasn't having any of it. "We don't eat until you do, *cara*. So get your sweet a-, um, *self* over here so the rest of us can chow down. The team needs to refuel. If we don't eat because you won't eat, we're damn good at heaping on guilt. So how 'bout you just park it on the bar stool and dig in?" He set the steaming-hot plate of food on the counter and motioned her over.

Wyatt had to smile because she finally conceded. Mendoza did have a way with women.

"Fine. Since you put it that way, I guess I don't have much choice. Just give me a second to untwist my arm," she grumbled, but she was smiling for the first time in a very long time as she rose and joined Mendoza in the kitchen.

Rafe grinned as he dished up another plate. "Not too painful, I hope."

"No," she admitted after tasting his creation. "Not painful at all. This is delicious."

Wyatt shot Rafe a look of gratitude as Sophie dug into her breakfast in earnest. Rafe nodded. *No problem.*

"Car door," Gabe said when they all turned toward the sound in the driveway.

He walked quickly to the window and hooked a finger on a shade to pull it back so he could see outside. "Doc and Green," he announced, then headed for Sophie's front door to unlock it and let them in.

23

"God love him!" Doc proclaimed, sniffing the air and following his nose to the kitchen. "Mendoza cooked."

Wyatt stood back as Doc barreled right past both him and Hugh, who scowled at both newcomers.

"Swear to God, Choirboy," Doc said as he accepted the plate Rafe shoved in his direction, oblivious to the angry undercurrents in the room, "there are days when I'd consider switching teams and marrying you just to cash in on some of your cookin'."

"You *so* did not say that," Green grumbled as he tossed his go bag on the floor just inside the foyer.

Joe spotted Hugh, then glanced at Wyatt. When Wyatt nodded, telling him all was well, he extended his hand, all the while giving Hugh the once-over. "Joe Green."

"Hugh Weber." Hugh returned Joe's handshake. "Yeah," he added when Green cut another glance at Wyatt, "Sophie's ex. But that's another story for another day. I'm here to help."

Joe nodded and jerked his head toward Doc, who

was shoveling in food as if it was his last meal. "That would be Luke Colter."

"Just call me Doc," Colter said with a nod in Hugh's general direction. "I'll be more sociable once I fill this hole in my belly. *Gawd*damn, Mendoza. You outdid yourself this time."

"B.J.'s recipe," Rafe said with a smile. "Joe, better get a plate before our growing boy aces you out of the rest of this."

"Do I have to offer to marry you, too?" Joe muttered as he walked into the kitchen.

Doc barked out a laugh. "D'you hear that, everybody? Joe cracked a joke. Jesus, Green. What's Stephanie done to you?"

"Just eat your damn breakfast," Joe said.

Wyatt knew the first time he'd met Joe Green that the man didn't like being the center of attention. If his silence on the subject was any indication, he didn't like talking about Steph, either, or the fact that the big, sullen warrior *had* loosened up since she'd become a part of his life.

The right woman could do that for a man, Wyatt thought, glancing at Sophie, who had finished her breakfast and was insisting that Joe take her stool. The right woman could have a man searching for and finding pieces of himself that life had broken and wondering if there was a prayer he could put them back together again.

Stephanie Tompkins had become the right woman for Joe. Just as Gabe and Sam and Rafe and Reed had found those pieces of themselves in their women. Strong women. Brave and true and above all else, women who knew exactly who they were and hadn't changed a thing about themselves to be the right women for their men.

He watched Sophie carry her plate to the sink and rinse it off before placing it in the dishwasher, and he realized again just how badly he wanted Sophie to be that woman for him. He had even begun to think there was a chance of that happening.

Then Hugh had walked in on them. Everything had changed in that moment. Sophie hadn't looked him in the eye since.

And Hugh—despite his outward show of anger, Hugh had hardly taken his eyes off her.

The certain knowledge that Hugh still loved his ex-wife rode over Wyatt's head like a storm cloud. Sure, on the surface, there appeared to be nothing but malice and anger and regret between them. Hate, even.

The only emotion stronger than hate was love—and love, he knew, could still burn behind the façade of hate.

Wyatt had to live with the possibility that Sophie might still be in love with Hugh. Just like he had to quit getting all twisted up about something he couldn't do a damn thing about. Like making an enemy out of an old friend and knowing neither one of them would fully recover from the loss.

What he *could* do was find that child.

He turned to Doc. "So tell us what you've got."

* * *

Against Mendoza's protests that he'd take care of it, Sophie shooed him out of the kitchen and busied herself cleaning up. She needed to do something with her hands other than wringing them as she listened to Doc's account of his and Green's latest foray into Soyopango, the gangland territory on the east side of San Salvador.

"The jungle drums must have been busy and loud, because word's apparently gotten around about our little playtime south of the city. Everywhere we went, we got the look. They knew who we were, knew what we'd done. Wasn't enough money in the Chase National Bank to make those suckers talk."

"So we resorted to another form of persuasion," Green said with a quiet intensity that sent a shiver down Sophie's spine.

"This piece-of-shit banger bolted out of an abandoned building just as we drove by," Doc went on. "He hadn't figured on running head-on into our SUV. Nice piece of driving, by the way," Doc said, giving Joe a nod.

"Anyway, once we convinced him that he needed to talk to us or we'd weld him to the grille and use him as a cattle catcher, it didn't take long to get him to roll on his buddies. Must be he didn't want to end up like the fat boy."

"Can you cut to the chase here, Colter?" Wyatt asked.

"Right. He told us about this house that Vincente Bonilla likes to use. Said he'd heard of some unspecified 'goods' held there for safekeeping. Figured it must be something big, because the big bangers closed ranks around it. Close as we could figure, this all happened about the time the girl disappeared. Anyway, he's done a few stints as lookout on the crib. Said he'd seen 'em going in and out of the building with food, thought he heard a child crying a couple of times."

Sophie froze in place, her hand gripped around a dish towel the moment Doc said the words *goods* and *safekeeping*. But when he mentioned that a child had been crying, her heart picked up several hard, heavy beats.

She dried her hands on the towel and joined them in the living room, where Doc bent over the city map that was still open on the coffee table. "Here," he said, leaning to the side when Hugh moved in to take a look.

"What do you think?" Wyatt asked Hugh.

"Fits," Hugh said reluctantly. "This whole area, ten to twenty square blocks, has all been claimed by Bonilla and the Mara Salvatrucha in the past few years. Besides this building, there are at least twenty, thirty other strongholds. But"—he met Wyatt's eyes—"even if this is our girl and even if MS-13 has stashed her in the city, you're never going to find her. She could be in any one of them."

"Then we hit every one of them," Wyatt said, baldly challenging Hugh. "What can you tell us about their security so we can figure out the best way to breach them?"

Hugh glared, then shook his head. "They'll be armed to the teeth. Lookouts all over the *barrio*. And there are hundreds of them."

And a handful of them, Sophie thought as Wyatt met Hugh's stare.

"Then we'll have to use our old standby force multiplier," Wyatt said, making it clear that he wasn't backing away. "Surprise and relentless, overwhelming force."

Hugh made a sound of disgust. "And you're still gonna end up dead." He cupped his palm over his jaw and swore under his breath. "Fuck me for a bleeding heart, I'll bite it right beside you. Never planned on rocking my way to the grave anyway."

Wyatt narrowed his eyes in reaction to Hugh's reluctant decision to go with them. Then a slow, pleased smile curved up one corner of his mouth.

When Hugh returned his smile, Sophie could see that they'd gone beyond truce to the "one for all and all for one" mentality that had seen them through more deadly confrontations than she wanted to think about. They were ready to face the fire again, side by side.

She bit on her lower lip until she thought it would bleed. One more time. One more time, these men — one who had once been the most important part of her life, one whose life meant as much to her as her own — were charging into danger. Together.

They were smiling — *smiling* damn it — over this second-chance reunion of their brotherhood, when there was every possibility that they could both die in the next twenty-four hours. They and four other brave men, all willing to give their lives so that good could triumph over evil.

* * *

The guys were outside, checking gear and weapons and getting ready to rumble, when Wyatt went looking for Sophie. Somewhere along the way, she had quietly disappeared. He understood why. Good-byes were never easy; under these circumstances, they were damn near unbearable.

He knew he should just go, but he couldn't make himself leave without telling her good-bye. He wasn't surprised to find her in Hope's room, but his heart damn near broke when he saw her there, standing in front of the oval mirror attached to a child's white dressing table.

Necklaces, hair clips, dozens of photos, and the typical clutter of a twelve-year-old hung from the mirror and filled the table. Posters of some American teenage pop stars hung on the walls. White stars floated down from the ceiling as if suspended from a dark blue sky.

"Sophie?"

It was a moment before she turned to face him. When she did, she was clutching a well-used, well-loved stuffed white bunny to her breast.

"It wasn't that long ago that Hope took Thumper with her everywhere." She buried her nose in the soft plush rabbit. "He still smells like she used to after her bath. Like baby powder and lotion." Her eyes filled. "She had such a small amount of time to be a little girl."

"She'll always be your little girl." Wyatt walked over and drew her into his arms.

She leaned into him and turned her cheek against his shoulder.

"Ask me how I know that," he said, giving her a gentle nudge that told her he wanted her to play along.

"How do you know?" she asked, obediently but with little enthusiasm.

"Because anytime I get to thinkin' I'm a little too big for my britches, Momma reminds me that once upon a time, she powdered my lily-white backside. Puts a man in his place, 'specially when she announces it in mixed company and lets everyone know that to her, I'll always be her little boy."

He felt her smile against his chest and hugged her hard. "It's going to be okay."

She pulled back far enough so she could look into his eyes. "Can you promise me that? Can you *promise* that when this is over, you, and Hugh, and the guys . . . that you'll all be okay? That Lola will be okay?"

No, he couldn't promise her. And he couldn't lie to her. The next several hours were going to be ugly. "Sophie—"

She touched her fingers to his lips. "Don't." Tears misted her eyes. "Just . . . just come back. All of you. Just come back."

He closed his eyes, covered her fingers with his, and pressed them against his lips. "Another thing Momma taught me," he whispered against her fingertips. "A Southern gentleman always does what a woman tells him to."

On a soft cry, she pressed deeper against him, lifted her mouth to his, and drew his head down for a kiss that was staggering in its urgency, stunning in its desperation. She tasted of desire and fear and a frantic need to will him to return to her. She felt like heaven and home as he wrapped his arms around her and drew her so tightly against him that she gasped against his mouth and squeaked.

Squeaked?

"Damn rabbit," he muttered, which finally made her laugh as he tugged Thumper out from between them and drew her back against him.

"Not good-bye," he whispered against her parted lips, and kissed her with all the love he wished he had the right to proclaim. "This is *not* good-bye."

But it felt like it.

Damn, it felt like it when he finally let her go.

He backed slowly out of the room, and her dark eyes—scared and searching yet determined to be strong—willed him to come back in one piece.

"This is so my favorite time of day to make house calls," Mendoza announced from the backseat of Wyatt's SUV as they cruised the Soyopango gangland territory. "Nothing says sneak attack like waltzing in under the cover of the noon-fucking-sun."

He had that right, Wyatt thought, appreciating the Choirboy's sarcasm as they ran recon on the first target on their list. Like Mendoza, Wyatt would have much preferred waiting until dark. They didn't have the luxury or the time, so the hope was to take advantage of *siesta* and catch their targets napping in the sweltering El Salvadoran heat.

The sun beat down like a bonfire; the humidity was so thick every breath felt like it was filled with swamp water. Functioning in this heat in full combat gear was going to be a bitch. Between the Kevlar body armor, extra ammo, and weaponry, each one of them was carrying a good forty pounds. They were all sweating in the sauna-like heat. And if they came back alive, they'd all be at least ten to fifteen pounds lighter in the water-weight department before the next twenty-four hours was over.

Twenty-four hours. That's how much time Lola had left. They were pinning all their hope of finding her on a list of probable MS-13 strongholds that Hugh had helped Wyatt isolate at Sophie's no more than two hours ago. Once their targets were set, it had taken most of those two hours to pull their plan together and then hit Hugh's munitions warehouse, where they'd bolstered their ordinance out of his inventory.

"Not to look a gift horse in the mouth"—Gabe had pulled Wyatt out of Weber's earshot before they'd left— "but you're sure this guy's a hundred percent solid?"

Wyatt got it. Gabe didn't know Hugh from a scud missile. He didn't trust him yet. But Wyatt did know Hugh. Regardless of the animosity between them over Sophie, regardless of Hugh's resistance to the attacks on the MS-13 hideouts, he knew he could still trust Hugh with his life.

The man riding shotgun beside Wyatt was a man he'd trust to guard his six at the gates of hell. He might not be the man Wyatt had known fifteen years ago— hell, Wyatt wasn't the same man, either—but the bond they'd forged as raw recruits in the rat-infested back streets of Mogadishu and a dozen other Third World hell holes had been sealed by blood.

"Yeah," Wyatt had told Gabe without hesitation. "I'm sure."

That was the end of the conversation. Gabe understood that kind of brotherhood. The BOIs lived it every mission. If they didn't, they died. Pig-simple.

And the bottom line was, Hugh knew the city. He not only lived in it, but he'd worked it for the past several years. He knew the gang mentality, their setup, their hierarchy. He knew where their cribs were, who called the shots in each district, and which heads needed to roll. If Hugh said targets X, Y, and Z were where they were most likely to find a hostage crib, then Wyatt was going through the door with him.

"That's the building," Hugh said, pointing out their first target to Wyatt. "The one on the corner."

PC vernacular would label it low-income housing. In the "calling a spade a spade" department, they were slum apartments. They'd driven by block after block of buildings just like this one, havens for MS-13, the gang's own urban jungle, heavily populated with civilians whose souls were as lost as theirs.

Sheer numbers gave the gang the protection of having a lot of innocent civilians around to give the *policía*—yeah, there was a joke—or, in this instance, Wyatt's detail pause for fear of collateral damage. It also provided an endless pool of lookouts. It was damn easy to recruit anyone for any job with the promise of drugs or money or MS-13's method of choice: a bullet in the head.

In this particular building, more windows were broken than intact. Graffiti and MS-13 gang signs smeared the first six feet or so of the grim cement-block structure. Apparently, the lack of extension ladders was the only thing keeping the upper four stories expletive-free.

"Mendoza."

"Already on it." Rafe interrupted Wyatt and raised Gabe on one of the commo radios Hugh had provided. "On target," he said into the mike.

"Roger that," Gabe answered almost immediately from the Suburban, which kept a respectable distance behind them with Green at the wheel. Wyatt would like to have had Doc with the team, but he couldn't risk leaving Sophie alone. It was too dangerous. And she was too close to the edge.

He could still see her standing in Hope's room when he'd left her, her arms wrapped tightly around her midsection as if she was holding herself together, her dark eyes haunted by fear and resignation.

They'd all piled into the vehicle and were about to pull out of the drive when she'd run out of the house.

"Bring her back," she'd said quietly, her gaze encompassing all five of them. "Bring them all back," she stated, those eyes lingering on Hugh and then on him.

There were so many things Wyatt wished he had said to her. He'd wanted to climb out of the SUV, pull her back into his arms, lose his hands in her hair, and feel her life blood pulse against him one more time. He'd wanted to tell her he loved her. Tell her that when this was over, he was coming for her. That Hugh had had his chance and had blown it. Now it was his turn. Now it was their time.

But he hadn't. For her sake, even for Hugh's sake, maybe even for his own sake.

He'd just left her standing there in the driveway, telling himself that if he didn't make it back, she'd be better off not knowing the depth of his feelings. Better off with Montoya, who was waiting in the wings and could give her a future that didn't start and end with the fear that the next time, he might not come home.

24

"Pretty quiet." Hugh's voice broke into Wyatt's thoughts about Sophie.

Wyatt shut down that part of his brain and scanned the AO as they cruised slowly by. Across the street, a kid—no more than ten or twelve, wearing baggy black shorts and a grimy blue tank—leaned against a broken-down chain-link fence, cell phone in hand. Talking to Mom? Not likely.

An old woman sat in a rusted-out lawn chair by the curb, holding a basket of half-rotted vegetables, hoping to make a sale in the sweltering sun. Right next to her, a crack whore huddled into herself in the gutter, her body shaking in the filth like it was fifty below.

Vehicle traffic was light; pedestrians were scarce. Wyatt would like to chalk it up to *siesta*. But he was smarter than that. This reeked of a setup.

"Too quiet," he agreed.

Jungle drums, Doc had said. Yeah, urban jungle drums in the form of cell phones, spreading the word that they were coming. He figured there were eyes everywhere.

"Rafe, tell Gabe we're going once more around the block. We'll regroup two streets up, figure out our approach."

Hugh snapped photos of the building with his cell phone as they passed, capturing the entry door, the side view, and the rear exit as they made a pass through the alley. When they met up again, those two passes were the sum total of their "eyes on target" recon.

It sucked. In the perfect world, they'd have sat through hours of briefings, made practice runs on a similar site, then spent more hours debriefing the mock op to see where they could improve. They didn't have that luxury. They didn't have shit.

He was asking a lot of his men. A lot of Hugh, who had made it clear he was opposed to this tactic and was as jumpy as hell. If Lola wasn't there, then Wyatt was going to ask them to do the impossible over and over again until they found her or kissed their asses good-bye trying. Multiple take-downs in one day in these conditions would not only be brutal, they could be deadly. Once the adrenaline burn set in, to a man, they'd have difficulty with even the most routine task. Fine muscle control went to hell. A simple job like reloading a shotgun became a chore. That was why muscle memory was so critical. That was why practice made perfect. And practice was exactly what they lacked on this op.

He met each man's face, and, even with Hugh's

RISK NO SECRETS 295

stone-faced reluctance, he knew that, to a man, they were the best at what they did. This op wouldn't be anything like the day before, when they'd gotten the drop on a clew of MS-13 rejects, so high on *ganja* and lulled by boredom that they couldn't tell their AKs from their asses.

No, these bad asses were ready for them. They could damn well be walking into an ambush—or ten.

"We've got to figure they know we're coming," Wyatt said as they huddled around the hood of his SUV.

"No shit," Mendoza muttered, stuffing two extra thirty-round mags for his M-4 into the ammo pouches on his vest.

Wyatt sketched the outline of the building in the dust on the hood.

"The crib is on the ground floor," Hugh said, grudgingly filling them in on what he knew of the gang stronghold. "Stairway is central, right inside the front entry. Stay left of the stairwell. Fourth door on the right should be ground zero."

"Gabe, I want you on the master key." Wyatt made an X in the dust over the area Hugh had marked as the front entry. "We meet resistance at this juncture, you know what to do. If the main entry is accessible, save it for door number four."

"Roger that." Gabe reached into the SUV for the sawed-off twelve-gauge shotgun. Whatever you called it—master key, Avon calling—the Mossberg 590 Persuader loaded with breaching rounds would blow any deadbolt, hinge, or lock. And if Lola was inside, the

breaching rounds stopped with the door. She wouldn't
be in any danger from that quarter.

Wyatt stuffed flash bangs into one pocket and, just in
case they needed them, handed a couple frag grenades
to Hugh, who took them without a word.

"Rafe, Joe, I want you on the rear entrance." Even
though each situation was different, the team knew the
logistics of a dynamic entry—which by design, philoso-
phy, and implementation, was to rescue hostages and
kill bad guys—like the backs of their hands. He didn't
have to tell them not to commit too early. They were
there for backup, and if things got too dicey, their job
was to sweep in and kill everything that twitched, right
down to the cockroaches. *Cockroaches* being the operative word here, because these MS-13 bastards were in-
sects.

"Hugh and I will make the front entry."

Wyatt trusted Gabe to cover their six. Gabe knew
the drill. Wyatt and Hugh would be damn vulnerable
from behind once they blew inside. Whether Gabe
stowed the shotgun behind his back on its sling and
transitioned to his M-4 or let loose with a breaching
round, Wyatt knew that anyone who crossed the Archangel's path would end up deader than last week's
news.

"Eyes peeled for booby traps," he warned them. "We
trip a mine, any kind of IED, it'll be all over but the
cleanup. Questions?" he added as the sun beat down
and their blood pumped through their veins like rocket
fuel.

"Yeah." Mendoza, apparently, felt the need to fill Doc's shoes. "Is it too fucking much to ask that they come up with air-conditioned Kevlar?"

"I'll tell Santa you want some for Christmas," Green grumbled.

"Jesus. Green made another joke," Mendoza said with a shocked grin. "Check him for a fever."

"You guys done?" Even though he appreciated their efforts to cut the tension, Wyatt shot them a glare. "Hugh?" Because he'd been silent, Wyatt addressed him directly. "You got nothing to add?"

Oh, he had a lot he wanted to say—Wyatt could see protest written all over his face. But he just shrugged and bowed to Wyatt's lead. "It's your show."

"Okay, ladies," Wyatt said after they made a quick commo check. "Hit 'em hard and fast. And you earn a fifteen-mile run in full gear if you end up with so much as a scratch."

"Love you, too, Papa Bear." Mendoza kissed the air in Wyatt's direction, then shifted to his game face.

"Lock and load." Gabe pumped the twelve-gauge once, loading a round into the chamber.

Game on.

Single file, with Gabe leading the way and Green pulling up the rear, they jogged along the pocked and pitted sidewalks. The word must have spread wide, because there wasn't a living soul outside in the sun within a three-block area. If there had been, one look at their detail, armed to the teeth in full combat gear, and they'd have dived into the closest rat hole.

When they reached the corner of the target building, Mendoza and Green peeled off, jogged down the side of the building, and disappeared down the alley.

"Keep alert," Wyatt said, and the three of them inched along the front of the building until they reached the central door.

Crunch time.

With their backs pressed to the hot cement exterior walls, they advanced closer.

All quiet on the western front.

Wyatt sucked in a deep breath.

Gabe's gaze was locked on his.

"Go," he said with a nod, and brought his M-4 to his shoulder. Beside him, Hugh did the same.

The entry door was solid wood, closed up tight. Gabe stood to the side, tried the handle. Locked.

No hesitation.

Boom! Boom! Boom!

He unloaded three breaching rounds, one at the door latch, one each on the two metal hinges holding the door to the metal frame.

Smoke was still curling out of the shotgun's barrel when Wyatt stepped up and slammed a boot heel into the door. The slab of scarred wood leaned on the broken hinges like a drunk on a bender, then fell to the floor with a crash of splintering wood and a cloud of fine dust and street dirt.

Leading with his rifle, Wyatt burst into the main hallway, ready to fire at the first thing that moved. Hugh was right beside him as they maneuvered through the fatal funnel, each clearing his section of the hall as they rushed toward the fourth door.

Wyatt had the fleeting thought that it was as if no time had passed since the two of them had cleared a rat hole together. No time. No regrets. No anger. They moved like the well-oiled team they'd always been, in complete sync, anticipating each other's moves, knowing exactly where they were in relation to each other.

"Clear right," Hugh said.

"Clear center." This from Gabe.

Wyatt secured his section. "Clear left."

Wyatt reached door number four first, waited the nano-second it took for Hugh and Gabe to get in place, then tried the handle.

When he found it locked, he nodded to Gabe, who shouldered the shotgun.

Boom!

The Mossberg blew the door open in one penetrating shot. Wyatt tossed in a flash bang, then charged into the room.

Hugh and Gabe stormed in behind him, weapons aimed as they moved through the dump of a living room, cleared it, then cleared both bedrooms, the bathroom, and the kitchen.

"What the fuck? Where are they?"

"Doesn't make sense," Wyatt said in response to Gabe's commentary on the empty apartment as the three of them wandered around the room, using the barrels of their M-4s to move aside torn curtains and stained sofa cushions.

"They've got the numbers," Wyatt continued. "They pride themselves on standing their ground. They protect their turf. Why wouldn't they make a stand?"

"Maybe because they were never here?" Gabe suggested with a hard look at Hugh.

"Oh, they were here," Hugh said, either choosing not to take insult at Gabe's veiled accusation or not catching it. "Smell that?"

Gabe snorted. "I smell gunpowder." He walked back into a bedroom for another look around.

Hugh shook his head, followed his nose back to the kitchen, and returned with the smoking butt of a joint pinched between his index finger and thumb. "Couldn't have been gone too long."

Mendoza and Green walked through the door just then and took in the empty apartment.

"No one went by us," Mendoza said. "What the hell's going on?"

"Wyatt." Wyatt turned at the sound of Gabe's voice. "Check it out."

Gabe walked out of the bedroom; a small heart-shaped disc hung from the delicate silver chain dangling from the tip of his index finger.

Wyatt reached for the necklace and held the heart to the light. He read the word *HOPE*, engraved in delicate script on the silver.

He flashed on a memory of the first time he'd seen Sophie's daughter. She'd been wearing a necklace exactly like this one. He hadn't been able to read the engraving then. Now he knew what it said. *LOLA.*

He clutched the fragile necklace in his fist. Such sweet innocence. Two little girls, best friends, wearing necklaces with each other's name. Thanks to these barbarian bastards, that innocence would be lost to both of them forever. One of them might even lose her life.

"She was here," he said, his heart pounding as a vicious anger burned through his gut. Anger so raw and visceral that nothing short of blood was going to assuage it.

"*Was* being the operative word," Hugh pointed out.

Wyatt gave Gabe a nod. "Destroy this shithole," he said.

"Wait." Hugh stopped him on his way to the door. "What's the point? Leave it. We don't have time."

And Wyatt didn't have time to argue or to wonder why Hugh questioned his order. "Destroy it," Wyatt repeated, and got the hell out of the building before he imploded along with the apartment that the guys were in the process of leveling to rubble. "Give the rats one less warren to hole up in.

"Where next?" he demanded of Hugh, who followed him back out onto the street.

"Again, what's the point?" Hugh asked.

"The point is, I'm going to find that child." Wyatt marched back to the SUV.

"Jesus. Don't you get it? They're ten steps ahead of us."

"Then we're just going to have to move faster!"

Hugh jerked open the passenger side of the SUV. "You're not going to find her."

Wyatt glared at him over the roof of the vehicle. "Watch me."

25

"That is *so* not a word!" Crystal protested, her eyes sparkling mad.

"It so *is* a word," Johnny argued, leaning away from the table and the board game, somehow managing to look indignant, wounded, and amused as hell when Crystal leveled her accusation. "Can I help it if I have the superior intellect when it comes to this stupid game?"

This stupid game was Scrabble, and watching the three of them—Johnny, Crystal, and Hope—huddled around the table in her library pulled at strings attached directly to Juliana's heart. Life. She loved being surrounded by it. And all this life filling the empty spaces in her home made her realize how much she'd missed having someone to share it with. And she loved how Hope had come out of her shell.

"Do you want to get the dictionary out, or should I?" Hope asked Crystal, grinning the way a twelve-year-old girl should be grinning when she was in the company of her biggest crush, namely Johnny, and her new grown-up BFF, namely Crystal.

"Go for it, girlfriend," Crystal said, exchanging a high-five with Hope, who giggled and looked toward Juliana for direction when she couldn't spot the dictionary.

"It's on the third shelf behind you," Juliana told her, then grinned again when Hope stuck her tongue out at Johnny, shrieked in delight, and scurried past him when he tried to grab her and keep her away from the dictionary.

Amazing, Juliana thought, that Hope could be in such deep, dopey, puppy-dog love with cute Johnny and yet adore Crystal, who was clearly the love of the gorgeous Texan's life. *Ah, youth*, she thought, smiling at the easy way Hope managed to compartmentalize her feelings so she could have the best of both worlds when it came to the Reeds.

"I'm telling you, it's a word," Johnny insisted, then shook a finger at Hope. "Don't crack the dictionary open, Princess. If you let Crystal sucker you into looking it up, it'll cost you points," he warned Hope with a wink that made her blush and smile even wider.

"You're just trying to trick me into believing you," Hope maintained, dropping the heavy dictionary onto the table.

"If you loved me, you *would* believe me," Johnny wheedled with a wounded puppy-dog look. "And you do love me, don't you, sweetie?"

"You're so full of it," Crystal sputtered.

"Yeah," Hope agreed, although it was clear she was practically melting under Johnny's sugar-sweet spell. "Full of it."

Reed made a show of clutching his heart and suffering the mortal wound she'd just inflicted, which sent Hope into another fit of giggles.

"They are so good for her," Juliana murmured, just loudly enough for Nate to hear. She was curled up on one end of her sofa, her feet tucked under her, a book open but unread in her lap, as she watched the shenanigans Johnny was pulling.

Nate sat on the far end of the sofa, going over a stack of BOI after-action reports. "*You're* good for her," he said simply, those few words relaying an unwavering belief in her that sent an involuntary but wonderful feeling of warmth flooding through her.

Actually, it was Hope who'd been good for Juliana. She saw so much of Angelina in the child. And where once Juliana hadn't let herself visit those memories of the daughter she'd lost, Hope's unexpected appearance in her life had opened her up to testing those memories again.

Soon it would be four years since she'd lost her husband and their daughter. Four long, lonely years. Lonely but for Gabe, who always kept in touch. Lonely but for Nate Black, whose solid, steady presence was both comforting and unsettling. And lonely, because at the end of the day, she was always there alone.

She glanced at Nate and smiled when Johnny tried to enlist him as an ally for the validity of his challenged word.

"Sorry. You're on your own, pal." Nate wasn't about to get dragged into the middle of that heated debate.

"Be glad, Reed, because if I had to pick a side, it sure as the world wouldn't be yours. You're pretty but not nearly as pretty as those two."

"And he says it's all about the team," Johnny grumbled, then went back to defending his word.

Although Nate had blown off his request to back him up, Juliana knew that Nate would go to the end of the earth for Johnny Reed. For all of his men.

And for her, she admitted, dropping her gaze and pretending to be engrossed in her book. After all, he'd been there for her since she'd lost Armando and Angelina.

Beside her, Nate continued to study his reports. She studied his profile, realized that she did that a lot these days. More than was probably wise. She found him fascinating in so many ways. Ways that were hard for her to admit to herself. Physically, he was a very appealing man. A passionate man.

A flash of memory hit her, and she felt herself blush as she remembered the way he'd looked, naked in her bed, his broad chest lightly dusted with dark hair, the corded muscles of his arms bulging, a healed bullet wound on his right shoulder, another on his left pec. The scars of a warrior.

In the background, the heated Scrabble debate continued amid much laughter and empty threats.

He glanced up, then at her, an inquisitive look in his beautiful eyes when he caught her watching him.

She smiled and went back to her book.

And she wondered, for the hundredth time, why she was fighting this.

"Damn," Crystal sputtered, looking up from the dictionary in disbelief. "Oenophlygia: the state of being drunk. It really is a word."

Johnny gloated unabashedly. "Just wouldn't listen, would you? Just couldn't stand that I might be way ahead of the game. Word to the wise," he added with a superior smirk. "Don't mess with a man of my experience in that arena."

Nate opened his eyes slowly, took a moment to focus, and realized he must have fallen asleep on the sofa in Juliana's library.

"You work too hard."

He turned his head and saw Juliana sitting beside him, a concerned smile tilting up the corners of her mouth. His heart did that *slam-thump* that it did every time she looked at him like that. "What time is it?"

"Late," she said. "The Reeds and Hope went to bed about an hour ago."

"So who won the Scrabble game?" he asked, stretching the kinks out of his neck.

"It's still a work in progress. Johnny was getting a little antsy—his leg was bothering him, I think—and Crystal called it."

"She's good for him." Nate scrubbed his hands over his face to rub away the lingering cobwebs. "Never thought I'd see any woman tame that outlaw."

"Is that what she's done? Tamed him?"

Her tone was playful, but something in her eyes set his senses on alert.

"Okay. Maybe *civilized him* fits better," he amended carefully.

"You're a very civilized man," she said, and for the life of him, he couldn't tell if she'd given him a compliment or a dressing down.

He sat forward, propped his elbows on his knees, stared at his clasped hands for a moment, and glanced at her. "Is that a good thing?" he asked, feeling a rich excitement, because it suddenly felt as if they were dancing around the heart of a discussion that they'd both avoided for a very long time.

She studied his face, drew a deep breath, and let it out. "I've always thought so."

He tilted his head and searched her eyes. And his heart damn near jumped out of his chest at what he saw there. She was flirting with him. And it was scaring her . . . just a little. Just enough to make it thrilling.

Something *was* happening here. The question was, was he too "civilized" to push for more?

"Do I hear a *but* at the end of that sentence?" he asked, deciding to go for it.

She hesitated, looked down at her hands, then lifted her chin. "*But* sometimes . . . sometimes I wish you weren't quite so controlled around me."

His heart kicked him again. Hard. And this was no longer a dance. "I thought you wanted control, Juliana. I thought you wanted restraint."

She pressed her lips together. "Yes, well, I've always thought I wanted that, too."

Over the years, he'd faced off against death too many

times to count. Facing this discussion and the mine field of emotions on the line, however, was far and away one of the hardest things he'd ever done. What if he wasn't reading her right? What if—

"Was I a fool to think that, Nate? Was I fool to keep you—keep 'us'—at a distance?"

He let out a breath that had been backed up in his chest since—hell, since the first time he'd laid eyes on her two years ago. This was hard for her. This was very, very hard for her.

"No bigger fool than I've been for letting you."

Tears filled her eyes, and he knew instinctively what put them there.

"He would want you to be happy, Juliana."

While she was a careful woman—careful with her trust, with her emotions, with her heart—she was also a woman without pretense. "I loved Armando for a long time," she said softly.

"And I expect you always will. I don't want to take that away from you."

She swallowed hard. A single tear trailed down her cheek. "Armando is my past." She finally looked at him, and what he saw in her eyes made his heart flat-out stop. "I want you to be my future. That is, if . . . if you want that, too."

"If I want?" He took her hand, then thought the hell with all this "civilized" behavior, and drew her onto his lap. "If I *want*? I have wanted nothing but you since the first time I saw you."

Her smile was radiant as she looped her arms around

his neck and pressed her forehead to his. "As long as we're confessing, I haven't had a good night's sleep since . . . well, since I slept with you in my bed."

She blushed, all pretty and pink, and, God, she made him feel like a kid. And not at all civilized. "I know it's been a while—seventeen months, two weeks, and one day, if you happen to be counting—but it's not the sleeping that I remember."

She laughed, then sighed in pleasure when his hands roamed her back. "I don't think a mature woman is supposed to feel this way."

"What way?"

"Giddy. Hot. Mostly hot."

He chuckled and cupped her face in his hands. "How about we go upstairs? I'll see what I can do to take care of that little . . . issue."

"In front of the children?"

The sound of Reed's voice had them jumping apart like kids caught with their hands in the cookie jar.

"Jesus, Reed! You've been stumping around this place like a bull on stilts for days. How the hell did you get in here without us hearing you?" Nate growled.

"I think maybe you were . . . preoccupied?" Johnny suggested with a grin that told Nate he couldn't wait to go back to bed and tell Crystal what he'd interrupted on Juliana's sofa.

Nate glared at him. "Buzz off."

"Right." He snagged the cell phone that had apparently brought him back to the library, took a couple thumping steps toward the door, then stopped and grinned over his shoulder. "'Bout damn time you two kids came to your senses."

"Reed!" Nate snarled.

"Buzzing, sir," Reed said dutifully, and headed back toward the door.

"And to think, I accused you of being too civilized."

Stark naked, flat on his back, breathing hard, and still recovering from the most *uncivilized* sex he'd ever had, Nate turned his head on the pillow.

Juliana lay beside him, her arms flung above her head, her beautiful breasts rising and falling with her attempts to catch her breath, her glorious body glistening with a light sheen of perspiration.

"Well, it was time to put that misnomer to bed. Past time to take *you* to bed. God, we've wasted so much time."

She turned her head, her brown eyes sultry and satisfied. "We can't look back. Only forward. And just so you know . . . you were so worth waiting for. That was . . ."

"Amazing," he finished for her.

"Yes, *mi amor*. Amazing." She made a soft sound of pure, wanton pleasure as she stretched and sighed and sent his blood pressure skyrocketing off the charts again.

Lush. There was no other word to describe Juliana Flores. No skinny model's body on this woman. There was flesh on her bones. Glorious, sensual flesh, soft in all the right places, curves a man could sink into and never want to come out.

And finally, she was his. He propped himself up on

an elbow so he could look his fill, claim what he'd been wanting for too damn long. No way in hell was he ever going to let anything come between them again.

He covered a full voluptuous breast with his hand and felt himself grow hard again when she arched into his touch, when her nipple tightened and pebbled against his palm.

"You are so damn beautiful." He lowered his head and, caressing the plump rise of her breast, skimmed his tongue over a taut, berry-pink nipple.

She sighed again and cupped his head in her hand, encouraging the contact by rolling to her side and sliding one long golden leg over his thigh. "I love how you touch me."

"Tell me where," he whispered against her nipple, then pulled away with a long, sucking stroke to admire the glistening dampness he'd left behind.

"Anywhere. Everywhere." She found his hand, brought it to her mouth, and kissed the backs of his knuckles. Then, with her dark gaze locked on his, she lowered his hand between their bodies, pressed it against the apex of her thighs, and rocked slowly against him.

His heart filled with love and longing and wonder. Finally, *finally*, he had the right to be with her this way.

He pressed her gently onto her back and knelt beside her, taking his time touching her, pleasing her, watching her move and breathe and wet her lips in anticipation of what he would do to her next.

"You know there's no going back from this." He lifted first one of her legs and then the other, so her knees were bent and parted, her heels pressed into the sheets. Then he moved between them, kissed the inside of each thigh, urging them wider apart as he made his way to the sweet, beckoning dampness of her mons. "This is forever, Juliana," he whispered as he breathed in the scent of woman and sex and desire. "Forever . . ."

She gasped and moved against his mouth when he parted her feminine folds with his fingers and found her center with his tongue.

"Forever," she managed on a breathless cry as he delved deep and devoted himself to ruining any small amount of control she might yet possess.

She was weeping softly by the time he'd finished with her, weeping and writhing and begging for mercy, pleading for release.

She came on a long, shuddering breath, her body tensing, her heartbeat slamming, when he moved up her body and kissed her, claiming her mouth and her soul as he entered in a long, driving stroke.

"Forever," she said again and again and again, as he pumped into her and drove them both beyond past regrets and toward the beginning of their future together.

26

"Fire in the hole!" Gabe made sure all the guys were ducked down behind the cover of their two vehicles, then set the charge of C-4 on the abandoned building that stood alone in the middle of a litter-strewn lot on the outskirts of the city.

The single-story warehouse blew like a Republican Guard munitions dump—only it hadn't been a munitions cache for Saddam's "elite" army. MS-13 was going to be a shitload of weapons and ammo lighter than they'd been two minutes ago.

"That ought to get Bonilla's attention," Mendoza said as the ordinance cooked off.

Hugh stood by, his arms crossed over his chest, his jaw clenched tight, as he stared at the smoke and dust swelling above the spot where the warehouse used to be. Wyatt still didn't get it. Didn't understand why Hugh was so adamantly opposed to their tactics, but Hugh's dogged reluctance wasn't going to stop him.

It was nearing nine p.m. During the course of the day, they'd raided four known MS-13 strongholds, all of them empty, all of them showing signs of very recent activity, most of them vacated so recently that the gang members hadn't had time to clean up after themselves.

Besides leveling each base of operations, so far, Wyatt and the guys had destroyed a huge meth lab and a surprisingly high-tech and high-dollar electronic communications network and had confiscated information on the weapons cache they'd just destroyed.

No, they hadn't found Lola, but each raid knocked another chunk off Bonilla's operation and led them closer. Wyatt could feel it.

He checked his watch, ignoring the sour look on Hugh's face.

"Call Doc," he told Mendoza. "Tell him to let Sophie know that we're okay and still looking. And tell her that we have every reason to believe that Lola's still alive," he added as an afterthought, touching his hand to the necklace he'd stuffed into the breast pocket of his Kevlar vest.

He should have made contact with Sophie sooner. Should make the call himself and talk to her directly. But he didn't trust himself to talk to her right now. He was on the down side of his fifth adrenaline overload of the day, and each time they'd come up empty, it had amplified the blood lust pent up inside him.

He was frustrated. He was pissed. He was exhausted. And he didn't want her to hear him that way.

Didn't trust that he wouldn't—

"Doc's not answering."

Wyatt jerked his gaze to Mendoza, whose scowl relayed his alarm. "Try the house phone."

Rafe dialed again, and they waited, the air thick with tension.

Several seconds passed before Mendoza shook his head.

Gabe's and Green's faces were set hard with concern. They both knew there was only one reason Doc wouldn't pick up: he couldn't.

No one said a word as they piled into their vehicles and headed back to Sophie's at warp speed, each and every one of them scared shitless that something bad—something very, very bad—had happened.

"I think I'm going to call it a night."

Doc looked up from the Sig he'd torn apart to clean. The pieces were spread out in all their oil-drenched glory on a newspaper on Sophie's coffee table.

She'd been pacing and fidgety all night. As wired as she was, he seriously doubted she could pull any Zs, but he wished her luck. "Look, I know you're worried, but don't be, okay? The guys know what they're doing. We should be hearing from Wyatt anytime now."

She lingered by the sofa. "It's killing you that you're not out there with them, isn't it?"

He grunted. "You kiddin' me? 'Bout time I pulled some light duty on this gig." He grinned up at her, but he didn't think she bought it.

Just like he didn't buy the notion that Wyatt and Sophie were just friends. He'd seen the way they looked at each other. Seen the strain Hugh Weber had added to the mix. He should keep his mouth shut. Knowing and doing, however, were two different things. He'd always been a gambler. No point in folding his cards now.

"You're the one, aren't you?"

Her gaze cut to his, her brows knitted in question.

"The one Wyatt's carried a torch for all these years."

Her checks flamed red, but she didn't deny or confirm his statement. Didn't matter. He knew.

"Okay, look," he said, sorry now that he'd put her on the spot. "I shouldn't be sticking my nose in where it doesn't belong. Just like it's none of my business what's going on between you and Wyatt now or what's going on between you and your ex, for that matter. But there's something you need to know. They don't come any better than the Papa Bear."

"I know that," she said softly.

"Yeah . . . well, there's something else you need to know."

"Look, Luke—"

He held up a hand, gently cutting her off. "Not my business. I know. But here's the deal. You could hurt him."

She closed her eyes and lowered her head. "I don't want to hurt him."

"I didn't think you did. Just makin' sure we're all on the same page." He smiled for her.

And because she was the woman he hoped she was, she smiled back.

His phone rang then, effectively getting them both

out of a tight spot. "There ya go," he said brightly.
"What'd I tell ya? That'll be Wyatt—"

The glass patio doors exploded in a hail of gunfire.

"Get down!" Doc grabbed the M-4 rifle and leaned
on the trigger, firing into the dark outside the shattered
glass doors, aiming for the muzzle flashes.

When the shooters momentarily backed off to take
cover, he sprang to his feet, grabbed Sophie, and shoved
her behind him, backing toward the kitchen, laying
down cover fire. When they reached the breakfast bar,
he pushed her behind it and dove down after her as five,
maybe six, AKs attacked again, the wrath of 7.62mm
rounds drilling into the house.

They hunkered down behind the counter as pictures danced off the walls; the TV screen exploded with
fire and pop; glassware shattered under the relentless
pounding as they swung their aim toward the kitchen.

Shit. Whoever it was had no intention of making polite conversation. He needed to get Sophie out of there
before they followed their ordinance through the door.

"Go for your SUV!" He had to yell to be heard above
the unremitting strafe of bullets, all the while hoping to
hell he could keep her covered while she crawled the
length of the kitchen floor to the door that led to the
garage.

"Go!" he repeated when she hesitated, then popped
up from behind the cover of the counter and fired off
several rounds. A shadowy figure went down. Score one
for the good guy.

The good guy needed to score real bad, because the

good guy could no longer ignore the fact that he'd been hit. Just like he couldn't count on adrenaline to keep him from fading.

He shook his head and tried to clear the spots that danced behind his eyes. No dice. And worse, right about the time the world started spinning, he realized he couldn't feel his left arm.

Fuck. Fuck!

His knees buckled. He dropped like a bag of sand, landing hard on his ass after sliding down the kitchen cabinets.

"Oh, God. Oh, God. Luke."

He leaned back against the cabinets and fought to keep conscious as Sophie's voice filtered through the cobwebs and the gunfire and a hot, searing pain in his gut.

"Luke . . . talk to me!"

He *was* talking, wasn't he? His mouth was moving . . . he swore it was . . . but he couldn't get any sound to come out.

"Jesus, oh, Jesus."

Why was she crying? Why were her hands red? With disjointed concentration, he squinted through a veil of murky shadows. Tears on her face. Red on her hands.

He felt as if he was a million miles away, couldn't understand why he couldn't see clearly. And why were her hands red again? Why was she—God . . . why was she hurting him? Why was she pressing on his gut with a pretty little towel that had green peppers and yellow squash and red . . . red . . . blood?

Ah. His blood.

QuickClot, he thought, but couldn't say the words. He needed QuickClot to stop the bleeding. To stop *his* bleeding.

Christ, oh, Christ, he'd saved so many men.

Couldn't . . . couldn't save . . . himself.

Couldn't . . . save . . . Sophie.

Wyatt was going to kill him.

"G-go," he managed one more time. She had to get out while she could.

And then, miraculously, she was gone. She screamed and just sort of flew away from him, then hovered above him, her terrified eyes surrounded by hard, tattooed faces. Men's faces. Men holding guns with barrels as black as death.

And then he lost her altogether.

He lost himself as the iron-hard stock of a rifle slammed into the side of his jaw, knocking him over sideways. His face hit the tile floor with a crack. The tile was hard and cold and slippery and running with blood.

The blood from his dead body. On a level he couldn't quite reach, he heard Sophie scream his name again. Heard the far-away sound of a phone. Ringing . . . ringing . . . ringing . . . as red faded slowly to white . . . white spilled silkily into gray . . . gray spun, thick and hazy, into black.

Cold, empty black . . .

They'd thrown a hood over her head, carried her outside, and dumped her into the trunk of a car. Sophie didn't know how long she'd been trapped in there. Long enough that when the trunk lid finally flew open, she gasped for breath.

She didn't know how much time had passed. Didn't know how many bruises she'd suffered. Didn't know if she could bear the guilt over Luke Colter's death or survive this night, when she was dragged out into the dark and hustled into a building. At least it felt as if she was inside a building. She couldn't tell. Couldn't get her bearings. It was all she could do to stay on her feet.

They'd tied her wrists together in front of her. The rope cut into her skin. She barely felt it, or the fingers banded around her upper arm like talons, as she was dragged to a stop.

Someone whipped off the hood. She blinked against the sudden light, willed her eyes to focus, then felt every muscle in her body freeze when she saw the man directly in front of her.

Vincente Bonilla. She'd seen pictures of him in newspaper articles about Mara Salvatrucha gang crimes. None of those grainy black-and-white shots, however, had conveyed the consuming evil in the MS-13 gang leader's face.

"You must be some woman for a man to go to such lengths to help you." Bonilla spoke from his "throne," where he held court like a medieval king in the middle of a squalid room in a derelict building that hosted more than one kind of rat. "Look at me when I talk to you, *chica*."

Not a chance. She was not his slave, and he was

not her master. She looked down at her hands instead, hands covered in Doc's blood that had dried to a rusty brown.

She closed her eyes and tried to block the picture of Luke bleeding out on her kitchen floor. He'd died for her. And for what? Bonilla was still going to kill her.

"I said, look at me when I talk to you, bitch!"

When she still refused to lift her head, the man holding her arm gripped her jaw and jerked her head up, forcing her to confront Bonilla.

"Yes," Bonilla said with a satisfied smile. "I can see why a man might choose to die for you. Later, *chica*, I hope to find out just how much you're worth."

She fought to keep her knees from folding. Forced herself to hold his gaze now, let him see her defiance.

Bonilla glanced at the man holding her and jerked his head in a quick nod. "Bring her to me."

The gangbanger dragged her forward and shoved her to within inches of Bonilla's tattooed face. The hand that had gripped her jaw fisted in her hair and jerked her head back. Pain stabbed through her neck.

She bit back a cry, wouldn't give Bonilla the satisfaction of knowing he'd hurt her.

His laugh was ugly as he reached out and drew his index finger along the side of her face. She knew what he was going to do before he did and swallowed back a gag when he slid his finger over her lips, then slipped it inside her mouth and stroked it across her tongue.

His smile was feral and amused. "You will be a fast learner," he promised. He leaned forward, pressing his foul mouth over hers and replacing his finger with his tongue.

Yeah, she thought when the bastard squeezed her breast with brutal pressure, *I'm a damn fast learner.*

She clamped her teeth down hard.

Bonilla jerked convulsively away from her and roared in pain. "Bitch!"

She'd known when she bit him that he'd make her pay for it. He didn't make her wait. He hauled back and slammed his closed fist into her jaw.

Crashing pain, consuming and electric, ripped through her head, and she felt herself falling. Felt another hideous onslaught of mind-shattering pain when she hit the filthy tile floor.

27

It was dark outside, but the lights were on inside when both vehicles roared to a screeching stop in Sophie's driveway. The front door stood wide open.

A cold fist clenched around Wyatt's heart and squeezed the breath out of him. Sheer adrenaline had him bolting out of the SUV, M-4 shouldered. He sprinted toward the door, peripherally aware of Green and Mendoza breaking right and running around the side of the house toward the backyard. Aware on a tactical level of Hugh and Gabe flanking him, automatically falling into assault entry mode, Wyatt fought a crippling fear of what they would find inside.

He stepped gingerly over the threshold, combat-alert, dread ratcheted up to overdrive. When he saw the devastation, shock sucked the breath out of his lungs like a vacuum.

Jesus.

Destroyed. Everything. Destroyed.

An overkill of holes riddled the walls in an abstract grid fashioned of bullets. Glass windows were shattered.

Art had been shot off the walls. Stuffing poked out of upholstered furniture that looked like it had been splattered with double buckshot. But a shotgun hadn't done this damage. This was the work of an automatic rifle.

This was the work of a kill squad.

Sophie.

All Wyatt could think about was Sophie.

"Clear right," Gabe shouted beside him.

"Clear left," Hugh followed suit, his voice tight with tension.

Wyatt crept slowly forward, afraid of what he'd find, afraid not to look.

"Dead banger," Green announced as he and Mendoza appeared out of the dark by the sliders. Rifles shouldered, they stepped over a body and walked through the destroyed patio doors into the house.

"Jesus," Rafe muttered when he saw the destruction.

Satisfied that the area was clear, Wyatt sprinted for the bedrooms. Adrenaline burned through his chest like hot wax. Hugh was right behind him, as frantic to find Sophie as Wyatt. Gabe followed on their heels as the three of them cleared the bedrooms.

Nothing. No one. No signs of a struggle in that part of the house.

"Doc. Oh, Jesus God, it's Doc!" Mendoza roared like wounded animal.

Wyatt raced back into the living room, following Mendoza's voice, then skidded to a stop when he saw the look in Joe Green's eyes. Joe stood just inside the kitchen, his gaze fixed on the floor behind the counter on a spot Wyatt couldn't see. What he *could* see were the heels of Mendoza's boots, toes down where he knelt on the floor.

Green shook his head, then dropped to his knees beside Mendoza's feet.

Wyatt sprinted around the counter and stopped dead in his tracks when he saw Colter on the floor.

Jesus, there was so much blood. Inching across the floor like spilled paint. Covering Mendoza's hands as he checked for vitals.

Wyatt's own blood turned to sludge.

"He's got a pulse." Mendoza's voice rose with guarded excitement as he leaned over their fallen brother. "Weak. Thready. Fast. And, fuck, barely there."

He pressed his cheek against Doc's nose. "He's breathing. Just barely. Get Doc's kit. His kit, his kit! Someone get his goddamn medic kit!" he shouted, just short of hysterical.

Wyatt joined Mendoza on the floor when Green bolted out of the kitchen in search of Doc's medical kit. "What do you want me to do?"

"I don't know. I don't fucking know!" Mendoza's eyes were wild with a fear bred by helplessness. "*Doc's* the Doc. *He* fixes this kind of shit. Shit!" He swore again, raked a shaking hand through his hair, then pulled himself together. "Okay. What would Doc do? Stop the bleeding. Gotta stop the bleeding, right? Gotta keep him from going into shock."

Wyatt didn't say it, but he was afraid it was already too late to worry about shock setting in. Doc's skin was pale, cool to the touch, and clammy. "Let's get him on his back," he said, forcing himself to push back his concern over Sophie.

Sophie, who was gone. Who was still alive—had to be alive. Otherwise, why would they take her?

He helped Mendoza carefully turn Doc onto his back, then sucked in a sickened breath when he saw the size of the hole in his side.

Jesus, how can he still be alive?

Mendoza swallowed hard and pulled his KA-Bar out of the sheath on his belt. He cut away the blood-soaked shirt surrounding the wound with shaking hands. "Get me a towel. Towel!" he demanded, frantic to save his friend.

Wyatt was already in the process of raiding Sophie's cabinet drawers. He grabbed a handful of dish towels and shoved them into Rafe's outstretched hand.

"Compression, right? It's all about compression." Mendoza pressed the stack of towels to the seeping hole in Doc's belly. "Where's that kit? Gotta be some Quick-Clot in there."

Green came flying back to the kitchen just then. He skidded on the blood and went down, full out on his side. Without missing a beat, he scrambled to his knees, ripped open the bag, and rammed around inside until he found the clotting agent they'd all seen Doc use to field treat wounds.

Only once, though, had they seen a wound this big. This bad. Wyatt glanced at Green as Mendoza worked frantically to stem the blood flow, applying the quick-clot and replacing the blood-soaked towels with trauma

dressings. Wyatt knew that Green and every one of the
BOIs in the room were thinking of Bryan Tompkins,
who had bled out in the mud and the rot and the gore
of Sierra Leone. They couldn't lose Doc, too.

"We've got to get him to a trauma center." Mendoza
glanced up at Wyatt, desperation clouding his eyes.

Wyatt looked to Hugh for information.

"You're wasting valuable time on a dead man. We
need to find Sophie!"

Only because he understood where Hugh was coming from did Wyatt resist planting a fist in his face.
"Where?" Wyatt demanded on a roar.

"Closest hospital is Rosales," Hugh said, having the
sense to back off. "It's a good forty minutes out."

Gabe stepped into the kitchen, carrying an armload
of sheets and bath towels. Green stood up and helped
him fold the sheets into a litter, while Wyatt and Rafe
carefully and quickly bound a bath towel around Doc's
torso in a makeshift compression bandage.

"He needs blood." The quiet desperation in Rafe's
tone laid bare the depth of his fear.

Each and every one of them had been patched up by
Doc at some point. Each and every one of them owed
him his life. Now Doc's life was hanging by a thread,
and they felt helpless to save him.

"He'll get it." Gabe laid a hand on Rafe's shoulder
and squeezed. SOP required that the team knew one
another's blood type. And while each man there would
bleed himself dry for Doc, the blood he would get
would be Gabe's. If he made it to a hospital.

"Let's get him loaded." They all gripped a corner of the sheet. "On three.

"Rafe, you need to go, too," Wyatt said after they'd carefully loaded Luke's limp body into the back of the Suburban.

Rafe gave a jerky nod, made a quick swipe at his eyes with the back of his hand, and climbed into the back with Doc.

"Call Nate. He needs to know."

Gabe nodded and climbed in behind the wheel.

Wyatt didn't have to look at Green's face to know he wanted to go with them to the hospital. Hell, so did Wyatt. But Sophie was out there somewhere. And he needed both Green and Hugh to help him get her back.

He stood in the dark, hot night, watched with a lump in his throat as Gabe sped off to the hospital, following Hugh's directions.

"Look, I'm sorry about your man," Hugh said, breaking into Wyatt's thoughts as he stood there wondering if he'd see Doc alive again. "But you'd just as well face it. Gut-shot like that? He's not going to make it."

Green spun around, got right in Hugh's face. "Shut the fuck up!"

They were all stretched wire-tight. Just when it looked as if Hugh might not have the sense to back down in the face of Green's rage, Wyatt's cell phone rang.

He didn't recognize the number on the digital read-out. A sick feeling boiled through his gut. He glanced at Hugh and flipped open the phone.

"Savage."

"Wyatt." Sophie. Scared.

Wyatt's heart slammed against his ribs. "Sophie, where are you? Are you hurt?"

A wild desperation filled Hugh's his eyes when he heard Sophie's name. He grabbed for the phone. Wyatt turned away from him, gripped the cell phone tighter against his ear, straining to hear her.

"No, I'm not hurt . . . but Doc . . . Wyatt, they killed—" That was all she got out before he heard sounds of a struggle.

"Wyatt Savage." A gravelly voice grated over the line. "So, I finally speak with the man who has torn apart my operation."

Bonilla. Wyatt fought to control his rage at the thought of Bonilla having his hands on Sophie.

"You hurt her, you're a dead man, Bonilla," he promised with stone-cold intent.

"Speaking of dead men. I trust you found yours where my men left him?"

A crippling wave of guilt swamped him. He'd wanted to smoke out Vincente Bonilla, but not at the cost of Doc's life.

"You have caused much trouble, Savage. Cost me much money and many resources. I am way behind you on the body count." A total void of emotion made Bonilla's words all the more chilling. "The beautiful Sophie Weber will be a good start on settling the score, I think. Unless you want to pay to get her back."

"I repeat. You hurt her, you're dead."

Bonilla laughed. "Perhaps we can negotiate a trade. Your life for hers would be a start, eh?"

"Sophie and the child," Wyatt demanded. "You want the money, you trade for both."

"Fine, but the price is double," Bonilla agreed.

"Name the place."

"La Cola del Diablo. Three hours. And come alone." The line went dead.

28

Hugh looked like a wild man when Wyatt hung up. "If that bastard hurts her, I'll kill him."

"You're going to have to stand in line." Wyatt rushed into the house. He dug through the rubble until he found the area maps on the floor. "La Cola del Diablo. What is it? Where is it?"

"Jesus." Hugh's face went pale. "La Cola del Diablo. The Devil's Tail."

Wyatt spread the maps out on the kitchen counter. "Show me."

Hugh joined Wyatt at the counter. "It's a spit of barren land in the middle of the jungle." He pointed to a spot on the map. "About an hour south of the city."

Wyatt scrubbed both hands over his face, his mind racing. "Why does he want to meet up there? Why not in the city, where he'd be in his element?"

"Because La Cola del Diablo is sacred ground to Mara Salvatrucha. They claimed it as gang territory years ago," Hugh said impatiently.

"Bastards don't know sacred from sacrilegious."

"Trust me, it's sacred to them. And they'd died protecting it. It's the ritual he's after. The Devil's Tail is Bonilla's killing ground. It's where he stages his ceremonial executions." Hugh looked worried. "What exactly did he say?"

"That if I wanted Sophie and Lola, I was to come alone and bring double the initial ransom."

"Fuck that," Joe said. "Even if you had the money, he's not going to let you walk away from that alive. He's not going to release Sophie or the girl, either."

"So we figure out a way to make that happen." Wyatt turned to Hugh. "You know how he thinks. How's he going to play this?"

Hugh rolled a shoulder. "He'll want to make it a spectacle, gather all of his lieutenants and put on a big show for them."

"That would explain why he gave me three hours. He needs time to gather the troops. What kind of numbers are we talking?"

Hugh cupped his nape and shook his head. "His elite force is made up of thirty or so, maybe. All of them have maimed, tortured, and murdered to reach their lofty status."

Wyatt nodded. "Okay. So he's pissed that we put the hurt on his operations, wants to kill me in front of his big mouths. The ones sure to spread the word about how big and bad he is to keep the ranks in line."

"And he'll want to do it ugly. Beef up his 'legend' status," said Joe.

Wyatt smiled with grim understanding. "Hell, he sees me as a recruiting tool."

"He *sees* you fucking dead," Hugh said. "And when the smoke clears, he'll still have Sophie."

"Like hell he will." Wyatt's phone rang again. Nate Black's number showed up on the readout. Wyatt swallowed hard, then answered. "You talked to Gabe?"

"Yeah. Doc's hanging on, but it's bad," Nate said. "Juliana's reaching out to the medical community there. She's tight with a trauma surgeon on staff at Rosales. He'll take care of him. Now, fill me in on what's happening."

That was Nate. He was hurting over Doc as badly as the rest of them, but he wasn't going to wallow in what they couldn't fix. The best thing any of them could do for Doc right now was to get the bastards who had done this to him. And the best thing he could do for Sophie and Lola was to keep a cool head.

Wyatt nutshelled the call from Bonilla, bringing Nate up to speed on what he'd be up against at La Cola del Diablo.

"What do you need from me?" Nate asked.

"The fucking moon, but I'll settle for a distraction. Something to get Bonilla to forget about Sophie and Lola long enough to give us a window to get them out of there. I don't suppose Uncle has any boots on the ground that you can reach out and put the touch on?"

The United States still had a number of Spec Ops units and resources stationed in El Salvador, the Army's

Special Forces—a.k.a. Green Berets, Green Beanies—
most notable. Nate was a former Marine, but he had
solid Army connections.

"What's our time frame?" Nate asked.

"A little less than three hours."

"Keep the line open. I'll be back in touch," Nate
said, and disconnected.

Sophie saw nothing but pitch dark, felt nothing but
stabbing, all-encompassing pain as they shoved the
hood over her head again. She was hauled roughly to
her feet, dragged back outside again, and shoved into
a vehicle. A van, she thought, recognizing the sound
of a door rolling on a track before it slammed shut. An
engine roared to life, and the vehicle started moving.

For long moments, she just lay on her side on the
cold metal floor of the van. Her head felt as if it had
been split with an axe. A throbbing ache pounded in
her jaw, warning her against opening her mouth in case
Bonilla had broken her jaw when he'd hit her.

She squinted into the dark. Saw nothing but black
cloth. Smelled nothing but dust and fear. Heard nothing but an incessant ringing in her ears, the beat of her
own heart . . . and the ragged sound of shallow breaths.

Not hers.

Oh, God. Someone or something was in here with her.

Her heart slammed inside her chest as she willed
herself to concentrate. She got more pain for her effort.

"Who . . . who's there?" she whispered.

Nothing.

"Who's there?" she whispered again, this time in Spanish.

An eternity passed in the space of several heartbeats before a weak, fragile voice whispered back, "Lola."

Wyatt headed straight for La Cola del Diablo, wanting to get ahead of Bonilla and his death squad and figure all angles. With the SUV hidden off-trail behind the Devil's Tail and away from the main access road, they'd scrambled to the top of the ridge at the edge of the jungle directly above and approximately twenty yards away from the section of land called La Cola del Diablo.

Hugh and Green were bellied down in the dirt beside Wyatt as he scanned the area with night-vision binoculars. The name was fitting. The Devil's Tail was a narrow strip of earth roughly three city blocks long but less than fifteen yards across at its widest point, down to maybe five yards at its narrow end. And yes, it very much resembled a tail.

An anomaly, Hugh had said. *Fuck, yeah.* In this area of El Salvador, every inch of soil that wasn't covered in asphalt or cement grew thick and solid with jungle. Hack three feet clean one day, and the next, the growth would have taken over like a cancer. Yet the black earth that made up La Cola del Diablo was as barren as an oil spill. Not one plant, not one tree, not one iota of life sprang from the tail as it snaked across the landscape.

It was spooky as hell.

"No one knows why," Hugh had told him as they sped out of town with Green at the wheel obliterating speed limits to get there ahead of Bonilla and his lieutenants. "And since MS-13 chases off any scientific expedition sent down to find out, it remains a mystery.

"Nothing supports it, but local legend claims La Cola del Diablo was the site of an ancient Mayan sacrificial altar. The story goes that so much blood was spilled and flowed down the length of the tail that the earth died. That's why it can no longer support life."

Wyatt figured a helluva lot more blood was going to be spilled before the night was over. He'd already resigned himself to the possibility that this desolate piece of ground might be his own killing ground. The chances were slim that he was walking away from this. But Sophie . . . somehow, he was getting her out of this alive.

His cell vibrated in his pocket. Nate.

He back-crawled off the ridge and answered. A few minutes later, he hung up and bellied back down between Joe and Hugh.

"What?" Joe asked.

"Nate's SF connections came through. We've got game."

"Fuck," Joe said after hearing the details.

Fuck was right. Their entire game plan hinged on a wish, a prayer, and how far Bonilla was willing to go to protect his sacred grounds. And on Wyatt pulling off the biggest bluff of his life.

He scrubbed a hand over his face and listened to the roar of arriving motorcycles, cars, and trucks as the gangbangers gathered via the offroad trail that led to the tip of the Devil's Tail in this hole in the jungle. Lights started flickering around the perimeter of La Cola del Diablo as Bonilla's bangers began forming loose lines on either side of the sacred ground, settling in for ringside seats to his execution.

Wyatt counted at least twenty so far, which meant a few more of Bonilla's elite had yet to arrive before the fun started.

"Check it out." Hugh's voice interrupted his thoughts.

A paneled van emerged out of a break in the jungle and crawled slowly up the length of the Tail. Wyatt followed the vehicle with his NV binoculars until it rolled to a stop at the thickest end of the Tail, where it appeared the action was going to go down. The driver's door opened, and a tank of a man squeezed out, lumbered slowly around to the passenger side, and opened the door.

"Fancies himself a fucking master of the universe," Green sputtered as Bonilla stepped out of the van. He wore his blue and white gang colors on a do rag tied around his head. His arms were bare. Leather bands were wrapped around his wrists. Ammo belts crisscrossed the network of gang tattoos covering his chest. Wyatt could make out a sheathed knife at his belt.

He looked like a bad imitation of a *bandito* villain straight out of a *Rambo* flick.

"*Guerrillas* gone wild," Wyatt muttered, and got a snort from Green that cut a chunk out of the tension.

The side panel of the van slid open. Wyatt bit back an oath when the "tank" reached inside and jerked a blindfolded Sophie roughly out of the vehicle. Unable to get her balance with her hands bound in front of her, she stumbled and fell to her knees.

Beside him, Hugh snarled between clenched teeth.

The child appeared next. Small, fragile. Terrified. Also blindfolded and bound.

Still on her knees, Sophie reached out, blindly groped the air. She must have called Lola's name, because the little girl turned abruptly and stumbled toward her, then huddled against her in the night.

"I count thirty individual lights now," Green said, locked in recon mode. "Hail, hail, the gang's all here."

"They've formed their ritual horseshoe in front of Bonilla," Hugh said, sounding relieved. "Bastards are so cocky they left their flank vulnerable."

Score one for the good guys. It was exactly the break they needed if Sophie was going to get away.

Wyatt lowered his field glasses and drew a deep breath. "Okay. You both know what to do."

"You're committing fucking suicide," Hugh said for the umpteenth time.

"Just be ready to move in and get them out of there." Wyatt backed away from the ridge. "And make it fast," he said as they parted ways, Wyatt heading for the narrow end of the Tail and Hugh and Joe circling around behind to where they'd hidden the SUV fifty yards from Bonilla's unprotected flank, "because if and when Nate's SF buddies deliver on their promise, they won't waste any time pulling the trigger."

*   *   *

Five minutes later, Wyatt walked out of the jungle and started up the length of the narrow Tail, holding his arms away from his body, palms up to show he wasn't carrying, aware that every banger present was watching every step he took. He didn't let himself think about anything but the man standing directly in front of him. He didn't let himself think about Joe Green's somber eyes before Wyatt had ordered him to drive the hell away from there as soon as they got Sophie and Lola clear. Didn't let himself think of his momma, sad-eyed and holding up as they played Taps at his funeral. Didn't think of Annie's little tow-headed toddler and feel the regret that he might never know what his own son might have looked like.

Most of all, he didn't let himself look at Sophie, because if he did, his heart would fucking fly right out of his chest, and then where the hell would he be? Bonilla wanted his heart. He was ready to give it, if he had to.

All of his senses were hyperaware of his surroundings. The triple-canopy trees rising high above, reaching wide at their apex, spanning across the sky, and in spots joining and entwining to form a leafy ceiling over the barren ground.

He breathed deep as he walked closer. Smelled jungle loam in the near distance juxtaposed with the pungent scent of his own sweat. And somewhere in the back of his mind, he smelled Sophie. Fresh from the shower, her dark hair wet and heavy in his hands. Aroused and needing him, her body liquid and giving beneath him. Her hands soft and greedy on his skin.

He stopped ten feet away from Bonilla. Made himself look at Sophie. They'd removed her blindfold and posed her beside Bonilla like a puppet. It had to piss Bonilla off something fierce that she hadn't submitted to him. Bruised and defiant, she stood with her shoulders pulled back, the child huddled against her side.

Bruised but not broken, he thought with pride, even though his gut clenched with rage at the sight of her swollen, discolored face.

He shifted his attention back to Bonilla's thugs, who circled the periphery of the makeshift gladiator-type arena, milling around like gnats on rancid meat. They were all armed to the teeth. Any one of them could take him out with one shot in very short order. Bonilla need only say the word, and Wyatt was a dead man.

He was counting on Bonilla wanting him all to himself. Hell, he was counting on a lot of things.

He glanced skyward, breathed deep, and started the show.

"If I'd known we were going to have such a big audience," Wyatt said, pinning Bonilla with a steely glare, "I'd have showered and shaved."

"If I had known you'd actually show up, I would have made certain you would have played to a larger crowd."

"Okay. This is all real nice and friendly, but we've had our chitchat moment, okay? I'm here. Now what?"

Bonilla's smile tightened. "Now you make me a million dollars richer."

"Yeah, about that. Couldn't find a bank open this time of night. Go figure. But then, this isn't really about the money tonight, is it? It's about you having your pant-ies in a twist because I've broken some of your toys and-fucked up your fun."

Bonilla's eyes narrowed. "Do you think, then, that insulting me and showing up empty-handed makes you a brave man or just a foolish one?"

"What I think," Wyatt said, choosing his words care-fully, "doesn't matter. What matters is that you let both the woman and the child go."

Bonilla made a sweeping glance at his lieutenants to show them how amused he was by Wyatt's demand. "Not only foolish but insane. Unless you've got an army hidden somewhere, you don't have the leverage to make any demands on me."

"Funny you should mention that." Wyatt smiled tightly. "The army was otherwise engaged. Well, most of it was. Lucky I didn't need most of it. Just a pair of birds with a couple of big guns."

29

Bonilla's smile faded, and Wyatt went in for the kill.

"Seriously. You didn't think I'd be stupid enough to come out here without backup," he pressed while he had Bonilla off balance and wondering. "Man in my line of work doesn't live too long without knowing how to make friends in high places."

Bonilla puffed out his chest. "How stupid do you think I am? The U.S. military is not going to get involved in your personal problem."

"Well, hell no. At least, not so that anyone would know. But let me tell you how this works. Back in the day when Uncle footed the bill for my *sanctioned* ops, I fudged my fair share of after-action reports for unauthorized missions. Boys will be boys, right? And boys get bored. We'd go out, have some fun with our high-tech toys, then write those little extracurricular raids up as routine training ops. No harm. No foul. No U.S. intervention where they weren't supposed to intervene. At least, none that any four-star in the Department of Defense would ever see and question.

"Anyway," he continued, knowing he had Bonilla wondering, "the SF boys down here still get bored, you know? They're always up for some off-the-books action." He glanced skyward, smiled, then met Bonilla's glare. "Like tonight."

Bonilla narrowed his eyes. "You're bluffing."

Damn, he hoped not.

"You a movie buff, Bonilla?" Wyatt asked casually, and prayed like hell that Nate's buddies came through. There hadn't been any opportunity to arrange commo, so he was flying blind. "Ever see *Black Hawk Down*? Those Little Bird light-attack gunships are amazing, right? Couple of those babies unload, oh, say, right *here*, and all that's going to be left of your sacred Devil's Tail is a shitload of spent M134 mini-gun shells and bloody banger body parts."

Every banger on the Tail was looking nervous and looking skyward now.

"I don't hear nothing," Bonilla said, calling Wyatt out.

Neither did Wyatt, but Nate said they'd be here, so they'd be here. The question was when. Someday—if he lived through this—he'd find out what kind of favors Nate had called in.

"Don't worry. They're up there. Silent as the wind— but then, you know that's how the Little Birds fly, don't you?"

Bonilla didn't want to buy it, but it was looking more and more like he was afraid not to.

"Okay, look," Wyatt said, and made a pretense of checking his watch. "Here's the deal. I need to give the birds a signal to back off in"—he tapped the watch face—"thirty seconds, or they're going to unload. Then there's not going to be anything left of you or your sacred ground but scorched earth and a big damn hole."

Bonilla eyed him with defiant suspicion. "You wouldn't risk getting the woman killed."

"You're going to kill her anyway," he said, making it clear that the fun and games were over. "If you don't let her go, at least I'll have the satisfaction of knowing you're going to die, too.

"Twenty-five seconds," he reminded Bonilla, and touched a finger to his ear, listening for commo from the Little Birds through an earpiece that was actually Joe's Bluetooth earbud.

"And what do I get if I let them go?" Bonilla asked abruptly.

Wyatt breathed his first breath of relief since he'd walked out of the jungle and stepped into Bonilla's lair. He was sniffing the bait.

"Simple. I call off the birds. You keep your sacred ground intact. And you get *me* in exchange for Sophie and the child."

Bonilla glared at him, still fighting with wanting to believe him.

"Eighteen seconds," Wyatt said, pouring on the pressure. *Fucking let them go*, he willed Bonilla silently. "Fifteen."

One of the lieutenants stepped forward and spoke to Bonilla in rapid-fire Spanish.

Wyatt didn't catch it all, but he got enough to know

it was a warning. They didn't want their sacred ground destroyed. They didn't want to die.

"If you know any prayers," Wyatt said, twisting the screws, "better say them in ten, nine . . ."

Come on, you sonofabitch. Bite.

"All right," Bonilla said, his tone urgent. "Call them off."

Wyatt tucked his chin into his collar and the infrared strobe he'd clipped there, hoping to hell it would pass as a commo mike in the dimly lit night. "Nightstalker One. Nightstalker Two. You are not cleared for gun runs. Repeat, *not* cleared. Stand by for further in thirty seconds—repeat—stand by for further or commence fire in thirty seconds."

He took a step toward Bonilla, his hand poised on his collar, a warning that he could rescind the order at any time. "Let them go. Now."

Bonilla glared, then nodded to his muscle man.

"Give her a flashlight," Wyatt demanded after the "tank" cut the bindings on Sophie's wrists.

Bonilla glared but nodded again, and one of the men handed her a flashlight.

Wyatt let himself look at Sophie then, willed himself not to buckle under the weight of the terror in her eyes.

"Go." He notched his chin toward Bonilla's unprotected flank, where Hugh and Joe had by God better be in position with the SUV to haul ass out of there. "Take Lola and go," he repeated.

Tension as tight as a zip line hummed over the back

of the Devil's Tail as tears and fear and yearning filled Sophie's eyes.

"It's okay," he assured her, and felt a staggering relief when she turned and, with Lola's hand gripped tightly in hers, started running.

Wyatt watched the beam from the mag-light bounce away from the crowd of bangers and finally disappear in the dark of the jungle behind them.

"Call them off!" Bonilla yelled, nervous that his thirty-second deadline was upon them.

"Nightstalker One. Nightstalker Two," Wyatt said into his fake mike, and played out the charade. "Hold fire. Repeat, hold all fire."

Bonilla's smile was smug and feral when Wyatt met his eyes again. "You actually think they can survive out there alone, in the dark with the night creatures?"

The unmistakable sound of the SUV roaring to life and then car doors slamming came from the direction Sophie had run with Lola.

Thank you, God!

They'd made it. Hugh and Joe had them and were driving them the hell away from there.

It was his turn to smile with smug satisfaction. "Yeah, well, I don't think the night creatures are going to be a problem."

Bonilla's expression changed from smug to seething rage when he realized he'd been had.

"So, Vincente." Wyatt tilted his head. "Looks like it comes down to you and me . . . and your band of merry miscreants," he added with a nod toward the bangers.

"You played me," Bonilla said, his fists clenched at his sides. "There are no gunships."

"Yeah, well, about that—"

Bonilla's roar cut him off. He charged like a mad bull, driving his head into Wyatt's gut like a battering ram. He landed on his back with Bonilla straddling him, his left hand wrapped around the hilt of a pipe knife, the blade dagger-sharp, narrow as a stiletto, long as a damn hammer handle.

Bonilla reared back and made a vicious swipe at him. Wyatt blocked the strike with a forearm, used the opportunity to knock Bonilla off balance and his weight for leverage, and flipped Bonilla onto his back.

The banger was agile and quick. A street brawler— more dangerous than a formally trained fighter because he wouldn't even pretend to fight by any rules. And Bonilla knew how to use Wyatt's weight against him.

He heaved and bucked and maneuvered Wyatt to his back again, until they were rolling over the dead, black dirt, the blade between them. The bullets in Bonilla's bandoliers dug into Wyatt's chest, gouged the hell out of his sternum.

He rolled to his back, using Bonilla's momentum against him, and while Bonilla was on the rise, Wyatt flipped him over his shoulder. Bonilla was still airborne when Wyatt shot to his feet. He reached into the leather knife sheath he'd tucked into his boot and whipped out his KA-Bar just as Bonilla flew at him again.

Fire burned the length of his left bicep as Bonilla connected with his blade. Wyatt rolled away from the attack; searing pain radiated down his arm to his elbow.

He pushed himself up and balanced on the balls of his feet. Ignoring the blood trailing down the fingers of his left hand, he hefted the KA-Bar in his right and looked for a way past Bonilla's defenses.

"The ground will run red with your blood before I'm finished with you," Bonilla taunted, his white teeth glinting through his smirk of satisfaction.

"What? This scratch? If that's the best you've got, you don't deserve to wear the gang colors."

It always amazed Wyatt that so many professed killers didn't get that fighting wasn't about being pissed off. Fighting was about mind over matter, inertia over brawn, calm over rage.

Bonilla was falling behind on all three. He roared again. Lunged again. Wyatt dodged left. He spun a full three-sixty, hooked out his foot on the back swing, and caught Bonilla hard on his shin. The gang leader crashed face-first into the dirt.

He was fast, though, and up on his feet again before Wyatt could move in. Ignoring the fire raging in his left arm, Wyatt assumed a wide-legged crouch, dancing his weight from one foot to the other, egging on Bonilla to strike again. He didn't disappoint him.

Bonilla charged in, shoulders high, and at the last second dove for Wyatt's left knee. The impact knocked him off-balance. Before he could recover, Bonilla tackled him to the ground. The knife sliced down again, straight for his throat. Wyatt jerked his head left, blocked with a forearm, and felt the tip of the blade slice his ear-lobe before slamming into the dirt beside his head.

He rolled again, bucked Bonilla off, and swung the blade all in one motion. When he felt it connect with bone and heard Bonilla's gasp of pain, he doubled his pressure on the blade, following through with his forward motion.

Bonilla groaned, and Wyatt hesitated, trying to get a read on the damage he'd done to Bonilla's ribs. It proved a crucial mistake. Propelled by pain and bone-deep survival instincts, Bonilla hauled back with a wild swing that caught Wyatt across his chest in a slashing diagonal slice that spanned from his right collarbone to just under his left pec.

Wyatt rolled again and rose to his knees, breathing hard as Bonilla struggled to rise to a sitting position. Wyatt didn't hesitate this time. He shot from his knees and, sucking air, flew the scant three feet to reach Bonilla.

His shoulder rammed into Bonilla's chest, slamming him to his back and knocking the wind out of him. Wyatt went in for the kill. He levered his left forearm over Bonilla's throat, choking off his air supply. Then he jammed the blade up and under Bonilla's ribs, ripping his diaphragm and severing the aorta.

Bonilla's eyes widened with shock, then narrowed with the realization that he was a dead man.

Dark eyes, pleading for life, locked on Wyatt's. A palsied hand reached up, grabbed at his shirt, fingers curling into a claw that never found purchase.

"That was for Sophie," Wyatt gritted. "This is for

Lola." He gave the knife one final hard twist, and Bonilla stopped breathing.

For a long moment, Wyatt couldn't move. He lay on top of the dead gang leader, panting for breath. He finally rolled off him, lay prostrate on the bloody ground, gathering strength, blood pumping from the adrenaline feed, head ringing from the blood loss.

And then the ground lit up like a football field.

The Little Birds had arrived, searchlights engaged.

Fuck. Holy fuck. He needed to get up. He needed to find cover. He needed . . . *shit.* He needed a bunker, but he wasn't going to get one. Weak from blood loss, all he could do was lie there under the whip of the rotor wash as the birds dropped closer and started leveling the field with a barrage of the M134 guns.

He covered his eyes with his arm to shield them against the blinding lights that lanced into the darkness.

This is it, he thought, and felt a calm settle over him unlike any he'd ever experienced.

This is the moment I am going to die.

He breathed deep of night and his own sweat and blood and gave himself over to fate. On one last concession to faith, he fumbled with the IR strobe he'd attached to his collar and flipped it on.

Not that it would save him now. He was bull's-eye center in the kill zone. The pilots were good, they'd be looking for his light. But they weren't that good. He knew it. They knew it. Just like he knew they'd do what they were best at, what they'd been trained to do: kill bad guys and break their toys.

The bangers had mobilized. They shouldered their AKs and fired skyward. Wyatt watched with a disconnected sort of awe as the belly of a Little Bird breached the opening in the canopy of trees, then dropped like a feather into the kill zone. Tracer rounds danced through the dark like a laser show. The earth erupted as fiery bursts from the guns peppered the Devil's Tail on either side of him, thundering through the night like black death.

Bangers screamed and swore and dropped under the onslaught of the M134 guns that roared like chainsaws and were every bit as destructive. Brass from thousands of spent shells rained down. It was like lying out in the open in a hailstorm, only the hot brass burned his skin and would never melt away to nothing.

This is it, he thought one last time when a gun run slammed shells into the dirt within a yard of his head. Then he closed his eyes and waited for the volley that would take him.

30

"For the last time, Sophie," Hugh ground out, "we need to get out of here."

"And for the last time, we are not leaving him!" Sophie glared at Hugh from the backseat, weary of the argument, determined to win.

Hugh sat behind the wheel of the SUV, engine running, his expression just short of savage. Once they'd escaped Bonilla and piled into the SUV, Hugh had driven no more than fifty yards away from the Devil's Tail when she had ordered, demanded, and, finally, near hysterics, screamed at him to stop.

When he hadn't complied, it was Joe who finally convinced him with a firm, concise threat. "Stop the fucking vehicle, or I'll blow your fucking head off."

That had been less than fifteen minutes ago, and the barrage of gunfire from the attack helicopters hadn't let up since.

Hugh had fallen into a sullen silence. Sophie had drawn her knees to her chest and lowered her head between them, praying for the gunfire to stop. But like the relentless whine of the choppers' turbo engines, the guns just kept firing and firing and firing.

Wyatt. Oh, God. Wyatt was out there, and it didn't matter how many times Joe Green told her he was wearing an infrared strobe that the pilot could see and therefore would not target, she didn't know how he could possibly survive the devastating excess of firepower.

Tears blurred her vision, but she tried to keep it together for Lola's sake. The little girl was already traumatized. So traumatized that when Joe Green had scooped her up in his arms and hustled her out of Bonilla's clutches, Lola had latched on to him like a monkey. She'd clung like Velcro ever since, and Joe—big, tough, ate-razor-blades-for-breakfast Joe—hadn't had the heart to pry her off his big body. He'd just held her, patted her little back with his big hand, and told her nobody was going to hurt her again.

"They've stopped," Green said into a sudden silence. *The guns have stopped!*

Sophie lifted her head. She looked out the window and up into a jungle canopy as black as onyx and watched the lights from the Little Birds fade away.

"We have to find him." She shoved open the SUV's rear door and stepped out into the dark. Wyatt was out there. Hurt. Possibly dying. She refused to believe he was dead.

Hugh piled out from behind the driver's seat and caught her when she would have run blindly into the dark. He jerked her around to face him. "He was already down, Sophie. Listen to me." He gave her a shake when she tried to pull away. "He was down in the middle of the kill zone. No one could have survived that attack."

She pulled against his hold on her arm. "We're not leaving him out there!"

"You heard the lady."

She whipped her head around and saw Joe, his arms still full of Lola, rounding the front of the vehicle and walking toward them.

"All right." Hugh heaved a deep breath. "But you're staying here. Tell her she's staying here," he said with a glance over his shoulder at Joe.

"He's right," Joe said over Lola's head. "The boys in the birds had to have lit up most of the bangers, but some of them could have scattered into the jungle. They could come out shooting at any time. You aren't going to do Wyatt or anyone else any good if you become a target."

He tried to hand the little girl over to Sophie, clearly intending to help Hugh search for Wyatt. But when Lola whimpered and clung tighter, a "What am I going to do?" look came over his face.

Hugh gave Joe a nod. "One of us needs to stay with Sophie and Lola. Looks like you're it."

Then Hugh grabbed a mag-light and an M-4 and headed back toward the Devil's Tail.

The pain told him he was alive. The pain and the sudden silence. It was that silence that had Wyatt finally opening his eyes to an empty sky.

The birds were gone. Mission accomplished.

And *damn*, he *was* alive while only inches away from where he lay, the earth smoked like the fires of hell.

"Wyatt!"

The voice came out of the distant dark, competing with the ringing in his ears. He listened, not sure if he'd imagined it.

"Savage!"

Not his imagination. It was Hugh. He recognized his voice.

He jerked upright, fought back a wave of dizziness, and squinted into the night. A bouncing white light danced toward him. A mag-light, growing closer as its beams swept the field. Searching.

On a grunt of pain, he rolled to his stomach, surprised that all of his limbs were attached and working. Another push, and he rose to his knees, then promptly sat back on his heels when another wave of dizziness swamped him.

"Over here!" he managed, surprised when his words sounded so faint.

Hugh sprinted over to his side, a hard look on his face. "I don't fucking believe it."

Wyatt grunted. "Makes two of us. Help me up." He held up a hand . . . and got a boot in his chest that slammed him to his back.

He gasped against the new insult of pain, then shook off the surprise and focused on Hugh's face. One look at his old friend's eyes, and he knew. *Jesus*. Everything came together in that heartbeat. Everything he hadn't wanted to see or believe about why Hugh had dragged his feet, fought him at every turn.

"Why couldn't you just die?" Hugh glared at him, his expression a mix of remorse and anger and wild-eyed desperation. "Why couldn't you just fucking die?"

How ironic was this? He'd survived Bonilla. Lived through the Little Bird air strike. Now he was going to die at the hands of a man he had once called brother.

"Not going to be easy killing me, huh?"

Hugh glared at him, the cold determination in his eyes drilling to the bone. "I've wanted you dead since I found you in my wife's bed."

"Yeah, I got that," Wyatt said, fighting through the pain of his knife wounds that paled in the face of Hugh's betrayal. "But that's not why you're going to kill me. This has to do with Bonilla, doesn't it?"

Hugh laughed grimly. "Always were too smart for me, Bear. When did you figure it out?"

"That you were in bed with Bonilla on Lola's kidnapping?" He shrugged, angry, disappointed, disillusioned, and soon, if Hugh had his way, dead. "Not soon enough. Wasn't until tonight, when Nate Black told me that our IO had discovered you were in El Salvador all along that it started to come together. Couldn't figure out why you'd let Sophie think you weren't here. But things had been working on me, you know? I guess I had a big blind spot when it came to you . . . being you've been like a brother to me and all."

Hugh's mouth tightened. Guilt and regret flashed across his face. Not enough, though. Not enough to stop him from pulling the trigger.

"Tell me something. Why didn't you just help her if you were here all along?" Wyatt asked, hoping that if he kept him talking, bought some time, he could figure a way out.

Hugh shook his head, a wild, desperate look in his eyes. "That turned out to be a bad call on my part."

"Because she called me in when she couldn't reach you," Wyatt surmised.

"Yeah," he said bitterly. "Because of that."

"Why?" Wyatt asked. "Why are you involved in this? Why abduct Lola?"

"It wasn't supposed to be Lola!" Hugh roared, and Wyatt saw more than just desperation and regret. He saw the desolate helplessness of a man on the edge. "It was supposed to be Hope."

"Your own child?"

"She's not my fucking kid!" He pointed the M-4 dead center at Wyatt's chest, his eyes beyond wild now and edging toward insanity. "Christ, it was supposed to be a cake walk. Sophie's old man would pay up, we got her back. End of story. Nobody was supposed to get hurt."

"But I showed up and threw a wrench in the gears." Wyatt struggled to raise himself on his elbows, gritted out the pain in both his arm and his chest. "Makes sense now. You've been pulling the strings on this all along. Had your thugs feed us bogus leads to steer us away from Bonilla. You sent us running around like chickens with our heads cut off."

"For your own damn good! I tried to save you. I tried to get you the hell out of the picture. But you couldn't stop yourself from playing hero, could you? Just couldn't leave it alone. Damn you! You almost got Sophie killed. And now . . . Jesus, Wyatt, now I'm going to have to kill you. Don't you see it? Don't you see that I've got to get you out of the picture?"

Wyatt could only stare, unable to comprehend what had happened to this man he had once trusted with his life. "Why didn't you tell me you were in trouble? I could have helped. I *would* have helped."

Hugh pushed out an ugly laugh. "You couldn't help. It was too late for anyone to help. They were going to kill me."

"Who?"

"What the fuck do you care?" Hugh roared.

"You have to ask that? After all we've been to each other?"

Hugh looked away, looked ashamed. "I got into some shit with the Bratva, all right? Some money shit. Fuckers were going to kill me if I didn't clear the slate."

Bratva. The Russian Mafia. "Jesus, Hugh."

"We can't all be Boy Scouts, Bear. We can't all lead charmed lives."

In the midst of the jumble of unbelievable conclusions, something occurred to him. "All those kidnappings. The ones you helped broker. They were all—"

"Staged," Hugh interrupted. "I worked a deal with

Bonilla; we split the ransoms. And don't you fucking look at me like that! I do what I have to do to get by." He shook his head again, a loose cannon with a very short fuse. "And I had a handle on it until you screwed things up. You should have left well enough alone. You should have just backed off when I told you to!" He took a step toward him, then backed away again, his actions disjointed and jerky, a man on the verge of losing it.

"The Hernandez girl," Wyatt said to keep him talking. "Were you a part of that, too?"

Hugh's silence was as good as an admission.

"I don't get it. If you needed the money, why give her up to us?"

"I didn't," Hugh said with loathing. "You weren't supposed to find her. You weren't supposed to *be* here," he said again, as if repeating it would make it go away. He drew the rifle to his shoulder and aimed down the sites.

"Why Sophie?" Wyatt asked abruptly, stalling for more time. "Why did you have to bring her into this?"

Hugh breathed deep, lowered the gun, and leveled Wyatt with a look of rage so potent it felt like a gut punch. "Again. I didn't. She wasn't supposed to get hurt. She wasn't supposed to be touched by this, but you pushed Bonilla past the limits. First by cutting him out of his ransom when you rescued the Hernandez girl, then with your commando raids on his cribs. You killed his men. You cost him money. You cost him face. And you cost me an alliance. And that, my *friend*, is why he took Sophie. To stick it to me for the trouble *you* caused."

"So you break bread with the devil and this is all *my* fault?"

"Fuck you and your righteous indignation," Hugh shot back. "You haven't been where I've been."

A wave of sorrow blindsided him—sorrow for who Hugh had been, for what they'd been to each other. Who was this man? This man who had been his best friend, who had been his equal. "That wasn't me in Mogadishu? Or in Lebanon? That wasn't me dragging your ass out of Beirut under fire?"

"Yeah, like I said, you were always the Boy Scout," Hugh acknowledged with a sour smile. "Always played by the rules, didn't you? Always bled red, white, and blue."

"So did you." Wyatt's grief played second only to disgust. "Christ, Hugh, what happened to you?"

"Things changed. I changed. I work for the money now, okay?" Hugh shouted as if that would somehow make things right.

"You had it all, brother."

"Oh, yeah. Right. I got the girl, didn't I?"

"You *lost* the girl," Wyatt pointed out.

"And I want her back!" Hugh screamed. "She would have come back, too. I would have gotten my share of the ransom to pay off Bravta, Lola would be safe, and—"

"And you'd be Sophie's hero again," Wyatt finished as the last bizarre puzzle piece fit into place.

"Goddamn right!" Hugh's eyes flashed conviction

and hatred, and in that moment, Wyatt understood that Hugh wasn't merely corrupt and lost, he was a little bit insane. "She doesn't love you," Hugh said. "She could never love you."

"Yeah, well, guess that's a moot point now, isn't it, being as how you've got the gun and all."

"Get up," Hugh ordered, motioning with the nose of the rifle. "Get up and run."

Wyatt managed to laugh. "So you can shoot me in the back? Make it look like a banger got me? Shit, Hugh, if I ran, I'd just die tired. And I'm already tired. Sorry, old friend. If you're going to do this, you're going to have to look me in the eye when you pull that trigger. And you're going to have to explain to Sophie why I'm dead."

"Drop the gun!"

Wyatt jerked his gaze just beyond Hugh's shoulder. *Sophie.*

Aw, God, he didn't want her to see this. And he didn't want to see her this way: her arms stretched out straight ahead of her, a Glock 19 clutched in a two-handed grip, her face twisted with fear and horror and a God-awful dread.

"Please, please, drop the gun," she begged as Joe Green walked silently up behind her, an H&K in one hand and Lola pressed against his chest with the other.

Wyatt caught the intent in Joe's stance and gave a quick, almost imperceptible shake of his head, a signal to hold his fire. As long as he was alive, he still had a chance to talk Hugh down from this.

"Please don't make me shoot you," Sophie pleaded again. There were tears in her eyes, tears in her voice, but her grip and her stance were rock-solid steady.

Hugh didn't move. Didn't turn around. Didn't lower the M-4 that was still pointed dead center on Wyatt's chest. But his face fell, then twisted into a mask of pain and defeat and regret.

"You always loved him, didn't you?" Hugh asked with a slow nod that said he already knew the answer.

"I loved *you*," Sophie said, her voice tremulous. "But you never got that. Or if you did, it wasn't enough for you. And then you . . . you changed, Hugh. You weren't the man I loved anymore."

An awful calm came over him as he stood there. A horrible look of utter defeat. "So now, you're willing to kill me to save him."

"I'm not willing to do anything. I don't want to kill you. Please don't make me do that," she begged on a tortured whisper that ripped Wyatt's heart in two.

Hugh's shoulders just seemed to collapse, as though everything holding him strong and tall deserted his body. As though everything that made him a man deserted his soul. And suddenly, Wyatt was more frightened for Hugh than he was for himself.

"It doesn't have to end like this," Wyatt said, trying to reason with him. "If you care anything about her, don't do this to her. You kill me, then she has to live with the fact that she didn't stop you. She kills you, she has to live with the knowledge that she pulled the trigger. You really care about her? Then put the gun down."

Hugh swallowed hard. His eyes misted with tears. "And what? Watch you walk away into the sunset with the girl?"

"Yeah, that," Wyatt said, hoping to reach him with an appeal to what was left of his integrity. "Man up. Be the man I know you are. Be the man who does the right thing."

"The right thing," Hugh repeated in a tone of echoing loss. "The right thing, from where I'm standing, looks like a lose-lose situation for me either way. So maybe I'll just do the only thing that matters."

Too late, Wyatt realized what Hugh was going to do. "No!" he yelled, and struggled to push to his feet.

But he couldn't reach him in time.

Hugh withdrew his Sig Sauer from his belt holster, stuck the barrel into his mouth, and pulled the trigger.

31

Wyatt had intimate knowledge of each and every hour of the night. It didn't get any darker than four a.m. And no hour was quite as empty. Even the woman lying beside him in a bed that smelled of her and clean sheets couldn't fill the void or ease the pain—both physical and emotional.

Just as there was little he could do to ease hers. He was a warm body in the dark in a cold, impersonal hotel room. Another heart beating. Another heart grieving for a man they had both loved and lost long before he'd ended his own life.

He knew she wasn't asleep. She was beyond exhaustion on all levels. Even Lola's happy reunion with her mother and family a few hours ago couldn't breach the cocoon of grief that surrounded Sophie. A long, soaking shower couldn't wash away the horror of Hugh's gruesome suicide.

They'd both asked themselves the inevitable questions.

Why didn't I see it?

Why didn't I recognize that he needed help?

Why did it have to come to this?

And they'd both given up on the answers.

Wyatt wanted to believe that Hugh hadn't taken the coward's way out. As he'd struggled to pick up Hugh's lifeless body and, with Joe's help, carried him out of that bloody battleground, he wanted to believe instead that Hugh had considered his actions the ultimate act of redemption. He'd relieved Sophie of an impossible choice. He'd spared Wyatt's life.

He could shade the picture any way he wanted, but the end was still the same. Hugh was dead. Wyatt couldn't help him now. Just like he couldn't help Sophie.

So he just held her. And held on to her. And prayed that a new dawn would bring new light to a tragedy they would both carry with them for the rest of their lives.

Wyatt stood looking out the windows of the hotel room, downing his third cup of room-service coffee, when Sophie walked out of the bathroom, hugging her arms around her waist. It seemed that daylight had only brought more sadness to her eyes and desolation to her bruised face.

He wanted to go to her. Wanted to pull her into his arms and tell her everything was going to be all right.

But they both knew it wouldn't be. He'd lost a friend who had once been like a brother. She'd lost a man she'd once chosen to share her life with. And nothing would ever be quite right again.

"Any news on Luke?" she asked.

He nodded. "Just talked with Gabe. It was touch-and-go, but he made it through the night. Surgery was as successful as could be, considering. Now it's a question of time. Doctors said the first forty-eight hours are the most critical. If he makes it through them . . . well, he's got a chance."

She nodded and looked toward the windows, her expression somewhere between relief and grief and hope and tears.

"I want to go back home," she said.

He nodded, understanding that she knew she couldn't go back yet. Not until they got a crew in to repair the damage Bonilla's thugs had done to the house. "Working on it," he said.

"And I want my baby back," she said without meeting his eyes.

Yeah. He was sure she did. "That was my next call," he said. "I wanted to make sure they were up."

She nodded, glanced at him, then away, embarrassed by the tears that started falling.

He swallowed hard and couldn't do it. Couldn't keep his distance. He went to her. Ignored the jagged pain shooting from under the dressings on his arm and across his chest and drew her against him.

And he let her cry. Let himself feel the depth of his own pain. For the friend Hugh had once been to him. For the husband he'd once been to her. For the chasm that Hugh's actions and suicide had sliced in the common ground between them that no bridge could ever span.

A knock on the door startled them both.

Sophie jerked out of his arms. Swiping at her cheeks with the back of her hand, she pulled herself together and walked to the door.

Wyatt knew who would be on the other side. He'd called Diego Montoya himself. He accepted that Montoya—the epitome of wealth, composure, and concern—was what Sophie needed now.

"*Mi amor*," Montoya said, his voice thick with emotion, and pulled her into his arms.

For a long moment, Wyatt made himself look at the picture they made standing there. Montoya tall and handsome, Sophie small and fragile in his embrace.

She fit there, he acknowledged with a pain in his chest that had nothing to do with the sixty stitches it had taken the ER doc to patch him up. Nothing to do with the ache in his bandaged arm that rivaled the ache in his chest.

Yeah, he thought, and quietly gathered his gear.

They fit.

He didn't.

That fact was never more obvious than when he walked out the door and she didn't utter a word to stop him.

Ten days later, Wyatt sat in a chair by Doc's hospital bed, legs stretched out in front of him, ankles crossed. He'd laced his fingers carefully over his sore chest and closed his eyes. The soft sounds of Doc's breathing—steady now and, thank God, no longer powered by a ventilator—gave him reason enough to relax and catch a little rest himself. The beep and blink of machines monitoring Doc's blood pressure and pulse and oxygen levels blended into the mix of hospital sounds and scents and reassured him that all was well.

At least, it looked as if it was going to be.

He wasn't certain what alerted him to another presence in the room, but one instant he was drifting and half-asleep, the next he was wide awake.

His eyes flew open. And there she was.

Sophie stood just inside the door, a vase of flowers in her hands and a soft smile on her face that relayed hello and hesitation and an edgy sort of expectancy that he couldn't quite get a read on.

"Hi," she whispered. Glancing at Doc, who remained sound asleep, she stepped a little farther into the room.

"Hi," Wyatt whispered back, sitting up straighter in the chair, trying his damnedest not to let her notice how hard it was to see her again. It had been only ten days. It felt like a decade. A decade during the ice age.

"How's he doing?" She crossed the room to the window and set the vase on the wide sill along with half a dozen other bouquets.

"Good." Her bruises had faded. The memory of how she'd gotten them hadn't. "He's, um, doing real good. Better than they expected for this stage in his recovery."

"Then he's going to be okay?"

He nodded again. "Yeah. He's a lucky man. Tough man," he amended when her eyes searched his expectantly. What was she looking for? He wanted to ask. Didn't dare.

"How's Hope?" he asked instead, because he cared and because any question was better than "What are you doing here?"

"Hope's amazing." Her face lit up; her smile was totally without reservation. "Of course, she's madly in love with your Johnny Reed, but since she also adores Crystal, the break to her heart is barely noticeable. Thank you so much," she added, her smile fading, "for putting Hope in their care. I couldn't see through the fear, but Johnny and Crystal, Nate, and Juliana, they were exactly what she needed. They were wonderful with her. She hasn't stopped talking about them since she's been home."

She stopped suddenly, as if she realized she was close to rambling, and cast a glance at Doc.

"Don't worry. You're not going to wake him," Wyatt assured her to assuage the guilt he saw in her eyes. "Someone dropped a tray outside the door a little while ago. Sounded like a plane crash. He never missed a snore."

She smiled, glanced at Doc again, then at the flowers, then back at Wyatt.

Nervous. She was nervous to find him here.

"Yeah, well, maybe . . . maybe I'll just go stretch my legs," he said, standing.

"I called Gabe," she said, stopping him cold. "He told me I would find you here."

Okay. Nervous but not surprised to see him. *Expecting* to see him.

"Yeah, well, someone's got to hang around to run interference with the hospital staff. Doc's not the best patient." If only he felt as casual as he managed to sound.

She nodded again, walked to the bed, fussed with the fold of the sheet, then stood with her back to him, saying nothing.

"You okay?" he asked finally.

She turned slowly, her eyes searching. "You left," she said.

He stared at her.

"You just . . . left," she repeated. "No word. No good-bye. I . . . I didn't know where you were. *How* you were. If . . . if you wanted to see me."

He swallowed thickly. "I thought it was what you wanted," he finally admitted. "For me to leave."

In fact, he'd known that was what she wanted. She'd stood and watched him go when he shouldered his duffel and walked out the door, hadn't she? Stood there beside Montoya and hadn't made a sound.

She searched his face, then averted her gaze to the flowers again, walked over to touch a finger to a velvety petal of a red rose. "Yes, well, I thought that might be what I wanted, too."

His heartbeat became the loudest sound in the room.

He should say something. Didn't trust himself.

"You have to know that I love you." She finally turned to face him.

The look in her eyes made his heart stop. He didn't see love there . . . did he? Hell, maybe, yeah, maybe that's exactly what he saw, but what struck him rock-hard was the conflict.

"But you don't want to," he surmised, and knew he was right when her eyes filled with tears.

"No. I didn't want to. I was scared, Wyatt. Scared and hurting. Hugh . . ." She stopped and swallowed, and the pain she felt over Hugh's betrayal and his violent suicide washed over her. "Hugh's death . . . I felt responsible, you know?"

"Yeah. I know."

He knew, because he felt the same sense of responsibility. It was wrong. Intellectually, he knew that. Figured she knew it, too. But emotionally, the guilt was still there. Would probably never go away.

"I married a warrior once," she said in a soft voice, forcing him to look at her. "I lived with Hugh's demons every bit as much as he did. And I don't know, Wyatt . . . I don't know if I'm strong enough to walk that minefield again."

Honest. Brutal. Blunt. No amount of regret in her voice could cover her fear.

"I'm not Hugh," he said, feeling defensive and defenseless in the same breath.

"No," she agreed. "You're not. And you never could be. I know that. Hugh had something inside him . . . something that ate at him . . . something that tore him apart. You were always . . . different in so many ways. But you're still a warrior at heart. Next op, next adventure, you'll be gone. Just like Hugh was always gone."

Wyatt leaned forward in the chair, propped his elbows on his thighs, and clasped his hands together. And he waited because he knew she had a lot more to say.

"I keep asking myself. Can I go through that again? Can I keep the home fires burning while you're off getting shot at? Can I live not knowing where you are, only that you're in constant danger? The truth is, I don't know."

He closed his eyes.

"I've had my fill of seeing guns lying around the house. Of jumping when the phone rings and praying it's not the worst possible news. I don't want to do that anymore. I want to spend the rest of my life coming home to see my man sitting on the sofa with . . . with . . . I don't know. A TV remote in his hand, bare feet crossed and propped on a coffee table, a beer or a glass of wine within reach. I want to be able to ask, 'How was your day?' and not know in advance that it most likely involved bullets and bad guys and near-death experiences that will eventually wake him up screaming in the night."

He finally looked at her. Tears filled her eyes, but she soldiered on, knowing it was hurting him, clear that it was hurting her, too.

"Even more, I want to be able to come home and know he's going to be there. That he's not bleeding and in pain in some godforsaken jungle, or worse, that he's already dead and forever gone from me."

Now was the time to tell her. Now was the moment to let her know that he'd been reevaluating the way he led his life. That he'd gone home to Georgia what now seemed like a lifetime ago but in fact was less than two weeks, to find answers to the questions that had been plaguing him for some time.

He was tired. He was empty. Played out. He missed things . . . things like the easy pace of the South. Like connecting with something other than adrenaline and danger. He wanted to see Annie's little guy grow. He wanted to know what it felt like to be Sam Lang, at home and at peace in Nevada with Abbie and their son. He wanted . . . hell, he wanted out. He'd paid his dues. He'd done his job. It was time for someone else— someone still hungry for the rush and the speed and the danger that had been a part of his life for longer than he could remember—to take up the slack.

Yeah. He should tell her all that. Right now. But he kept seeing her with Montoya. And he knew that Montoya could give her everything a busted-up shadow warrior couldn't.

He finally looked up at her. She was waiting for him to say something. Maybe to try to convince her he could be that man.

"You're right," he said instead, and knew he was saying good-bye to the best thing he'd ever wanted in his life. "You deserve all that. Montoya could give it to you."

She blinked, then shook her head as if she hadn't heard him right. "I don't love Montoya. You weren't listening. I love *you*. Damn me for a fool, but I want *you*."

He stood slowly, not trusting himself to believe her words, unable to deny the truth that he saw in her eyes.

"So, if you're willing . . . if you can help me through

it, I'll wait it out," she said, walking into his arms. "I won't like it. In fact, I'll hate it most of the time, but I'm going to hang on to the thought that you can't do this forever. Someday, you'll have to give it up."

He buried his face in her hair as love rushed in and rolled over every conceivable roadblock that even attempted to throw a barrier between them. "How about tomorrow?"

She pulled away from him, her hands clutching his forearms. Dark eyes searched his with a heady mix of disbelief, hope, and love. "What did you say?"

"I said, how about I hang it up tomorrow? Okay, maybe two weeks from tomorrow. I owe Nate at least a two-week notice."

"You're . . . you're serious." Her smile was radiant through the tears spilling down her cheeks.

"As a heart attack," he said. "I'm done, Sophie. And not just for you. For me. I . . . I'm just done," he said, and felt the weight of a thousand tons of spent cartridges lift from his shoulders. "That's why I was in Georgia when you found me. I'd gone home to face the fact that I wanted out and to figure out how to deal with it."

"But you left me," she pointed out. "Ten days, Wyatt. Not one word."

"I was playing the hero, okay? I was clearing the way for you and Montoya. I wanted you to be happy."

"You make me happy."

He finally smiled, finally believed this was happening. "Well, it's a damn good thing," he said, "because honestly? I hit the wall today. I was coming after you. I thought I could walk away, but the truth is, I couldn't. Not this time." He brushed his thumb over her wet cheek. "I love you. I want you in my life. I want to *be* your life."

She hugged him so hard he flinched at the tenderness in his stitches and lost his balance. They landed back in the chair with a thud, her body sprawled across his lap.

Fire burned through the knife wounds. He didn't care. All he cared about was her. Holding her. Feeling her heat and her tears and her life blood beating through her body and knowing there were no secrets between them anymore.

"Why don't you two nice kids get a room? Leave an injured man to rest in peace."

Sophie gasped. Wyatt grinned and held her tight when she would have scrambled to her feet.

"You're supposed to be asleep," he said, glancing at Doc.

"What, and miss all the good stuff?"

Yeah, Wyatt thought, looking from one man he loved like a brother to the one woman he loved more than life. This was definitely the good stuff.

Epilogue

They decided on a spring wedding. They wanted to start their lives together during a season of hope and renewal and promise. May in Georgia provided all that and more. And they'd both needed the nine months to heal.

The colors and the scents filling the day were pure South. Margaret Savage's gardens were in riotous bloom. Streamers of Spanish moss dripped from the wide-spreading branches of the majestic live oak lording over the backyard of the only home Wyatt had ever known. It seemed fitting, then, that the only woman he'd ever loved stood beside him, her dark hair dappled by sunlight and shadows and a delicate halo of baby's breath and lace.

"Ladies and gentlemen." Pastor Bob Larson beamed over his Bible at the gathered crowd. "It is my pleasure to present to you Mr. and Mrs. Wyatt Savage."

No polite round of applause from this crew. Oh, no. Wyatt and Sophie were met with a rowdy roar of "Hoorays!" and "Lock and loads!" and shrill, happy whistles, with Johnny Reed and Doc leading the way.

Besides the BOI contingent that had turned out in force, family and special friends also joined the celebration. Robert and Ann Tompkins had flown in from Virginia to help them celebrate their special day. Carrie Granger was among the first to offer her congratulations as they stood in a receiving line of well-wishers.

"I'm so happy for you both." Carrie's smile was genuine and generous.

"Glad you could make it, sugar," Wyatt said, hugging her.

"Are you kidding me? The whole county's buzzing about all the 'dangerous' men who checked into Sara Parker's B&B yesterday. No way was I going to miss this action."

Wyatt snorted. "One of them is bound to end up with a lamp shade on his head before the day is over. We'll see how dangerous they look then."

She smiled again and squeezed his hand. "And no way was I going to miss seeing you so happy."

"I like your friends," Sophie said later as they relaxed in a wooden glider on the quiet end of Margaret's manicured yard filled with lawn chairs and tables overflowing with traditional Southern dishes. And while the champagne fountain was seeing its fair share of action, the busiest spot of all was the keg of beer that had been wrapped in an old quilt to keep it cool. "And I love your family."

"You do know that my mother hasn't stopped smiling since I told her about us nine months ago." He searched the crowded lawn of laughing and chatting people and found Margaret Savage, beaming and full of vitality in a violet lace dress, talking with the pastor and his wife as far away from the keg as she could possibly steer them.

"Well, that makes two very happy Savage women."

Oh, he liked the sound of that. And the sound of the laughter that surrounded them.

"I hope those guys don't get out of hand," he said with a nod toward Doc, who was back in fine form. Apparently, he was also well educated on the workings of a pony keg, because in between telling tall tales to Wyatt's dad and flirting with Carrie, Doc had taken charge of the spray nozzle and was topping off everyone's glass.

"You're not disappointed that we didn't make this a big, formal affair?" He folded her hand in his and brought it to his lips, damn proud of the way their wedding bands looked twined together.

"I loved our ceremony," she insisted. "It was perfect. My parents are loving it, too." She smiled in the direction of her mom and dad, who were visiting with Robert and Ann Tompkins. "We're not formal people, Wyatt. This is much more . . . real," she said, finally settling on the right word as Hope, pretty in a pink dress, went sailing by with Sam's niece—now adopted daughter—Tina. The little girls were laughing and chasing Annie's monster child, Will, who hadn't lost any steam since last summer when Wyatt had first met his terror of a nephew.

Wyatt no longer worried about depriving Sophie of the things Montoya could have given her. She'd long ago made him a believer that she was comfortable in whatever world they created, as long as they were together.

"And you're good with turning the Baylor School over to Maris for the time being?"

"Couldn't be in better hands," she said, smiling for him. "She'll do a wonderful job. Besides, I'll be making regular trips back. Hope's not going to let me get by too long without taking her to see Lola. How about you?" she asked, looking up at him. "You're really okay leaving the BOIs?"

"I'll admit, I'm a little . . . unsettled about it right now. But give me a few months," he said, with as much honesty as he could. "Let me get past the adjustment curve, and then we'll see. For now, I'm all about settlin' back into Georgia time, sugar. I'm all about settlin' in with you."

"I'm liking the sound of that."

He was, too. Yeah, he would miss the good guys. They were his brothers. The bad guys? Not so much.

"The band's about to start up," he said when he saw the Talbot boys, a popular local trio, set up their equipment on the back porch. "Hope you like country."

"I've been known to hum along to a little Waylon and Willie."

"Let's just hope Reed doesn't decide to make his country debut," he said with a nod toward Johnny, who was deep in conversation with Brad Talbot over his Martin guitar.

She laughed. "*That* I want to hear."

"No," he assured her. "You don't."

A few minutes later, when the band struck up the first chords of Kenny Chesney's "You Had Me from

Hello," the crowd erupted in more whistles and cheers, and expectant eyes turned to Wyatt and Sophie.

"Guess they're playing our song, sugar." He stood and held out his hand. "Me and my two left feet would love to have this dance."

She took his hand and let him lead her to the brick patio before moving into his arms. "Dancing's not about footwork, darling man."

He loved the playful sparkle in her eyes. "No?"

"Oh, no." She looped her arms around his neck, pressed close against him, and swayed to the music. "It's about the contact."

Then she tipped her head back and kissed him. Kissed him like they were alone in the dark on a dance floor. Kissed him until he forgot that they weren't.

Didn't take long before he got a reminder.

Another round of loud whistles and applause finally had him coming up for air. A tap on his shoulder had him growling a succinct "Get lost."

"Yeah, right." Doc just laughed and swept a grinning Sophie into his arms and danced her across the patio.

I'm the luckiest man alive, Wyatt thought as he stood at the edge of the makeshift dance floor and watched another man dance away with his wife. He was surrounded by friends and family. He was loved by a woman he adored. And as of today, he officially had a daughter.

Hope was a born nurturer, he thought, becoming used to the pride he felt when he watched her with his sister's boy and Sam's little Bryan. Like her mother, he realized, shifting his attention to Sophie again, who was laughing in Doc's arms. Not for much longer, though, by the looks of things. Rafe, Johnny, Gabe, and Sam looked like they were ready to move in and take their turns giving Sophie an earful about the best ways to domesticate a Papa Bear, while Rafe's B.J., Johnny's Crystal, Gabe's Jenna, and Sam's Abbie were huddled together around a table, sipping champagne and catching up.

Joe and Steph stood aside from the crowd, wrapped up in their own little world. They were still falling, Wyatt realized. Still exploring this "crazy little thing called love."

Nate and Juliana caught his attention then, as they sort of swayed to the music but mostly just stood still, bodies close, eyes only for each other. The guys had all known that Nate and Juliana were crazy about each other. What they hadn't known was that when their fearless leader finally took the plunge, he'd dive this deep.

The song ended, and Sam politely delivered Sophie back to Wyatt's side.

"She's too good for you, Bear," the tall rancher said with a wink at Sophie.

Wyatt wrapped an arm around her waist. "Tell me something I don't know."

"Okay." Sam leaned in close. "We're pregnant again."

Wyatt did a double-take. The look on Sam's face said he was over the moon. "Congratulations, man. Wow. That was fast."

"Yeah, well, when you're good at something . . ." Sam let the line trail off when surprised and happy squeals erupted from the table where the wives were gathered. "I'm guessing Abbie just shared the news."

"Lot of hugging going on," Wyatt observed as the women rose to embrace a beaming Abbie.

"Congratulations, Sam," Sophie said. "I'll just go extend my congratulations to Abbie."

"Tell me something," Wyatt said, watching the four women envelop Sophie in the circle of their love, "how'd we get so damn lucky?"

Sam grunted. "I stopped asking that question a long time ago. Now I just go with it and thank the powers that be that that woman is a part of my life."

Yeah, Wyatt thought as the spring sunshine warmed his shoulders and the love of his wife warmed his heart, it was time to just go with it.

"You knew it was going to happen," Rafe said a couple of hours later.

"Yep. He's been itching to roll up his sleeves and break out the poker chips," Wyatt agreed as they stood side by side, watching Doc lure anyone within winking distance over to a picnic table where he was setting up shop.

"Help me finance my trip," Doc teased Jenna Jones. "You know you just love to lose to me, darlin'."

"That's my wife you're calling darlin'," Gabe muttered as he pulled out a chair and sat down at the table.

"Jealous? Sorry, *darlin*'." Doc winked at Gabe. "From now on, I'll save the pet names just for you."

"Can anyone join this game?" Wyatt's sister, Annie, made herself at home at the table.

"You're in trouble now, Colter," Wyatt warned Doc. "Go get 'em, Spanky."

"Finance what trip?" Joe stood with his arm over Stephanie's shoulders, watching the action.

"Eat your hearts out, ladies and gents. I'm taking a long overdue vacation to Italy, where I plan to gorge myself on pasta and gelato and soak up the local culture."

The latter part of his statement was met by grunts of laughter.

"Fine. Laugh, you Neanderthals," Doc countered around the unlit cigar he'd tucked in the side of his mouth. "While you all wouldn't recognize culture if it bit you on the ass—you ladies, of course, are excluded from that statement—I happen to appreciate the fine arts."

More chuckles.

"And when I'm not taking in the local color," Doc went on, refusing to fall to their insults, "I'll be lying in the sun on the Amalfi Coast in the arms of some warm, willing woman. No guns. No bad guys. No stress."

"Speaking of stress." Wyatt pulled Sophie away from what promised to be an all-nighter. "I don't think anyone would miss us if we slipped away."

Secure in the knowledge that Hope was in Margaret Savage's loving care, she took his hand and followed him.

The little inn where Wyatt had reserved a room for the night was only fifteen miles from the Savage farm where the party was still running full tilt. Here, in this room, in this bed with Sophie, however, they were a world away. Their world away. Their lifetime. Finally.

"Do you know that in the entire world," he whispered, pressing his lips against the inside of her thigh just below the spot where she was warm and damp and needing him, "there is nothing as soft . . . nothing as silky . . . nothing," he repeated gruffly when she sighed and shuddered and opened for him, "as amazing as this spot . . . right here? Right"—he bussed his nose against her heat, kissed her there—"here," he murmured, and opened his mouth over her.

Drinking her in.

Coaxing her higher.

Leading her toward a long, lush climax.

"Wyatt."

His name escaped on a whisper of breath as she gripped the sheets at her hips and rose to meet his mouth, to urge him to take her wherever he wanted to go with her.

He loved her this way. Desperate. Gasping. Her taut muscles quivering, her body arching and wet and giving.

She was in a hurry. He had no intention of rushing this. He'd waited a lifetime for the privilege of loving this woman. So no, he wasn't rushing a damn thing.

He wanted her wild. He wanted her screaming and teetering on the brink of sanity. Wanted to take her places only he could take her. Steal her breath. Feed her fire. Discover secrets about her sensuality that she had never risked with anyone but him . . . then make her pleasure last forever.

"Please," she begged, then caught her breath on a moan when he slid one broad hand beneath her hips and angled her deeper against his mouth.

"Please!" A ragged cry this time when he cupped her breast, then finessed the tight bud of her nipple between his finger and thumb to the rhythm of his tongue and sent her over the sharp, searing edge of sensation.

She poured into his mouth like honey, her muscles clenching wire-tight, her body straining to capture and savor the electric ride before she dissolved in a boneless sigh.

Love, rich and rare and beyond anything he had ever imagined, filled him as he slid up her body and filled her. Pressing deep. Moving slow.

There was time now. Time to savor and sink into her heat, time to wait for her to recover, then respond, then rally to meet him stroke for stroke, heartbeat for heartbeat.

"I never knew," she whispered as he moved fluidly above her. "I never knew love could be this good."

She lifted a hand, stroked his hair, guided his face so she could see his eyes. So that he could see hers.

And what he saw when he looked into the beautiful brown eyes staring back at him was much more than love. Much more, even, than life. He saw forever.

Sexy suspense that sizzles

FROM POCKET BOOKS!

Laura Griffin
THREAD OF FEAR
She says this will be her last case.
A killer plans to make sure it is.

**Don't miss the electrifying trilogy from
New York Times bestselling author Cindy Gerard!**

SHOW NO MERCY
The sultry heat hides the deadliest threats—
and exposes the deepest desires.

TAKE NO PRISONERS
A dangerous attraction—spurred by revenge—
reveals a savage threat that can't be ignored.

WHISPER NO LIES
An indecent proposal reveals a simmering desire—
with deadly consequences.

Available wherever books are sold or at www.simonandschuster.com

19582

Love a good book? So do we!
Pick up a bestselling Romance from Pocket Books.

≈≈≈

FEEL THE HEAT
A BLACK OPS, INC. NOVEL
Cindy Gerard
A relentless enemy…
A merciless temptation.

UNTRACEABLE
Laura Griffin
Be careful what you look for…
You just might find it.

MAKE HER PAY
Roxanne St. Claire
A BULLET CATCHERS NOVEL
Sometimes it takes a thief to catch a thief…

OUR LITTLE SECRET
Starr Ambrose
Keeping secrets can be deadly
…or delicious.

A DIFFERENT LIGHT
Mariah Stewart
The beloved classic—now revised and
revisited by the bestselling author!

≈≈≈

Available wherever books are sold or at
www.simonandschuster.com

22184